LT Graham
Graham, Heather
The night is alive /

34028083563628
OF $33.99   ocn844726350
                        08/15/13

THE NIGHT IS ALIVE

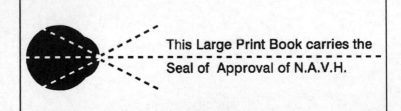

This Large Print Book carries the
Seal of Approval of N.A.V.H.

THE NIGHT IS ALIVE

HEATHER GRAHAM

THORNDIKE PRESS

A part of Gale, Cengage Learning

Detroit • New York • San Francisco • New Haven, Conn • Waterville, Maine • London

GALE
CENGAGE Learning·

Copyright © 2013 by Heather Graham Pozzessere.
Krewe of Hunters Series.
Thorndike Press, a part of Gale, Cengage Learning.

Thorndike Press® Large Print Core.
The text of this Large Print edition is unabridged.
Other aspects of the book may vary from the original edition.
Set in 16 pt. Plantin.

LIBRARY OF CONGRESS CIP DATA ON FILE.
CATALOGUING IN PUBLICATION FOR THIS BOOK
IS AVAILABLE FROM THE LIBRARY OF CONGRESS

ISBN-13: 978-1-4104-5974-9 (hardcover)
ISBN-10: 1-4104-5974-8 (hardcover)

Published in 2013 by arrangement with Harlequin Books S.A.

Printed in the United States of America
1 2 3 4 5 6 7 17 16 15 14 13

To Savannah!

For family trips, ghost hunts, a road trip with Pablo the cat, an incredible stay at the 17hundred90 Inn and Restaurant, the hearse tour, and so many more wonderful times!

And to my children,
Jason, Shayne, Derek, Bryee-Annon, and Chynna and the magic they added to the city with their imaginations each time we traveled through.

PROLOGUE

Then

Abby didn't know why she awoke; she might have heard a sound in the night. Whatever it was, she'd gone from being curled up, enjoying a dream about the great tenth birthday party she was going to have at her grandparents' tavern, the Dragonslayer, to being pulled out of her dream, as if she needed to be awake. And aware.

There was someone in her room, she thought. Someone with a kind, handsome face staring down at her, eyes filled with great concern.

Then the face was gone and she was instantly wide-awake.

And scared.

She slipped from her bed and out of the room in the apartment above the Dragonslayer, running to the door in the little hallway that led to her grandparents' suite. Neither of them was in bed.

That scared her more. Her grandparents weren't in their bed.

She instantly knew she should be quiet. The fear she felt was instinctive, and she tiptoed in bare feet down the curving metal stairs to the ground floor.

Halfway there, she stopped. Her heart seemed to squeeze and her whole body froze.

She wasn't afraid of the tavern, she never had been. It was filled with old ships' wheels, countless figureheads, paintings, etchings, maps and more. The elegant beauties, dragons and mythical creatures that gazed down at her from the walls were part of her heritage.

No, she wasn't afraid of anything in the Dragonslayer, but . . .

Someone was there, someone who shouldn't be. He was standing at the entry, looking through the cut-glass window on the front door, and it wasn't her grandpa Gus.

He was tall, and beneath his tricorn hat, his rich black hair fell down his back in curls. He had a neatly manicured beard and mustache. His black boots were tight on his calves over tan breeches. He wore a crimson overcoat with elegant buttons that matched those on his vest, and a white shirt with lace at the throat and sleeves. He seemed im-

8

probably imposing as he stood there — as if nothing could pass by him. She couldn't see his eyes in the darkness, but she knew their color.

Just as she knew him.

He was the man who'd been standing by the bed, watching over her.

She'd seen images of him dozens of times. He'd been loved — and hated. He'd sailed the seas on a constant quest for adventure, some said. For his own riches, according to others. He'd never killed a man, although he'd made good on many threats regarding severe thrashings. He'd kidnapped a wealthy man's daughter and held her for a fortune, but when she was rescued, the girl had wanted to go back to her captor. He never broke his word.

Of course, despite his sense of honor, he'd been hunted. He had been the pirate, Blue Anderson. He was her umpteen-great-great-uncle.

Had been.

He was dead. He had been dead for more than two hundred and fifty years.

But there he was — standing in the darkness, watching whatever was happening outside the door. Watching with intense interest.

He looked up at her suddenly, as if he re-

9

alized she was there.

He studied her for a moment and then he smiled, inclining his head curiously and nodding.

He could tell that she saw him.

If she'd been able to move, she would have. She would have screamed and gone running back to her room to hide under the bed.

But she couldn't move. She could hardly breathe, much less scream.

He smiled again, tipped his tricorn hat, glanced outside one more time and then slowly disappeared.

As he did, she heard the door open. Her eyes darted to it with fear.

It was her grandparents coming back into the building. But it had to be about four in the morning, and they didn't go out at 4:00 a.m. From the stairway window — she hadn't managed to move yet — she realized there were flashing lights in the parking lot.

Flashing lights. The kind police cars had.

"Not to worry. They got him, Brenda, my love," Gus told her grandmother.

"Yes, but . . . Oh, Gus! That horrible man might have gotten in." Her grandmother sounded worried. She was such a wonderful grandmother — different from most, perhaps; she wasn't much of a cookie baker.

10

But she came to all of Abby's school events. She loved to dress up, she read stories and acted out all the characters. She was slim and energetic, too; she loved a long bike ride.

"Hey, so what? He would've stolen what little cash we have in the register. But he didn't get in. We woke up, we called the police, all is good," Gus said. He looked up then — just as Blue had done, but of course, she couldn't *really* have seen Blue. That would've been seeing a . . .

A ghost.

"Hey, munchkin, what are you doing up?" Gus called to her.

She willed her frozen lungs to function. "I woke up," she said. Her voice sounded funny, and she forced herself to move. "I — I just woke up. And I couldn't find you."

"It's okay, now, Abby. Everything's okay. You can go back to sleep," Gus told her.

"What happened?" she asked.

Her grandmother turned to her grandfather, and Gus answered. "A thief trying to break in, baby. But the police got him. We're fine."

"Back to bed, child!" her grandmother said. She smiled to lighten the sternness of her words. "It's late. Or early. Whichever. Time for young'uns to be asleep! What

11

would your parents say about the way we keep you up?"

"Mom and Dad wouldn't mind. Mom always says you're the best. She said that if you and Gus weren't so wonderful, she'd never be able to travel with Dad as much as she does. Not many kids are so lucky. I get to stay with *you.*" Her father worked for a major tech company and traveled frequently. She had a room at the tavern with almost as much stuff in it as her room in the house on Chippewa Square.

"Be that as it may!" her grandmother began. "I want you back in your bed. It's a school night."

Abby gave her grandfather a wide-eyed look. He was an easier mark than her grandmother. She couldn't possibly go back to bed — alone. Not yet.

"Come on down. We'll have a cup of tea, and then we'll go back to bed. How's that?"

She managed to nod. And to come running the rest of the way down the stairs.

"Abigail Anderson!" Brenda said sternly. "I told you not to run around barefoot! Glasses do break, my darling, and even when we clean up, you can't be sure we get all the little slivers."

"Leave her be right now, Brenda," Gus suggested.

Brenda wagged a finger at her. "Tonight. Just tonight. You follow the tavern rules — *my* rules, young lady — or you don't stay here anymore!"

"Yes, ma'am," Abby said.

Brenda spun on Gus. "And you! Don't go putting a shot of whiskey in her tea to calm her down, do you hear me? She's barely ten."

"Oh, Brenda, it's what our parents did for us —"

"And nowadays, it's considered child abuse. You two behave. I'm going back up."

She caught Abby's chin and gave her a kiss on the cheek before she went up the winding staircase.

Gus winked at Abby. "Come into the kitchen," he said. "We'll brew some tea."

In the tavern's large, modernized kitchen, she sat on a stool and watched Gus place the kettle on a burner and bring out the makings for tea. There was a bottle of whiskey on one of the top shelves. He hesitated, and then shrugged. "One little nip. Cured me of colds, stubbed toes and a broken heart, and I had a wonderful mother, God bless her!" He crossed himself and looked upward. "Now, think you'll be able to sleep after this?"

She nodded enthusiastically. A few minutes later, he'd made tea — with a "nip" of whiskey in it for the two of them. He brought the cups out front and they sat together beneath the figureheads and other artifacts. She cherished these occasions with him; there weren't many.

"So, why are you scared?"

"You weren't there," she said.

He ruffled her hair. "I wasn't gone. I'd die before I'd leave you, munchkin, you know that."

She nodded again and sipped her tea. It was sweet and good with a lot of milk and sugar. Whatever else was in it, she couldn't tell.

"Something's bothering you," he said.

"Well, Gus, of course!" she said. She didn't know why she called him Gus, since she called her grandmother Nana.

He sighed and turned to her and stroked her face. "A bad man was trying to break in. But we heard him . . . saw him. Called the police, they came right away and now all is well."

She bit her lip. She couldn't get rid of the image of the dead pirate watching her grandparents through the door. Watching *her.*

"What is it?" Gus persisted.

"How did you know someone was trying

14

to break in, Gus?" she asked him.

He looked away from her quickly. "Ah, just heard him."

"Gus . . ."

He studied her, as if trying to read her mind. She was afraid to speak, afraid to say she'd seen a ghost. She was almost *ten,* and she didn't want him thinking she was a scaredy-cat baby. Or worse — having mental problems. Benny Adkins had acted weird at school, and they'd taken him out and sent him to some kind of special home for children.

She didn't have to speak. Gus sipped his tea thoughtfully. Eventually he said, "You saw old Blue, didn't you?"

Her heart thumped. "What?"

"I guess I was about your age when I saw him for the first time," Gus said. "Where was he?"

"Blue?" she whispered.

Something about the somber tenderness in her grandfather's eyes made her believe it was going to be all right. She could admit to him what she'd seen.

"I — I think he was over my bed. I think . . . maybe he . . . I think he was making sure I was all right. But I was scared and I jumped out of bed and I came running down the stairs. I saw him standing

15

there . . . at the entry."

He didn't laugh or tell her she was crazy or seeing things. He nodded gravely and smiled at her. "Don't be afraid of Blue. He's kind of like a guardian angel for us. Some of us see him — some of us in the family — but the rest of the world? I don't know. We don't see him often. I figure we're very lucky, but also that others wouldn't understand. So let's keep it a secret, okay?"

"Did he wake you up, Gus? Is that how you knew the tavern was in danger?"

"He woke me up. Yes. I hadn't seen him in years and years. Hey, this is between us. Drink that tea now so you can get some sleep."

"But —"

"Abby," he said, "don't tell people that you see Blue. They'll think you're some kind of fake or crazy, one or the other. And seeing Blue is . . . well, it's special. So, just know that if he's around, he's looking after you."

She nodded.

"We won't speak about it unless we're alone, okay?"

"Okay."

She drank her tea and they went back to bed. She was surprised she fell asleep easily and that she wasn't afraid.

16

But she wasn't. The way her grandfather had explained it . . . Blue was looking after her.

The next day, although her family tried to keep the facts from her, Abby learned that the man who was trying to get in had broken into a tavern in Charleston a few nights before — and killed the owner. Thanks to her grandparents calling the police so quickly and quietly, they'd never have to find out what their fate might have been had he gotten in. And thanks to them, he'd been apprehended.

Thanks to Blue, she thought.

But she didn't see the pirate in the tavern again, and as the years went by, she convinced herself that she'd seen him standing there because she knew so much about him, because actors portrayed Blue all the time, and because she'd been so frightened.

Once, when she was thirteen, she talked to Gus about it. "I never saw him after that night," she said.

And Gus had smiled and put an arm around her shoulders. "He comes when we need him, Abby. He comes when we need him. He made an appearance during the American Revolution when a family member needed to escape after spying on the British. And he came during the Civil

17

War . . . and he came again when an Anderson was hiding from a fed during prohibition," Gus admitted dryly. "Blue watches, you know. And he finds the one who sees him, and . . . well, he's not on call. God save us all from ghost hunters. I won't let them in here. Blue isn't a séance away. Like I said, he comes when he's needed."

She saw him the night her mother died of pneumonia, and again two years later when her father died, his heart having given out. Blue stood in the cemetery and watched solemnly as they were buried, and Abby felt his touch on her hair as she sobbed each time.

She thought she saw him at her bedside, occasionally, just watching over her.

But life was busy. Years passed, and her memory of Blue faded and settled back into history, exactly where it belonged.

1

"Mr. Gordon, how were you able to find Joshua Madsen when the police were completely baffled as to where Bradford Stiles was keeping the child?"

That was the first question shouted, but there were dozens of reporters in front of the Richmond police station where Malachi Gordon had just finished the interviews and paperwork that completed the Stiles case as far as he was concerned. They were like a flock of ring-billed seagulls with their microphones.

Should've had someone sneak me out the back, he thought.

He raised a hand. "Please. It's been a long day and night for everyone involved."

At his side, Detective Andrew Collins supported his efforts to escape. "Everyone who worked this case is drained. There'll be a police spokesperson out shortly. Let Mr. Gordon pass!"

That didn't stop the barrage of questions or change the fact that Malachi felt as if he was being attacked by a flock of birds as he and Andy Collins made their way to the street and his SUV.

"Sorry," Andy muttered. "Should have —"

"Yeah, yeah, should've gotten me out through the back. Or maybe I could've called for a 'Beam me up, Scotty!' " Malachi said. "Not to worry — my mistake. I guess we're all worn out."

They reached the car, which was behind a police fence so the reporters couldn't follow them that far. As Malachi slid into the driver's seat, Andy asked, "How the hell *did* you find that cabin in the woods?"

"Pure luck, I think. We'd all fanned out. I just got to it first. It's my neck of the woods, so I pretty much knew where it *couldn't* be," Malachi said.

"Well, another few hours and . . . That boy owes you his life."

Malachi shook his head. "Everyone worked on this."

"But his mom came to you — and the case broke once you were on it," Andy said. "You know, if you admitted you were a psychic, no one would think less of you. I mean, yeah, some of those guys can be jerks, and they like to tease you about your voodoo powers and all that, but —"

"I can't admit I'm a psychic, Andy, because I'm not," Malachi told him. "I'm going to go home and get some sleep. You need to do the same."

"Sure thing. Thanks, Malachi."

"Yep," Malachi said. He hesitated. On a case like this, cops could be hard-asses. Big tough guys, they still felt fear. Not fear of a junkie or a drug dealer or even a brutal killer, but fear of what they didn't know or didn't understand. After he'd left the force in New Orleans, he'd preferred to work on his own for that very reason. As a P.I., he didn't mind working with them; he just didn't want to be one of them. That way when the ribbing got bad, he could always walk out.

Some cops, though, like Andy, were all right. They didn't understand. Maybe they were even a little afraid. But they were willing to accept any help they could get, and they weren't afraid to be grateful for it.

"Andy," he said, "thanks to you and your lieutenant for letting me in on this, and for listening to me. The kid owes *you* his life."

"Hell, yeah!" Andy said.

Grinning, Malachi waved to him and revved the car into gear, leaving the parking lot. He headed out of the city then, anxious to get away. He'd never expected the publicity that would come with this case. He'd taken it on because Joshua Madsen's mother, Cindy, had come to him. She had broken his heart. Joshua had been abducted during the two-block walk from his school bus to his home yesterday afternoon. A neighbor had seen a nondescript white van pull away, and when that news came out, police had immediately suspected Stiles, the Puppy Killer, as he'd been called.

Stiles didn't kill puppies; he used puppies to lure young people to his van. They'd rescued a litter of golden retriever pups and their mom when they'd found Stiles and Joshua Madsen.

Malachi didn't consider himself particularly brilliant in finding Stiles. The police investigative work had been excellent. They'd narrowed down the white vans in the city, thanks to the keen eye of the neighbor who'd managed to give them a partial on the license plate. Soil found on one of the victims had placed him in a certain area.

Malachi had known the area.

And he lived not twenty miles away in a home that was over two-and-a-half centuries old and came complete with pocket doors so that it could serve as a tavern, way station, home and hideout when need be. And it also came with Zachary Albright, Revolutionary spy and resident ghost.

No need to try explaining *that* to Andy, even if they were friends, or any of the other cops. Because, frankly, Zachary didn't have all the answers; being dead didn't make him omniscient. Just like he'd been in life, Zachary was a passionate man with a strong sense of right and wrong. He wandered the grounds, and he'd been the one to note the reclusive hunting lodge near the river. He'd suggested it to Malachi, and Malachi had remembered it — yes, the perfect place to bring a victim. Cries couldn't be heard and the sure-flowing water was always ready to wash away an abundance of evidence.

It occurred to him that he really shouldn't be thanked; he'd been observing the comings and goings on the trail when he was spotted by Stiles. He'd been forced to kill Stiles or be killed himself. The trail had led to a rundown shack but there'd been no sign of the missing boy. Police had searched the woods. Because of the "hideaway" in his own home — floorboards that lifted to reveal a six-by-six hidden room below — he'd begun to tear apart the shack. And he'd found Joshua Madsen, bound hand and foot, dehydrated, unconscious . . . but still alive.

Kids were resilient, he told himself. And this time, Stiles hadn't had a chance to abuse the boy. They got him to the hospital and he'd been returned to the loving arms of his family. He'd make it, Malachi believed, without carrying the kind of abuse that might have made him an abuser himself.

Malachi wished he could say that about all kids who were abducted.

It was late, past midnight, and once he took the ramp off I-64, the country road that would take him home was dark. He turned down the air-conditioning in his car. Summer was quickly changing into fall.

He pulled into his drive and entered the old house he'd inherited from his uncle, an academic who'd never married, thus leaving him the place in his will. Malachi had spent time with him there from when he was a kid. He'd loved it, and his parents had owned a home just minutes away in a suburb of Richmond. He usually kept the pocket doors open. While the original structure had been maintained, it was also a home. It had always been a home, even when the original inhabitants had opened it as a tavern because of the economy. Yep, things didn't really change. Back in the 1700s, sometimes the only way to survive had been to serve up good old country fare and lots of locally brewed ale and use the home itself as income.

Malachi picked up his mail and dropped his keys on the side table as he walked in. He was immediately accosted by Zachary. Once, Malachi had been unnerved by the ghost. Now he was accustomed to Zachary, clad in the black frock coat and silk vest in which he'd been buried out back in the family cemetery.

"You found him?" Zachary asked anxiously.

"We did. Thank you. If you hadn't mentioned that place —"

"You would've thought of it. Eventually."

"And the kid might have been dead by then."

"Your jacket!" Zachary said. He touched Malachi's arm. Malachi felt the movement of air around him, nothing else.

"The killer fired at me."

"Good God, man, he was close!"

"Too close. I shot back. He's dead."

"Quite fine!"

Malachi shook his head. "I didn't mean to kill him. We hadn't found the boy yet. But I assumed someone built the shack on the lines of old places like this, and I was right. Joshua Madsen was in the hideaway."

"So you saved him. Are you injured?"

"Only my pride. I didn't think Stiles had seen me. I was trying to watch the place and get closer, and I didn't realize he'd come out back. Not until the bullet grazed my shoulder. I liked this jacket — not as much as uninjured flesh, but —"

"Then, all ended well," Zachary broke in, pleased. "I'm out to tell Genevieve!"

The ghost turned and left him, moving through what was now the kitchen and outside, dissolving through the walls. He was heading to the small family cemetery in back, Malachi knew. Zachary's wife and children were there — the three who'd died as infants and the three who'd survived childhood diseases to adulthood. Many of his grandchildren and great-grandchildren were there, too. Malachi had asked him once why he stayed around when he missed his Genevieve so much. Zachary had told him, "I believe I will know when it's time for me to follow my love."

Malachi never reminded him that he hadn't known when it was time to hide from the British during the Revolution. Zachary had been caught spying. They'd intended to hang him but he'd escaped and yet, in escaping, he'd been mortally wounded and had died in the arms of his Genevieve, right in the house, in front of the large stone hearth.

Then again, Malachi mused, he hadn't been that bright himself. Stiles had almost caught him in the chest with a .45.

He walked into the kitchen to pour himself a shot of his favorite single-malt Scotch. As he did so, there was a tap at his door. He immediately stiffened.

Aw, come on! His address wasn't public. The damned reporters hadn't found him out here, had they?

He decided to ignore the summons and remained unwaveringly focused on his shot of Scotch.

His phone rang. He glanced at his caller ID as he passed it. The number was unavailable, so he didn't answer. The ringing stopped.

The pounding at the door began again.

Swearing, he strode over to it. He lifted the little cover on the peephole and looked out. He was ready to swing the door open, oh-so-ready to berate whoever was knocking at this time of night.

He stopped, surprised by the sight of three somber and distinguished-looking men in suits. One was elderly — possibly around eighty or so. The other two were tall and appeared to have Native American blood in their backgrounds, though mixed with some kind of Northern European ancestry.

The elderly man held a cell phone. He hit the keys.

Malachi's cell began ringing again.

Seriously, what the hell? These guys had his number and they knew where to find him.

He opened the door and scowled at the three of them.

"Mr. Gordon, we're sorry to disturb you, but we've been trying to reach you," the elderly gentleman said. He held up his cell phone with a shrug.

"I've been a little busy," Malachi said. "And it is —" he looked at his watch "— almost 3:00 a.m. Who are you? I don't mean to be rude, but I've had a long day and a longer night. What do you want?"

"Your unusual talent, Mr. Gordon," the elderly man said, offering his hand. "My name is Adam Harrison. These are agents Jackson Crow and Logan Raintree."

"Uh, great, nice to meet you. What unusual talent?"

"The kind explained by your roommate," one of the other men said. Raintree, Malachi thought.

"My roommate?" Malachi said.

Raintree indicated someone who stood behind Malachi.

Malachi turned. Zachary was back in the house, watching him — and the newcomers — with obvious amusement.

"I believe these gentlemen see me, Malachi," Zachary said.

"Yes, we see you," the man introduced as Crow acknowledged. "May we come in, please? You had a long and fruitful day, and we're pretty sure you don't intend to stop when it comes to protecting the innocent who are in imminent danger."

"We believe we can make you an offer you can't refuse," Adam Harrison said.

Harrison. Malachi thought he knew the name. Harrison had been around a long time; he was known for solving some horrible crimes, some cases that . . .

Were unusual.

That had some kind of . . .

Ghosts.

He opened the door. "Okay, come on in, but I was about to have a Scotch. You can join me or not. I'll listen to you — but that's it. I'll listen."

Harrison walked in, followed by the other two. Malachi closed the door behind them.

They saw Zachary.

He asked them to go ahead and sit down in the old parlor by the huge stone hearth. Back in the kitchen, he scooped ice into glasses and poured Scotch.

He paused, then added a second shot to his own.

He had a feeling his life was about to change.

"One day I'll fall, but I will fall to the law on the high seas, and not to the likes of you, Scurvy Pete! I will go with my ship — and not with the dregs of the sea!"

"To the death, Blue Anderson! To the death!"

The two young fencer/actors played out the battle between Blue Anderson and Scurvy Pete Martin with passion and panache on a raised all-weather stage at the far side of the Dragonslayer parking lot. They were decked out in full pirate gear, colorful flared and embellished jackets swirling around them as they accomplished each choreographed step.

The wench they fought over — a British admiral's daughter named Missy Tweed — cowered in a corner while they fought. She was customarily played by a pretty young blonde from the local arts academy. Eyewitness accounts of the encounter in the river between the two pirates described Blue as a hero, even if he'd been a pirate. But Blue was known for being a staunch Englishman above all else; he didn't mind sacking a non-British ship of her treasure, and he only went to battle against enemies of the Crown. Blue swore he'd never be caught, nor would he abandon his crew. He never *was* caught; he sailed away one summer when storms were rampant and wasn't seen again.

The tourist performance — and come-on for the restaurant — ended with the death of Scurvy Pete, and Blue's announcement, "The lady may bring riches, but she'll not be disrespected whilst in my, er, care!" Abigail applauded with the others. She knew the two young actors playing the parts. Blue was played by Roger English, an old friend; they'd graduated from high school together. Without his long dark braided wig and beard, he had sandy-blond hair and deep brown, expressive eyes. Roger, who was an avid fan of Savannah's history, also ran one of the best ghost tours in the city.

She smiled, thinking about old times. Even as a kid, he'd loved to tell scary stories, some from history and some he'd made up. It had all paid off for him in the end.

Scurvy Pete was played by Paul Westermark, who'd gradated in the class before them. Paul sometimes worked for Roger, but he was also an accomplished vocalist and guitarist and spent many nights playing local venues.

While their audience, collected from passersby on the street and those who knew that the two pirates performed on Saturdays, grouped around to congratulate them on their performance or ask "pirate" questions, Abby hurried around to the front to reach the restaurant.

She was anxious.

Come home. I need you.

That cryptic summons had come from Gus Anderson, her grandfather, and had brought Abigail Anderson driving down from Virginia. He hadn't wanted to talk to her about "the situation" on the phone; he needed to see her in person. She feared the worst. Gus was in his early nineties and even if he was in excellent shape for his age, he was certainly no spring chicken. And while she would've dropped anything in the world to come home if he was in trouble, she couldn't help but marvel at his timing. She'd finished at the academy, and she was now waiting for her actual assignment. That made it a perfect time for her to drive home.

Gus's restaurant, the Dragonslayer tavern,

sat right on the river, just as it had since 1758. Abby had arrived in time to see the end of one of the three performances given every Saturday, this one donc as the tavern closed after lunch to prepare for the dinner crowd. Whether the show brought diners to the restaurant or not, Gus didn't really care. As a youth, he'd played his great-great — however many greats — uncle in the shows; now, he simply loved his restaurant. They weren't the only "pirate" restaurant in town, and they weren't the most famous. But they were, as far as preservation went, filled with integrity. Diners could get great stories from Gus if they were intrigued by the old-time lure of the establishment.

Approaching the restaurant was part of the charm to Abby, and part of the allure of coming home. Driving the streets with their majestic moss-covered and stately oaks, she always felt a little thrill when she saw the Dragonslayer appear before her. She'd grown up in Savannah, and had often stayed at the Dragonslayer. It wasn't that her family didn't have a house, and a lovely house at that, on a nearby square, almost as historic as the restaurant itself. But, as a child, she'd spent days and nights with her grandparents, who'd maintained their apartment right above the tavern where famous men had come for two and a half centuries. She'd been regaled with tales of the pirate days, when her ancestor had built the pub and where his brother — the infamous Blue Anderson — had been known to slip in and shanghai many a ne'er-do-well.

The Dragonslayer never changed. It was lovingly maintained, but it never changed. Its edifice appeared much as it had in the 1750s. There were probably far more adult trees surrounding it now, with their mystical sweep of dripping moss, but other than that, she could well imagine stepping back in time. Of course, that would mean slop pots, pigs, chickens and other animals crowding what was now the parking lot, and a horrendous smell in the midst of a summer like this. But still, there was a touch of magic about a place imbued with history. Gus called it living history — each new generation being a part of the past and creating more history.

She hurried toward the building, anxious to see her grandfather, dreading whatever problem he might have that had brought him to say, "I need you." A problem he didn't want to discuss on the phone.

A covered porch with old wooden benches for diners awaiting their tables had been part of the original building. Now steps and a ramp led up to the porch. Near the old double doors to the entry Gus kept the typical wire bin that offered promo materials, maps of the historic section and a free local community paper. The community paper was on the top tier of the bin; Gus's clientele were locals as often as they were visitors. Even distracted as she was, she noticed the blazing headline in the paper.

Second Body Found; Police Seek Any Information!

She picked up the paper, surprised that she hadn't seen anything on the news regarding a murder in Savannah. She glanced over the article as she reached for the old iron ring that opened the door.

She learned that tourists leaving an Irish bar around the bend on the river had found the first victim, a young woman. This morning, the second victim, a businessman from Iowa, had come ashore down by one of the coffeehouses. The reporter asked: Is a River Rat killing in the city? Abby flinched; she had a feeling the moniker would stick.

Were these deaths related?

The victimology was different — one woman, one man. But both had been tourists or visitors, which meant they didn't know the city.

Since she'd just come from her FBI classes, it was hard not to speculate on the situation. But while part of her mind wondered if it was the kind of case she might be called in on if the local police invited the feds to take part, she was still too worried about Gus to give the horrible matter her full attention. She folded the paper and slipped it into the large canvas carryall she had over her shoulder. Gus first, paper later.

Pulling off her sunglasses, she stepped through the door. Lights were ablaze inside, but they didn't compare with the sun burning outside in the late-summer heat of Savannah.

"Abby!"

She'd barely stepped in when she heard Macy Sterling, Gus's day manager, call her name. Macy came from behind the reservation desk to throw both arms around her in an enthusiastic hug. "Hey, Gus said you were coming today! He's been talking about nothing else all morning. I'm so glad! Seems like forever since you've been here!"

Macy was an attractive woman in her early forties with bright green eyes and sable hair swept up in a chignon. She'd worked for Gus since her mid-twenties and she was a family friend as well as employee. Like all employees here, she was dressed up in Dragonslayer traditional costume, that being pirate mode. Macy made a beautiful wench. She had a lovely figure and did her white cotton blouse, black leggings, boots and red vest proud.

"It's great to be here," Abby told her. "But it hasn't been *that* long. Only about six months. I did my basic training, twenty weeks, and then I graduated. And after that, I was assigned to more behavioral classes and desk duty. Fortunately, I was in a sort of holding pattern so I could come home now. They're working on permanent assignments for everyone in my class and my current supervisor told me I could take a break."

"Well, last time you were here, it was just for a day, and Gus hoarded you selfishly. I hope you have more time this trip. We miss you."

"Thanks," Abby said. "And I miss you all when I'm gone. And this place, for sure!" She took a minute to appreciate the bar; it had been there from the beginning and had actually been constructed from the planks of an old ship. Now, of course, it was lovingly tended with wood polish.

The walls were adorned with antique figureheads and pirate flags. An old ship's wheel separated the entry from the bar area to the left — as well as the steps to the second floor — and the restaurant rooms to the right. The old secondary stairs, cut out of stone, were seldom used now. They led down to the basement and the "secret" passage to the river and were guarded by rails and a life-size robotic mannequin of a 1700s pirate, namely Blue Anderson.

"Oh!" Macy dropped a kiss on her cheek. "I should've said congratulations! You passed! I was so sorry we couldn't attend the ceremony. Our little girl is really all grown up now."

"Yes, let's hope so, since I'm twenty-six," Abby said, smiling. "I mean, if any of us ever really grows up completely."

Macy studied her as proudly as a parent. "Tell me more. How are you? How's living there? Who are you dating? *Do* people still date? How's the great state of Virginia?" Macy fired questions at her.

Abby laughed. "I'm fine. I rent a little house in a rural district not far from work — it's historic. The 'history' thing must've gotten into my blood. I love living there. Yes, I believe people still date, but not me. I've been too busy. And Virginia is hot as Savannah," she said, trying to answer Macy's questions in order.

Macy held her at arm's length, studying her.

"Where's your hair? You didn't chop off your hair, did you? One day, you mark my words, you'll get old and you'll have to dye it, so you need to have lots of that glorious color while you can!" Macy said.

Yes, it was good to be home.

"My hair's all here, Macy," she said. "Just swept up because it's hot as hell on my neck," she said. She'd heard that her hair color came down to her from Gus and his family; apparently Blue Anderson, the pirate brother, had enjoyed the same coloring. But whether his moniker had come from the blue-black hair color that appeared in the Anderson clan every so often or the brilliant color of his eyes, no one really knew. Or because he had a reputation for the "black and blue" he could inflict on those who defied his orders . . .

"We'll catch up some more later," she said, then asked, "but where's Gus?"

"Hmm, I'm not sure. He was up in the office. You want to wait for him there? Oh, are you hungry? Shall I have the cooks whip something up? You drove five-hundred-plus miles, and you *are* the heir to a wonderful restaurant!"

"No, I've eaten, thanks. I stopped at the

North-South Carolina border," Abby told her. "I'm going to run up to the office, okay? If he's not there, I'll wait for him."

"You bet!" Macy gave her another fierce hug. She returned it.

She turned to hurry up the stairs but before she could do so, she was hailed from the bar.

"Abby! Why, Abby's here, just as old Gus said!"

Abby knew the voice well.

"Bootsie!" she said, turning back to greet the man sitting at the end of the bar with two other familiar faces. Together the three looked every bit the rakish pirate crew. Young compared to her grandfather, Bootsie was still close to seventy — and yet seemed ageless. He had a thick hard-muscled chest and arms like a linebacker. He'd been a fixture on his bar stool as long as she could remember, and if any man had ever resembled an old pirate, it was Bootsie. His real name was Bob Lanigan; he'd been in the marines, followed by the merchant marines, and then he'd captained one of the ships that ran along the river. He'd had a sweet, long-suffering wife who'd indulged his whims and waited patiently at home for whenever he chose to return, but Betty had died about a year ago and Bootsie now

40

spent much of his time on the bar stool. He had a thick thatch of long white hair, a white beard — and a peg leg. He'd lost his left leg from the knee down when he was in the service, and he didn't "cotton to" any of the new technology. While he owned a number of new, very real-looking prosthetics, his peg leg was just fine for him. Abby only remembered seeing him without it once or twice.

If he wore an eye patch, he'd be perfect for the role of pirate, but thankfully, Bootsie still had both eyes.

"Look at you, lass! Beautiful! Didn't I tell you she'd grow up beautiful?" he asked Dirk Johansen, one of his companions at the bar. Dirk was the "whippersnapper" of Bootsie's group of cronies. He was in his late forties and still sailing. A lean, fit man, he often resembled a staff member at the Dragon-slayer, since he typically came in straight off one of his "pirate cruises" on the *Black Swan.* He was handsome and distinguished, an eternal bachelor, or so it seemed. Abby was pretty sure that Macy had maintained a secret crush on him for years. They would have made a handsome couple.

Dirk smiled at her as he replied to the statement. "Bootsie, she's been a beautiful young woman for quite a while now. Abby, welcome home. It's always wonderful to see you."

"Cheers!" said the third member of their group, Aldous Brentwood. Aldous was several times a millionaire from his own — and his family's — maritime efforts. He was in his mid-fifties, but hard work had kept him toned. He shaved his head bald, had bright blue eyes and wore a single gold earring in his left lobe. Like Bootsie, he could easily pass for a pirate, or, Abby thought, the character for the Mr. Clean line of household products.

"Bootsie, Dirk, Aldous," Abby said, giving each a quick hug and kiss on the cheek.

"Gus misses you terribly when you're away," Dirk said.

"And he grins for a week when you're coming back!" Aldous told her.

"Well, I'm here now. I figured I'd find him on a bar stool with you gentlemen. So where's my favorite old grouch? I was on my way up to see if he's in the office," she said.

"He might be up there. I'm not sure." Bootsie shrugged. "He let me in when the kitchen staff started arriving at ten. We sat and talked for a while and he did keep looking at his watch, telling me about where you'd be on your drive."

"I saw him right at opening," Dirk offered.

"Yeah, I did, too, but I didn't see him after that," Aldous said.

Sullivan, the lunchtime bartender, a handsome thirty-year-old with green eyes and flaming red hair, plus a neatly coiffed mustache and beard, came by to check on his "barflies" as the three referred to themselves. He smiled at Abby; she didn't know him well. He'd only worked for her grandfather about four years and she'd been gone most of that time. His given name was Jerry, but he went by Sullivan.

"Abby, he said something earlier about working on the books, so you're probably right. He's got to be up in his office. I haven't seen him since before the lunch crowd started coming in."

"Thanks, Sullivan," Abby said. "And, gentlemen, see you later," she told the three older men seated at the bar.

They responded with an out-of-sync chorus of "Aye, Abby," "See you, Abby," "Glad you're here!"

She smiled and walked over to the winding iron stairway that had been there forever and was watchfully maintained, since it was still used on a daily basis.

The second floor of the establishment had a low ceiling. No food was stored on the upper level, but a long room housed wine, spirits, kitchen utensils and other restaurant supplies. The second floor also had a nice lounge for the employees with lockers and closets full of costumes so no one had to come as a pirate or wench and leave as a pirate or wench. On one side of Gus's office was the apartment he'd lived in with her grandmother until Brenda Anderson's death eight years ago. Now he remained there alone. It had a little sitting room and access to a balcony that looked over the rear grounds and out to the river. Beside the sitting room were the two bedrooms, the one Abby had always slept in and the one her grandfather now maintained for himself. On the other side of Gus's office was the manager's office, shared by Macy and Grant Green, the night manager.

Gus wasn't in his office nor was he in the manager's office. She tried his apartment door. It was open, but Gus was nowhere to be seen. The room was sparse and spotless. The only pictures on the walls here were images of his family.

Abby called his name as she hurried through the apartment, and then went out to check the supply room, as well. She walked past carefully stored rows of different liquors and the wine vault. There were boxes marked Dragonslayer plates, salad bowls and glasses, tablecloths and more, but none of the employees were up there now.

"Gus!" Abby called again, but all she heard in return was the distant sound of the "pirate" track that played during lunch hours.

Frustrated, she went into the lounge, but she seemed to be the only person on the second floor. Abby walked back to Gus's office and sat at his desk. Despite his age, Gus had entered the age of technology with gusto; he had a new computer, a printer and, to the side, a file cabinet. There was a little office carrier filled with incoming and outgoing mail. She looked anxiously at the incoming mail, hoping she wouldn't find a stack of doctors' bills. She didn't — most of the mail was solicitation letters. She knew he read most of it, always looking to see if there was something the restaurant could use.

"No important mail from doctors or diagnostic clinics," she murmured aloud.

She didn't think it was anything to do with his health that had made him summon her in such a manner, and yet couldn't help being concerned. And curious. Gus had an impressive history. He'd served in the navy during World War II, then he'd returned to Savannah — where he was guaranteed to make a living since his family owned the restaurant — to join the police force. But when his father passed away, he'd left the force to concentrate on the Dragonslayer. She'd admired him all her life. It was thanks to Gus that she'd gone to the FBI academy; he'd encouraged her in every action she'd ever wanted to take. He hadn't pushed her toward law enforcement, but he'd told her she was smart and could do anything she wanted to do.

There was nothing on his desk giving her any indication that something might be wrong with Gus.

Had he run out to do an errand? She drummed her fingers on the desk and then took the newspaper from her handbag to study the article on the murders.

Both victims had drowned. Both had been found with their hands tied behind their backs. Police were withholding other information, as it was an ongoing investigation. Next of kin had been notified, and anyone with any information regarding either victim was urged to contact law enforcement.

She set the paper down, then started, certain she'd heard a sound coming from the storage area — but she'd just been there. At the rear of the storage area was a wrought-iron stairway from the back of the dining area to the second floor. It was far narrower than the main staircase and it was gated. Diners were prohibited from taking those stairs, as was the staff, she reminded herself. Gus didn't consider them safe. At one time, they'd allowed pirates who were drinking, wenching and enjoying their liberty in Savannah to escape quickly from the upstairs to the underground passage that led to the river and their ships. While Robert Anderson — brother of Blue, and Abby's direct ancestor — had been a legitimate businessman, he and his pirate brother were known to be close and Blue Anderson was known to have frequented the tavern. British officers were prone to burst in on the Dragonslayer in search of Blue, and thus the easy escape route.

Thanks to the secret passage, they'd never caught Blue — or any of his men — at the tavern.

The door to the passage was covered with a grating now. Before, it had been hidden under wooden planks that matched the rest of the floor. Now it was a curiosity and guarded by chains, a locked metal grate and the robotic Blue Anderson. Blue was set up beside the grate, and diners loved to have their pictures taken with him.

Abby stood up, then walked down the hall to the storage room. The lights remained on as they always did during business hours. She moved silently along the rows of modern chrome restaurant equipment and boxes to the back of the room.

Halfway there, she paused.

Her heart seemed to rise to her throat and catch there.

Blue! She could see him. He was standing right by the winding iron stairs. He beckoned to her and went down them.

She might have been a kid again, frozen there. For long moments, she wasn't sure she was even breathing.

He only comes when he's needed, Gus had told her.

Abby came to life. She sprinted across the room and to the stairs.

A chain stretched across the iron railing of the landing here; it was in place as it should have been.

Abby slid underneath it and quickly followed the winding steps to the main floor.

A few diners lingered, but she'd been quiet and hadn't been noticed. The grating was in place. She knelt down — and saw that the lock was open.

Heedless of anyone who might see her,

Abby lifted the grating. It was dark below. There were lights, but Gus kept them off except for the ones directly by the grate. She hurried down the stairs, calling his name. "Gus!"

She reached the bottom and the dank tunnel that led out to the river.

"Gus!"

Someone seemed to be ahead of her. A shadow moving almost as one with the darkness.

She followed.

And then, ten feet along the tunnel, she found him.

Gus.

She fell to her knees at his side. "Gus, Gus, Gus!"

He didn't answer. He didn't feel her touch when she felt for a pulse, for any sign that he was breathing.

He was so cold!

Yes, cold, she realized, horrified and heartbroken.

Stone-cold dead.

2

Augustus Anderson was laid to rest a week after his death at the city's incredibly beautiful Bonaventure Cemetery.

Abby's family had a plot there, a group of tombstones that ran the gamut from the mid-1800s, when the cemetery was founded, to the last burial before this one, when her father had passed away. A lovely low fence surrounded the small plot. The number of people who'd come to the church ceremony and now to the cemetery to honor Gus was almost overwhelming. The crowd didn't fit into the actual plot area and many waited on the other side of the fence, listening to Father McFey as he spoke his final words over the coffin and Gus was left to rest in peace.

Abby barely heard the service. Despite the fact that he'd been gone a week, she was in no less a state of mental turmoil. Friends had sympathetically reminded her of his age and that he'd died quickly and hadn't suffered a long and debilitating illness, which would have mortified him. She didn't need to be told. She knew she was blessed that she'd had him for so many years — and that he'd been lucky to have led such a robust and healthy life.

All of that was true.

But it wasn't right. What had *happened* wasn't right.

Gus, she was certain, had been murdered.

Making the suggestion to the police had merely brought her more sympathy.

Gus had been as old as the hills. She'd recognized the looks that the officers who were called to the scene had given her.

Poor girl's lost her only living relative. She just came out of the academy at Quantico, and she can't accept an old — old! — man dying, so she had to turn it into a mystery.

An autopsy had revealed that he'd died because his heart had given out.

She believed that. But his heart had given out for a *reason.*

Gus had expected her; he'd been anxious to see her. Gus never got up and suddenly decided he needed to go down into the old pirate tunnels — he hadn't been down there for years. To ensure that the tunnel remained safe and supported the structures above, he sent workers down every few months. He maintained the tunnel because of its historic value. It wasn't a place he went for exercise or to commune with his ancestors or anything of the kind.

She'd tried to be logical. Gus had been very old. She'd heard of a number of cases like his, cases in which someone had led a long and healthy life, and just dropped dead. Young runners occasionally dropped dead, for God's sake.

She couldn't forget how and when it had happened. Couldn't forget what he'd said.

Come home. I need you.

She wished now that she'd insisted he talk to her over the phone, that she'd demanded he provide *some* sort of explanation.

But she hadn't.

And still his words haunted her. If she didn't discover *why* he'd said those words to her, they'd haunt her for the rest of her life.

She suddenly realized that everyone was silent, that Father McFey was looking at her. He'd finished with the ceremony, and everyone was waiting for her.

She held the folded American flag that had draped his coffin, since he'd seen military service in two wars, and a single rose. She was supposed to drop the rose on the coffin, allow others to do the same thing and officially end the burial of a man who had become an icon.

It seemed that half of Savannah had come out for the occasion. They needed to get back to their lives.

She needed to figure out how to organize hers.

She walked over to the coffin, which still sat above the ground; they wouldn't lower it into the earth until she and the rest of the mourners were gone.

The soprano from Gus's church was singing "Amazing Grace" as they finished and Abby was aware that Macy — and several other people — were sniffing and trying to hold back sobs.

Abby didn't cry; she'd cried herself out over the past week. She stood and touched the coffin and spoke to him within her own mind.

Thank you, Gus. Love you, Gus. Thank you for loving me the way you did. You will always be a part of me, with me. I will never forget you. . . .

She set her rose on the coffin and stepped back, gazing into the crowd. As she'd expected, Blue Anderson was there, across from the coffin, a little to the left, behind Gus's old cronies — Bootsie, Dirk and Aldous. The men had dressed in their best suits for the occasion. But even in their tailored and proper attire, they looked like pirates. Bootsie had his peg leg, of course, and Aldous was still bald, still wore his earring.

Maybe the pirate resemblance came from the fact that Blue Anderson, in his splendid frock coat and sweeping pirate hat, stood behind them.

She stared gravely at Blue. He nodded to her, a gesture of consolation that somehow seemed reassuring.

Father McFey took her arm and led her from the burial site. A uniformed chauffeur waited to open the door to the black limo that would take her back to the Dragonslayer. Those who could join them would be there for a repast in honor of Gus.

It was what he'd wanted; he had let his wishes be known in his will. He'd wanted to lie next to his wife and his son, Abby's father, and he'd wanted "Amazing Grace" and Father McFey. He'd left explicit instructions. *And then bring our friends back to the Dragonslayer. Please laugh with them and remember the wonderful events in my life. Celebrate for me, for I was blessed, and life comes to an end for us all.*

She turned before getting into the car. A

very tall man she didn't know leaned against another car, a silver SUV. He hadn't come to the grave site, she thought. But he'd been watching — he'd watched the burial rites, just as he watched her now.

He was interesting-looking, certainly. He appeared to be six-three or -four. He was appropriately dressed for a funeral in a dark suede jacket, white shirt and a dark vest. Black hair was neatly clipped, with one swatch that sat slightly low over his forehead. She couldn't see his eyes because he was wearing sunglasses but she knew he was watching her.

An old friend of Gus's? Or a new one? Definitely someone she hadn't met.

But he hadn't really taken part in the service. He'd stood at a distance, as if he had needed to watch — and still meant to be respectful. Odd, to say the least.

"Ms. Anderson?"

She realized she'd been staring at him when the driver suggested that she enter the car.

She was alone on the short drive back to the Dragonslayer. Macy had gone on ahead to see that they were set up for the reception to follow the service. Reception? No, party. Gus had insisted they celebrate his life, not the passing of it.

She thought about the week since his death and the funeral. Many people considered that a long time, but there'd been an autopsy and she'd wanted to arrange for those who'd loved Gus — some of them from out of town — to show up for the service.

The parking lot was half-full when the limo drove up to let Abby out. She wasn't sure why she felt she needed more fortitude for Gus's party than she had for the church or the graveside service. She knew a lot of people were going to cry — party or no — but she felt drained of tears, numb. Gus's death was the end of her world as she'd known it.

"Hey!"

When she walked in, she almost smiled. The first people she saw were Gus's old cohorts already at the bar. Bootsie, Dirk and Aldous.

They had teacups in front of them but she knew the tea had been spiked with whiskey — Gus's favorite drink and cure-all.

They swung their stools around to greet her, all raising their cups. "Abby!"

She felt oddly as if they were saluting a monarch. Maybe they were afraid she'd oust them from their seats at the bar.

"Hey, guys," she said.

Aldous reached for something and came over to her. She noted the way his bald head shimmered in the tavern's lights. His blue eyes seemed gray, sad, solemn.

He'd collected another cup from the bar. "We had it ready for you," he said. "We thought we'd have a private toast before you got caught up in all the craziness. Gus was one of a kind. A lot of people loved him. But I think we're going to miss him the most, the four of us."

"Thanks, Aldous," she said, taking the cup from him. She lifted it. "To Gus!"

"To Gus! Long may his legend live!" Bootsie said.

She gave Aldous a kiss on the cheek and walked over to do the same with Bootsie and Dirk. "You guys all okay, workwise?" She looked specifically at Dirk. His "pirate" ship went out every day. Dirk loved to play the pirate master of ceremonies and he was very good at it.

"It's handled. I have the crew taking care of everything. No way I wouldn't honor Gus," Dirk told her.

Macy came striding over to her. "Abby, the mayor wants to convey his condolences and the chief of police is here." She glanced at the men. "If I can steal you away for a minute."

"See you in a bit, guys," she said as she accompanied Macy.

And so continued what already felt like a long day.

She was cordial to the chief, despite the fact that she wasn't feeling especially fond of the local police at the moment. She supposed she couldn't blame them. Her insistence that something was wrong with the circumstances of an old man's death couldn't compare with some of the very real and obvious crimes they were facing.

And the autopsy did conclude that Gus had died of a heart attack, not surprising for someone of his age who wanted to crawl around in historic tunnels as if he were a young man.

But that was the point they *weren't* getting. Gus didn't crawl around in tunnels!

Fine. There was very little she could do about their lack of interest in the tunnels. She'd contacted the officer in charge of her assignment at Quantico, who didn't seem to have much understanding of her situation. An old man had died. It happened; that was life. But, of course, she should take whatever time she needed and report in as soon as possible, let them know when she'd be returning.

And she'd probably be in a boatload of

trouble when she *did* return for an assignment. Because she'd gone over her supervisor's head to contact another FBI unit leader.

Jackson Crow.

Crow was in charge of a special section of the agency; he and his people were based in a field office of their own in Arlington, Virginia. From there, they were sent across the country.

At the regular offices, they were referred to as the "ghost busters." Despite that reference, they were held in awe by most of the other agents. They had a spectacular record of solving cases. She knew about Jackson Crow because he was a legend at the agency; he'd solved cases with various units before being asked to form a special one dedicated to situations that were . . . out of the ordinary.

They were officially known as the Krewe of Hunters. She assumed that was because the first assignment as a new unit had been in New Orleans, when the wife of a U.S. senator had mysteriously died.

Abby didn't want any ghosts "busted." She wanted someone to believe that her grandfather had been onto something, that he'd needed to speak with her for a very real reason. And from what she understood, while there were rumors about the Krewe agents having "special" abilities, they worked with evidence and cold hard facts. Even so, Jackson's units had often been called in when cases involved historic properties that were supposedly haunted.

Heart attack or not, she was convinced Gus had been murdered. His heart had stopped because he'd been startled or come upon some sight so horrible that he'd died of shock. She hoped that her email to Jackson Crow, filled with information on the history of Savannah and the Dragonslayer, would bring him out to investigate. She wasn't sure how she could make a federal case out of the death of a Georgian in Georgia, but she couldn't let it rest. She owed Gus way more than that.

So, as she greeted the local law and government personnel who'd turned out in respect for Gus, she was polite and circumspect. She moved from one to another, thanking them all.

She didn't mention again her belief that he'd been murdered. She didn't need more pitying stares from those who thought she was a little crazy with grief — or suspected that, fresh from the academy, she'd try to create problems between federal and local law enforcement.

Luckily, the people she didn't know didn't stay long. An hour and a half later, she found herself at a table near the life-size image of Blue Anderson, still sipping the spiked tea Aldous had handed her, with Grant Green, the night manager, and a couple of her old friends, Roger English and Paul Westermark. She'd seen Roger and Paul portraying Blue Anderson and Scurvy Pete Martin when she'd arrived a week ago.

"I thought he was immortal," Roger said, sighing. "Lord, I loved that man. He knew how to keep the fun and magic in history. When we were kids, remember, he'd let us dress up? Sometimes we'd pretend to be captives that Blue had taken. Or mates running around, trying to shanghai other men down to the ships."

"Never, ever paid us late." Paul smiled. "I remember during one of the storms that hit Savannah a few years back, Gus had us go and do a whole pirate day for a bunch of kids at one of the shelters. He just did it out of the goodness of his heart."

"He put me in a wig and dressed me up as a silly maiden in distress for that one," Grant Green recalled, sipping on a beer. "Gus was the best. The day I applied to work here, I hadn't even filled out a form and he was short a server, so he stuck an order pad in my hand and said, 'Just sing some kind of pirate song if you mess up — you'll be fine!' "

"Gus was like that," Abby said.

"Ah, Gus!" Grant said sadly. "He was a force of nature. I don't think any of us believed we'd ever really lose him."

She could see that Macy was thanking some of Gus's church friends and saying goodbye. She should have gotten up and joined her.

She couldn't quite manage it.

As she watched, Jerry Sullivan came to the table, bearing a fresh cup.

"New one for you," Sullivan told her. "The one you're holding must be iced tea by now." He shrugged. "Gus did think that a shot of whiskey in hot tea solved all." He grinned at her, green eyes sympathetic. "It's kind of an Irish thing — I know, 'cause of my folks."

"My great-grandfather married an Irish girl in the 1890s, fresh from Ellis Island, or so I heard." Abby smiled back, accepting the tea. She had a feeling that Sullivan had heavily spiked this cup.

He had, but it was good. It burned as she swallowed it, warming her stomach, and then seemed to move outward to her limbs.

"Thanks, Sullivan."

62

"My pleasure," he said, and went back to work.

She watched him leave. Twisting, she saw that someone was standing at the bar with her grandfather's trio of cronies.

"Excuse me," she murmured, rising from the table and heading to the bar.

Before she even came near, she realized that the man was the same one who'd been watching her at the cemetery — few people were that tall with hair quite so dark. She wasn't sure why, but it seemed that her heart was racing a little as she walked to the bar.

"Here's our girl now," Bootsie said affectionately. "Our Abby, more beautiful every day, the finest wench ever to grace such an illustrious tavern."

"Yep, here I am," Abby said dryly, slipping in between him and Dirk.

She faced the unknown man. He was minus his sunglasses. His eyes were green, sharp and enhanced by the darkness of his well-defined brows. His features were striking. Weathered, hardened, bronzed, but striking. His chin was a solid square while his cheekbones were high. He had the look of someone who'd seen the harder side of life — but had come out swinging. Still, his dress was entirely appropriate and she had a feeling he'd be courteous and polite.

"Ms. Anderson," he said, offering her a hand. "My name is Malachi Gordon. I'm here from the bureau."

"Oh," she said, taking his hand. Fed? Yes, he could be a fed. But she doubted it. A fed would've shown up in a more standard suit, wouldn't he?

"Thank you. It wasn't necessary for the bureau to send a representative. Only a few friends in my classes ever met Gus, and the agency sent a beautiful wreath," Abby explained.

"I'm here to see you, Ms. Anderson," he said.

She was curious but didn't want to ask any more in front of the others. She wondered what this was about. Did the agency believe a death in a family could have such a negative effect on an agent that he or she was rendered less able for duty?

"Thank you for being here," she said, assuming he'd clarify later.

"We've been giving him a history of the Dragonslayer," Aldous said.

"And telling him about Gus," Bootsie added.

The trio lifted their cups again. "To Gus!" they said in unison.

Malachi Gordon smiled at Abby. She

smiled in return.

"This is an incredible place," he said. "Well-preserved — and yet alive. Living history is always the best."

"Yes, well, people do love pirates."

"Thank God!" Dirk shrugged and said, "I make my living by running a pirate ship that we take out for tourists every day. We do birthday parties and other occasions, too." He produced a card from his wallet to hand the newcomer. "Abby's worked on her over the years. Go figure — she made a great pirate and now she's a federal agent."

"Well, who ever said there weren't a few pirates among the feds?" Malachi Gordon asked lightly.

That was very amusing to her grandfather's friends; they all laughed. Glancing around, Abby saw that Roger and Paul were about to leave and she excused herself to say goodbye to them. She'd try to catch the fed on his own soon.

Roger and Paul were old friends and both hugged her warmly. She walked out front with them. "Hey, your freebie newspapers were delivered," Roger said, picking up the bundle to open them and lay them on top of the stand. As he did, she noticed the headline.

A *third* murder? she wondered, itching to pick up the paper and find out what was going on.

Or . . . a *fourth*? Had Gus been murdered by the same person who'd killed three people found in or near the river?

Was her mind going haywire because she was a new graduate from the academy who'd just taken classes taught by a premier behavioral specialist? *Was* she looking for a mystery where none existed?

But . . . Savannah's murder rate for the past few years had been low for a city of its size. Any large city battled violent crime and Savannah had seen its share. But this . . .

"Hey, you'll be heading back to Virginia," Roger reminded her. He took her by the shoulders, his eyes meeting hers. "You have to worry about *you* right now, Ms. Anderson."

"What are you going to do?" Paul asked her. "You've inherited the Dragonslayer. You wouldn't close down the tavern, would you?"

"No, no, of course not," she said. "Don't worry."

"That's going to be tough — you being an absentee owner," Paul pointed out.

"Macy has it down pat," Abby said. "We have great bartenders, cooks and waitstaff. I'm sure it's all going to work out. That's been the least of . . ." Her voice trailed off. She didn't want to say *worries*. "That's . . . well, not what I've worried about," she said.

"Yeah, sorry, kid. So sorry," Roger murmured. "I know how much you loved Gus."

"We really loved him, too, you know?" Paul said.

She nodded. "Of course. I know."

Abby went back inside. One of their newest waitresses — a girl named Julie whom Abby had just met — was cleaning up in the dining rooms. The staff who'd been there the longest hadn't really worked that day, other than stepping in to help get a few things loaded into the bus carts. They'd come as mourners.

She looked around; there was no sign of Malachi Gordon.

"Everyone's left?" she asked Julie.

"There are a few of us still tidying up in the kitchen. It's back to full service tomorrow, or so I was told," Julie said. She hesitated. She was young and sweet, a student at the design school. "I mean, I'm sorry — that's your call now. But, um, that's what I was told."

"Yes, we're back to regular hours, Julie.

Thanks." Abby smiled. "And thanks for getting everything picked up."

"Yeah, a real sad thing about Gus. He was so good to all of us."

"That's great to hear, even though it's something I know — that Gus was great to work for," Abby said.

She turned and went back to the front. Sullivan was behind the bar. Macy was collecting glasses that had been left at the tall bar tables.

Aldous, Dirk and Bootsie remained on their bar stools.

"What happened to your new friend?" she asked him. "The man from the bureau?"

Dirk frowned. "I don't know. Maybe he took off. He wasn't actually a friend of yours, right? Just a rep from the government?"

"I'd thought he'd speak with me again before he left," Abby said. "But . . . I guess not."

Bootsie stood, his peg leg wobbling. "Listen, Abby, we know today's been hard on you. Now, the boys and I, we can hang around here as long as you like. Or, better still, we can take you off somewhere else and give you a break from this place."

She shook her head. "No, thanks. It's okay. To be honest, I'm looking forward to

68

some time alone."

"Alone?" Bootsie said, surprised.

"Do you want us to walk you to your parents' house?" Dirk asked her. "I mean, do you *really* want to stay here right now? You have that beautiful house on the square. . . ."

"She should come with us," Aldous said. "The house is where . . . and this is where . . ." He broke off. *The house was where her parents had died; this was where Gus had just died.*

"I love my house — it's beautiful. I really should rent it out again." The previous tenants had been a writer and his family, and they'd gone back to New York a few months ago. She'd rented the place furnished. Not sure what she wanted to do with it yet, she'd brought over some extra clothes and retrieved boxes of her old belongings from the basement, returning them to her childhood bedroom. "I'm not unhappy in either the house or the Dragonslayer, guys. I have good memories here — and there. I'm fine. Just need a little time to take a deep breath now that the funeral's over, and then get everything in order. So . . . out with the three of you! Go wander along the riverfront and give another innkeeper your business tonight. Come back tomorrow. With or without Gus, this remains your place. I don't know what I'd do if I came home and didn't find the three of you here. But for now, scat!"

They looked like a group of fathers forced to leave their children for a first day at school.

"Hey, come on now. Out, out," Abby told them.

They finally left her with a bit more grumbling and a lot of hugs.

Sullivan cleared his throat. "I'll just get these last glasses. . . ."

"No, no, Sullivan, that's all right. I've got it. I'd like something to do," Abby said.

"I'm exhausted," Macy said. "Grant's upstairs. He's checking on supplies for the week. After that, I think he plans on leaving for the night. But, Abby, I don't feel you should be alone here."

"I've spent most of my life here!"

Macy walked behind the bar to get her purse. "All right," she said with obvious reluctance. "Make sure you lock up. The city can be scary. I don't ever remember so many people —"

"Dying?" Sullivan finished. "Come on, Macy. Abby doesn't want us here. I'll walk you home."

Macy nodded as she stood behind the bar,

looking at Abby. "You have my number. If anything comes up. Or if you just need to talk . . ."

"You were both wonderful to Gus. He loved you and appreciated your loyalty to the Dragonslayer. And so do I. Now, I'm fine. You two go on home."

"You know you control the music from behind the bar," Sullivan said.

"I know," Abby assured him.

"I wish Gus had gotten a solid alarm system for this place." Macy glanced at Abby and flushed. "I'm not criticizing. He had cameras put in the front and over by the parking lot, and there's an emergency police buzzer behind the bar. Most of the downstairs windows are sealed now, but . . ."

"He thought his security installations were a big deal. State of the art. He started them more than fifteen years ago, when we were nearly broken into," Abby said. "But, Macy, don't worry. I'll see about getting a real alarm system before I go back to Virginia," Abby promised. She looked up; she heard Grant coming down from the offices upstairs. He joined them, giving her a hug.

She loved Grant. He'd worked for Gus, first as a pirate entertainer. Grant had spent seven years getting his hospitality degree, he'd told her some time ago. He couldn't

71

decide between acting, modeling and going into the restaurant or hotel business. Once he had his degree in hand, the first person to really believe in him had been Gus.

"I heard the words *alarm system,*" Grant said. "I have brochures up in my office. Gus asked me to look into a good system just a few days ago," Grant said.

"Then we'll take care of it," Abby promised. "Grant, sometime tomorrow, if you want to go through the different companies with me, that'd be great."

"Absolutely," Grant said. "I'm going to head out now — if you're sure you're okay."

Grant, who was gay, had been with his partner, Alden Blaine, for well over ten years. Alden worked for the fire department and had left the tavern earlier, since he had an early call the next day.

"Go home, yes, go home. My Lord, getting you people out of here is a real project."

At last, with everyone still protesting, she got them all out the door.

As she closed and locked it, she smiled, wondering what they were worried about; she'd been staying here every night since she'd arrived, and — except for today — the Dragonslayer didn't close until 2:00 a.m. That meant the staff never left until three or four. She'd been going to bed much earlier, leaving Grant to lock up.

And she'd been fine.

Maybe it was the fact that people were here so late — and that the first of the setup crews were usually in by six in the morning, although they didn't open until eleven. So there were only a few hours when she'd been alone and despite, or because of, the circumstances she'd come home to, she'd been sound asleep during those hours.

They were probably worried about what she might imagine in the darkness, worried that she'd be afraid.

But she wasn't afraid. She knew what they didn't know.

Blue Anderson watched over the Dragon-slayer.

In the days that had followed her grand-father's death, she'd hoped Blue would make an appearance. She'd hoped as well, that she'd be haunted by her grandfather.

But no one had appeared to her, upstairs or down, by day or night. Blue had stood by the burial site in the graveyard, though. . . .

With the door finally closed and locked, Abby walked around the downstairs. Figure-heads from ships of many centuries stared down at her. She walked past the hostess stand and behind the bar, gathering up the last of the glasses as she did so.

A copy of the day's paper lay on the bar. She set the glasses by the sanitizer and picked it up.

There was no mention of a serial killer in the article; it stated simply that the body of Felicia Shepherd, twenty-two, had been found on the river embankment by the bridge. The cause of her death would be determined by the medical examiner.

Thoughtfully, Abby walked back to the hostess stand and searched through the papers collected there until she came to the one she had picked up the day she arrived.

The first victim had also been a young woman, aged twenty-five. Her name was Ruth Seymour and she'd come to Savannah on vacation. She'd wanted to stay in the historic city for a night on her own before meeting up with friends at Hilton Head. She had checked into her bed-and-breakfast — the clerk remembered her as bubbly and charming — and that was the last anyone could remember seeing her until her body was discovered.

The second victim was Rupert Holloway, a salesman for a mobile phone company. He never arrived at his hotel. His wife told police he'd planned to meet business associates on the riverfront for lunch.

The associates had gone to lunch; Rupert Holloway had not. He had next appeared on the river embankment — dead.

No cause of death was mentioned for Holloway, either. An autopsy had been pending for both at the time the article was written.

"Foul play suspected," she read aloud.

She set the first paper down and picked up the most recent one.

Abby didn't care what the police were saying. Ruth Seymour, Rupert Holloway and now Felicia Shepherd were all out-of-towners, all found by the river.

Serial killer.

She shook her head. The victimology was so different. A serial killer usually liked a type. With Ted Bundy, it had been young women with long dark hair. Jeffrey Dahmer had gone for boys or young men. Some killers preyed on couples.

Maybe he was after young women — and the businessman had been a mistake or had stumbled upon him when he'd been engaged in some other illegal act?

"Ms. Anderson?"

Abby was so startled by the voice that she screamed and threw the newspaper in the air. She swung around.

To her astonishment, she wasn't alone.

She'd locked herself in, all right, but

75

somehow she'd managed to lock herself in before confirming that everyone else was out.

It was the agent, and he was staring at her from the left dining room. But the lights had been dimmed in the dining rooms, so he would've known they were closing.

He hadn't gone, after all.

He walked toward her quickly, apologizing as he did. "I didn't mean to scare you."

"What the hell are you still doing here?" she demanded. "You did scare me — you scared me out of my wits."

"I might have frightened you because of the circumstances," he said. "You did just come from the academy, right?"

"What's that supposed to mean, Mr. Gordon?" she asked. "A certain amount of fear is healthy for all of us. It keeps us from being reckless."

"That's the line at the academy, is it?" he asked.

She frowned. A small trickle of fear assailed her again. Who the hell *was* this man? She didn't know him; he'd *said* that he'd come from the FBI but he'd done nothing to prove it.

"You don't remember the academy?" she asked him.

"Remember it? I never went to it."

There was, she knew, a gun below the bar in the strongbox. A nice safe place during the business day — hard to get to right now. And this guy was probably a full six-foot-four, lean, muscled and hard as nails.

Unease slithered alone her spine.

Serial killer?

He didn't look like a serial killer.

But, of course, she *had* just come through the academy, as he'd said. So she was well aware that a serial killer could be charming, credible and handsome. They'd seen enough examples of that.

"I'm sorry. You really are frightened. And you're thinking that getting your gun from under the bar won't be easy, and since it was your grandfather's funeral service today, you aren't carrying your regulation Glock," he said.

"I've been around this place since I was a kid, Mr. Gordon — or whoever you are. I'm lethal with a broken bottle and I can grab one and smash it before you can blink!"

He smiled and shook his head, frowning. "I told you, I'm so sorry. I didn't mean to scare you."

"Then perhaps you shouldn't have been hiding in a darkened restaurant. If you needed to speak with me, you might have stayed around and done so instead of just vanishing."

"I wasn't hiding in a darkened restaurant — and I didn't vanish."

Abby arched her brows and looked toward the dining room.

"I went down into the tunnel," he told her. He took a step toward the bar. She reached for a bottle and held it by the neck. He stopped, lifting his hands, smiling grimly. "Your grandfather did die in the tunnel, right?"

"The grate from the restaurant to the tunnel is locked." She could tell that her voice sounded thin.

"Perhaps it's supposed to be," he said. "It wasn't."

"That tunnel is almost pitch-black." Her voice was growing even tighter and thinner.

And while she wasn't armed, she realized he did have a gun worn discreetly beneath his jacket. She wasn't sure what kind, because the flap of his jacket was covering it.

Her fingers tightened around the neck of the bottle she held.

He reached into his pants pocket; she drew back, slamming the bottle against the wall.

He let out a sigh and stepped back again. "Man, that's going to be a bitch for someone to clean up," he said. "I was only getting my light. It's finger-size but casts a glow big and strong enough to light up Pluto."

He held up a small flashlight. To add insult to injury, he turned it on. It nearly blinded her.

"What were you doing in the tunnel?" she asked.

"Investigating, Ms. Anderson. That's what you wanted, right? You think your grandfather was murdered. I'm here to investigate."

She shook her head in denial. "No one paid any attention to me," she told him. "And you just said you hadn't been to the academy —"

"I haven't been. Yet. I'm here on a trial basis."

"I don't understand."

"At the moment, I'm a consultant. I've been asked to join the Krewe and we're seeing if I work out as a Krewe member. Whether they like me enough — and whether I like the job enough to accept it."

Wary, Abby said, "Mr. Gordon, you really need to leave. You haven't been through the academy, so no one I know sent you. And I'll see to it that the grating is locked. Thank you so much for letting me know it isn't. Now . . ."

"Now — yes, now. Can we please have a discussion? A rational discussion. Look, you're the one who sent for help!" he said irritably.

"Talk about what? I don't know who you are or what you're doing here if you don't have the credentials —"

"I was sent here because *you* asked for help!"

"But —"

"I have a copy of your email, Ms. Anderson. I'll show you, as long as you don't drag the whole bar down if I reach into a pocket again. You wrote to Jackson Crow, from the Krewe of Hunters. Jackson Crow sent me. Take me or leave me, Ms. Anderson, but I'm your man. If I agree you've got the right kind of problem — and there *is* a strong possibility that your grandfather was murdered, possibly in connection with those murders you were just reading about — then more Krewe members will step in. For now, you've got me."

Abby swallowed. There were a number of agents in the Krewes who'd been with the FBI for some time now. This man was saying he hadn't even gone to the academy.

"You're not an agent?" she asked in a whisper.

"Not yet."

"Oh, Lord," she said shaking. "Then . . . then what *are* your credentials?"

"Ah," he murmured. "Well, I'm a private investigator legitimately licensed. At one time I was a detective with the New Orleans police. And now I'm legitimately on the books as a consultant to the feds. Perhaps most important, Ms. Anderson, I just had a conversation with an ancestor of yours. Calls himself Blue. Will that do for starters?"

3

Maybe he shouldn't have mentioned the fact that he'd seen Blue Anderson, Malachi thought. But, then again, the young woman seemed to think he was a serial killer himself, so he had to say *something.*

It hadn't occurred to him that the place would have emptied out by the time he came back. But the tunnel had fascinated him, and he'd followed it from the tavern to the riverbank and back more than once, marveling at the pirates who had constructed the escape — or kidnapping or shanghai — route. Once in the tavern again, he'd had no choice but to make himself known.

Or maybe he should just have told her he was an agent. Except that he wasn't. Not yet. If he chose to accept an appointment with the Krewe of Hunters, then, yes, he'd have to go through a course at the academy. But he was still skeptical.

And neither had he expected to be sent out on his own. But, apparently, that was the way Adam Harrison, Jackson Crow and Logan Raintree felt it should be done.

Sort of like a baptism by fire.

Malachi was game, though. Especially after he'd read about the two bodies that were discovered on the riverbank. He hadn't been convinced that the death of a man in his nineties was murder, but since the man's granddaughter had just graduated from the academy and had written such an impassioned letter, someone needed to come out here. And these recent murders did give a degree of credence to her beliefs.

So it was a test. For them, and as he'd said, for him. A chance to find out if he was really willing to join a unit or "create his own," as he'd been offered. They needed more units in Jackson Crow's specialized area and apparently they thought he was a man who could head up another one.

Actually, it didn't seem like a bad deal. Work with people who didn't think he was crazy *or* that he was a psychic. Trying to convince some people that he *wasn't* a psychic was as hard as convincing others that he did have certain . . . talents.

As Abby Anderson stared at him, Malachi tried to sum her up. She was tall, a stunning woman with a headful of the darkest, richest black hair he'd ever seen and eyes so blue they appeared to be violet or black. Her features were delicate and beautifully chiseled, and while she was lithe and fit, she was still well-endowed. Slim and yet curvy — hard to achieve.

She had to have ability and intelligence; he refused to believe she could have made it through the academy without both. What agents sometimes lacked, in Malachi's opinion, was imagination and vision. Though not, he had quickly discovered, the agents who wound up in what Adam Harrison had created — the Krewe of Hunters or, as it was generally called now, the Krewes. There was the original Krewe and then the Texas Krewe, although even adding a second was proving to be insufficient. Adam Harrison had told him passionately that it wasn't a calling that came to just anyone. No two ways about it, forming a new Krewe was difficult. Very few people had the talents they needed — *and* the ability to physically and mentally work in law enforcement.

She continued to stare at him as time ticked by. She seemed almost frozen, as if she were in a tableau. He feared she had to be in shock, although she didn't reveal her emotions.

"Hello?" he said, somewhat awkwardly. "Look, Ms. Anderson, I know what I'm doing around a crime scene and I generally know what I'm doing around people. Alive *and* dead. No, I don't see hundreds of ghosts walking the streets, but when someone's hanging around a place like this the way your Blue Anderson seems to be doing, it's usually for a reason, like safeguarding someone."

Was he wrong? Had she never seen the ghost of the pirate? If not, he'd just shown himself to be a real quack in her eyes.

No, in her email to Jackson she'd stated there was a ghost at the tavern, a ghost reportedly seen through the centuries. She hadn't come out and said *she'd* seen the ghost, but reading between the lines, he was certain she had.

And even if she did think he was a quack, so what? He still wasn't completely sure he wanted to be here or be part of this. He'd spent the past five years working for himself and he liked it that way. Maybe he should've started off with the fact that he'd served in the military and been a cop in New Orleans for several years before Marie's death from cancer, when he'd come home to his family property in Virginia. That was when he'd chosen to work for himself, getting a P.I. license.

Now . . .

"He *spoke* to you?" she whispered.

"Ah, there's life behind those eyes!" he murmured. "Yes, it seems to take him a great deal of effort. I don't believe he's practiced at speaking."

"Practiced?" she asked, sounding startled. "*Practiced?* Ghosts have to practice . . . being ghosts?"

Curious. She didn't seem worried that he'd seen the ghost. She was worried — or maybe confused — about its being a *practiced* ghost.

Jackson Crow had been certain, reading her email, that Abigail Anderson was of their own kind. A communicator, as Jackson referred to people who saw more than others did.

"Ms. Anderson, in my own experience, those who remain behind meet the same difficulties we do in life. Some are shy and don't do much more than watch. They never manage to speak to the living, move objects, even make a room cold. Some discover that they can learn to speak, to move objects — and they *can* even create a cold wind. Just like some of us on earth speak many languages while others are lucky to speak one. And some can barely walk, while others have athletic talent and prowess or perform in dance or join the Cirque de Soleil. Every ghost is an individual, just as each of us is."

"And you . . . saw Blue. And *spoke* to him?"

"Yes."

"I don't believe you. He hardly ever appears. He's never spoken."

"Not to you, perhaps."

"I'm his descendent!" she said indignantly.

He shrugged. "Well, have you ever tried speaking to him?"

She straightened, glaring at him with hostile, narrowed eyes.

No, Malachi decided, it didn't seem he'd gone about this the right way at all.

"So, you're old friends. Where is he now?" she asked.

"Certainly not old friends," Malachi said. "And I haven't met a ghost yet who appears on demand. I'm sure he's around somewhere, though. I don't think he leaves these premises. At least not often."

"And you spoke with him where, exactly?" she asked.

"In the tunnel."

"What did he say?"

"I didn't know he was there at first. He

put a hand on my shoulder and said, 'This is where he died. He was strong of heart. His death was not so simple.' "

She stared at him with such incredulity, Malachi found himself growing irritated. She saw Blue herself.

"Mr. Gordon, even if you are for real, I wish you'd leave right now. My grandfather died. We buried him today. But you know that. You were watching."

He stared back at her. "I can leave, or we can get started. Your grandfather called you because he suspected something or knew something — at least, that's what you wrote to Agent Crow." He tapped the newspaper. "So Gus is dead, possibly a victim, and there are three more — in a city where the murder rate is customarily quite low. Four victims in a short period of time. Do you want to sit there doubting me, or do you want to piece together what we know? Shouldn't take long. It isn't a lot."

"Almost nothing," she agreed after a moment, disgust in her tone. She picked up the newspaper behind the bar. "Another girl dead, found on the riverbank. The police haven't released cause of death, and when I tried to speak with them, I got nowhere. I tried to tell them Gus hadn't just died — that there had to be someone else down there in the tunnel, someone who *caused* him to die." She shook her head, studying him. "Look, you're not even an agent. How are you going to get any information?"

He smiled. "I honestly have a private investigator's license and I am now on the federal payroll as a consultant. Feel free to check that out. Call Jackson Crow. I think he'll be expecting you."

"Call him? I don't have a number. All I could find in the material I have from Quantico was an email address. And I couldn't reach him on an official line now. It's nearly eight!"

"I have his cell number. And he might be in the office, anyway. He works long hours."

"Right. So I could be calling anyone!"

He smiled at that. "Ever suspicious. That should make you a good agent, but you do have to go with your gut and trust someone at some point."

"I'm really not seeing why that should be you," she said.

"Ouch."

"You could have approached me earlier — while there were still people here."

"As you said, your grandfather's funeral was today. And then, I wasn't sure whether you wanted to advertise the fact that you'd called in . . . the ghost investigators."

89

"Give me that number," she said, pulling her cell phone out of her pocket.

He rattled off the numbers and she dialed. She watched him as she spoke. "Mr. Jackson Crow, please."

Malachi could hear the deep murmur of Crow's voice from where he stood.

"If you're Jackson Crow, would you by any wild chance still be at work?" She was silent for a minute. "I see. Then . . . would you be good enough to call me back on an official line?"

Jackson murmured something again. She pressed the end button on her phone and studied him while she waited for it to ring. When it did, she looked at the exchange. After she'd answered, Malachi could once again hear the deep timbre of Crow's voice as he spoke to Abby Anderson.

She thanked Crow, then ended the call. She frowned slightly, but now there seemed to be a touch of wonder in her eyes.

"He said that once we get an initial investigation going, he'll come down himself."

Malachi nodded.

"He said you do know what you're doing."

Malachi laughed at that. "I've been working as a P.I. I needed to be on my own. But I was a cop, up until about four years ago

90

in the city of New Orleans. I have a connection in the homicide department here."

"A connection?" she asked. For the first time he heard a touch of hope in her voice. "What kind of a connection."

He smiled at that. "Detective David Caswell, homicide. My ex-partner. Have you met him?"

"No."

He pulled a card out of his pocket and handed it to her. "That's David's card. Keep it with you. He's a great guy. He married a woman from Savannah about a year ago and moved up here. But when we were both working in New Orleans, he was my partner."

He waited.

She was still looking at him, as if he were an alien who'd suddenly landed in the tavern. Or . . . a ghost.

He sighed. "So, I guess you're with me — or on your own."

She was silent for another minute. "All right, then," she said at last. "We'll work together. I've lived here most of my life, and I've gone through all the real training, but you have the connections. You said you wanted to get started. What do you want to do?"

"Let's compile the little that we do know

about the victims. Then we'll figure out what we want to ask when we get in to see David. This is your city. Tomorrow I want to see where the bodies were discovered."

"Blue Anderson just showed you where I found my grandfather," she said huskily.

He took out his notepad and pen. A number of law enforcement professionals were now using their smartphones as notebooks, but he still preferred a pen and pad. Maybe actually writing the words gave him time to think about them. "Our first victim, Ruth Seymour, was a young woman who loved the city. She came to Savannah happy, excited and ready to enjoy a bit of history searching on her own before meeting her friends. She did check into her bed-and-breakfast — her car was found in their parking lot. Next victim was Rupert Holloway from Iowa. It's easy to understand why no immediate connection was made with the first victim, since Rupert was a man and in the city on business. Ms. Seymour would have been searching out tourist haunts. But a mobile phone exec? I'm not so sure. He was due to see business associates for lunch on the river — but he never showed. Our third victim was a student in the city. Her hometown was Memphis, Tennessee. So far, we don't know where she was last seen, only that her body was discovered on the river-bank."

"So, they have in common that they were all found by the river," Abby said. "Plus they were from out of town."

He nodded.

"And," she said slowly, "you think that my grandfather died because he knew something about the murders or the murderer."

"Probably. You found him in the tunnel. The tunnel leads down to the river and a dock. Well, not exactly. There's landfill now, but basically, when you follow the twists and turns of the tunnel, you come out at the very edge of the Dragonslayer property — about a hundred yards from the embankment and another fifty from the dock."

"But . . . Gus really didn't spend his time walking around in the tunnel," Abby said.

"No. So he went down there for a reason," Malachi said. He closed his notebook. "I'll pick you up tomorrow around ten. We'll have a talk with David and you can show me around the city, the river and the docks."

"All right."

He waited. He thought she'd ask him where he was staying. She didn't.

"Well, then, lock me out, Ms. Anderson. I made sure that both grates — at the entrance to the tunnel here and at the riverbank — were secured and bolted." He glanced around. "There should be a better alarm system here."

"We've been fine. And don't even suggest that we'd harbor a murderer here!" Abby said indignantly.

He raised a brow. "Hard to say, isn't it — when you don't know who the murderer might be."

She didn't respond to that but said, "Allow me to show you out."

As Malachi walked to the door, she followed. "This is a big, rambling place for you to stay alone, Ms. Anderson."

She smiled at him. "Blue's here, isn't he? I'm not alone. Good night, Mr. Gordon." She closed the door and he heard her lock it. Bemused, he headed out to the parking lot for his car. He wasn't particularly good with people anymore, he realized.

But then again, that was why he'd worked on his own for the past four years.

"Hey!" Abby said aloud when the door was closed. "Blue Anderson! Why don't you speak to me?"

She got no reply and the tavern was silent. Glancing at her watch, she saw that it had grown late. Well, not *that* late. It was only eight-thirty. Still, she'd been up most of the

94

previous night. She needed to get some sleep. Looking around one last time — wary in case anything had been left unsecured — she decided she should pack it in for the night and go to bed.

Jackson Crow had responded. She should've been elated.

But . . .

He'd sent her a rookie!

She told herself she should be grateful that she received a reply at all — even if it came in the form of Malachi Gordon. The man who claimed he'd spoken to Blue. Well, Crow had told her on the phone that if she and Malachi found a situation in which the Krewe could be of real assistance, he'd come himself and he'd bring more associates. Gordon also claimed to have an in with the police, which could help. And, if she needed someone intimidating, the man was tall and did have a strange air of authority about him. He wore his suit well; he was ruggedly attractive, which could be good with the right people.

She hoped he didn't usually walk around claiming he'd just spoken with the local ghost.

Abby cleaned up the mess she'd made when she'd broken the liquor to create a makeshift weapon. Then she went upstairs, but rather than turning in, she walked back to Gus's office. She'd started to go through his papers and invoices during the past week, but had been continually interrupted by someone needing an answer to a restaurant or bar question — or people who wanted to tell her how sorry they were about Gus and then tried to make her feel better by mentioning his age and reminding her that he'd led a good life.

Now she sat back behind his desk and picked up a sheaf of papers.

Invoices from liquor companies.

She looked around, feeling the silence of the tavern weigh down on her.

"Blue?" she said again.

But the ghost of her ancestor didn't appear.

She looked back at the papers in her hands. She saw Gus's handwriting on some of them. One note indicated that a certain flavor of vodka had not gone over well with his customers. Another said that the salesman now working for a particular company was one of the best he'd ever met.

As she began to leaf through them, another paper slipped down to the desk, smaller and different from the invoices. It was a sheet ripped from a small notepad. She quickly read the words he'd written, almost as if he'd been thinking out loud and had scribbled them down.

The murders. Am I right? Call Abby.

Just as she read the words, she heard the loud ship's buzzer that was the tavern's doorbell.

It startled her so much that she jumped and the sheets she'd been reading flew into the air, wafting back down in disarray.

Glad that she hadn't gotten into her pajamas yet, and wondering who would come by when most of the city knew the tavern had been closed in honor of Gus, she started to run down the stairs. She hesitated, ran back up to her room and opened the little dresser next to her bed, retrieving her service Glock and sliding it beneath her jacket. Then she ran down the stairs again to the front door. She looked through the ship's portal to see who was calling.

The man standing outside appeared to be about forty; he was of medium height with sandy-brown hair and was wearing a blue suit with a white shirt and a tie that had been loosened.

Cop, she thought instantly. *Plainclothes cop.*

That was instinct, but she couldn't be sure.

"Yes? The tavern's closed," she called.

"Ms. Anderson?"

"Yes."

"I'm sorry to bother you, but I have a few questions."

"Badge?" she said.

He produced his credentials. His badge looked real, as did the ID he flashed with it.

Abby opened the front door. The cop seemed uncomfortable. "Detective Peters, Ms. Anderson. I just remembered seeing in the papers that you were closed today for your grandfather's funeral."

She nodded. "Can I help you?"

"I'm here about this girl," he said, showing her a picture. "Her name is —"

"Helen Long," Abby said. "Yes, I know her. She works for a friend of my grandfather's, Dirk Johansen. He does pirate ship tours and she plays a pirate wench."

"She's missing," Peters said. "Her roommate called it in this morning."

Abby frowned. "Dirk was here all day. He didn't mention that she was missing."

"He might not know yet," Peters told her. "Helen Long was off today, and she was off yesterday. She had lunch here with friends. Do you remember seeing her?"

Abby nodded. Like so many people, Helen had made a point of approaching her to express her condolences. She hadn't really known Gus that well. She'd only worked for Dirk for about a month. Helen had grown up in Atlanta but come to Savannah to be an extra in a pirate movie, since the exterior shots were filmed in the city. She'd been waiting to see if she'd gotten a part in another movie about to be filmed down in New Iberia, and she'd been honest with Dirk about her intentions.

"I did see her. She had lunch here, yes."

"Do you remember seeing her leave?" he asked.

"Yes. Wait, no — she was with some girlfriends and they left first. She stayed at the bar awhile longer. I don't know when she left. I went back upstairs after I talked to her," Abby explained. "But my staff and a few customers might be able to tell you more. Dirk was here himself at the time, sitting with Bootsie — Bob Lanigan — and Aldous Brentwood. My bartender, Jerry Sullivan, was on, as was the day manager, Macy Sterling. I'm sure they'd be more helpful." Abby paused, wondering about something. "Helen's been missing since she was seen at lunch yesterday? I thought you had to wait until an adult was gone for more than twenty-four hours before you filed a report."

"Usually," Peters agreed. "But . . . we've had a few people go missing and then turn up dead. Like I said, her roommate called it in when she woke up this morning. Helen never came home last night. And she hasn't shown up today. So —" he cleared his throat "— we're starting early with this one."

"I see. I'm glad," Abby told him. "She's a sweet girl, Detective. I wish I could help you. And you should speak with my staff and my customers. They may know more."

"I'll do that tomorrow, thank you. And if you can think of anyone else who might've seen her, please get in touch." He passed her a card, which she tucked into her pocket.

"Of course!"

"Well, then, good night," Peters said. He looked as if he wanted to say more. "I'm sorry," he said again, "but this was the last place her girlfriends saw her, so . . ."

"If you want to search these premises, you're more than welcome to do so," she assured him.

"I'll try to speak with your people first," Peters said. "Someone might've seen her leave — and they might've seen who she left with."

"I hope so. I have a list of numbers. You can call them now, if you wish. It's really not that late."

"Thank you."

Abby hurried back behind the bar and found the list Sullivan kept there of their regulars. He was a good bartender and liked to memorize their drinks. Then she moved over to the host stand to find the sheet with staff contact information, as well. Peters waited politely at the door. She gave him the pages and he thanked her.

Abby locked the door again and stood there for a moment. Where the hell was Blue?

Not making an appearance that night, it seemed. Wearily she went back upstairs, sorted out the papers that had flown everywhere and sat back down.

Helen.

She felt horrible. *She knew Helen.*

So far, those who'd disappeared had taken a few days to be discovered.

Maybe there was still hope.

She stared down at the paper that was back in her hands, written in Gus's broad scrawl.

The murders. Am I right? Call Abby.

This time, as she reflected, she nearly jumped sky-high again when the office phone on the desk began to ring.

Once again, papers flew.

"Abby!" It was Dirk Johansen. She knew why he had to be calling. . . .

"Hi, Dirk."

"Oh, my God! My actress — my pirate wench — Helen. She's missing," he said.

"I know, Dirk. I'm so sorry."

"You know?"

"A detective was just here. Apparently, she was last seen having lunch at the tavern."

His voice was thick. "Yeah, that's the last time I saw her, too. I told the cops that," he added.

"Did you see her leave?"

"Yep. She was teasing about the pirate days with Aldous, Bootsie and me . . . and Sullivan. Then she looked at her watch and said she had an appointment. She didn't say who with. She just went running out."

"Did she have a boyfriend?"

"No, she was actually doing some online dating. She said she'd met at least six guys and found one, maybe, worth a relationship."

"I'm sure that'll help the police."

"Do you think she might've taken off on

some romantic spree?" Dirk asked hope-fully.

"Sure, maybe," Abby lied. "Dirk, what's going to be important is that you think of any bit of information that might give the authorities some leads to follow."

"Right, right . . . her roommate must have her computer. That should help."

"Yes, I bet it will."

An awkward silence followed. Then Abby said, "Dirk, I'm going to get some sleep. In the morning —" She hesitated, thinking about Gordon. The hell with him. He'd have to play it her way. "In the morning, I'll be your personal agent. We'll find her. How about that?" The local police might not be impressed with her, but Dirk might want her help.

"Yeah, um, well, actually, that was what I was going to ask you," Dirk said.

"To help you?"

"I need you to be my wench."

"What?"

"I don't have a wench for tomorrow. Helen shared the job with Chrissy Sutton, and Chrissy is in Atlanta, visiting her mom. She won't be back until late tomorrow night."

Great. She thought she might be wanted for her investigative skills.

103

Dirk wanted a wench.

"Oh, my God. She's missing. I'm terrified for her. But . . . I still have to keep it going, keep others working."

But maybe it wasn't a bad idea. She could talk with shipmates who knew Helen; she could hang out at the dock.

"Sure, Dirk. I'll be your wench."

"I hate to ask you after . . . after Gus and all, but . . ."

"I'll be there, Dirk. What time?"

"Ship leaves for the first run at ten. We're back at one. Second run at three. Last one leaves right at sunset. I'll need you to show up at about nine for costuming and a few instructions."

"Okay, Dirk."

"Bless you, Abby."

She started to reply but he'd already hung up.

Abby let her head fall on the table. Gus . . . She'd been sick about Gus.

But two young women and a man had also died. Now Helen was gone. . . .

She really needed help. And what she'd gotten was Malachi Gordon. Maybe he did have a few talents with the dead. But whoever had taken Helen had to be alive.

Very much alive — and very busy in the beautiful city of Savannah.

■ ■ ■ ■

Dirk's *Black Swan* was a beautiful ship. She was a schooner with one large square-rigged mainmast; her figurehead was that of a mermaid crowned with pearls. Topside was the great helm on the forecastle and behind it was a stage of about twenty by thirty feet, surrounded by seating at the inner hull. There were barrels around, advertising rum or gunpowder, and Dirk's parrot, Achilles, sat on a little perch in the center of the stage. Toward the aft, down a few steps, was a snack shop that also offered gifts and souvenirs, and passengers could step atop the sterncastle, above the captain's quarters, to catch a great view of the riverfront.

Malachi Gordon had called Abby bright and early — at 7:00 a.m. — to make sure she'd be ready for their planned excursion of the city and the river. She began to tell him about Helen's disappearance but he already knew. When she explained that not only was she helping out an old friend but she'd get a chance to be on the pirate ship and the docks, he wasn't angry. Nor was he disappointed. He just said he'd catch up with her.

Dressed in pirate gear, custom-made by a

costumer to resemble the real thing rather than a contemporary Halloween fashion, Abby stood with Dirk's two main performers, Jack Winston and Blake Stewart. "Don't worry about anything, Abby," Jack said. "Dirk really runs the show. Our characters serve grog — to the adults — and soda to the kids. It's fun, honestly. Blake and I get into a fight over you, we split up some treasure and we have a few songs. All you do is respond and react."

"I'll do my best," Abby said.

He grinned. "Well, you're a child of the Dragonslayer. You've been a pirate before, I'm sure."

"Aye, mate, we're all pirates at heart, aren't we?" she responded.

He smiled again. "They'll be boarding soon. The concept is that they're all prisoners being held for a fine ransom. We're good to them because they might be worth a lot." He grimaced as he added, "Dirk's character is probably based on Blue Anderson."

"Could be," Abby said.

"Just greet people as they come up the gangplank," he told her, turning to walk back to the dock himself; he took tickets there with Dirk.

Abby looked around. Besides the performers, there were four men and two young women dressed up to man the ship. Un-piratelike, Dirk had plenty of automatic winches to deal with his sails. She watched as they made last-minute preparations to move the ship out onto the river.

She turned to see that their third per-former, Blake Stewart, was seated at one of the benches by the hull. He seemed some-how lost. She thought he was young, maybe around twenty-one, the age Dirk required for anyone serving on his ship, since a lot of his money was made on alcohol.

Young and, yes, lost.

She sat down next to him and he gazed at her with wide brown eyes. "Nice of you to do this," he said.

"It'll be fun, won't it?"

He nodded but he didn't smile.

"You're worried about Helen?"

Again, he nodded. "It's not like her. Did you ever meet Helen? She's very respon-sible. She really wants to be an actress. She told me once that work ethic is everything. If she's not here, it's because something's wrong."

"You really care about her."

He flushed and said, "I'm crazy about her. But she won't go out with me. Said it's no good to date people you work with, and besides, she doesn't expect to be here forever. So, instead, she went online." His expression was a little desperate. "Who knows what kind of crazy she might've met online?"

"Don't give up hope, Blake."

He changed his tone abruptly. "Showtime — captives aboard." He pointed to the gangplank and went straight into action, putting on his best pirate face as he greeted those boarding the ship. "Step lively, step lively! Now, no trouble from you landlubbers, and there be smooth sailing ahead. Eh! And that means you, my fine lad!" He stopped a boy of about ten who was getting on and reached for his ear, pulling out a "pirate coin." "Ah, we'll be watching you! *You* are the treasure, lad! The ransom we'll be getting for a fine lad like you. Don't be trying to out-pirate a pirate!"

The *Black Swan* took a maximum of fifty people per trip. Soon all had boarded and the crew rushed about to set sail. During the first twenty minutes, Abby dipped grog and soda, warned the passengers of dire consequences if they should act up and, as much as possible, talked to the crew.

Everyone, it seemed, loved Helen Long.

No one could fathom where she might have gone.

All of them feared the worst; she was just

so responsible.

When they were full out on the river, a good breeze sprang up. Dirk suddenly clanged a bell, calling attention to the show that was about to start. It began with Dirk and the parrot as he told his tale of being a poor lad, shanghaied into the ways of pirate life. He spoke to individual members of the crowd, asking questions, interacting. The parrot was perfectly trained to make wisecracks to him and he responded, bringing delighted giggles from the children aboard. Then he picked up his guitar and sang a sea shanty — and as his rollicking song came to an end, his two key pirates, Jack and Blake, began a loud and boisterous argument, cutting into Dirk's territory.

"I say you leave her be — the wench is mine!" Blake shouted.

"Not so says the wench!" Jack argued.

"That's you!" one of the crew whispered to Abby.

She strode forward between them. "Ah, cut the whining, ye scurvy lot!" she told them. "This wench belongs to no man!"

"Um, yes, you do!" Blake said.

"I don't belong to any man. I can sail these seas on my own!" she declared.

"Technically," Jack said, addressing the crowd, "we're not sailing the seas at all. This is a river."

Abby waited for the laughter to die down. "River, lake, ocean, sea — mud puddle! I can manage it on my own. However . . ." She walked to each man and touched his face. "I don't mind bringing on a mate who can prove his prowess should we be boarded!"

"Ah, fight!" Jack cried.

"To the death!" Blake roared back.

Dirk stepped between them. "First touch!" he commanded. "Jeez, it's hard to get good help these days, even for a pirate! Just first touch — I need you wretched blackguards alive!"

Abby watched as the two of them went into their swashbuckling duel. In the end, Jack made the first contact, and while Blake muttered and the parrot ridiculed him, he sheepishly began to ask people where they were from, and what their opinions of the fray might have been.

"Hey," Blake called. "This group is from Florida. They're demanding a recount!"

Dirk knew right when to let the laughter fade and step in. "Recount? Recount? How can I recount? The count was one!"

Abby moved around the crowd. "We have a birthday here!" she called, after speaking with a wide-eyed little girl. "Her name is Jade."

"A birthday? A birthday?" Dirk shouted. "Well, then!" He picked up his guitar and began to strum "Happy Birthday," and everyone on the ship seemed to sing along.

Blake found a couple celebrating their anniversary; she ran over with more grog. Jack spoke to a young man about to head off for basic training; she rushed over with two cups of grog as they all assured him he might need both, and then applauded his service to his country.

Abby came upon a young man with wild dark hair, sunglasses and a ridiculous shirt. "And what are you celebrating, sir? Where are you from?"

She couldn't really see his face — not with the glasses he wore and the baseball cap that sat low on his forehead. Despite that, she could tell he had heavy dark eyebrows.

"Just vacation," he said. "And I'm from the great Commonwealth of Virginia."

"Virginia!" Dirk said, and broke into, "Carry me back to old Virginny."

They continued with the festivities, Jack hauling out a pirate chest next and providing young and old alike with trinkets. Handing a pack of chocolate doubloons to a small child, Abby noted the Virginian had left his seat and was chatting with crew members.

Then he disappeared down the steps into the galley and snack bar below.

A passenger asked her a question about Dirk's pirate flag and she took the time to explain how pirates created their own flags. When she could, she slipped toward the steps and made a quick getaway to the deck below.

There was a counter at the far end. The price of the cruise included one glass of grog or soda and chips; hungry passengers could buy hot dogs, hamburgers, veggie burgers or salad — and beer or other beverages if they weren't fond of grog. There were tables alongside a central shelf that held pirate flags, eye patches, "doubloons" and other souvenirs. She glanced at the tables, which were empty. People tended to gather there while the ship moved out to the river and back, rather than during the height of the pirate festivities.

No one on either side.

Abby walked up to the man tending the snack bar and asked, "Hey, I just saw one of the passengers wander this way. Did you see where he went?"

"Um, yeah, below, down to the magazine. Of course, we don't really carry any powder or guns down there now. It's food storage, mostly," he said cheerfully.

"Why would a passenger go down there?" Abby asked.

"Oh, Wiley — one of the crew — was talking to him. This guy owns a similar outfit up in Myrtle Beach and was fascinated to hear about Dirk's bilge pumps. They're probably down there by now."

"Thanks," Abby said. She headed to the side of the counter, where a velvet rope blocked off the stairs down to the level below. She walked into the vast magazine. It was piled high with all manner of supplies, not just food but costumes, giveaways, makeup and wigs. There were bunks against the inner hulls, as well; Dirk let his workers sleep on board when they needed a place to stay.

"Hello?" Abby said. No one answered. She hurried up and down the length of the magazine. The place was deserted. Searching as she went, she found the hatch to the bilge below and opened it, climbing down the little ladder that led to the lowest area of the ship, where the two sides met at the keel. The bilge was dry. She could hear the pumps working.

No one was there.

Frustrated, she returned to the action topside. She didn't see the man who'd said he was from Virginia — and who had then disappeared.

"Where ya been, lass?" Dirk roared over to her. " 'Tis time to make certain we'll be getting the ransom from this lot of landlubbers!"

He was playing a pirate captain; he was supposed to sound gruff. But she thought he was irritated with the fact that she hadn't been on deck — and in sight.

"Captain, we've gotten the ransom for all of them!" she told him.

"We did?"

"They paid it before they got on board!"

"Aw, well, then, I guess we'll be bringing them back in," Dirk said.

A little boy jumped up and cried out, "No! I want to stay on the ship and be a pirate!"

Dirk was good. He walked over to the boy and pulled an eye patch from his pocket. "There you go, laddie! Now you're an honorary pirate!"

The *Black Swan* returned to the dock. Abby kept up her act — but kept looking for the man in the baseball cap, too. She didn't see him. Had he somehow disappeared off the ship?

Was that what had happened to Helen?

They reached the dock, and the *Black Swan* was tied up at her mooring. The passengers — all happy — said their goodbyes. Dirk reminded Abby that they'd leave again at three. He seemed to be impatient with her, but he didn't ask her where she'd been. She was a gift horse, after all.

She walked down the dock and pulled out her cell phone, placing a call to Malachi Gordon. He answered after the first ring.

"Have you found out anything?"

"I don't know," he said.

"Where are you now?"

"Behind you."

She turned around. She saw him on the phone.

He was the Virginian tourist with the baseball cap and sunglasses.

4

Once again, Abby Anderson stared at him, her frown intense, her manner completely unnerved and highly irritated.

"What the hell are you doing?" she demanded in a harsh whisper, coming up to him.

He arched one of his heavy dark brows and felt the spirit gum on it tighten. "You said you thought it was important to be on the ship. So I thought that it was important, too."

"You were supposed to be investigating the murders — seeing your friend, David Caswell, and finding out what's going on."

"I did see David," he told her. "I met him for coffee at eight. Weird situation. He's investigating the murders, but the other detective — the man you met last night — has been assigned the missing-person situation. So he's asked that he be paired up with Ben Peters. All the stations and all law

116

enforcement officers in the area have been alerted about the murders, but my friend David is the head of the task force. I learned a great deal today — before boarding the ship."

That didn't seem to make her happy. "Why are you in this ridiculous getup?" she asked.

"I'd met Dirk. I didn't want him to know I was on board, observing."

She turned around and started walking toward the end of the dock.

He followed her. "Hey!"

She spun on him. She made a good wench, he thought. A pirate hat with little pearl strings attached sat over her forehead. She wore boots, black leggings, a long-sleeved blouse, fitted red vest and frock coat — male attire, which certainly might have been chosen by a woman who found herself sailing the seas. She had long shapely legs and the boots added to her height. The color of her eyes was so rich and deep a blue that it was mesmerizing, especially when framed by the near-ebony darkness of her hair. He was surprised to feel something stir in him. But she stirred more than his senses; she seemed to touch something deeper than the simple lust that biology and nature dictated. She had passion. She seemed to breathe vitality.

"Do you enjoy sneaking up on me, playing dress-up?"

He cast his head to the side with a small, amused smile. "I often worked undercover when I was in New Orleans and, quite frankly, I used disguises in my work as a private investigator. As a matter of fact, Jackson Crow actually mentioned that some members of his unit have found their acting talents to be of use. In a way, acting is part of human behavior. I'm sure you've learned that criminals, especially psychopaths, have a tendency to act incredibly sane and rational. *We* need to be able to play certain parts, as well. And while you're busy commenting on me, you might take a look in a mirror. I think you're dressed up, too?"

"Not to make a fool of anyone," she muttered.

He frowned. "I wasn't trying to make a fool of you, Ms. Anderson. I was trying to take a ride on the high seas — or river, as it may be — and get a take on the man who owns the ship. A man you might not see with open eyes because he's been a friend for so long," Malachi said.

Abby gasped. "Dirk? You think *Dirk* could be guilty of . . . this? Of . . . of anything?" she asked.

Malachi caught her arm and walked her down the dock toward the street. "Ms. Anderson, as I told you, the first thing I did this morning was meet with my friend, David Caswell. And I discovered several things about the deaths. The victims had marks at their wrists that indicated they'd been bound, probably with heavy rope, according to the medical examiner. They all showed signs of blunt force trauma. In other words, they were hit on the head. But in all three cases, the actual cause of death was drowning. So, Ms. Anderson, it looks as if they were held captive, knocked out — and then forced into the water. Water . . . hmm. That could mean a ship. Look at it this way. They'd been bound and — metaphorically, at least — forced to walk the plank. That kind of implies a 'pirate' might have wanted them dead, or they might have met their end off the deck of a pirate ship."

Abby stared at him. "Oh, no! All right — maybe. But they could've gone off a rowboat or . . . or an oil tanker just as easily."

"Yes," Malachi said, "they could have. But how likely is that?"

She shook her head. "I've known Dirk most of my life. This is his livelihood. Why would he suddenly go insane and start killing people off his ship — especially without any of us seeing a change in him?"

"No one ever really knows another human being," Malachi said simply.

"Oh, I think I would've noticed bodies popping up in my city over the years!"

"People sometimes crack, Ms. Anderson. Strain, pressure. All the same, no one completely understands the human brain. It's the most wonderful computer in the world — but just like a computer it can short-circuit. And I didn't say your friend was the killer. I merely thought it prudent to investigate. Under the circumstances."

"And you knew I was on that ship."

"I'm not trying to fight you, Ms. Anderson. I'm not trying to go against you. Look!" he said with exasperation. "I'm here because you wrote to Jackson Crow. I'm here to help you."

"If you're going to stalk me, you can quit calling me Ms. Anderson. It's Abby," she said. "And —"

She broke off suddenly, blue eyes growing large as saucers as she stared past him.

"Abby?" he said.

She didn't respond. She was still staring.

"Helen?" she whispered, her voice thick.

Malachi spun around to see where she was pointing.

She was looking at the water, to the far

side of the dock. They'd done a good job in the past years, cleaning up the river, but it was impossible to stop a certain amount of natural growth and unnatural garbage from cresting the water and drifting up against the embankment.

There was sea grass or fungus, a plastic soda bottle someone had tossed away and a few cigarette butts. Oil slick covered the water right at the docks, creating little curlicues of blue and purple on the water.

And caught there, just by one of the pilings for the dock, was a body.

Facedown, it appeared to be a woman — long strands of river-sodden hair fanned out from the head. And it appeared that she'd just washed up.

On the slim chance that she might be alive, Malachi took his phone out of his pocket and let it fall on the deck before he dove into the river. Surfacing by the body, he quickly turned her over.

It was indeed a woman. That was all he could really tell as he looked at her face.

And she was dead. River life had already been eating at her flesh. The tip of her nose was gone and her flesh was icy cold and a grotesque shade of gray.

He looked up the five or six feet from the water to where Abby stood on the dock. She was almost as gray as the corpse.

"Call 9-1-1," he told her.

Despite her pallor, she was functioning. "I already did."

"Is it Helen?" he asked her.

"I wouldn't begin to know," she said, "she doesn't even look . . . real."

An hour later, the corpse was in an ambulance bound for the morgue, crime scene techs were scouring the water and the embankment, and police divers had been dispatched to see if any evidence might remain in the water. Shaken, Dirk had canceled his afternoon and evening pirate cruises, rescheduling or refunding the money of those who'd bought tickets. Abby sat with Malachi Gordon — who had cast off all vestiges of a costume — at a desk in police headquarters.

She liked Malachi's former partner from the get-go.

David Caswell's desk was surrounded by others. There was a fair amount of activity at the station. A hooker was arguing with her arresting officer and two other cops were trying to deal with a junkie on a bad trip.

David had arrived at the dock soon after the initial response team had cordoned off the area and plucked Malachi and the corpse from the water. About six-one, sandy-haired, green-eyed, he was serious without being somber, smart and probing without being aggressive or demanding. Abby thought he had to be in his early thirties. He spoke with a slow, smooth Southern accent that matched his steadfast but easy manner.

Maybe he didn't have to be demanding; he knew he'd get a straight story from Malachi, no matter what the story — and there really wasn't much of it.

"Your statements are being typed up. You can sign them and get out of here for now," Caswell told them. "I figure you want to attend the autopsy?" he asked Malachi.

Malachi, hands clasped in front of him, nodded.

"It'll be scheduled for later today. I'll call you when I know the exact time. Before I let you go, can we run through what happened? Ms. Anderson . . ." He paused, looking at Abby, and smiled. "Or is it Agent Anderson?"

She smiled. "I just realized it is. Agent Anderson. I am official. But please call me Abby."

"Okay, Abby. So you were working on your friend's pirate boat because his usual actress is the young lady reported as missing. Helen Long." He studied her. It wasn't that costumes and pageantry didn't abound in Savannah. But it could also be a very conservative, old Southern city. She was hardly dressed as a respectable young local in her plumed hat, frock coat, breeches and boots.

"Yes, I was being his wench for today. He's very upset. Dirk is a great employer. He provides sleeping space when his people need it. He takes on part-time help so his employees can go to school if they choose. He really cares about Helen," Abby said.

"But . . . he couldn't say that the girl we found in the water was Helen, right?"

"No. I couldn't tell you, either," Abby added. "And I knew her. I'd met her several times," she said. "I don't *think* it was Helen. But I can't be sure. The body . . ." Her voice trailed off. She had to be better about things like this; she'd been through an autopsy, for God's sake. She'd passed the academy with flying colors.

"Hey," Malachi said, looking over at her. "No matter how long you chase the bad guys, death can still tear you up. And if you get to where it doesn't . . . then you need to reassess what you're doing."

"Yeah, thanks," she said huskily.

"So you were working on the ship, the ship came back in to berth, you were walking down the dock and you just happened to stop and see the body," Caswell said.

"I was behind her. I'd called out to her," Malachi explained. "It was while we were standing there talking that Abby saw the body and . . ."

"And you dove in," Caswell finished.

Malachi raised his hands. "We could only see her from the top. She was facedown, but the pirate ship and some small boats had just come in, so — I doubted it — but . . . she might have been alive. Better to try than to find out you might have saved someone."

"Always," David murmured. "Now . . . this may change things," he said, leaning toward them. "The powers that be wanted to handle the situation on their own, but now with another murder . . . I think they'll ask for federal help, if you want to give the right people a heads-up."

Malachi nodded in acknowledgment. "Anything else you can tell us?"

"When you sign the statements, I'll give you a copy of the notes I've compiled. Then do me a favor and get out of here. I don't want any resentment if we do go official — or if we don't. You know how cops can be

— I don't want them to think the feds were snooping around before they were asked in. Some officers take it to mean they're being judged, that they weren't considered competent at their jobs and therefore the federal government had to step in. It's not conducive to constructive work and everyone does need to work together."

"What lines of investigation are you working on right now?" Malachi asked.

"Searching for Helen? We've got her computer and we're following up on the online dating angle. That was Peters's case," he said, and hesitated. "It might be mine now. We've gone through the cell phone records on the others, tried to figure out if there was someone they were meeting. We're retracing their steps. And we're still waiting for lab reports from Forensics, although the autopsy procedures have been completed on Ruth Seymour, Rupert Holloway and Felicia Shepherd."

"Do you have any suspects?" Malachi asked.

"No — not a one. We have our tech guys working on tracing the men Helen Long met through the online dating service, as I said. That's it. We don't have anything solid. Ruth Seymour checked into her B and B, and no one remembers seeing her after. She was a tourist, of course, and wouldn't be known by locals, but we've had her picture all over. Same with Rupert Holloway. He was due at a meeting at a restaurant on the riverfront. He never made it. Felicia Shepherd left her apartment, presumably to go to class. She said goodbye to her roommate — and that was it."

"They disappeared on foot, right?"

"Yes. Felicia's car was in her parking space at the complex, Rupert Holloway's was in the garage at the hotel, Ruth Seymour's car was in the drive at the B and B."

Ten minutes later they left the station. They were in Malachi's car heading back toward the Dragonslayer. He drove an Explorer, and while the interior was clean, it looked as if he'd driven on some rough roads.

"So what now?" Abby said, flipping through her files.

"First, I'm getting dry clothes."

"Oh!" She'd forgotten that he must be sodden; he hadn't had anything other than a towel provided by one of the crime scene techs. "Yes, you must be miserably wet."

"I'm almost dry but I feel like my clothes are glued to my skin. If you don't mind, we'll stop by my hotel. I'll only be a minute."

"Where are you staying?" she asked.

"The 17hundred90 Inn and Restaurant," he replied. "Hey, it's supposed to be one of the most haunted in Savannah."

Abby nodded. "I love the bar area and the restaurant. There's a great fireplace — nice to sit around on a chilly night. The house was actually built in 1820, but that was a disastrous year for the city. A fire wiped out half of it and an epidemic of yellow fever killed whole families, so I guess someone liked 1790 better and used that year to name the place. The ghost of Anna haunts it, you know."

"Anna, who threw herself from the window when her lover deserted her," Malachi said. "In my room — 204. Hey, I knew I was staying down here. Might as well go for an intriguing room."

"Have you seen Anna?"

"No, not yet," he told her. "Well, other than the fact that the owners have a fantastic sense of joining in with the city fun. There's a mannequin of her in the window. I pass her every time I come in and out of the room."

"The tour guides love it when they go by," Abby agreed.

Malachi managed to find parking quickly. Abby went into the bar while he walked up to his room. As she entered, she realized that she was still in pirate attire — a number of stares came her way, and before she could get far, a couple of children asked to have a picture taken with her. She complied and finally entered the bar. A friend of hers was bartending and laughed as she explained that she hadn't had time to change. She noticed that a lot of people were talking about the situation in the city in hushed voices. The media was broadcasting the fact that another body had been found by the river.

Abby ordered a cup of tea to sip while she waited. Locals frequented the bar and met visitors to the city there.

She didn't particularly want to become involved in a conversation right now and took her tea to one of the plush chairs near the fireplace, the folder with notes from David in her hand. When she looked through them, she discovered the autopsy reports on all but the newest victim. The women, she saw, had engaged in sexual activity before their deaths, but whether it had been coerced or consenting, the M.E. had not been able to determine. The bodies had been too compromised. No fluids had been recovered, so DNA matches from semen wouldn't be possible.

She frowned, reading that. If a serial killer was a rapist as well, it seemed strange that he'd chosen a male victim. She leafed through the next report, and learned that the male victim, Rupert Holloway, hadn't shown any signs of sexual assault.

But if her grandfather had been a victim of the same killer, was he surprised by him in the tunnel to the point of having a heart attack? Or perhaps forced to move quickly in an attempt to escape and that had brought it on?

She looked up. Malachi had reappeared. He'd evidently taken a shower because his dark hair was damp and slicked back. She noted the clean scent that emanated from him and the color of his eyes and the way he stood. And, as she'd told herself before, he could certainly appear intimidating.

He was wearing jeans, a tailored shirt and a lightweight taupe jacket. She saw that he wore a shoulder holster and suspected that he was seldom without his weapon. *She* was without hers. Pirate wenches didn't run around with Glocks. But in the days to come, she had to remember that she was an agent, which meant having her weapon available at all times. She'd asked for help that had turned out to be Malachi, and if she wanted to carry her weight, she had to behave like an agent.

He could disguise himself, too. First, he'd caught her unaware from out of the shadows. Then she'd spoken to him on the ship and not even known who he was!

"Ready," he said lightly. "I'm assuming you might want to change? But maybe not. That pirate garb is quite fetching."

She took a last sip of her tea and rose. She was glad she was fairly tall; in the pirate boots, she didn't feel short against his height. Abby wasn't sure why that mattered. But it did, probably because she felt that she'd been taken in by him a few times. Of course, maybe he really hadn't *meant* to make her feel like a fool. Maybe he'd just accomplished the feat by accident.

"I think I will give up the pirate attire for now," she said. "Shall we go back to the Dragonslayer?"

During the short drive, Malachi asked Abby if she'd seen anything in the files to draw her attention. She told him what she'd read, and then realized that he must have known the cause of death — and the fact that the women had engaged in sex, which was most likely *not* consensual. He would also know that the man had not been molested. After all, he'd spent an hour with his detective friend.

"Makes you wonder, doesn't it?" she asked.

"If there are two killers?" Malachi asked, glancing over at her. "I don't know. My guess is that the murders are being done by the same person. The disposal of the bodies is what makes me think so."

"Yeah, I agree," Abby said thoughtfully. "And cause of death — drowning — is the same in each case."

When they arrived at the Dragonslayer, Dirk Johansen was at the bar with Bootsie and Aldous. He'd obviously had a drink to calm his nerves.

Macy met her at the door. "He's pretty upset," she murmured. "But then, from what I understand, you found the body. And it might be Helen Long!"

"I don't think it's Helen," Abby said softly. She saw that Macy was studying Malachi. "Hello, there. You were at the funeral, right?"

Abby made the introductions. "Macy, this is Malachi Gordon. Malachi, Macy Sterling."

"How do you do, and yes, I was here yesterday," Malachi told her. "I'm a friend of a friend of Abby's at the agency."

"Oh, oh, oh!" Macy said. "A fed."

"Technically, I'm more of a fed than he

is," Abby couldn't resist pointing out. A smile of amusement glimmered on Malachi's face. He didn't say a word. She sensed that he wasn't being polite, he really didn't care if he was an agent or a detective or an investigator. He was interested in the job, not the title.

"Well, we're glad you're here," Macy said, shaking his hand. Macy liked him, Abby thought. Or, at least, admired his appearance. She had that look she wore when she found a man attractive.

"Thank you," Malachi said, bowing slightly.

"I'm going up to change," Abby announced. "Malachi, come on up and you can wait in Gus's office."

"It's your office now," Macy said.

"It will always be Gus's office," Abby said. Macy seemed a little stricken and Abby quickly added with a smile, "Okay, let's call it Gus's and my office. How about that?"

Macy smiled.

Abby strode over to the bar. Aldous glanced at her and nodded at Dirk, who was staring down into his drink, then shook his head sadly. Abby set a hand on Dirk's shoulder. "Dirk?"

Dirk looked up at her. "That could be Helen," he said. "That could be Helen. That blond hair . . . Helen has blond hair that streams around her like that."

"Dirk, you couldn't really tell if the hair was blond or not," Abby told him. "The woman we found was light-haired, but . . . I know Helen, Dirk. I don't think it was her. I wouldn't lie to you."

"I've been trying to contact her family," he said. "The police have been trying. . . . I have no idea what to say to them, but I've got a reprieve. They're on safari in Kenya. It'll be another week before they can be reached. Oh, Lord — I pray we find her, alive, before then."

Malachi's phone rang and he excused himself to answer it.

"This is horrible, so horrible," Dirk moaned as Abby tried to comfort him.

Malachi came back over to them. "That was Detective Caswell," he said. "The medical examiner's office has the young woman cleaned up. He says she's still pretty rough to look at, but they've gotten all the river gunk off her and he wants you to come down and see if you recognize her. I told him Abby could probably come make the same identification. He suggested you both come."

"I'll change first," Abby said.

"I'll go." Dirk's voice broke. "She worked

for me. I owe her."

Aldous and Bootsie each set a hand on his shoulders. They reminded Abby of the Three Musketeers — one for all, and all for one. It must be nice to have such close and steadfast friends. She didn't lack friends but a friendship like theirs, like the one they'd shared with Gus, was pretty special.

"Be right back." She ran up the stairs, stopping to throw the file folder of notes David Caswell had given them into the bottom drawer of Gus's desk. Something made her hide it beneath a stack of other papers.

She paused, looking around the room. "Blue?" She waited. "Gus?" she said hopefully.

But she spoke to the air.

Leaving the office, she hurried to her own room to dress. She put on one of her white tailored blouses and lightweight blue pantsuits. She was going to the morgue. It felt important to dress properly.

Malachi found a perch on the bar stool next to Bootsie. Sullivan asked if he wanted anything; he decided that if he was going to sit there commiserating with the tavern's intriguing trio of barflies, he should have a drink so he ordered a light beer.

"Sad business," he said. "But, Dirk, this

135

might not be Helen. Abby doesn't seem to think it is. Still, it'll be best to know for sure."

Bootsie turned to him. "Yeah, I guess so. I mean, you can hope the girl just went off on a whirlwind romance, but . . ."

"Helen was responsible," Dirk said. He lifted his glass. "Ah, Helen."

Dirk might be a little too far gone to recognize anyone, Malachi thought.

"Dirk, did Ms. Long have any tattoos or birthmarks? Anything that might help if her face is too . . . damaged?"

"Damaged?" Aldous repeated with a shudder.

"Um," Dirk said thoughtfully. "She, uh, did say she had a tattoo. But she never said what it was — or where it was. She liked to tease her pirate cast mates aboard the *Black Swan.* Make them guess. They were a phenomenal group of young people to work with — Helen, Jack and Blake. They got along so well." He shook his head. "Blake had a major crush on Helen. She liked him well enough, but said she wouldn't date anyone she worked with. Would that she had!"

"We don't know that it's Helen," Malachi repeated.

"And if it's not — then where *is* Helen?"

Aldous asked. He stared at Malachi and, in turn, Malachi stared at him. He was definitely unique and hard to miss, a big, powerful man with his shiny head and gold earring.

"Hopefully, alive and well somewhere," Malachi said. He gave Aldous a smile. "Sir, do you work on the pirate ship now and then? You've certainly got the look."

"Hereditary baldness," Aldous told him. "Sometimes — say, around St. Patrick's Day — the city gets crazy busy and then I work with my friend here."

"You're a captain, as well, though? Different kind of ship, if I remember our conversation from before," Malachi said.

"My family's been in the shipping trade for generations. We were bringing goods back and forth from the Old World before the colonies became a nation. I own Brentwood Shipping. We have ships all over the world. My dad was old school. I started work as a deckhand on a nine-hundred-and-six-foot container vessel. I've sailed on almost everything known to man, but these days, I mostly use my little fishing boat. She's a thirty-three-foot Boston whaler with a fine cabin and a galley. I can take her out for a few days on my own when I feel I need the water beneath me. But, yeah, there's fun

137

in playing a pirate. I'm still on the company board, but I already put in my time. Now, I do the world a favor and give people jobs to keep the company afloat."

"That's a good thing. We all need jobs," Malachi said.

"What about you? You spend a lot of time on the water?" Bootsie asked.

"I spent some time with friends on shrimp boats down in Louisiana," he answered. "And I've been on a cruise — does that count?"

Dirk managed a smile. "Hardly! You've got to have the wheel in your hands, really feel the power of the water, even on a river. Feel the wind whip around when you aren't sure you can fight your way back to the docks. Now *that's* being on the water."

"Hear, hear!" Bootsie shouted as he thumped the bar with his fist.

"Then you gentlemen have it all over me," Malachi said, smiling. "What about you, Bootsie?"

"Hey, I'm living on borrowed time here. I'm nearly as old as Gus! But, yeah, give me a chance and I'll be a pirate!"

Just then Abby came back down the steps, out of her pirate attire. She was now in a customary business suit, the kind worn by agents running all over Quantico and D.C.

But there was no way to tone down her beauty or inner vitality. It might have been her coloring — or it might've been that she had a passion for life. She had dearly loved Gus; that was plain. But she loved her city, too. She'd made that clear when she'd told him so enthusiastically about the inn where he was staying.

She looked at him, then looked at the beer in front of him. He'd barely touched it. He raised his glass and saluted her, showing her that only a few sips were gone.

"Want me to drive?" she whispered, coming up beside him.

"I think I'm fine."

"You shouldn't *think*. You should know."

"I swear — two sips."

"I'll drive," she said. "Dirk, let's do this, okay?"

They walked outside and Malachi headed for his SUV. She was headed to the parking lot. She frowned at him, and he grinned and lifted his hands. "Okay."

Amused, he followed her and Dirk to the car, choosing to take the backseat.

"Hey, big man, you can take the front," Dirk said.

"It's all right. I fold well. And we're not going that far."

When they reached the coroner's office,

Malachi found that David was there, waiting for them.

"Dr. Tierney has the case," he told them. "He wants someone to come in, rather than just viewing the remains on the screen. She's really ripped up. An identification might take some time if we have to go through dental records or DNA."

"You okay, Dirk? You can do this?" he asked the man.

"I can go in alone, Dirk," Abby said.

Dirk shook his head and squared his shoulders. They were led down a hallway and into a pristine autopsy room. The smell of chemicals was strong, but as they approached the gurney, so was the smell of death.

Tierney was a man of about fifty, medium in height and weight, with brown eyes, huge spectacles that made them appear bigger and a mask over his mouth and nose.

"We're ready," David said.

Tierney lifted the sheet that covered the corpse.

Malachi found himself thinking that the poor girl now resembled something that might have been created for the final scene of a horror movie — a mermaid beaten and destroyed or some other creature brought low. He shivered, remembering what he'd

140

felt when he'd turned her over in the water and realized that hope had been gone for some time. She'd hit a propeller somewhere in the river, it seemed, since chunks of her flesh were gone. Her face had been attacked by fish and crabs. Very little remained of her nose or lips.

He wondered if even the girl's mother would recognize her.

"Oh, God!" Dirk exclaimed, and turned away.

David looked at Abby. Abby was white and pinched, but she didn't turn away. "Can you tell?" David asked her.

To Malachi's surprise, Abby nodded. "It's not Helen," she said.

"And you know that because . . . ?"

She pointed to the corpse's left breast — in relatively good condition. "Helen had a tiny clover tattooed right there. She told a bunch of the girls about it one day, as long as we swore not to say anything to the guys she worked with. She liked to tease them, telling them she had one somewhere, but they'd have to guess where, and when she had all their guesses, maybe she'd tell them. And the hair . . . I don't think that's the shade of Helen's hair. She was almost platinum. This girl had a manicure and Helen didn't manicure her nails. She always said wenches didn't use polish."

"Okay, then." David let out a sigh. "We're still looking for Helen. And we have to find out who this poor girl might be. I'll get them started on missing-person reports back at the office. Thank you for coming in."

Malachi didn't want to leave yet. He walked closer to the table and stared at the dead woman. What he saw now might help him later when they were further along in the investigation. "Death was by drowning?" he asked.

"Her lungs were filled with water from the river," Dr. Tierney said. "They've scraped her nails, searched for trace evidence . . . but I don't know. She was in the river about a day and a half to two days, until she washed up near the dock."

"So, she died around the time Helen Long disappeared," Malachi said.

Tierney glanced at David.

David shrugged. "That timing sounds about right," he said.

Malachi didn't want to act like a ghoul but he wanted to touch the body. He moved closer and leaned over her, trying to study the remains of her face. He touched her arm; she was cold and he felt no sense of her. But he noticed something he hadn't seen before. Perhaps it was a detail the medical examiner's office and the police had wanted to keep quiet.

Her hands were darkened and curled at her side but there was something odd about her left hand. Malachi raised his brows at Tierney and touched the icy hand. He looked at Tierney.

Tierney returned his look with a fierce frown.

Malachi straightened. "May I see the other corpses?" he asked.

Tierney swung around to face David.

"He's one of my old partners, Doc. And now Mr. Gordon is a consultant with the FBI. I would appreciate it if you'd help us."

Tierney hesitated and pulled back his sleeve. "It's late," he muttered.

"Please," Malachi said.

"Can I . . . May I get out of here?" Dirk pleaded.

"Abby?" Malachi asked.

She wanted to stay and help — that was clear in her eyes — but it was obvious that she was the one who needed to be with Dirk.

"I'll take you home, Dirk," she said.

"I'll take Mr. Johansen for a coffee across the street. We'll wait for you," David offered.

"Abby should be here since she just graduated from the academy. She's an FBI agent now."

"So I've heard," Tierney murmured. It didn't sound as if he was impressed. Malachi made a point of grinning at her. *Learn to live with it,* he told her silently.

Whether she understood his message or not, she handled it. "Thank you. I believe it's important that we see all the victims."

David left with Dirk.

When they were gone, Malachi spoke to Tierney. "She's missing her ring finger. It wasn't gnawed off, it was cut off," he said.

"We're not letting that information out," Tierney said curtly.

"I understand." Malachi nodded. "Is it the same with the other corpses?"

"Yes."

Tierney walked over to a wall with numbered sliding doors and placards in little slots. He went straight to drawer nine. A handwritten name tag read *Ruth Seymour.*

He pulled the drawer back and gently removed the sheet from her face.

Ruth had fared better than the unknown girl they'd just seen. Most of her face was intact. Malachi saw the mark of some kind of bondage that had been described in the autopsy notes. He also saw that the ring finger on her left hand had been severed at

144

the knuckle.

"Head injury is here," Tierney told him, pointing.

She'd been struck on the back of the skull — one solid blow.

"It would've knocked her out?" Malachi asked.

"Probably came close to fracturing the skull, so, yes, likely she would've been knocked out. But if you look at the wound closely, you can see there's healing. So she regained consciousness again — a day, a few days? — before she was killed," Tierney explained.

That made something cold curl up inside his gut. Dead was dead — but he wondered what torture she'd gone through before death.

"What about Rupert Holloway?" he asked.

"That was different. As far as I can tell, Holloway was knocked out and killed soon after. Maybe a few hours later, somewhere in that time frame, at any rate. Both young women were kept alive longer. I assume you've read the reports. Although I can't state it definitively, I believe both were sexually molested, and killed later. I don't think they were in any condition to fight off the rapist. They were probably knocked out and held until they annoyed their attacker — or he tired of them. Ms. Shepherd was the last victim found before today. She's right here."

She could have been anyone. "How did you ID her?" Malachi asked.

"Fingerprints. They were on file at her school. It's a safety measure taken there."

"She's missing the ring finger?"

"Yes."

Malachi looked at Abby. She was stoic, watching, listening, betraying sorrow but allowing little else to show on her face.

Tierney went over the young woman's injuries.

Malachi moved closer to inspect the corpse again, touching the body. And again, he had no sense of anyone remaining.

"Mr. Rupert Holloway is the last of our recent victims. You don't want to visit the entire morgue, do you?" Tierney obviously wanted to be on his way.

"Just these victims," Malachi said. "Mr. Holloway, please."

Rupert Holloway was in nearly the same shape as their Jane Doe, and his head wound was worse; the skull had been fractured. "He might still have been out cold when he was tossed in the river," Tierney said.

"But he's missing his ring finger, as well."

Tierney looked uncomfortable. "Yes.

Taken while he was still alive — as with the others."

"Any other marks on him?" Malachi asked.

"Just one. On his back. Help me roll him and I'll show you."

He obliged; Rupert Holloway had been a big man.

Low on his back there was a wound, which was sharp and broad.

"Not serrated," Abby commented.

"No, it was made by a smooth blade," Tierney said. "Now, if that's all . . ."

"That's all, Dr. Tierney. Thank you so much for your time."

He led Abby out. They removed the scrubs they'd donned and left them in the appropriate receptacles.

"Definitely a serial killer," Abby said. She shuddered and looked at him apologetically. She was ashen, although she'd held up well. "Why . . . why the fingers? Is there a significance to the ring finger? Are they trophies?"

"Possibly. And I can't begin to fathom if there's a symbolic reason of some kind for the ring finger. Does it have anything to do with wedding or engagement rings? Holloway was married, but the others . . ." He shrugged. "I don't know." As he spoke, he watched something come alive in her eyes.

"I'm an idiot," she said.

"Why?"

She flushed. "I mean, there is a symbolic reason for the ring finger. Pirates used to cut off the ring fingers of their hostages specifically to steal their rings. Blackbeard supposedly cut off his own ring finger as a warning to others to leave him alone."

"Then it *is* symbolic," Malachi said.

"Yes, I believe that has to be it. But still, the killing of Rupert Holloway was different from the others. The injury on his back is completely unlike the injuries on the women. What do you think the blade was?" Abby asked. "And why that mark left there?"

"At the small of his back?" Malachi mused thoughtfully. "A pirate sword, Agent Anderson. I'm willing to bet that wound was made by a sword."

5

"It's not Helen. It's not Helen," Dirk repeated. He'd said the words dozens of times during the drive back to the Dragon-slayer.

"No, Dirk, it's not Helen," Abby assured him.

"Oh, my God! Did you see her face?"

They reached the parking lot and Abby put the car in Park. Malachi was out of the backseat, opening the door for Dirk. When Dirk stood in front of him, he steadied the man with a hand at his elbow. "Not Helen, Dirk. So if you can think of anything at all that might help us find her, it could save her life."

"What if he's doing that to her — to Helen — right now?" Dirk asked.

"Dirk, the poor girl looks so bad because of what the creatures in the river did to her. Helen could be alive. She's a bright girl, and if anyone can manage to stay alive, *she* can. I'll tell you what might help. You let the police do a thorough search of the *Black Swan,*" Malachi said.

"A search?" Dirk asked blankly.

By then, Abby had come around the car. "If they search the *Black Swan,* Dirk, they might find something Helen left on the ship. A note, a scrap of paper, a card — something."

She watched Dirk carefully — although she couldn't believe anything evil of him, not in a thousand years.

His expression didn't change. "If it'll help, hell, yeah, search the ship."

Malachi might have been surprised by Dirk's easy agreement; if he was, he didn't show it.

"That's fine, Dirk, thank you. I'm going to call my buddy David back and ask him to get a team in there, okay? You'll have to give David official permission."

Dirk nodded. "Anything that'll help," he said. He looked back at Abby. "It *will* help, right?"

"It will," she said.

"Call him. That detective. Tell him I'll sign anything he needs."

"Thank you," Abby said.

Dirk left the two of them, striding for the bar. He stopped and turned back. "You two just saw all that and don't need a drink?" he demanded.

"We're coming," Abby said.

She looked at Malachi. "Honestly, it *can't* be Dirk. You figure someone's kidnapping people, taking them on a pirate ship. With the women, he's making them behave like captives — forcing them to have sex as if they'd been seized by pirates. And because he has a pirate ship, you're thinking Dirk."

He shrugged. "Abby, yes, obviously, I'm thinking Dirk. Helen worked for him, Helen is gone. And he runs a pirate ship."

"If someone is going to search the *Black Swan,* shouldn't it be us?" Abby asked him.

"Get permission from your friend," he told her.

Abby whirled around and ran, catching up with Dirk just before he got to the door. He seemed perplexed but told her she was welcome on the ship anytime, any day. He handed her his keys; the gate down at the dock where the *Black Swan* berthed would be locked.

She ran back to Malachi. "Let's go!" She dashed by him.

"Hey!" he called after her.

"Faster to walk than to find a parking place on the river. Come on!"

It was only a matter of blocks to the marina. Abby used the key Dirk had given her to open the gate. She waited for Malachi, and tried not to remember how she'd seen the body here earlier. There was no crime scene tape; it wouldn't have served much purpose. She assumed the techs had looked for anything they possibly could, considering that the body had floated in the river for a day or two.

Malachi entered behind her. "Relock it," he warned.

She did. They hurried on down the dock. Malachi passed by her and jumped onto the deck of the *Black Swan.* The little gangplank that tourists used to board was on the ship, taken up at night to discourage anyone who might make it onto the dock.

Malachi stretched out his hand. She hesitated only briefly and accepted it to join him on board the ship.

Dock lights lit up the main part of the forecastle and performance area. Abby hurried on to the restaurant area and the restrooms. Employee lockers were in an anteroom. She turned on lights as she went in and heard Malachi behind her, searching the snack stand and environs.

She found Helen's locker, which was open. But on inspection of its contents yielded nothing except for a sweater, a makeup bag, a brush and Helen's costume.

Frustrated, Abby closed the locker.

The others were open and she decided to search them, as well. She felt awkward — as if she were sticking her nose where she really had no right — but Blake Stewart and Jack Winston worked with Helen. They were friends, and Blake had been in love with Helen. It had to be done.

But their lockers yielded nothing, either. There was a small costume and prop area next to them. She went through the swords and guns used by the players, touching each one. None was real. The blades were plastic, although they'd been artfully created to appear real.

She left the lockers, disappointed, and discovered that Malachi was no longer in the snack shop.

"Malachi?"

"Down in the magazine!" he called to her.

She hurried to the below deck and found him by one of the hammocks against the inner hull, placed there for the use of the cast and crew.

"Anything?" she asked.

"Maybe." He handed her a folded pamphlet.

"It's a tour map," she said. "Actually, this particular map is printed and put out by a friend of mine. You might have met him at the Dragonslayer yesterday. I went to high school with him — he was a major player in our drama department and a huge history buff. He does ghost tours here in the city and they're supposed to be some of the best."

"Roger English," Malachi said.

"Yes. You did meet him, then."

"No. His name is on the map. It's advertising for his tours."

"And you think Helen might have had it? The map, I mean."

He nodded. "I do. Because this looks like a woman's handwriting — small, neat, lots of curlicues. I know there's a young woman working on the crew, but the probability that it's Helen's is high. And she's marked something. Here." He pointed at a location on the map.

"Let me see it, please."

Abby took the map from him. It had real streets and real places, but they were sketched out cartoon-style. There was a checkmark on the map and in the border was written, "Meet here."

"What do you think?"

Abby shook her head. "That isn't any particular place, but there's an old church nearby. It was deconsecrated years ago and was a restaurant and nightclub for a while. Right now, it's just empty. A private restoration group bought it about a year ago, but they haven't started working on it yet."

"Interesting," he murmured.

"But you thought people were being snatched on the river," Abby said.

"I do believe the victims are being taken out *to* the river. But . . . we have nothing that tells us where they're being taken *from*. They're dying on it, yes — but how are they getting there?"

"Rupert Holloway was supposed to be meeting friends right here at the riverfront," she reminded him.

"Yes, but no one saw him here. Or, even if he *was* taken down here, it doesn't mean the women were kidnapped on the river. Can we go there? You know this part of the city."

"Of course we can go there. But that precise area is just the sidewalk," Abby said. "Except that . . . well, I could talk to Roger. He knows Savannah even better than I do. Maybe he can see something that I'm not seeing."

"Tell me more about Roger."

"Like I said, he's a friend from high school. I'm positive he's not a suspect. If he were going to kill anyone, it would be over a prime role in a pirate movie or in an argument on the history of Savannah. Roger, well, I've known him all my life. And I can't see him taking any . . . any physical trophies. He passed out at school when we were donating blood during an emergency blood drive."

Malachi's phone rang, and he answered it. "David," he told her.

"Yes," he went on, "we're down in the magazine. Coming up. We'll leave it to your fine crew now, my friend." He ended the call.

"Investigators are here. They can finish. I think we might have found something useful. He folded the map and put it in his pocket.

"You're not going to give it to the cops?" she asked him.

"I'll tell David the location, and he can send a car to check it out. I say we leave the rest of this to the experts and head back. I might have a surprise for you," he added.

"You know, I'm not really in the mood for surprises. I have had the longest two days in history."

He smiled slowly. Abby realized she was getting to like that smile; she was even coming to understand his strange ways. He could be unerringly polite, especially when someone else was acting like an idiot, and manage to get what he needed. He gave information out, but held on to what he felt he needed. Close to him, alone down in the magazine, she was aware of how attractive he was. Old-fashioned courtesy, combined with rugged masculinity, would make him appealing to most women.

Maybe she was one of them.

She stepped back. She tried to remind herself that he'd made a fool of her a few times, and yet . . . he'd seemed so puzzled that she'd felt that way.

"I'll talk to David as we leave. Let's get back to the Dragonslayer." He looked at his watch. "It's after nine now. I'm ready for that drink Dirk suggested. And I won't be driving to my hotel. I can easily walk, but I won't have to. I'm sure I can catch a ride."

"Malachi!"

They heard his name shouted. He stepped past her and hurried up to the deck. As she followed him, he turned back for her, helping her make the hop-over to the dock. David was at the gate with a five-man crew of investigators, and they walked down to meet him, opening the gate to allow them all entrance before handing him the key.

"Anything?" David asked.

"No blood or guts," Malachi said, waiting

until David's team went by.

When they had, he said, "We found a map. May or may not have been Helen's." He produced it and showed David. "You might want a man or two to check out the area."

"That's the middle of a sidewalk."

"So Abby told me. But it is marked on the map," Malachi said. "Okay if I hang on to this?" When David nodded, he folded it, returning it to his pocket.

"There may be something in the area — a restaurant, someplace Helen might've gone to meet someone," Abby explained. "And, actually, it could have been anyone's map, but since we're grasping at straws here . . ."

She let her voice fade. David shook his head, lowering it. "Yeah. We are grasping at straws, but we need to grasp quickly."

"That's why I suggested searching the *Black Swan* — tonight," Malachi said.

"But then you beat me to it."

"We haven't got the forensic talents to find what your crew might," Malachi told him. "We just did a run-through. After all, we already spent hours on the ship."

"Hmm. I'm reconsidering the map. How about handing it over?" David asked.

Malachi smiled serenely. "What map? Do you have a map, Abby? Did I mention a map? Lousy memory," he said.

David looked at Abby. She looked at Malachi, who guilelessly returned her stare.

"I don't have a map," she said.

David groaned. "Yeah, okay. You hold on to it, Malachi. See what vibes or whatever it gives you." He wagged a finger. "You should be grateful, my freelancing friend, that I've seen you in action before and that I'm willing to turn a blind eye to the way you ignore procedure. So, X marks the spot. I'll send a car tonight. And they'll call me and say that I sent them to stare at the middle of a sidewalk."

"Probably. But it's worth a shot, right? Call me if there's anything."

"Yes, I will," David said. "And you do the same."

"Let's go back to the Dragonslayer, Abby," Malachi suggested. "Let the detective get on with his work."

As they headed to the tavern, David called after him. "Don't forget. Call if you discover anything!"

"You know it," Malachi called back.

He kept walking; he had long strides, but Abby kept up with him. "Are you running for that drink you said you need?" she asked.

"What? Oh, sorry. I was just thinking."

"Yes?"

"We should call your friend. The tour-guide-slash-mapmaker, Roger English. It's his map Helen had."

"You can pick up that map at any souvenir store in the city."

"Still, it's his map. We'll have him show us around the city."

"I know the city!"

"You said you didn't know it like he does."

"True," she agreed. "Roger's always been a fanatic, obsessed with the city." She smiled. "Gus occasionally let him stay at the Dragonslayer, just because he loved it so much."

"Can you call him?"

"Of course, but I might not need to. He hangs around the Dragonslayer after his tours sometimes. They end around nine."

"Good."

Malachi opened the door to the tavern for her. Once they'd stepped inside, he walked up to Grant Green, on duty at the host stand as night manager. Trying to keep an eye on him, Abby went to the bar where Dirk was, as usual, seated between his two old friends, Bootsie and Aldous.

"Anything?" he asked her anxiously.

"Not that we could find, Dirk, but the police are there now."

"Yes, I told Detective Caswell that I was happy for him to search," Dirk said.

"I keep telling him we're going to find her." Bootsie yawned. "Hate to leave you, my friend, but I am *old.*"

"I'm fine," Dirk told him.

"I can stay a bit longer," Aldous said. "Hell, twenty years ago, I could've sat up all night."

"Good, you have another drink with him, Aldous. I need to get some sleep. Good night, all." Bootsie left, his peg leg making a little thump with every other step.

Dirk should have been bleary-eyed, considering the amount of time he'd spent in the bar that day, but he seemed to be all right. Abby cast a glance at Sullivan and raised her brows. Sullivan inclined his head with a secretive smile; that was his way of telling her that he'd promised Dirk the Dragonslayer would be picking up his drinks that day — and then Sullivan had watered them down to keep Dirk from keeling off his bar stool.

She smiled her thanks, then patted Aldous and Dirk on the back. "Take it easy, you two."

"We're okay. We'll stumble home together soon," Aldous assured her.

She nodded. Aldous sipped his drinks slowly and looked after his friends. He and Dirk both lived nearby, a few blocks from the Dragonslayer.

She turned, but Malachi was no longer there. Grant Green was giving directions to a couple who wanted to see the Colonial Park Cemetery, in the heart of the old town. They wanted to visit it the following day. She smiled and thanked them for coming to the Dragonslayer as they left, then asked Grant, "Where did Malachi go?"

Grant pointed to the dining room, where a group sat at one of the large round tables near the grate to the tunnel and the image of Blue Anderson. Malachi had taken a seat with them. There was an empty chair beside him.

As if he sensed her watching him, Malachi rose and beckoned her over.

She approached the table. All four of the people there — two men and two women — stood, too. The women were blonde, one petite and one tall. The men were both dark-haired, slim, handsome. They looked like a who's who of beautiful people.

Malachi smiled broadly as she reached the group. "I told you I had a surprise for you. One I thought you'd like. And these lovely people are it. The blonde across from you is Katya Sokolov. To your left is Angela Hawkins. Next to her, we have our illusionist and magician extraordinaire, Will Chan, and here, by me, Jackson Crow."

She was startled and told herself she should have recognized him from the pictures she'd seen of him, and now, of course, she did. *Crow.*

A surprise.

And she *was* surprised. Jackson Crow himself, now a legend in the agency, had arrived.

He was a striking man with his evident mixture of heritage. She shook his hand, and then met Angela, Will and Kat. She sat down in the chair held for her between Malachi and Jackson Crow, and the others sat, as well.

"You came," she said, staring at Jackson Crow. She'd never met him. She just knew his name, had seen his picture. Everyone at Quantico knew who he was. They whispered about him, sometimes in a teasing fashion, and sometimes with awe. Either way, his record spoke for itself.

"Malachi said this is a situation that warrants some extra help," Crow told her. "I figured we'd put Will to work with the pirates, since he's an excellent actor and magician. Kat is a pathologist. She'll see if anything's missing as far as the autopsies are concerned. Angela and I will work the computer angles and interview those who were last seen with the victims, leaving you and Malachi free to delve into the city. You're the expert on Savannah. I've got a meeting first thing tomorrow with Detective Caswell and the task force to give them some idea of what we think we're looking at — and who we might be looking for. And then we'll all buckle down to try to locate the missing girl."

Abby nodded. "I'm glad. So glad. Her life has got to be the priority right now."

"Of course." Angela spoke quietly.

"I'm grateful that you came in force!" Abby said.

"Agent Anderson, there have been a number of bodies found. Only a fool wouldn't think that warranted serious attention," Jackson Crow told her.

"But do you believe what I was trying to explain — that my grandfather was murdered?" Abby asked.

Crow nodded. "With the message he sent you, and his death right before your arrival? Yes, I do. Something is going on here. We'll do everything in our power to find out what. And I don't expect our hands to be tied. Two of the victims were from other states, which gives us jurisdiction — although I hate to step in uninvited. But because Malachi has a good relationship with the detective in charge, I believe an invite is in the works."

Across the table, Angela Hawkins leaned in. "The Dragonslayer is incredible. What a wonderful place — and what a fascinating history."

"The food is excellent, too," Kat Sokolov added.

"Thank you. I'm glad you've enjoyed it," Abby said.

"We have," Jackson said. "For now, however, we're going to get the check. There's a girl out there — and she might still be alive. Everyone will be starting early." He glanced around, as if looking for the waitress.

Abby shook her head. "Dinner is on the house," she insisted.

"This is your business, Agent Anderson. We don't take advantage," Jackson Crow told her.

"Please! You've come here. Let me offer what I can. Which, by the way, is a house," she said.

"We do have rooms booked," Jackson responded. "But thank you."

"Jackson," Will said. "It might be wise to accept. We'll have space and privacy."

"Yes, you can cancel your hotel rooms," Abby urged.

"We don't want to put you out. We only

165

need two rooms — except that I thought we should assign someone here, too," he said.

"I've been staying at the Dragonslayer since I came back," Abby said. "And not to worry. I'm fine. I've spent time here all my life. But I also have a home — a family home — on Chippewa Square." She shrugged. "It happens to be available. And there's no reason to incur taxpayer expenses that don't need to be incurred." Abby realized that Malachi had remained quiet; he'd been watching her all the while. He didn't appear angry, just bemused.

"We don't take chances," Jackson said. "Malachi, do you want to stay here? I'm sure Agent Anderson has a couch somewhere. And, if you really don't mind, Agent Anderson, we will take you up on your offer. We do, as a group and as individuals, tend to prefer the historic and the private — places with plenty of room to meet, without probing eyes. Detective Caswell will set us up with a room at the police station, but we still like having some private space — when we can get it."

"I'm fine on a couch. Or a floor," Malachi said.

"And you are sure you want to offer this invitation?" Crow asked Abby.

They were leaving Malachi here?

Maybe that made sense. Malachi had already seen Blue. And she hadn't seen him since he'd led her to her grandfather's corpse.

"Um, yes, of course." Abby turned to look at Malachi. "You don't have to sleep on a floor or a couch," she told him. "I can give you my grandfather's room."

"That certainly sounds more comfortable," Malachi said. He still appeared a bit bemused. Of course he did. Now that Jackson Crow had arrived, she was all hospitality. "I've been staying a few blocks away at a hotel on the riverfront, so moving over will take ten minutes." He spoke softly to Jackson. "We have a lead. At least, I *think* it's a lead. We found a map with an X. Abby has a friend who's a city expert, and we're meeting up with him in the morning to see what we can find."

"I'll be speaking with the task force," Jackson Crow said, "and we'll compare notes later."

Abby got a piece of paper and wrote down the address of her house on the square. "There are a few things there — coffee in the freezer, dry creamer, but not much else. I went over one day last week, checking up on the place, and everything's in order." She hesitated, looking at the group. "I was thinking I'd rent it out again when I leave here to get my assignment."

"The rest of your family is gone?" Angela asked her.

Abby nodded. "Yes, it was Gus and me for a while there," she said.

"I'm sorry." Angela didn't add that her grandfather had been old, and Abby was glad of it.

"All right, then," Jackson said, rising. "We'll go to your house now."

"I haven't stayed at the house in years, and it's been empty for a while. Oh, it won't be terrible — no moldy sheets or anything like that. They're in the hall closet in sealed bags. I can come with you, to get you in, but —"

"No need," Malachi said. "You need to see if your tour-guide buddy is here."

Abby retrieved her house keys and handed them to Jackson.

"We'll see you both tomorrow. In the meantime, we'll keep in contact on our cell phones," he instructed. "And, like I said, we're careful in this unit. That's why we check out a situation, and then work in numbers when warranted. We'll say good-night now." Jackson Crow left a tip on the table. Abby started to dispute, to assure him she'd handle it.

168

"Ah, well, the least we can do is reward our excellent server," Jackson said.

Abby nodded, and the group walked to the door. Malachi told her he'd pick up his bags at the hotel while the restaurant was still in full swing.

When they were gone, she realized that Grant Green was standing right at her back. "Okay, give!" he said.

"Give?"

"A cool-looking, authoritative . . . mysterious group of people! So, who are they?"

She couldn't see any reason to lie to him. "FBI."

"I knew it!" he said. "I knew it." Then he grew serious. "So they're here to help? Thank God. I mean, bodies don't usually pop up like that in this city. We have our criminal element, but who doesn't? I'm glad they've — Oh, man, is it true? Do cops and FBI agents really not get along? Do the cops get resentful when the FBI is called in?"

She smiled. "Grant, I have no idea. I've never been with a group that's been called in. Actually, I haven't been with a group at all. I was ready to be given an assignment . . . but then, well, Gus. And my superior back in Virginia told me to check in when I'd taken care of my family affairs."

"Keep me posted!" he told her.

"I will," she promised. "Hey, Roger doesn't happen to be in here, huh? I don't see him at the bar."

"Yeah, he's here." Grant lowered his voice to a conspiratorial whisper. "He's with a date."

"A date? Impressive."

"They're in the far dining room."

"Should I interrupt?" Abby wondered.

"It's your place. You can just wander by and ask if everything's all right. By the way, are you having the actors do the reenactment this Saturday? I'll need to call them."

"Grant, you and Macy manage the place," she reminded him. "*You* decide."

"Still have to know the new owner's mind," Grant told her.

"I'm an absentee owner, and I think you two do a great job managing the place."

He gave her a hug. "Macy and I get along well, and we'll make sure you're never disappointed." She hugged him back, and then disentangled herself. "I'm going to swing over and say hello to Roger."

Roger was in a little nook in the far dining room. He was leaning over the table, close to his date, a pretty girl with dark brown hair and a sweet gamine face.

The girl saw Abby first and indicated to Roger that someone was coming. He pulled

170

back, said, "Hi, Abby," and started to get up.

"Sit, Roger, I'm just stopping by to see how everything's going," she said.

"Fabulous." He widened his eyes at her. "Abby Anderson, this is Bianca Salzburg. Bianca, Abby, who owns this place."

"Pleased to meet you. And it's wonderful," Bianca said.

"Thanks. I'm glad to hear that. Do you two need anything?"

"Nope. You hire the best. Which includes me," he told his date. "You'll see when I play Blue Anderson on Saturday." He looked at Abby. "*Am* I playing Blue on Saturday?"

"Of course," she said. "Grant will confirm with you. Oh, I wanted to ask you something, too. I have a friend in town — well, friends. One of the guys wants a tour of Savannah from someone who really knows it."

"Well, that would be you," Roger said.

She shook her head. "I don't know it the way you do. Can I book a private tour tomorrow?"

"For you?" he asked, perplexed, curious — and, she thought, a little flattered.

"Yes, for me. And the friend I mentioned. You might've met him, since he's been hanging around here. His name is Malachi Gordon. I'll tell you more tomorrow. If you can do it."

"Sure. Anything for you, kid. It'll be fun." He smiled and glanced at his date. "Abby and I used to love exploring places — especially places we weren't really supposed to go. Gus dragged us out of that tunnel time and time again. We liked to play pirate. Except Abby never wanted to play captive — she always had to be a pirate herself. Like Anne Bonney."

"Wow. That was a lot of years ago!" Abby said. "So tomorrow. Nine. Ten?"

"Ten works better for me."

"Thanks, Roger."

"I'll see you here."

"Okay." Abby nodded. "Bianca, it was very nice to meet you. You're new to the area?"

"I'm here to find an apartment. I work for a delivery company, and I'm being transferred from Chicago."

"Well, then, welcome to Savannah." Abby made her way back to the bar. Grant was going over the following day's reservations at the host stand. Aldous and Dirk were gone. "Aldous left with Dirk, didn't he?" she asked.

"Yeah, they were kind of cute as they went

out, big pirate-kind-of-guy leaning on bald, gold-earringed guy. Don't worry, Aldous said he'd walk Dirk straight to his house."

"Thank you, Grant." Abby went to the bar and took a seat. There were no more customers and Sullivan was sterilizing the bar glasses, then hanging them on the wooden racks.

"You okay?" he asked her.

"Yeah, I'm good, thanks."

"So, you've brought in a bunch of FBI agents?"

Surprised, she frowned at him.

He laughed. "You told Grant. That's like posting something on Facebook. And the one guy, Malachi Gordon, introduced himself to us the other day."

Abby laughed. "I didn't exactly *bring in* a bunch of FBI. Malachi Gordon showed up because of Gus's funeral," she said. That was true. Let them think he was a representative of the agency, there to show his respects. "But, Sullivan, four bodies have been found — three, and then the one today. At least two of the victims were from other states. One was a college girl. And we don't know about the last."

"That's really sad, Abby. What do *you* think is going on? What did they teach you at FBI school?"

"I'd have the same suspicions now whether I'd gone to the academy or not," Abby said. She wasn't giving anything away by stating the obvious. "I suspect there's a serial killer in Savannah."

"Yeah?" He stopped what he was doing and rested his elbows on the bar. "I don't get it, though. Three women, one man. And . . ."

"And?"

"You went crazy when you found him," he said gently. "If there's a serial killer, why would he go after Gus — and how did he get into the tunnel?"

"I have no idea, Sullivan. Maybe I *was* a little crazy. Gus was everything to me," Abby said.

One thing she'd learned: an agent shouldn't share thoughts or information with anyone other than those also working the case, unless someone was at risk. Information in the wrong hands could be dangerous.

Not that she considered Sullivan a suspect. It would've been impossible for the man to slink through the restaurant, since he was always behind the bar.

"I'm so sorry, Abby. You know we all loved him," he was saying.

"Thanks. I do know that."

He touched her cheek, a brotherly gesture. "Be careful, okay?" he said huskily.

"I am careful. And guess what? I excelled in marksmanship. I'll be fine. Thanks, Sullivan."

He backed away, looking toward the door. "Hmm. Your FBI man is back — with a suitcase."

"Yeah, he's going to be staying here."

"Oh?" Sullivan said. A smile twitched his lips.

"No *oh,*" she told him. "Helen Long was last seen here, and we're near the river, that's all."

"Now that's a shame," Sullivan teased. "That it's just business, I mean."

"Sullivan," she warned.

"Tall, dark and handsome. Has a nice aura about him, full of confidence. You could do a hell of a lot worse, you know. Hmm. You *have* done worse."

"Hey!"

"Just sayin'. You always dated pretty boys. Not up to par. And from what I've seen in the past few years, you date someone for a few months, then you're bored."

"That's not true! I've been focused on my career, that's all."

Malachi was coming to join her at the bar. She frowned fiercely at Sullivan.

"Well, then, just jump his bones. Everybody's life is better with some hot sex in it," Sullivan told her.

"Stop it!"

He made a show of buttoning his lips. Malachi slid his suitcase up beside his bar stool. "I'm . . . back," he said a little lamely. "Everything okay here?"

"Right as rain," Sullivan said before she could respond.

"Come on up. I'll show you Gus's room." Abby smiled sweetly at her bartender.

"Yep, and don't worry about anything," Sullivan said. "Grant and I will see that the place is locked up tight."

"Thanks," Abby said.

Malachi smiled at Sullivan, got his bag and followed her up the stairs. She flicked on the light as she opened the door to the apartment. "I talked to Roger English. We're all set to meet him in the morning."

"Good," Malachi said absently. He stepped into the apartment and glanced around. "Nice." He walked in, noted the little coffee nook and moved into the center of the living room area. He went straight to the balcony. "Do you mind if I look out?" he asked her.

"Of course not."

He opened the door and stepped onto the

balcony. Leaning, he looked to the left. She followed him.

"So you grew up here?" he asked.

"Here, and at our family's house on Chippewa Square," she said. "When my parents died — my mom and then my dad — I spent my time here with Gus. And my grandmother, of course, when she was still with us."

"It's hard to lose family," he said, but he didn't elaborate.

A moment later, he gave his attention to the view. "You can see the river from here."

"You can," Abby agreed. "Of course, if they build up anymore, it'll block the view."

"It's pretty," he said. "And made sense for old pirates."

"And maybe new pirates?"

He turned and looked at her. "You're worried that this place is somehow being used. But because a woman was last seen here doesn't mean the Dragonslayer has anything to do with what's going on."

"What about Gus?" she asked.

He was thoughtful for a minute and then said, "Kat will go over the M.E.'s records for Gus. I believe he did die of a heart attack — but the heart attack might have been brought on when he accosted someone or vice versa. Whatever happened, it won't happen again. With your blessing, Will Chan will set up a camera system in the tunnel. No one will get down there by *any* means without being seen. Does that make you feel better?"

"Yes, thank you." She hesitated. "How did you wind up on this case? You said you're not an agent, that you're a consultant."

He shrugged. "I was recently part of a high-profile case in Virginia. Then Jackson Crow, Logan Raintree and a man named Adam Harrison — you probably know he started the whole Krewe of Hunters branch — came to see me. I told you, this is on a trial basis. And . . ." He paused, lowering his head, smiling slightly. "I'd been working alone since I left New Orleans because I got tired telling fellow workers that I'm not a psychic. Most people want to lock you away when you tell them you came up with some of your deductive reasoning because of a ghost — and therefore you don't tell them. Jackson apparently knew what I was doing because he'd studied the work I'd done. After I got to spend time with him, Logan and the other agents, I felt right at home. As if I'd found my people, so to speak. Jackson sent me down here to see what's going on, and I let him know what I've learned. They work in groups, which is why the others have joined us."

"I'm glad," she said. "Did you leave New Orleans because you lost your partner — David Caswell?"

He looked back out at the night.

"No. I left New Orleans when my wife died. It was her home and I always saw it through her eyes. When she was gone, I couldn't stay anymore."

"I'm sorry," she told him.

He turned to her. "It was a long time ago now. We all lose people, and we learn to go on. That's life — and death. So, show me Gus's room. I'll get that bag put away. And maybe we should try to grab a couple of hours' sleep, because during those few hours in between shifts when this place is empty, I'm going to want a private tour. If you're up to it . . . ? Maybe old Blue will let himself be known when it's just you and me."

"Definitely. Gus's room is over here."

She led him down the little hall within the apartment to the first door. Stepping inside, she switched on the light. The old captain's bed was just as it had been. She'd spent some time in the week since he'd died cleaning up, gathering up his clothes and donating them to the Salvation Army. Gus had been almost fanatically clean, but she'd given the room a once-over, too. It was decorated with ships' lamps, a whaling harpoon and other memorabilia from the sea. The walls were paneled, very much like a ship's cabin.

Malachi nodded approvingly. He set his suitcase on the floor and said, "I guess you accept that I'm more or less legitimate now?"

"Yes, I do."

He studied her for a minute, and offered her a smile. "I think you're legitimate, too, you know."

"Thanks." She felt strange, looking at him there, feeling that subtle smile of his as if it were a caress.

And liking it.

She stepped back into the hallway. *Tall, dark and* very *handsome.*

He was suddenly far too appealing.

"Okay, then . . . see you in a few hours," she told him.

She turned and walked the few steps down the hall that led to her own bedroom. She quickly walked in, leaned against the door and realized she was shaking. And she knew then that she was impossibly attracted to him.

Sleep. Oh, hell, yeah. Sure thing.

"Blue, you're supposed to come when we

need help!" she whispered aloud. "And, Blue, I definitely need some help now!"

6

It was a good thing he'd never really needed much sleep, Malachi thought.

He'd lain in bed, staring at the ceiling, going over everything he'd seen and everyone he'd met since he arrived. He hadn't wanted to alarm Abby, but he couldn't help assuming that the Dragonslayer had been used in some way. Either that or the killer was a patron of the tavern.

Dirk. Most obvious suspect. He ran a pirate ship. He played a pirate daily.

Sullivan? The bartender knew the place like few others.

Aldous, Bootsie, Grant, Macy. Bootsie was an old man. Macy was a woman, which didn't clear her, but the sexual activity the women had engaged in — rape? — before death had been with a man. Still, she could be in on it. A facilitator.

He wasn't going to be able to sleep, so he got up and studied Gus's room. It made him wish he'd had the opportunity to know the man. He'd evidently loved the river and history and ships. His room wasn't furnished with reproduction pieces; the lamps and harpoons and other paraphernalia were original, probably worth a small fortune.

When he opened the old sea chest at the foot of the bed, he saw that it contained neatly folded blankets. Wandering around the small space, he discovered that the room didn't have a closet, just an old oak armoire, but it had been emptied except for a few shirts and a woolen captain's coat.

There was one dresser in the room. On top of it sat a few pictures. One he guessed was Abby as a child with her parents. Another was of Abby and, surely, Gus. Another was Abby's college graduation photo. She was young and beautiful, and her eyes were filled with the bright light of one anticipating the future.

She still had that look about her, but now it was tempered by loss. The important people in her family had died. She'd made it through the academy and certainly seen enough of the brutality that could exist. It hadn't silenced the resilient, vibrant chord of life within her; she'd seen something wrong in her grandfather's death and was determined to get to the root of it.

And, she knew there was more in the world than what was seen by most people. Maybe she hadn't had a lot of experience — but then, you didn't really need a lot. Once you'd experienced the dead appearing before you or speaking to you, you recognized that it was possible.

He paused for a moment before opening the first drawer. Although he'd already been prying, he murmured, "Forgive me, Gus, I have to see if there's anything here that will help us."

The first drawer held neatly folded briefs and nothing more. It didn't seem that Abby had gotten around to going through Gus's more personal items.

In the second drawer he found T-shirts and two sets of long underwear. Savannah, on the river, could get damply cold in winter.

Third drawer contained jeans. He looked under them.

There was a newspaper neatly folded beneath the several layers of jeans. Malachi glanced at the date — three months earlier. He studied the paper. A brief article on the bottom of the front page had a headline that read Savannah Underground!

He scanned the article, which was interesting; apparently, years ago, Savannah had teemed with life below the surface.

He started to put the jeans back, deciding that, with more time, he'd refer back to the article. As he held the jeans, he felt something in one of the pockets.

He pulled out a small plastic bag. There was a Post-it stuck to the bag with a note. "Police. Found at bottom of tunnel ladder. Must get to right person."

Curious, Malachi examined the contents of the bag. He couldn't figure out what the object was and then a chill seemed to settle in his bones. The . . . thing was small and oddly dark, as if it were growing charred. He had to open the bag and let it spill out before he saw what it was.

A finger. Presumably a ring finger. Decaying. He looked at the note again. It had to mean that Gus had found the finger and meant to give it to the police. But he'd wanted to talk to his granddaughter — someone he trusted. Gus had known or suspected something.

"Hello?" Abby tapped at his door. He opened it.

"I heard you rummaging around," she said. "So I knew you were awake. I wanted to tell you that Grant and Sullivan are gone. The Dragonslayer's empty except for the two of us."

He didn't reply right away.

"What is it?" she asked.

"Gus was onto something."

"What?"

He hesitated. "Gus found a . . . um, finger. He found a finger at the bottom of the tunnel. He knew that someone who had some involvement with the murders had been in the tunnel. Except the police never released the fact that the ring finger of the left hand had been taken from each of the victims. So he probably didn't know exactly what he'd found — which was why he wanted to talk to you."

Abby lowered her head. "He died," she said dully, "because I didn't get here fast enough."

"Abby," he said, lifting her chin, "he died because it was his time. He died doing what was right, and that would've been important to Gus."

She nodded and he released her. "You're right, even though you didn't know him."

"I wish I had, but I know that much about him."

He realized she was far too close. She smelled sweetly of soap and shampoo, and he was surprised that it was suddenly so difficult for him to separate a coworker from someone . . .

Someone he wanted.

"What should we do with the finger?"

He stepped awkwardly back as her words broke through his thoughts. "Give it to Kat," he said. "She'll tell us whether it's new and showing some kind of decay or if it's been in the tunnel for ages."

"Unlikely — since this killer is taking fingers."

"I agree. But we'll give it to Kat," he said. "All right."

He paused for a minute. "We'll deal with it tomorrow."

"And then we'll give it to the cops, right?"

He nodded. "Okay, now show me the Dragonslayer," he said.

She led him through the upstairs first, leaving the family apartment behind to show him Gus's office, the manager's office, the employee lounge, lockers and restroom. They went to the supply room and she showed him the stairs that went down to the dining room below.

Only the night-lights were on. When they went down the stairs, they were greeted by the image of Blue Anderson standing guard over the grate that led to the tunnel below. The robotic mannequin — handsomely crafted — was eerie in the half-light.

But it wasn't the Blue he'd met the night

187

he arrived.

"You've been in the bar and the dining rooms," Abby told him. "Oh, and the kitchen is reached through the server entrance over there." She paused and pointed to a doorway. "It's always open. Gus thought diners had a right to see where their food was cooked. And there's a little service window that opens to the bar."

He gazed carefully around. "If someone knew the routine here — the hours of business, when people were where — it would be possible for that person to be upstairs, maybe, in the storeroom, and come down those stairs . . . and all the way to the tunnel."

"But we keep the grating locked," Abby said.

"It wasn't locked when I got here."

She knew he was right. "The lock on the grate is a combination lock Gus had for years."

"And you really don't know who — or just how many people — might have the combination."

"That's true," she admitted. "New lock in the morning."

"I think we're okay for tonight," he said. "But tomorrow I'll go out and get a combination lock. How many people have keys to the tavern?"

"Grant, Macy, our morning chef and Sullivan. That's as far as I know. I don't think Gus would have given the keys to anyone else. When I was a child, we were almost broken into one night." She hesitated. "That's when I saw Blue for the first time. He woke my grandfather. I heard them and came out of bed and looked downstairs — my grandparents were outside with the police by then — and I saw Blue standing by the door. My grandfather suggested I not mention that I'd seen him to anyone else. I never did. Until now . . ."

"I never talked about seeing people, either," Malachi told her. "I had — have — a few friends who suspect I see things that they don't. They tend to think I'm a real psychic, regardless of what I say. Or they accept the work I'm able to do, know I don't want to explain and let it go at that. Like David. As far as others are concerned, I avoid the topic. Too many people want stock tips and that's something I truly can't give," he added dryly. "Look, I'm a really early riser. I'll run out to buy a new lock, and I'll make sure that Jackson and the group get in here to set up some cameras. That's something we almost always do in this kind of investigation. It's possible that the killer will realize the Dragonslayer has been identified and try something else. But it's also possible that . . ."

He paused, looking at her and wondering if he should go on.

"Possible that?" she urged. She'd stiffened, and he felt she expected his answer, but dreaded hearing it.

"A victim might appear," he said flatly.

"What?" she whispered.

He drew in a breath, hoping he wasn't going to sound ghoulish. "It was important for me to touch the victims today. Sometimes, the dead actually talk on the autopsy table. Kat Sokolov can tell you more about that. I may be repeating what you might already know or suspect, but . . . we should think about it. From what most of us have discovered, ghosts don't like to be with their mortal remains if they're trapped on this plane for whatever reason. But if they do stay behind, they may appear where they feel they can find someone to help them achieve justice. If any of the victims did somehow come through here, they could be caught on camera."

She stared at him, her eyes stricken.

"You okay? You don't need to fear the dead."

"It's one thing to think about Blue hanging around the tavern — he's my ancestor and he obviously stayed because he loves the family and loves the tavern. But . . ."

"Murder victims only stay because they need help," he said.

Abby nodded. "And they just might be caught on camera."

"Don't worry. I sleep lightly and I'm just a few steps away."

He was surprised when her smile was deep and real.

"Funny how things go, huh? You pissed me off when I first met you. That wasn't very long ago, and tonight I'm *really* glad you're here!"

"Let's go up, shall we?"

"Yes, let's go up," she said.

She walked ahead of him, directly for the stairs. When they were both back in the apartment, she locked the door to the outer hallway. It was a good measure, even if they were alone in the restaurant. She walked down the hall to her room, beyond the door that led to Gus's. She hesitated there. "Good night."

He found himself hesitating, too. "Good night."

She started to speak, but paused again. "I, uh, meant what I said. I truly am grateful that you're here."

"I'm truly grateful that you let me be here. Though I *am* curious now."

"About?"

"Your home on Chippewa Square."

"It's pretty," she told him. "You'll see."

"Well, good night."

"Good night," she said. That time, she walked in and closed her door.

Malachi did the same. He smiled as he did so. There was something about her . . .

As he'd said, he was very glad he was there.

Again he lay awake for hours, trying to concentrate on the case and put all the facts in order. Three female victims now, and one male. The killer, to Malachi's mind, had killed Rupert Holloway for coming too close, so the victimology didn't completely fit. That meant the killer was after pretty young women.

Those who might be seen the way women were once seen, as damsels. Lovely young women as prizes.

They'd all been found in the river.

As if forced to walk the plank, at least, symbolically.

And then there was Gus. Dead in the tunnel.

He looked around the room in the dim light, once more wishing he could have met the man. He imagined him as temperate, prone to liking people. But he'd lived a long time and been through a lot. He loved the river, history, antiques — and his granddaughter. She'd grown up with confidence and ability and the strength to choose her own path in life.

"She's a beauty, Gus," he said aloud. "And a strong, smart person. I couldn't know you, but I'm proud to know her."

He realized that his thoughts were going in a direction he'd never expected when he'd headed down to Savannah. But there was no denying she had a beauty any man would instantly admire and somewhere in his heart — or libido — instantly desire. He'd lost Marie five years ago. When she'd died, they'd been young and madly, almost insanely, in love. While he'd engaged in a few brief relationships since her death, he'd never really known any of the women and nothing between them had ever done more than touch the surface of his emotions.

Maybe this was different because of the ghost thing.

And maybe it was because of the way she looked. Or the fire that seemed to simmer within her, a passion for laughter as well as justice.

At some point, he dozed. He wasn't sure

if he opened his eyes and saw Blue Anderson there, standing over him, and then walking to the window — or if he dreamed it. He managed to get some sleep.

His phone rang early around 7:00 a.m. It was Kat Sokolov.

"Did I wake you?" she asked.

"Not really. Yes, but I need to get up." He liked Kat. But he liked Will, too, and the other members of the Krewes he'd been brought in to meet after Adam, Logan and Jackson had brought him to their offices. She was the tiniest, cutest little blonde and didn't look like any medical examiner he'd ever met. But she certainly knew what she was doing.

"I just wanted to let you know I'm heading to the morgue. I'll be attending at the next autopsy," she said.

"I hope the local guy, Dr. Tierney, likes you better than he seemed to like me," he told her.

He heard the soft sound of her laughter. "Not to worry. Adam Harrison has done his magic. We're officially invited in. Jackson and Angela will be down at the local station, giving a heads-up on what we believe, based on what we've seen and learned from you and Abby."

"We're looking for a would-be pirate,"

Malachi said quietly, "who likes to take the ring finger of the left hand as a souvenir. And . . . I, uh, have a finger to give you."

"What?"

"Gus was onto something. I think the killer lost one of his trophies in the tunnel, and Gus found it before he had any idea of what was going on. It might be why he asked Abby to come down here."

"You found it where?"

"In one of his drawers. I need to get it to you."

"I'll run by for it," she said. "Maybe pirates liked to make necklaces out of the bones of people they killed? I'll research my pirate lore," Kat promised him. "Oh, and Will's taking over for Dirk this morning as head pirate on the *Black Swan* to keep an eye on that ship. And Dirk."

"The guy really does seem devastated," Malachi said.

"And I gather he can be a very good actor — as a pirate, at least."

"Excellent plan. And I've heard Jackson gets along well with the local police."

"He has his ways. Not that he has a lot to say yet. They're probably looking for a white male, with or without a companion," Kat said. "Someone who knows the river."

"And has a boat or a ship, or access to

one," Malachi added.

"Big river," Kat said.

"Yes, it is. Keep me posted."

"Back at ya."

Malachi checked his watch. Time for a cup of coffee before starting the day. In fact, he could smell coffee coming from nearby, not from the restaurant below.

He showered quickly, thinking all the while about the clues they had — his thoughts disrupted now and then by another that intruded. *Abby.*

He was glad he was going to spend the day with her.

Abby selected two coffee cups and two small plates from the overhead kitchen cabinet. They actually had time for breakfast.

She toasted a couple of bagels, and Malachi spread cream cheese on them while she poured coffee. "You doing okay?" he asked her.

She glanced at him. He seemed exceptionally appealing as he stood in the tiny kitchen area of the apartment. Fresh from the shower, his hair was dark and slick. His hazel eyes were set somberly upon her and seemed to speak of a depth she couldn't begin to understand. She wondered about his past — the wife he'd lost — and she suddenly wanted to know everything about him.

"I'm fine," she told him.

"I can't stop thinking about your grandfather — wishing I'd known him."

She smiled. "He was great."

"I can tell," he said softly.

She put one of the cups of coffee in front of him. "Thanks." She watched him for a moment. "You're not going to comfort me by telling me that he was old and lived a full life?"

"Does someone having been old make you miss them any less?" he asked.

"No."

"It does, however, help if you know that someone did lead a full life. And it should also help if you know just what you meant to him — that you were the most important person in his life. That's what life is all about. The grief remains, but there's consolation in those things."

"What about you?" she asked. She was pushing it, she thought, but her curiosity was beginning to consume her. "How did you cope? What happened to your wife?"

"Cancer. One day she was fine and then, within a year, she was dead."

"I'm sorry."

"I appreciate that. And time has helped,

as they say."

"So . . . you coped."

"I didn't, not really. New Orleans was her home. I loved living there, loved the music, the food, the architecture. You name it, I loved it. But when she died . . . I quit the police force and the city. I left. I can't bear to go back, even though I loved her family, too. I returned to Virginia, moved into my old family home, and . . ." His voice trailed off as he looked toward the windows and the river.

"And?"

He shrugged. "I realized that in my state of mind, I wouldn't be able to play well with others. So I got licensed and became a private investigator."

"But that *is* coping," she said.

He smiled. It was a crooked, rueful smile, and she yearned to walk over to him and stroke his cheek.

"*You're* coping," he told her. "You're on fire. Going after the killer."

"But you can't go after cancer. No one can."

He shrugged again. "I guess I know that — knew that. I went after God for a while. Didn't work. But . . . ah, well. I have an ancestor who hangs around, too. Doesn't hesitate to speak his mind. He fought a revolution and saw friends die right and left, and wasn't interested in my self-pity. So . . . I started really using whatever this ability is that we have. I pursued bad guys. I tried to save lives and sometimes succeeded. That does help."

Abby made a point of keeping her distance from him. She didn't think she'd ever wanted to touch another person so badly.

"With any luck, we'll save Helen Long," she said.

"Luck — and work," he agreed. He flicked a glance at his watch. "We meet your friend soon? Where?"

"In front of the tavern. But not until ten."

Macy was at the host stand when they went down. She greeted them both, acting a little perplexed. "Good morning," she said. "You came in earlier?" she asked Malachi.

He leaned on the stand and gave her a charming smile. "I'm staying here."

"Oh. Oh, uh . . ." Macy looked at Abby. Abby just smiled, too.

"Macy, you'll see some of my colleagues here in a few hours," Malachi told her. "They'll be setting up some security cameras. If they need it, you'll lend them a hand?"

"Of course," she said, sounding flustered.

He thanked her and turned to head out of

the building.

"What's going on?" Macy whispered to Abby.

Abby merely shrugged and smiled. She quickly joined Malachi outside.

"She thinks we're sleeping together," he said. "Did you set her straight?"

"I don't know what she thinks. I just followed you. Is there a reason you walked out?"

He nodded. "Kat's coming by."

"Oh." She lifted a questioning brow — and then she remembered. The finger. *"Oh."*

A moment later, a dark SUV swung into the lot. Malachi headed for it, reached into his pocket and produced the finger wrapped in a clean silk handkerchief Abby had given him.

"I may be able to match it to a body," Kat said.

"I hope so. I also hope it doesn't mean there are more bodies out there."

Kat nodded and waved to Abby. He stepped back from the SUV and she drove off.

"It's almost nine, so I'm going out to see if I can buy a better lock. Should be back in half an hour or so."

Abby spent the time he was gone organizing more of Gus's papers. By 9:45, she was too anxious to do anything but wait for Malachi downstairs.

He returned just as she stepped outside. "Got it. I'll leave it in the car until we're back. Good timing — that's your friend's car, right?" As he spoke, Roger waved at them from across the parking lot.

Abby waved back. "Be prepared," she warned Malachi, smiling. "You're in for a *tour*. I don't think Roger can help himself. He should be an ambassador."

"That's exactly what I want," Malachi said. He paused as Roger drew closer. "What I want are the ins and outs tourists don't usually get. The city secrets," he told her.

"And no faith in me, huh?" she asked.

"Eternal faith in you, Ms. Anderson. But Roger English made the map that Helen Long might've had in her possession."

"True. And he probably does know more than I do. It's my home, my heritage, and I love Savannah. But Roger is a fanatic."

He smiled, head slightly bent, and she liked the way he looked at her. He might see the world through mocking eyes, but if so, he seemed to mock himself first and there was something charming about that. Then again, he seemed more and more charming to her as time went by.

And, of course, she was more and more intrigued by him.

Not to mention attracted . . .

"Hey!" Roger said, walking up and shaking Malachi's extended hand. "I'm Roger English, best guide in the city. I'm totally yours for the day, my minions are handling all else . . . and where shall we go from here?"

"Malachi Gordon, Roger. And the answer is everywhere — the public city and the hidden city," Malachi told him.

"You're with the feds."

"Yep."

"And you're taking a tour?" he asked politely.

Malachi grinned at that. "Yeah, with the feds, hoping to catch a killer. I think it's the killer's city, so I need to know it, too."

"You're with the right man!" Roger studied Malachi for a minute, hands on his hips. "Yeah, I guess that makes sense. Okay, well . . . we can walk first, if you're up to it. My favorite secret is about four blocks up, but I thought we'd walk along the riverfront and start with Colonial Park Cemetery," he said, glancing at Abby.

"Fine with me," she said.

"Well, you've been in the Dragonslayer, of course," Roger began.

"Coming to know it well," Malachi told him.

"The city has another famous restaurant along the same lines," Roger said. "The Pirates' House. Tourists, children . . . everyone loves it. People get off the highway and come to Savannah to dine there. Children grow up and bring their children. Oh." He looked at Abby apologetically.

"I love Pirates' House, too," Abby said, laughing, "almost as much as I love the Dragonslayer."

"Okay, I'll talk while we walk along the riverfront. You'll notice our shops, the monuments, the hotels — the riverfront is the heart of everything. The city of Savannah was established in 1733 and it's known as our country's first planned city. It was the first capital of colonial Georgia and, later, the state of Georgia. General James Oglethorpe named the thirteenth and final colony Georgia after King George. He arrived at the city via the ship *Anne* with one hundred and twenty settlers. He and his company landed on a high bluff above the Savannah River and he dreamed of a port to rival the best. Oglethorpe's original plan was for total religious freedom and no slavery, but with the marshes to create rich rice fields, his concept of no slaves didn't last too long. However, the planning of the city gives us the unique beauty of her riverfront and the squares we still have today. Streets are built on a grid with squares providing public meeting places and lovely little areas to enjoy. Today, the downtown area is one of the largest National Historic Landmark areas in North America."

"Very impressive," Malachi said.

"We'll get to the squares and more landmarks later. We'll start with Colonial Park Cemetery. It was the first graveyard for Christ Church Parish, and we'll enter by Alercorn and Oglethorpe. More than seven hundred dead from the 1820 yellow fever epidemic rest here, along with a signer of the Declaration of Independence, Button Gwinnett. And, sadly, a number of those killed in duels are buried here, as well. There's one really great restored stone. Come on, we'll find it."

Roger had walked them down the river and then up and through the streets until they reached the regal arched entry, surmounted by a noble eagle. A number of tourists and tour groups were in the cemetery. Roger didn't even see them; he walked among stones, aboveground sarcophagi, family vaults, mausoleums and memorials to get to his objective. He read aloud, " 'He fell in a duel on the 16th of January, 1815, by the hand of a man who, a short time ago, would have been friendless but for him. . . . By his untimely death the prop of a Mother's age is broken: The hope and consolation of Sisters is destroyed, the pride of Brothers humbled in the dust and a whole family, happy until then, overwhelmed with affliction.' We are looking at the 1815 headstone of James Wilde. Sad, huh? Facing all the dangers of those early days, men still shot one another down in the streets." He grinned at them for a minute. "Nowadays you just have to go on Facebook and unfriend people who piss you off!"

"True, and much less gruesome," Abby agreed.

"Save the mother, the sisters and brothers a lot of heartache," Malachi added.

"Now," Roger continued, "most Americans know that during the Civil War, General William Tecumseh Sherman began his March to the Sea. He pursued a scorched-earth policy, believing that the only way to beat the Confederacy was to bring her to her knees. So he razed Atlanta and headed on east. When he got to Savannah, the city surrendered, which meant he didn't have to burn down Savannah. Colonial Park Cemetery was closed to burials in 1853, so there are no Civil War soldiers buried here. But the Civil War left a lasting mark on the cemetery. As I said, Sherman didn't burn the city. Instead, he wrote a telegram to President Lincoln, presenting him with Savannah as a Christmas gift in December of 1864. Today, we're grateful. But here's something interesting. Union troops filled the city with few places to billet. Many were forced to stay here in the graveyard. So, in some instances, they tossed corpses out of the mausoleums and family vaults. Bored, they scratched out the dates on a number of tombs, so in some instances, you can find a grave for someone who was born in 1820, but died in 1777. Names were changed, stones were moved around. They say the cemetery is, to this day, riddled with ghosts, dismayed by the way their graves were so rudely desecrated and disturbed. Now, it was pretty cold, so I'm guessing sometimes the Union soldiers were bitter and that sometimes, when they threw a corpse out for an enclosed place to sleep, it was just because the poor suckers were freezing."

"Sad story," Malachi said. "But if the dead were asleep . . ."

"*If* they were asleep?" Roger echoed.

"Well, if they'd really gone on, they wouldn't much care, would they?"

Roger frowned suddenly. "Hey!" he said. Abby saw that he was looking at one of the tour groups.

"Roger? What's wrong?" Abby asked.

"Huh?" His attention still on the group, he glanced back at her.

"What's wrong?" Abby repeated.

"My date from last night is cheating on me!"

"What do you mean?"

"She's out with another tour group!" Roger said indignantly. "You met her last night. Bianca. She's with that group over there. Excuse me. I'll be right back."

He trotted off. "Ah, young love," Malachi murmured, watching him go.

Then he gestured in the opposite direction. "See them?" he asked softly.

"Them?"

Malachi pointed again. "An elderly couple there, on the bench. He's holding her hand very tenderly. They still seem to be in love, a feat during any era. And there . . . far over there past the bench. Seems to be a lumbering fellow . . . a huge lumbering fellow. Lord, he must be almost seven feet tall. He's acting furtive, as if he's scared. . . ."

She stared out at the far side of the cemetery; she didn't see what he saw. She was about to tell him that, but then, looking where he looked, listening to his words, she felt she did begin to see.

The elderly couple . . . They were in Revolutionary-era clothing. He wore a wig and she wore a cap over her white hair. They did hold each other tenderly.

And the bumbling man who seemed frightened, who seemed to stumble around . . .

She gasped suddenly. The big man was legend — the pure stuff of ghost stories!

Malachi turned to her. "You see them. You could have seen them all along. You didn't know to look for them. Despite what Roger said, not many people haunt a graveyard. Why would they? They didn't live here. But those two. Perhaps they're upset by something written on a stone or some desecration committed during the Civil War and never righted."

She didn't reply to that; she pointed at the other man. "Rene Asche Rondolier," she said. "All the ghost tours talk about him. He was mentally slow. He was accused of killing animals as a child. Whether he did or didn't, no one's ever established. His parents tried to keep him on their property behind a huge brick fence, or so the story goes. I often wonder if he was mentally deficient and therefore an automatic whipping boy at a time when a lot of the populace was still superstitious. People made fun of him or they feared him. He was accused of killing two local girls — their bodies were found here in the cemetery. The local people chased him down to the swamps and lynched him. Afterward, the murders continued, and I don't believe the real killer was ever caught. But Rene had already been hanged for the crimes."

"Poor man. Sure looks like he's weeping and still afraid," Malachi said.

"I don't know if what we hear about his reputation was true, or if it's been enhanced over the years," Abby said. "What *is* true is that his family owned property that's now part of the cemetery. It expanded in the late 1700s to allow for . . . well, more time and more dead."

"Maybe we should try to speak with him sometime," Malachi suggested. "And the older couple. There might be a way to find out why they're still here."

Abby looked at him. "Why is Blue still here, do you think?"

"Maybe he was here for Gus. Or maybe he's here for you, to help you learn exactly what happened to Gus."

Roger came back to join them.

"You okay?" Malachi asked him.

"Yeah, sure. Bianca just knew I'd be busy with you two today and she wanted to see some of the sights. We'll meet up later. Okay. Now we can walk through the city and I can tell you tales as we go. We can visit Christ Church, or the Juliette Gordon Low birthplace or —"

"How about secret Savannah?" Malachi said. "Secret is the most interesting. What do you know about tunnels?"

"Ah!" Roger brightened. "You've heard that the city is riddled with tunnels?"

"Secret tunnels," Malachi said.

"Yeah, and if you're game, I know where we'll find some of the best!"

7

"Malachi, there are so many tunnels to choose from," Roger said happily. "Come on, let's start walking toward the south again."

"The south," Malachi repeated. He pulled the map he'd found on the *Black Swan* out of his pocket. "Are we going in this direction?"

"Yeah, we can head there. We'll stand on that spot marked *X* and I can tell you more." He moved at a brisk pace and they followed a step or two behind. He paused to look back. "There are lots of tunnels. Some more like catacombs. One I've discovered recently that Abby probably doesn't even know about. Seriously, like I said, the city is riddled with them."

"I know there are tunnels. I didn't know the city was *riddled* with them," Abby said. "We have the shanghai tunnel at the Dragonslayer that leads to the river. There's one at the Pirates' House restaurant, too. And there are houses with tunnels that were part of the Underground Railroad during the Civil War. And, of course, the tunnels near Candler Hospital, but I know they're off-limits."

"Yes, there are the Candler Hospital tunnels — truly fascinating, and with very little written history, especially on how and when they were built. Most believe it was during the Civil War. There was once an underground morgue, and autopsies were done there. Some historians note that it was cooler underground, so perhaps it was an attempt to stop the yellow fever and malaria epidemics that used to strike. Oh, and there are the catacombs under an old abandoned church called Saint Sebastian's."

He suddenly stopped walking. "We're on X marks the spot," he told them.

"Do you know why anyone would have marked this spot on your map?" Malachi asked.

"Well, we're standing over a tunnel. Other than that? No. There's nothing here but sidewalk. And some pretty moss-draped oaks next to us."

"The church is right there," Abby murmured.

"The church? Saint Sebastian's? The

church you were just talking about?" Malachi asked.

"None other," Roger told him, obviously gleeful that his knowledge of the city and its history was being fully appreciated. "The church and the tunnels will not be found on official tours. The city's had a problem at various times with vagrants crawling in. In fact, you can find *historic* beer cans and cigarette butts at the entries to many of the tunnels," he said, not hiding his sarcasm.

Abby glanced at Malachi. "*X* equals underground," she said. "It doesn't sound like Helen. I mean, crawling around underneath the ground does *not* sound like Helen."

"Helen Long?" Roger looked a little ashen.

"We think this was her map," Malachi told him.

Roger nodded, clearly perplexed. "Yeah, I gave it to her, but I never saw her mark the map," he said. "She was just asking me about taking a good tour of the city. She was hoping to leave soon. She's driven — really wants to act. But she was asking me about the old church. She said she'd talked to someone who was thinking of buying it, as it hasn't been renovated since the nightclub or worked on by the private company that bought it for historical preservation. This guy she knows wanted to make something out of it like a year-round haunted house. Pirate-themed."

"How did she hear about it? As far as I knew, it was off the beaten tourist and business track," Abby said.

"This guy she met, I guess." Roger shrugged. "Maybe someone who'd taken the tour out on the *Black Swan.* Helen's a sweetheart. Kids love her on that ship. Adults, too. Especially guys."

Malachi nodded. "How about showing us the church?" he suggested.

"I can show it to you — and the catacombs and tunnels, which are kind of one and the same. But it's against the law since it's private property. Oh, wait — you *are* the law, aren't you?"

"Sure," Malachi said, looking at Abby. "Well, we really are the law, although I'm still a consultant. But you're the real deal."

"So are you," she said softly. Her voice, her sincerity, stirred something within him.

"Okay," Roger said, turning back to them. "Let's go around to the side. Casually, of course. There's an old, small iron door that was used for ice delivery. We can crawl through that and then through the hallway. Just be careful, okay. I'd rather not draw attention to us as we creep around private property."

"We shall creep with incredible agility, and quietly," Malachi said.

They crossed the street. It was actually easy to disappear into the many trees that surrounded the old church. Slipping around the side, Malachi realized that at one time there'd been a delivery path there; he could imagine the horse-drawn wagon that would have carried the ice blocks, could see where it must have parked for the few minutes it took the driver to make his delivery. The ice delivery "door" was about four feet off the ground and had a massive dark metal hatch that opened to allow for a space of about three feet by two.

"You can get in?" Roger asked. He gripped the handle. It was old, hadn't been oiled in forever and didn't budge. Malachi stepped past him. "Let me give it a try," he said.

"I *have* opened it before," Roger told him. "Seemed to be easier then."

Malachi gripped the handle, got it into the open position, then braced a foot against the building and pulled hard. When the door gave, he had to jump back quickly to keep from falling.

"I'll pop through first. Make sure there are no spiders or snakes!" Roger told Abby.

"You're afraid of spiders and snakes?" Malachi asked her.

"I'm not particularly fond of either, but I don't freak out."

"You used to scream like a girl when you saw a spider," Roger said.

"I *am* a girl, but I haven't screamed at a spider in years," Abby insisted. Roger merely smiled, then hiked himself up and eased his body through the opening. Abby glanced at Malachi and followed Roger, and then Malachi followed her.

He had to crawl through the old, lined wooden icebox, and when he did, he stood in a room that was shadowed and empty. After a moment his eyes adjusted and he saw something that looked like a contemporary counter against the wall. There were cups covered in spiderwebs; the floor was gritty with dust.

"Come this way," Roger said. "There's a hall that leads to the main church."

Malachi set a hand on the small of Abby's back as they started through the shadows to a door. There were drapes on the few windows down the hallway, shredded and torn in places. Daylight glinted through the rips and tears.

They came to a door that opened into the side of the main church. There were no longer pews that faced the altar, but the steps to the altar and the altar on its dais

216

still stood. Here, there was light that seemed to spew into the interior in a number of colors. Stained-glass windows remained, none had been damaged or altered. Biblical scenes were represented in the glass, beautifully executed. Above the altar, Christ looked down at Mary Magdalene and his mother, Mary, surrounded by lambs. To one side was John the Baptist, to another, the archangel Gabriel.

The glass windows marched down both sides of the church. The blues in the glass were rich and deep, as were the crimsons. The light they admitted was eerie.

Tables had replaced the pews. When it was a nightclub, the owners had played on the religious symbols and added to them with an ironic and diabolical twist — bats dangled from the ceiling.

"The tunnel entrance is up on the dais and behind the altar," Roger said.

They trailed after him.

It wasn't quite as odd an entry as the one by which they'd entered. A little wooden fence surrounded a grate; they opened the entrance and then Roger bent down to lift a hatch. A steep narrow stairway led to the darkness below.

"Father Liam O'Leary is in the coffin directly beneath the altar," Roger said. "The

Irish Catholics liked to take their cues from Rome, I guess, and the Vatican. There are a number of coffins on biers just below here — glass encased. Sort of creepy. I've got a little penlight. Anyone else have anything?" he asked.

"Yeah," Abby said, producing her key chain and a small flashlight. Malachi drew the light he'd used that first night out of his pocket.

"Prepared, huh?" Roger joked.

"Me and the Boy Scouts," Malachi said. He shined his light over the circular room, directly beneath the altar where they were standing. Not surprising, it was dank and musty, and there seemed to be a verdant smell of the earth around them. He walked over to one of the coffins. The lid was glass; beneath it lay the decaying body of a priest in his vestments. His skin was growing brown as it stretched over the bone. Malachi dusted the grit and grime off the bronze plaque before him. His name had, indeed, been Liam O'Leary and he'd been born in County Cork in 1744 and died in Savannah, Georgia, in March of 1793, beloved of his "lambs."

"First priest here," Roger told him. "And around the room you have several more of the especially beloved fellows who served the faithful. I'm surprised they weren't dug up — or carted out — when the church sold the property in the late 1890s and the building was deconsecrated. Could've been bureaucratic error, red tape, whatever. Seems strange and sad that these guys were down here while people were up above them drinking 'Exceptionally Bloody Marys' and watching vampire bats dance over their heads."

Malachi and Abby both nodded.

"When I first started exploring down here, I was shocked," Roger said. "And I didn't even know there were catacombs or tunnels — until I leaned against the wall and it turned out someone had just boarded up the entry. I practically went through. But there are five tunnels leading out from here, with lots of corpses lining them. Again, kind of like the Christian catacombs in Ancient Rome. Savannah started off English, of course, but had a large Irish population from the beginning. Man, you should come for Saint Patrick's Day! But that's beside the point. These people were *very* Catholic. And when the church was established here, they emulated Rome."

"Five entries — by each of the five dead priests?" Malachi guessed.

Roger nodded. "After I found the first, I

tapped around the room and found the rest of them. Those three —" he pointed across from Father O'Leary "— must've caved in decades ago. The other trunks go on and on. It gets damper and damper as they head under the streets to the river. So . . ." He let the word hang as he lifted his flashlight to look at Malachi's face. "You can pick door number one or door number two."

"I think we should head out from behind our good Father O'Leary — what say you, Ms. Anderson?"

"I'm sure the good father would not lead us astray," she said.

He smiled and raised his own flashlight. The beam played over Roger, standing between two of the glass-domed coffins and their decaying priests, and then over Abby. She appeared to be pale, almost ethereal with her jet-black hair and deep eyes. She would've been a perfect image, he thought wryly, when the place was a vampire-themed nightclub.

"Just push that piece of plasterboard aside. That's the entrance," Roger told them.

Malachi lifted the loose piece of wood — plastered over and painted white to blend with the wall — and moved it to one side.

The first tunnel yawned directly before them.

"You can see why they don't want the average tourist family with their four-year-old running around down here," Roger said.

"Yeah." Abby glanced at Malachi and then trained her light down the tunnel, which seemed to stretch ahead endlessly. She stepped forward and he followed. Roger quickly came up behind him.

Each side of the wall had shelving dug into it, and each shelf had been the burial point for one Christian soul. The shrouds on the bodies had long ago turned as dark and murky as the earth on which they rested; they seemed to have gone back into it, giving true meaning to the Biblical term *dust to dust*.

It was eerie and sad. Here and there, tree and brush roots were crawling through as if they reached down to embrace the last mortal remains of those who lay here, forgotten by time.

"We're going toward the river," Abby commented, walking ahead of him.

"Yes, you can feel that it's growing damper."

"Some experts believe there are even more tunnels underneath the ground than those we know about," Roger said. "They know of some that were part of a real 'underground' railroad during the Civil War — but in those days, they would've used anything. I'm thinking those hidden doors, like the one we came through, were put up during the Civil War."

"It's certainly a valid theory," Malachi said.

They moved slowly. The dark was so complete that their lights made the surrounding blackness seem even deeper.

Suddenly, while walking ahead of him, Abby let out a startled shriek, threw up her hands and dropped her flashlight.

"What is it?" Malachi demanded, rushing up behind her. Her arms flapped in the darkness.

"Hey," he said quietly, holding her. He felt the beat of her heart, felt her frantic breathing.

And her warmth, the way she started and then eased as he held her.

"They were all over me!" she said. "Sorry — ugh. I've got to get it off."

He smoothed her face, removing strands of web. Raising his light, he saw the web in her hair and smoothed it away, too.

"Spiderwebs!" Roger said, and laughed. "Nothing but spiderwebs. I told you, Abby screams like a girl when it comes to spiders and snakes!"

"I'm sorry," Abby murmured. "I did scream because I walked right into a big web. It was all over my face — my eyes and mouth."

"It's a creepy feeling," Malachi said. "Whether you're a girl or not," he teased.

She grinned. "I feel like an idiot."

"Don't — I might have screamed like a girl, too." Malachi spoke reassuringly. "Nothing to be embarrassed about."

"Seriously?" Roger asked. "Corpses melting into the earth don't bother you, but a little old spider can drive you nuts?"

"Ah, but spiders are alive and bite. Corpses lay where they're left," Malachi said.

"Until the zombie apocalypse." Abby laughed nervously. "But since I'm not a big believer in zombies, yeah, spiders are scarier. You can get a nasty bite from a brown recluse, you know."

"Yeah, okay, whatever you say, Abs." Roger retrieved her fallen flashlight and handed it to her. Abby turned — and crashed into a wall of earth.

"Watch it," Roger said. "There's a funny curve here. I think this is where the Saint Sebastian's catacombs ended. We make a little twist to the right — and I'm pretty sure it's where, long ago, another church stood. I checked the old records. There was a Lutheran church here from about 1790 to 1830. It burned to the ground and there's just parkland on top of us now."

They made the turn. The earth was dug out a little differently — three shelves to a wall instead of four and there were no corpses in them.

Casting the beam of his flashlight around, Malachi said, "These shelves seem to be empty."

"They were probably dug out, and the dead reinterred, after the church burned down. They might've been brought to Bonaventure Cemetery. I do know that the dead from some churches were reinterred, or whatever one calls it."

"That makes sense," Malachi agreed.

"They're . . . not all empty," Abby said. She was across from Malachi, inspecting the middle shelf. She brought her light up, illuminating the space, and gasped.

"Abby!" Roger shook his head, laughing. "There are going to be spiders down here!"

She turned. Her eyes, bluer than the sky, were caught in the glow of the light.

"It's not a spider," she said. "It's a corpse."

"There are corpses all over!" Roger protested.

"Not like this," Abby said, and her tone was weak.

Malachi moved past her, hunkering down to get a good look at the body on the middle shelf that had been dug into the earth by hands that had lived in a far past day.

There was, indeed, a "fresh" corpse on the shelf.

It was that of a young woman. He had little medical training, but he'd seen his share of corpses.

He estimated that this one had been there about a month. She had bloated and browned, her skin tightening over her frame. She'd worn a baby-doll dress and still had one shoe; the other was missing.

The third finger on her left hand was missing, too.

"Well, that's not going to be much of a secret tunnel anymore," Roger said, leaning against the trunk of Jackson Crow's car.

They'd been down there for a long time after discovering the corpse. Malachi had called it in to Jackson Crow, and Jackson had arrived with David Caswell and Kat Sokolov. They'd all been down in the tunnels waiting for Kat. She'd brought a medical bag and had gloved her hands and made a cursory inspection of the corpse where she lay.

Two crime scene techs had come behind them, bearing a litter. Scoops of earth were taken, bright lights beamed within the tunnel and the corpse was photographed from every conceivable angle. They'd been asked if they'd moved anything at all and, of course, they hadn't. With David, Jackson, Malachi, Kat and two crime scene techs down in the tunnel, it had grown crowded. Roger and Abby had moved back through the tunnels to the priestly vault beneath the altar, and then up to the main church and out into the sunlight.

"Don't go anywhere," Malachi had said to Roger. "The paperwork awaits."

"Roger, the tunnel couldn't have been *your* secret. Someone else has definitely been down there," Abby said.

He smiled at her. "Thank God you said that! I was hoping you didn't think I managed to get that corpse down there. Oh, well, if I *had* put the corpse there, I wouldn't have taken you down to find it. Unless, of course, I was trying to throw you off by bringing you down there to discover the corpse. Oh! Hey, don't get any ideas! I obviously watch too many police shows on TV. I swear — I haven't been down that far in ages. I've known about the tunnels under the church. A lot of the other guides in town know about them, too, but . . . mostly, we honor the city's rulings on what we can and can't show people. Like I said, it's private property, so trespassing is against the law. I wouldn't bring the average tourist down there. You know that, right? You believe me?"

"Of course I believe you, Roger," Abby said.

"Oh, Lord! Are the police going to believe me?"

"I can't tell you what other people will believe, but as far as I know, there isn't anyone out there who thinks you've been running around murdering tourists."

"No. I wouldn't murder tourists. I make my living off tourists." Roger shook his head. "I'm not the type to murder tourists because they gave a lousy tip or didn't tip at all. I mean, there've been a few I wanted to slap, but even then . . . survival wins out!"

"Roger, I've wanted to slap a few tourists over the years, too," Abby said, obviously trying to lighten the tone. As she spoke, the main doors to the church opened and the two crime scene techs appeared, bearing the litter holding the corpse — now covered with a clean white sheet — out to the ambulance. The others emerged into the sunlight behind them. Kat Sokolov waved and headed for the ambulance; she wasn't letting this corpse out of her sight. Jackson Crow, Malachi and David Caswell strode toward them.

"Can you come down to the station and sign statements?" David asked Roger and Abby. "No way out of record keeping."

"Of course," Abby said.

"Uh, yeah, sure." Roger looked at Malachi and winced. "I did tell you that these tunnels aren't on the beaten tourist path."

Malachi patted his shoulder. "Not to worry. I told David that I insisted on going down there and that we were on federal law enforcement business. Your reputation as a tour guide will remain absolutely spotless."

"Thanks," Roger said a little huskily.

"Pile in," Jackson told them. "I've got my old federal-issue SUV. We'll all fit."

They did pile in; David Caswell and Jackson Crow were in front.

Abby was in the back between Malachi and Roger. Despite Malachi's words, Roger was still agitated. He seemed nervous the entire time they were at the station, although Malachi did most of the talking and they were both merely asked if they had anything to add. When Malachi was asked why he'd felt it was important to get down into the tunnels, he said flatly, "I believe that the person or persons killing young women in Savannah now thinks of himself as some kind of pirate. I believe that he — or he and his accomplice — kidnaps these young women and brings them through to the river via the various tunnels."

Eventually, the statements were signed and they were free to go. Jackson drove back to the Dragonslayer.

"Wow. Lord. Oh, God," Roger moaned when they pulled into the parking lot at the tavern. He looked at Abby as if everything that had happened today was finally hitting him. "There was a *dead girl* in the tunnel. Not long dead. Newly dead."

She laid a hand on his arm. "You brought us there and we found her. That's a good thing, Roger."

"She's *dead.* How can that be good?"

"Finding her could help us catch the killer," Abby replied.

"She'll still be dead," Roger said dully.

"But," Malachi added, "the fact that her body's been found could bring some solace to her family. For those left behind, there's comfort in knowing that a killer is brought to justice."

Roger got out of the car. "Uh, did you want more of a tour?" he asked.

"Not today," Malachi said. "But if I have any questions about the city, I'll call you."

"Yeah, all right. I'll probably be in the Dragonslayer later," Roger muttered. "Might see you then."

They watched him walk to his car. "That was good of you," Abby told Malachi. "It was really kind of you to speak to him the way you did. I know he was afraid he was a suspect."

Malachi looked at her. "He *is* a suspect," he said.

Abby frowned.

"Everyone's a suspect right now," Jackson explained. "Let's go into the Dragonslayer. We'll see what Will's managed with the cameras so far."

Abby walked slowly toward the restaurant. She had a sick feeling inside. She believed in Roger; they'd gone to high school together!

But she believed in Dirk as well, and their other customers and Macy and . . .

It didn't have to be anyone close to her. Maybe the Dragonslayer had been used, just as, perhaps, the *Black Swan* had been used.

She took a deep breath and entered the restaurant.

It was after lunch but before dinner. Will Chan was at the bar talking to Dirk, Aldous and Bootsie.

Malachi walked over as if he'd known the four of them all his life. "Hey, Dirk. How are you? Have you heard that our Mr. Chan's a fine actor and magician?"

Dirk nodded absently. "I'm all right," he said. He didn't look all right. He was parchment-white. He turned to Malachi anxiously. "According to the TV news, another body was just found in a tunnel. A woman."

"It wasn't Helen," Malachi assured him.

"But how do you know?" Dirk asked.

"Poor girl was dead long before Helen disappeared," Malachi told him. He rested a hand on Dirk's shoulder. "The bad news is that a number of young women have lost their lives. The good news is that the local police and the feds are working hard on the case. The streets will be full of police and agents who know what they're looking for and I'd bet money that, with these combined efforts, the truth will come out and the killer will be caught."

Dirk nodded. "Did you work today?" Malachi asked him.

"I took the first tour group out. I let the guys handle the second. My other actress was back so . . . I'm okay."

"Yeah, he's doing fine," Bootsie said.

"I was telling him that if he wanted, I'd head out with him tomorrow," Will put in. "I'd love to play pirate."

"The tours are fun," Abby said. She felt as though she was playing a part at that moment. Pretending everything was normal. Pretending that the Dragonslayer would go on as it always had, and that Gus would be there in spirit. Women were not dead and missing — and Gus had not been suspicious of anything before he died.

Malachi's phone rang and he answered it, stepping aside. When he hung up, he and Jackson seemed to share some kind of intuitive exchange.

"I've got to run out," Malachi said.

"We'll show Abby the cameras we've got set up." Jackson nodded to Will, who nodded back.

"See you all later," Malachi told them. He offered her a strange smile. She sensed that he was trying to tell her he wasn't avoiding her, but that he didn't want to be heard by anyone else. That the connection between them was private. She smiled in return.

As he left the restaurant, Macy came up to her. "Have you eaten anything?" she asked.

"I'm not hungry right now. I'll eat soon, Macy, I promise," Abby replied.

"We're going to show her what I've been up to all day," Will explained to Macy. He slipped an arm around Abby's shoulders. "Come and see your new security system. We'll start upstairs."

He headed up the stairs, Abby behind him and Jackson at her heels. "First camera," Will said, "covers the hall here, in front of the apartment. It'll show up on computer screens in the parlor area of the apartment, and in the living room at your house." He opened the door to the apartment. A large screen, divided into eight sections, was set up on a portable table with a chair in front of it. "Down at the bottom — with the strange light filter — that's the tunnel. Here, upper left, you have the hall. Then you have the storage room and the employee lockers and lounge area. Below that you've got the bar and the front entry, and the two back-to-back dining rooms. Your last camera covers the outside, the whole structure of the building. I want to make sure we can see anyone trying to get in through any other entrance."

"That's fantastic. Very high-tech," Abby said.

"Thanks. I do love computers and cameras," Will told her. "But I plan to be on Dirk's ship tomorrow. We'll have Kat and

Angela manning these cameras, just watching what's going on — and trying to see if anything *is* going on. Frankly, I think this guy moves around. I think he uses different routes to get to the river."

"You're right," Abby murmured.

"The cameras will help." Will smiled at her. "I guess you have a guardian angel of sorts."

"Oh?"

Will looked at Jackson.

"The pirate," Jackson said, smiling, too.

"Did you get Blue on film?" she asked incredulously.

Will shook his head. "He passed by while I was setting up the camera in the tunnel. He didn't speak to me, but he nodded, as if he approved."

"I haven't seen him. I haven't seen Blue since he led me to Gus," Abby said.

"I assume he's keeping watch. That's what he does for the Dragonslayer. He really is your guardian angel," Jackson said. "We've all learned that there's really no point in questioning how and when the dead choose to communicate with us. Or why some stay — and some leave. We just work with them whenever they're willing to work with us."

Abby nodded. "Thank you for coming here."

■ ■ ■ ■

"We're looking at very much the same thing as with the other killings," Kat told Malachi. "She was struck on the head. But the actual cause of death was drowning. And, as I'm sure you already noted, third finger of the left hand is gone. I'd say she's been dead a good three to four weeks. Do you see the marks on her wrists? They suggest she was bound by some kind of rough rope. But, you'll notice, there are bruises on her arms. I think she fought back."

Malachi nodded. This poor girl didn't look real anymore.

"Has she been identified?" he asked.

"The police are going through missing-person reports," Kat said, "and Jackson has sent what information we have to the national database back at the offices. So far, we don't have an identity for her."

"That would probably put her into the same category as the other women," Malachi said slowly. "She was a tourist, perhaps on her own. Or maybe she was here looking for work. Maybe she was just passing through — so people are searching for her somewhere else."

"I wish there was more I could say, more

235

I could tell you."

Malachi took a step closer to the corpse, setting his hand gently on her arm. He felt nothing except her cold, lifeless skin.

"I tried that," Kat murmured.

Malachi nodded; he wasn't surprised.

"I'm going over the other autopsies, looking for anything," Kat said. "Oh, there's one other thing I should tell you. We did match the finger to a victim."

For a moment, he blanked. "Who?" he asked.

"It belonged to the first victim, Ruth Seymour."

"The killer must have been carrying it around," Malachi said.

"David has all the information for the reports. He was disturbed, of course, that Gus hadn't called the police. But it's too late to ask Gus why he didn't. Maybe he was afraid he'd be a suspect himself? We'll never know. But at least we found out where the finger belongs."

"Thanks, Kat." He sighed. "I'll get back to the Dragonslayer now. There's something forming in my mind. I'm not sure yet what it is. But —"

"Hurry it up if you can," Kat broke in. "We have a girl out there who might still be alive."

"I know," Malachi said. "I know."

Jackson Crow left the Dragonslayer to head back to Abby's house on Chippewa Square to meet up with Angela. They were doing character studies on everyone associated with or working in the area of the river. He didn't tell Abby that they were concentrating on employees and frequent customers of Dirk's tour ship and the Dragonslayer. He didn't need to tell her, she knew.

Alone in the apartment, Abby watched everything revealed by the newly installed cameras. She was fascinated as she went from screen to screen; once the dinner hours began, customers came and went.

Bootsie, Aldous and Dirk remained at the bar. When he wasn't busy with other customers, Sullivan hung out there and chatted with them.

She watched as Macy spoke with Grant Green, giving him the day's report. She could see Macy go up the stairs and into the manager's office. Macy gathered up her belongings. She hesitated at the door to the apartment as if she meant to knock, but didn't. Instead, she walked downstairs, obviously preparing to leave.

Abby thought about stopping her; she didn't.

As she stared at one of the screens, she gasped. She'd been looking at the dining room with the grate to the tunnel and the image of Blue Anderson. But as she watched, Blue seemed to step out of his own image. He peered into the grate, then slipped through.

Abby jumped up and hurried down the stairs. Luckily, it was growing later by then. There were a few diners but none near the image of Blue. Rather than taking the main stairway, she hurried to the back of the storage room and came down the winding stone steps. At the grate, she fell to her knees and opened the combination lock that held the grating closed. She'd moved casually, but quickly and silently. With the grate open, she caught hold of the sides and slid down, hopping the last foot. It was dark in the tunnel but she'd come with her light and her Glock — she wasn't taking chances.

She shone the light over the tunnel.

There was something — someone — in the shadows.

She lifted the light higher.

For a moment, it was as if she saw Blue in the flesh, he was that solid and real to her. He seemed to stand there in living color.

"Blue." She whispered his name.

He looked at her, then turned and walked

toward the river. Then he paused and looked back. He seemed to be waiting for her to follow.

She did.

The tunnel twisted and meandered and came to an end near the Savannah River. At one time, the entrance had been even closer to the river, but now it opened onto grass and parkland. The original hatch had been welded shut, but ancient, metal, ladderlike steps led up to the newer hatch.

She was in the area where she'd found Gus.

Abby tried not to remember finding him and realizing he was dead.

Determined, she fumbled with the grate and pushed at it; years ago, it had been set over the tunnel for public safety. It was supposed to be sealed. At first, she thought it was, that it wouldn't give, wouldn't budge.

Then, to her amazement, it did.

She pushed hard and hoisted herself out. She heard the lap of water against the supporting wall.

She hurried over to the wall, staring at the river.

She could see something there. Something in the darkness of the water.

Something that . . . moved.

Abby cried out and forgot everything else.

She kicked off her shoes and removed her jacket and plunged into the Savannah River.

8

Leaving the morgue, Malachi drove straight back to the Dragonslayer. The historic district of Savannah was beautiful, even by night. Great oaks dripped moss onto streets where the architecture whispered of the past. Flowers bloomed copiously in beautifully grown yards and night-lights lay gently all around.

When he'd parked, he wasn't ready to go in.

He sat remembering all the times he felt he'd been cursed with his strange ability to talk to the dead. In his generation, it had been his and his alone. Zachary had told him once that his grandmother had been able to talk to spirits and she'd explained to him that it was just like sound. Some folks could simply see and hear what others couldn't quite grasp or get into their field of vision.

He'd quickly learned not to talk about it.

But when he'd seen the dead and the dead had been able to help him, show him where to go — show him how to stop a dangerous situation — he'd had no recourse but to act. And so people had thought he was psychic. Friends had trusted him for whatever it was they believed he had. Luckily, the jerks and idiots had left him alone, either scornful or intimidated. He didn't care which.

In New Orleans, he'd gotten lucky, being partnered with David Caswell. Caswell could be a by-the-book cop, but he was also a big believer in "gut" reactions and in hunches. Malachi had trusted in David's intuition; in turn, David had trusted him and never pressed when Malachi had known where to go to help someone, especially after the summer of storms, when a dead man had led them to his children, alive and well and praying for rescue.

The problem with this kind of "talent" was that you never knew when it would kick in. And, of course, you couldn't explain to the living that ghosts were *like* the living; they could only tell you about a situation if they'd been there at the time. Or if they'd seen something. Blue, for instance, could only point him to the killer if he knew who the killer was. Blue was aware that the tun-

nel had been used recently. He'd known
Gus was in the tunnel and he had led Abby
there. But unless he'd actually seen the
killer . . .

Parking, Malachi started for the restaurant. But as he approached it, he paused. A
few late-nighters were walking toward the
front door.

They didn't see the pirate standing there,
the man in the frock coat with the rakish
hat and pitch-black hair.

Blue Anderson.

But Malachi saw him and saw him clearly.
Blue, he thought, was waiting for him.

He stood still but the pirate didn't come
any closer. Malachi strode toward him, hoping no one was watching from inside.

When he reached Blue, he heard the
crackling whistle of the man's voice on the
air — or he heard it in his own mind, he
was never sure.

"The river. Abby is at the river. He went
through this tunnel . . . in the midst of the
flurry over Gus. I did not see him . . . just
the leaving. And I saw the boat . . . saw the
rowboat out. When the rowboat is out, the
bodies appear. Abby is out there."

"Where, Blue, where?" Malachi asked
anxiously. Abby was a trained agent. She
knew how to use a Glock and she surely

had it with her.

Blue drew a pattern in the air. "The little park — little patch of ground by the river, by the embankment. Go now."

He didn't need to be told twice. He began to run, heedless of the fact that he ran past the rear of several other businesses and dashed between parked cars and a monument, then tore across a street where he might have been hit by oncoming traffic.

He reached the place; he knew it, of course. He'd followed the tunnel to its end when he had first arrived. He'd checked the hatch, put in by the city years ago.

The hatch was unsealed?

It wasn't just unsealed, it had been thrown open.

He turned toward the river. There was someone in it — someone swimming, towing another person. He raced to the water, digging for his phone, then called Jackson and told him where he was and what was happening. Then he threw the phone aside and dove into the water.

Abby seemed to be a strong swimmer but she was slowing down. She had a young woman in a life-saving hold as she swam toward the embankment. He made his way to her with strong, hard strokes, swimming as quickly as he could. The current was fierce that night.

She seemed startled as he approached her. He saw her eyes widen with alarm. He could almost see her mind working as she weighed her options in fighting off an attacker while preserving the life of the victim. He saw the woman she held; she was unconscious — possibly dead. A trickle of blood streamed through the water but he couldn't figure out its source. As the water sloshed around them, he saw that the skin on the woman's wrists was raw and red, badly chafed.

She'd recently been bound. And she was bleeding — she might be alive.

He realized that Abby was trying to kick away from him.

"It's me, it's Malachi!" he said.

He saw relief flood her face.

"I'll take over," he told her.

He had no idea how far she'd swum out, and knowing her as he was beginning to know her, she would have made it in with her burden.

But she was tiring.

When she nodded, he slipped his arm around the woman's torso and Abby eased her hold. The woman seemed to be dressed in voluminous clothing; in fact, the weight of her clothes was enough to have drowned her.

The sound of sirens was loud in the night. Abby began to swim toward the embankment and he followed. River water lapped into his mouth, and as he neared the embankment, he felt sea grass pull at his feet. But he was there.

He saw Jackson leaning over the supporting wall, grasping Abby's arms. Abby was hauled up. "Hang on!" Jackson called to him. A moment later, he saw paramedics and police divers. Two more men jumped in, as well as a floating stretcher. The rescue team relieved him of his burden. He saw Jackson reaching down again and he grasped his friend's arms, grateful for the assistance.

Abby stood near him, shivering. He walked over to her without thinking and put his arms around her. He felt chilly in the night air, as well. They were both cold, but together, they seemed warmer.

They watched in silence as the rescue workers hoisted the stretcher from the water. When the stretcher and the woman on it were brought up, the EMTs started artificial respiration. He listened to the counts as two men worked together, trying to breathe life into the victim.

Water suddenly spurted from the woman's lips.

"She's alive?" Abby whispered.

"She's alive," an EMT said.

Malachi saw the river-diluted blood that was smeared on much of her tangled clothing. He winced, suspecting what it signified.

Abby began to shake in earnest.

Malachi held her more tightly. "Pretty incredible, Abby," he told her. "A few more minutes in that river with all that clothing tangled around her . . . She wouldn't have stood a chance."

Abby looked at him, her blue eyes enormous against the ashen color of her face.

"It's Helen, Malachi. It's Helen Long. And thank God, she's alive."

Hard to believe how quickly the media arrived on the scene.

Or maybe not. The newscasters followed calls for police and rescue vehicles.

David Caswell moved to keep the media at bay, but before anyone could decide what information to keep secret, someone had guessed that the missing Helen Long had been found, and reporters immediately began setting up, even while rescue personnel and police worked the scene.

Abby stood there shivering, watching it all, grateful for Malachi at her side. And grateful that David was shielding them from inquisitive — and sometimes aggressive —

reporters.

The situation seemed personal to her, very personal. She was grateful; they'd saved a woman.

They'd saved a woman she knew.

Helen Long was rushed to the hospital, and Jackson climbed into the ambulance to drive with her. Soaking wet, Abby and Malachi again made the drive to the police station, where David Caswell met them. Encased in blankets, they gave more statements.

David kept them as briefly as possible. He looked at Abby curiously and asked how she'd known Helen was in the river. Abby told him she hadn't known — she'd just been there and seen the disturbance in the water. They called Jackson at the hospital before they left; Helen Long was still unconscious. But the doctors hoped she'd make a complete recovery.

When they returned to the Dragonslayer, Grant Green and Sullivan were just shutting down, and Abby realized they'd gone into the wee hours of the morning.

It had been a long day. They'd found the body of one dead woman — unknown, but surely loved and missed, and there would be sad news for a family somewhere.

But, she reminded herself again, they'd

also saved a woman. Someone she knew and even considered a friend.

"Oh, my God, you both look like bloody hell!" Grant told them.

"We took a swim," Malachi said. He didn't mention Helen, but Abby knew everyone would hear about it soon enough. No need to come up with something clever to explain their sodden shape.

"A good swim. We found Helen," Abby said.

"You *found* her?" Sullivan demanded.

"She was in the river," Abby explained.

"You just found her — in the river?" Grant asked. "I mean, that's wonderful! I haven't had the news on. Oh, no, wait, is she . . . dead?" he asked, the last word a whisper.

Abby shook her head. "She's alive. They've taken her to the hospital."

"Then . . . then she'll be able to tell them what happened," Grant said. "Thank God! The cops will catch this bastard. Maybe he'll resist arrest and they'll have to shoot him. That would be justice!"

"Grant, we have courts for justice, but, yes, we hope she'll be able to tell the police what happened to her," Abby said.

"She hasn't said anything yet?" Sullivan asked.

"She isn't conscious," Malachi answered.

Sullivan let out a sigh. "But she will regain consciousness?"

"They're hoping for a full recovery," Abby told him.

"Thank God!" Grant breathed.

"Yes, thank God," Sullivan echoed.

"Well." Grant wrinkled his nose and stepped back. "They've done a lot to clean up that river, but you two are pretty disgusting. Abby, that hairstyle — plastered to your face — is not your best. We'll finish locking up. You two go take showers. And get some sleep. We'll take care of this place. Go on."

"Going now," Abby said.

She turned and started up the stairs. "Good night, you two," Malachi said. He followed Abby and they went into the apartment together.

"It's not locked," Malachi noted.

"I rushed out," Abby said.

"I'll just take a quick look around, huh?"

She nodded. Malachi went down the hall. His "look" wasn't really that quick. She heard him open doors and she was pretty sure he checked under the beds. When he returned to the living room, he headed straight to the bank of cameras. He knew how to use the equipment, running through the time they'd been out, scanning it all, screen by screen. He sat back after a minute.

"Nope, no one even tried this door. Sullivan came up at about nine to get two bottles of bourbon. Grant came and worked in the office for a while. . . . Everyone else just worked. All seems well here." He looked over at her. "Why did you go to the river?"

"I saw a shadow by the grating — it was Blue. He led me all the way through the tunnel and to the river. Malachi, the hatch was open. It should have been sealed."

Malachi drummed his fingers on the computer desk. "When you found Gus, he was at the end of the tunnel."

"Yes."

"The police and emergency crews came, didn't they?"

"Yes, but . . . well, no one checked the hatch."

Malachi pulled out his cell. He called David and winced when his friend answered, then covered his phone. "Sounds like I woke him and he's cranky," he said. But she could dimly hear David's voice; he might've just fallen asleep, but he was already awake, telling Malachi he'd get crews right on it.

He walked over to the apartment door and locked it. Smiling, he said, "Despite Grant's comment, I'm not sure you *could* find a bad hairstyle, Agent Anderson. Even dank from the river, you don't look bad."

"Thank you. We're locked in, so we're fine, aren't we?" she asked him.

"We are," he assured her. "And I have some news."

"What?"

"We found out about the finger — from Gus's drawer," he said.

"Oh?"

"It belonged to Ruth Seymour. The first victim."

"Gus couldn't have known that!"

"No, I don't believe he could have. But I do believe he called you because of it."

"Why not the police?" she murmured.

"He must have been worried — and perhaps he knew you'd never suspect him of such brutality, but the police might. Still . . . I don't think it would've changed anything if he *had* called them."

She nodded.

"You're okay?"

"Of course. I know Gus was doing his best." She gave him a weak smile. "I'm going to have a shower."

"I'll go do the same," he said.

Abby walked down the hallway to her own room. She stripped, but before she went into the shower, she tended to her Glock. This wasn't a night she wanted to discover that she'd damaged her service weapon.

When she was sure it had dried properly and was back in good shooting order, she set it in a drawer of her bedside table, then finally walked into the shower. The heat that suffused her, the sense of being clean again, was almost sinfully delicious.

When she emerged, she slipped into a terry robe and returned to the living room. A figurehead gazed sternly down at her from the far wall; she smiled, looking at the various flags that adorned the walls. Gus had loved his heritage, loved this place.

She loved it, too. No monstrous killer making use of it would change that. She would find him.

She sat down to check the screens. There was no movement anywhere in or near the Dragonslayer.

As Malachi came out of Gus's room, she stood up. She saw that he was wearing a blue terry robe, his dark hair slicked back and wet. "Everything okay?" he asked her huskily.

"Quiet. Just like it should be."

She sat at the computer table again and he leaned over her to study the screens. She became very aware of the heat of his body and couldn't help thinking that he might be naked under the robe. She was naked under hers. . . . She focused on his face as he watched the screen. She noted again the character that seemed etched in the rugged planes of his cheekbones and jaw. She felt the vitality of his muscles.

"Looks good," he agreed. "And these same screens are on at your home. Someone will be up all night — they'll take shifts."

"We don't have to take a shift?" she asked him.

He shook his head. "We're the principal agents," he told her. "I admit I'm new to this, too, but I did spend some time getting to know the people in both Krewes. Usually there are one — or sometimes two — agents closest to what's happening. The people most connected to the situation. That's us, in other words. So . . . we sleep when we can. The others cover the watches and do the research on people, places or possible suspects."

She wasn't really listening. There was something exceptionally compelling about the scent of soap on newly washed male flesh. There was something about . . . him.

He looked from the screen, into her eyes. She saw a sudden change in their mercurial hazel color.

Time passed, and then he touched her face, his fingers caressing and following the lines of her cheeks and jaw. She stood up, coming straight into his arms, and when his hands fell away, it was only because he needed them to pull her against him.

He kissed her, a pressure on her lips that was, at first, a request. She drew closer to him, responding, parting her lips, welcoming his tongue. Arousal swept through her, and she continued to feel the hunger of his lips, his touch. They seemed to stand there for an eternity, their kiss going on and on. It was as if a kiss were a brand-new thing, as if they'd invented it.

But in time, the kiss wasn't enough, and she felt his hands under her robe, moving along her skin. His touch was almost . . . reverential. She threaded her fingers through his hair, moved closer and closer to him. And as they stumbled in their haste to touch and kiss again and again he whispered, "Bedroom."

She whispered back, "Mine."

He inhaled sharply, his teeth grating. "Wait. We have to slow down. I'm not —"

She smiled. "I am. I wasn't planning on anything, but I'm on the Pill."

He returned her smile.

They made their way down the hall, still touching, still kissing, crashing into a wall here and there. Finally they reached her bedroom and they fell onto the softness of her bed, the robes a tangle around them. Straddling her, Malachi wrangled out of his robe and helped remove hers. He paused for a minute, and she wasn't sure what went through his mind. She didn't care; she rose against him, loving the feel of her breasts against the heat of his chest. Again, they kissed, still kissing as they eased back down.

She felt him slide down the length of her body. She felt his touch, so evocative, so arousing that she was nearly delirious. Her life had been the Dragonslayer and the academy for so long . . . but she knew that wouldn't have mattered. Nothing would have mattered. There were people who changed reality for others, created magic for them, and Malachi was that magic for her. She had never wanted anyone so much, never felt so afire, so hungry. And his every touch fulfilled her. His intimacy brought her almost to the brink, teased her and let her slip to become almost insanely aroused again. And then, he thrust deeply into her, filled her, and his movements elicited that same fevered urgency.

The world around her seemed to spin, to disappear, and yet to become achingly real. She was fascinated by his touch. His hair, the wicked movement of his muscles. She arched and writhed against him until the fire within her seemed to explode. She felt him explode within her as well, and for a moment, she simply luxuriated in the sensation of winding down. When she did, she felt the coolness of the air around them and she smiled. Sex wasn't new; it was as old as life on earth. And yet she couldn't help feeling that they had somehow reinvented the wonder of it all that night.

She smoothed back a lock of her hair and curled up against his chest. "Is . . . was that allowed?" she asked.

She saw the curve of his lips. "I didn't ask anyone's permission."

"Yes, but . . ."

"I think it's okay. Jackson is with Angela. Will is with Kat. We have two other couples in the teams. Maybe it has to do with our unique talents." He rolled so that they faced each other. "And maybe it's because, somehow, these situations just bring us together with the most fascinating people in the country."

She smiled again and leaned back, staring up at the ceiling. "I'm fascinating?"

"Entirely."

"You're a bit unusual yourself, you know."

"I certainly hope so."

"I'd never have imagined . . ."

He rose up on one elbow, gazing down at

her. "Actually, I'd never imagined *any* of this. I made a rather awkward start of it. My social graces may be a bit . . . lacking."

"That's okay," she said. "Your other skills aren't."

He leaned down and kissed her once more. She'd never, ever believed a kiss could be so deep, *do* so much, enter her every cell.

That kiss . . .

They began making love again, more slowly at first, and then more frantically, and when they'd finished she lay in his arms. She thought they'd talk afterward, but they didn't. Exhaustion must have overwhelmed her. She fell into a deep, dreamless sleep.

She didn't hear when the kitchen crew arrived in the morning.

She didn't awaken until she felt Malachi bolt up and go running out to the living area. Then she became aware of the sound of a ringing phone.

A minute later, he returned to the bedroom, pausing naked and perfect in the doorway. His tone was strange — anxiety combined with regret. "We've got to get moving," he told her. "Helen Long is conscious and talking. We have to get to the hospital."

■ ■ ■ ■

Jackson was there to meet them when they arrived.

"How is she?" Abby asked.

"She's doing all right. She's suffering from dehydration more than anything else."

"What has she said so far?" Malachi asked.

"Very little. She's only been conscious for a couple of hours, and David asked her what she remembered, who hurt her, but she still seemed disoriented. David thought she might be better once Abby got here," Jackson said. "And she might have had enough time now to reorient and remember at least some of what happened."

"Let's hope so," Abby said.

Malachi nodded and looked at Jackson. "Was I right about what I saw? She was bleeding in the water. I figured she had to be alive but I couldn't see the injury. Was her ring finger taken?"

"Yes. She cried for a while when she realized that. In fact, the hospital staff had to sedate her. She's calmer now, but still lucid," Jackson told them. "There was a plastic surgeon on duty and he explained that they could do a prosthetic that she'd hardly notice. Then, of course, she cried because she's grateful to be alive." He turned to Abby. "She knows you saved her, although she can't figure out how you knew she'd be in the middle of the river."

"I saw movement," Abby murmured.

Jackson didn't question that. "Did you notice what she was wearing?" he asked.

"A lot of fabric," Malachi said. "Let me guess — she was dressed as a wench?"

Jackson nodded. "She was wearing a costume like the one she wears when she works on the *Black Swan.*"

"Let's see if we can get her to tell us anything," Malachi said.

Helen Long's hospital room was fairly large, which was a good thing since David Caswell, Jackson Crow, Abby and Malachi were all huddled in it, trying to be mindful of the patient but eager to hear what she had to say.

Malachi was aware of the hum of the IV monitors, of the hospital staff tending to the sick and injured. Outside the door was a chair; an officer would sit there day and night. They feared that whoever had wanted Helen dead would know where she was — and come back to finish the job.

Helen looked pale as she lay against the pillows. She was weak, but her eyes were bright and her mind seemed to be clear.

"Helen, Abby is here now. She'd like to talk to you. I know you can do it," Jackson said gently.

Helen looked at Abby and tried to smile. "Thank you!" she whispered.

"Helen, thank *you.* You made it," Abby said.

Helen's eyes touched Malachi's for a minute. "And thank you."

"My pleasure," he told her. "You're a survivor, Helen. And we believe in your strength. You're going to help us catch him."

"Maybe." Helen glanced down at her bandaged hand. It looked as if tears were welling in her eyes again but she blinked them furiously away.

Abby said, "Please, Helen, tell us — how did he get you? Or how did *they* get you? Please, help us catch him."

"I don't think you can catch him," she whispered.

"Tell us what happened," Malachi urged.

Helen took a deep breath and began. "I met a man on the *Black Swan* one day. He told me he wanted to bring a tourist attraction to Savannah. He wanted to open a haunted house. A pirate-themed haunted house. He was nice — just pleasant, not lecherous — and when we spoke, he was easy to talk to. He asked me if I could make

261

any suggestions about properties that might be available and would work for a haunted house. I told him I knew the best guide in the city — Roger, of course — and that I knew where he might find the perfect spot. I said he'd have to follow certain historical guidelines, especially since it's owned by a private restoration society. But the society hasn't had the funds to restore it. Anyway, I got one of Roger's maps and I remembered what I'd learned about the old church. Roger and I had talked about it. I had his map, I walked around, using it, and I was going to get together with the man I met on the *Black Swan.* It was . . . before Gus's funeral, after we were all talking one afternoon — at the Dragonslayer."

"Everyone remembers that day," Abby said.

"Well, I thought we were meeting in the parking lot at the tavern, but I didn't see him. Instead, there was a note on my car, along with his business card. He said to meet him at the church."

"Helen," Malachi asked urgently, "what did this man look like?"

"I . . . I don't know. He was just a businessman. Maybe about six feet tall? I guess he was getting started early on his whole pirate-theme thing. He had long hair and a beard and mustache. Dark. You could barely see his face."

"Did you know him? Had you ever seen him before?"

Helen frowned. "There was something familiar about him . . . I feel I *should* have known him, but I didn't. Or maybe he reminded me of someone I knew, but I couldn't place who it was."

"What was his name?" Malachi asked.

Helen frowned. "Chris . . . Chris Condent. Christopher on the card, I think. He told me to call him Chris."

Malachi didn't allow a flicker of change on his face but his mind was racing. *Chris . . . Christopher Condent.* Christopher Condent had been a pirate, active from about 1718 to 1720. After taking a great prize, he retired from the sea and lived in France until a ripe old age. He'd become very rich by taking his ill-gotten gains and investing them in a career as a merchant.

"So," Malachi said, "you found the note on your car with the man's business card, telling you to go to the church. What then?"

"I went there — and I was surprised. The church door was open. I figured the man had gotten hold of the owners or one of the owner's representatives and been given a key," Helen explained.

"And then?" Abby asked.

Helen let out a long breath. "I went in." She stopped speaking and just stared ahead.

"Helen?" Malachi said quietly.

She didn't move; she didn't seem to hear.

Abby moved closer and squeezed her hand. "Helen, please, go on."

Helen shook her head. Tears gathered in her eyes.

"What?" Abby said very softly. "What happened then?"

"I don't know," Helen said. "I walked in and suddenly I felt a searing pain in my head. Someone or something had hit me. I didn't see anything, anything at all."

She fell silent again, her expression anguished.

Malachi nodded at Abby, and she understood what he meant. Helen knew her, trusted her. She was the one who could probe where the rest of them couldn't.

"You were hit — and you were unconscious. But . . . you came to?"

"I was tied up. My wrists were bound. And I was in a cabin. A ship's cabin. At least, I think it was a ship's cabin. It seemed like I could hear water . . . and whistles and ships' horns. It was dark, really dark. There were portholes or windows but they were covered and I couldn't move to try to see out."

Abby sat on the bed next to Helen. "I know this is hard, but it's important. What happened next?"

"He came in," Helen said. "He came in . . . and he was horrible."

"I'm so sorry, Helen," Abby murmured.

"He . . . told me I was a captive. A pirate's captive. So I'd better be good. Captives who caused problems didn't live very long. He said he'd put out the call for my ransom, but if I gave him any trouble, if I tried to escape . . . he'd kill me."

"Did you recognize this guy? Was it the businessman you met?" Abby asked.

Helen stared at Abby. "I — I don't know. I really don't know if they were the same."

"What do you mean, Helen?" Abby asked.

"It was . . . the pirate. The real pirate."

"Helen," Malachi said, "was it someone acting as a pirate? You said that this Chris Condent wanted to open a pirate-themed haunted house."

Helen shook her head, growing agitated. "He wasn't Chris Condent anymore. He was the pirate, the *real* pirate. That's who kidnapped me. And I *had* seen him before. He was very big and he had dark hair. Rich, dark hair. And blue eyes." She took a shuddering breath. "It was the pirate, Abby. The pirate from the Dragonslayer."

She paused, as if waiting for Abby's comprehension.

"It was Blue," she said. "The pirate, Blue Anderson."

9

They left the hospital soon after Helen Long stated that she believed she'd been kidnapped and attacked by a pirate who had been dead for well over two hundred years.

Because it was private and they could watch the Dragonslayer on the screens at Abby's home on Chippewa Square, they returned there. David Caswell met with the group and they went through everything they knew.

The house on Chippewa had been built in the early 1800s and had come to Abby's family in the 1850s. Built in the colonial style, it had a handsome porch with eight white pillars standing sentinel. The house wasn't huge; the front door opened into a hall that stretched to the rear door and small yard. A staircase led to the second floor. There were three bedrooms and a den upstairs — a nursery in days gone by — while on the ground floor, to the left, was a large formal dining room and the pantry-now-kitchen, while the onetime kitchen out in the yard had been turned into a little summer house. The formal parlor was to the right of the front door with the old music room behind it.

Malachi hadn't seen her actual home yet, and he was curious. It was evident that Abby hadn't spent much time there in recent years. It was impeccably clean, although not much had been changed, the television in the old music room was as old as the stereo system. The upholstery was colonial-style, as was the furniture throughout the house, except for one massive recliner.

"My father's. He loved it. He watched Sunday football from that chair every week," Abby told Malachi.

"My dad had one of those chairs, too," Malachi said. "I admit I'm fond of it. I watch football on Sunday from that chair, too. And a few other shows, of course."

"I like the chair. Reminds me of my dad. He was great. So was my mother. They were typical parents, I guess. My mom loved to bake and cook and she had a little business making designer baby clothes. She made all kinds of things, of course, but she especially loved baby clothes. I think she would've liked a houseful of children. . . . She was always the mom in charge of food drives at school and she collected for the Red Cross. She was the epitome of the Southern lady." Abby paused, a look of fond nostalgia on her face. "They both represented the very best of Southern hospitality. My dad worked for a tech company but he spent as much time at the Dragonslayer as he could. He loved the history, but he was practical. He used to say there was money to be made on the legend of Blue, and it might as well be made by the Anderson family."

"But they raised a daughter intent on being a federal agent," Malachi commented.

"They raised me to reach for whatever I wanted, whether that was a rocket scientist or a stay-at-home mom."

"That's the best," Malachi said. "That's how kids *should* be raised."

She nodded. Although she'd been talking to him, she seemed distracted.

They'd left the others in the large formal dining room, where the computer banks and screens had been set up, when Abby set off to show him the rest of the house. And while she'd shown him around with casual enthusiasm, he thought it was forced.

"I enjoy hearing about your family, but what is it? What's tearing at you?"

She frowned at him, hurt, confused, indignant. "My ancestor is *not* attacking women and throwing them in the river!" she said.

"Abby, we all know the ghost of Blue is not doing this," he said.

"Didn't you tell me ghosts . . . could be different? Some were shy, some talked, some hid . . . So who's to say that some haven't gotten almost-mortal power — and the ability to hurt people. But I'm positive Blue isn't one of them!"

"Abby," he said, aching to draw her to him, but it wasn't the time or the place. "Abby, I'm sure some ghosts never make contact with anyone. They might be there, but they never show themselves. Others are outgoing and curious and seek out those who might see them. Some can create cold spells or learn a certain ability to move objects. But to my knowledge, there isn't a ghost out there with the strength or *energy* to physically attack human beings — to bind them with rope and throw them in the river. No one believes that Blue Anderson is after people."

Abby let out a breath. "So, you agree it's someone dressing up as Blue," she said.

"That I don't doubt. Let's go see the others, discuss what we're all thinking and what

270

moves we should make today."

Abby smiled. "It's a good day so far. Helen's awake."

"It *is* a good day," he said. "Come on. I have some info I should be sharing with everyone."

In the dining room, they discovered Kat and Angela seated at the side of the room, where they could watch the screens.

Jackson was at one of the computers, a sheaf of papers in front of him.

"Where's Will?" Malachi asked.

"He went off to spend the day on the *Black Swan,*" Kat said.

"Glad to hear it." Malachi pulled out a chair for Abby, taking a seat himself.

"Anything going on at the Dragonslayer?" he asked.

"Macy's arrived. She's at the host stand. Looks like she's checking reservations. Sullivan is hanging glasses. Bootsie just came hobbling in. He's alone — no Aldous or Dirk at the moment — but David called Dirk to let him know he could see Helen, just for a few minutes. He's not going out on any of the pirate voyages today. Will's going to work with his cast instead," Angela told them.

"It looks like business as usual at the Dragonslayer," Kat said.

"All right." Malachi sat forward, folding his hands on the table. "There's something I happened to catch because I started researching when I first came down here — Savannah and then the Dragonslayer and pirates in general. The name Helen Long gave us was *Christopher Condent.* I know David Caswell is searching local records to see if anyone with that name was registered at a hotel or bed-and-breakfast or used a credit card at a restaurant, gas station, shop or any other venue. I don't believe he'll find such a person. I think the man Helen met chose the name because it was that of a real pirate, one who survived his days of piracy to become a rich man and live happily in France after his career on the high seas. My guess is that he intends to 'retire' from piracy one day and live on his proceeds, so to speak. The real Condent was born in the 1690s, fled Jamaica in 1718 when Woods Rogers came in and went on to practice all kinds of atrocities. He cut off the ears and noses of many of his captives and tortured others. He was known to be brutal to those he captured. Karma didn't ever catch up with him. He and his men captured an Arab ship worth a fortune and Condent went on to negotiate a pardon with the governor of Bourbon. He became a merchant and died fat and wealthy in France in 1770. I'm telling you all this history — or legend, whichever it might be — because I think our killer specifically picked this pirate. This was a man who practiced atrocities, got away with it and prospered. Supposedly, he was the man behind the ever-popular Jolly Roger flags. His own flag had a row of three skulls."

"If this person wants to be a pirate and retire happily — after doing horrendously cruel and brutal things — why would Helen have thought she was attacked by Blue?" Abby asked him. "Blue was revered as a gentleman pirate. He never hurt anyone, he didn't rape his female captives and he had a strict code for his men."

"I believe this guy dresses up as Blue because Blue's such a famous pirate in Savannah. Blue's image is used at the Dragonslayer, and there are shops with his image worked into their décor. There's a wooden image of him down by the river, with the face cut out so people can stick their own faces in for their pictures. Then, looking at the psychology of it —" he glanced at Jackson, who nodded, clearly intrigued by Malachi's theory "— he may resent Blue, since the real Blue didn't behave the way this creep thinks a pirate should. He didn't rape, torture or murder. This killer may find it amusing to think that if he's ever seen, people will believe Blue is somehow walking the streets again and that his reputation was a lie because he was as vicious as the rest."

"What's consistent is that he has to kill his victims by forcing them off his ship or boat — or whatever conveyance he has them on," Abby said slowly. She looked around the room, as if assuring herself that they wanted to hear her opinions. "So, we're back to the river. He uses the underground, not so much to get his victims to the docks, but because he figures a pirate would use the tunnels to secure captives or shanghai crew members."

Jackson nodded. "I also think this man is no tourist or newcomer to the city. I think he's known and that, until now, if he were caught in costume, he'd be able to explain it easily. He'd claim he was going to help out a friend — like Dirk — on a ship."

"Or . . . he *is* Dirk," Malachi said.

Abby raised her eyebrows. "Don't you believe that if Dirk was guilty, he'd stay away from Helen?" she asked.

Malachi shrugged. "Not necessarily. He might be confident in his disguise."

Abby fell silent.

"I'm not accusing Dirk. I'm just saying

274

he's not off the suspect list."

"I'll take Dirk," Jackson said quietly. "Probe into his past and find out about his every movement over the past month and, more important, the past few days. Find out exactly where he was when Helen went missing."

"He was at the Dragonslayer," Abby said.

Malachi cleared his throat. "He was with Bootsie, Sullivan, Macy, Aldous, your buddy Roger English and others when Helen was there. Which is the last time she was seen. They all said they'd seen her. But we don't know now just how long any of those people were there."

Abby was silent again. Malachi saw that Kat and Angela were watching her with sympathy; it was a difficult thing to learn that those you believed in might not be all that they seemed.

"Savannah is filled with ships, boats, yachts — and ship's captains," Abby said stubbornly.

"We realize that, and we've been pulling names and working on investigating ships, their schedules and their crews. But, so far, the victims we know have something in common," Jackson said.

"What?" Abby asked.

"They all made meal purchases at the

Dragonslayer within a few days of their disappearances." Jackson looked at the sheet in front of him. "Even Rupert Holloway. He ate at the Dragonslayer two nights before he disappeared."

Abby was frustrated. She felt she should be doing more. Perhaps going back to the Dragonslayer, confronting the image of Blue Anderson and demanding he show up, have a conversation with her. She wanted to yell at him and make sure he understood that she needed his help because people had been killed. And if their killer was doing terrible things while pretending to be him, his reputation was being tarnished. He'd been a good pirate — good at piracy and good in that he'd followed a moral code. He didn't act with wanton cruelty, the way many had.

She was still learning about ghosts, of course. And yelling at one would probably prove as effective as yelling at the air.

She and Malachi were at the riverfront. They were due to have another interview with Helen Long in a few hours. In the meanwhile, Jackson had suggested they wander down by the river and get something to eat. She was hungry, since their meals had been irregular over the past few days.

They dined on bangers and mash at one of her favorite Irish pubs. From their vantage point on the outside patio, they could see one of the reproduction paddle wheelers heading out on the river. Gulls squawked and thronged the walks and the air; tourists ambled in and out of the shops on the riverfront.

"Paddle wheelers," Abby said. "Has anyone checked into those?"

"Jackson had the police make thorough sweeps. Not one of the captains or owners refused. They cooperated. I don't believe we're looking for a paddleboat. No, we're looking for a sailing ship," Malachi said. "Or maybe a rowboat."

"How are we ever going to find it now?" Abby asked.

"Whoever's doing this must still have been on the river when you saw Helen," he pointed out.

She frowned at that. "I don't remember seeing any vessels. I saw Helen because . . . she was a shadow. She was a shadow on the river, but there was movement. I didn't really think. I plunged in."

"She was lucky you did. Although plunging in without thinking isn't such a good idea most of the time," Malachi told her.

Abby ignored that. "One day you'll have

to really see this city," Abby said, changing the subject. "Savannah is so beautiful. We've been to Colonial Park Cemetery but Bonaventure is one of the loveliest, most gracious cemeteries I've ever seen."

"I was there," he reminded her.

"Oh. Right. Gus's funeral," she said.

"I'd actually been there before."

"Oh! I'm sorry. A lot of people visit the city, of course, and you're not that far away, so . . ."

"I don't know Savannah like you do," he said. He swallowed a long drink of iced tea and set his glass down. "Excellent bangers and mash, by the way."

She nodded. "They have great Irish music here, too. And you really should have lunch at Mrs. Wilkes's. Every morning at eleven — and I mean *every* morning — a crowd forms. It's 107 West Jones. When you go in, tourist or local, you sit at a big table with strangers and you leave with a bunch of new friends. The food's superb. Gus and my folks used to take me there when Sema Wilkes was still alive, and she was wonderful." She took a deep breath. "There are *so many* historic homes all over Savannah. There's the Historic Savannah Theater, Juliette Gordon Low's birthplace, the Massie Heritage Center, and you should

take a carriage ride down the streets and
—"

He reached across the table and touched
her hand. "I will do all those things," he
promised.

She nodded, wondering why she suddenly
felt as if she'd known him for a long time.
She really knew so little about him. . . .

Except, she knew she wanted to wake up
beside him again. She'd be disconsolate if
he never touched her again, if she couldn't
study his eyes or the way he smiled. Or
watch him when he was working something
out — by logic or intuition.

Abby looked down, feeling she'd gushed
too much. She didn't need to be defensive;
Savannah was a gem of a city.

"Virginia is great, too," she said.

He laughed. "Virginia *is* great. I love
Richmond. The White House of the Confederacy, Hollywood Cemetery and all the old
Civil War memorials . . . My part of Virginia
is pretty remote. But I think you'd like it."

She started to answer him; she wanted to
talk about Virginia, or anything else rather
than what was going on between them. But
before she could say a word, she was startled
by the presence of someone beside their
table.

It was Roger English. "Hey, you two

okay?" he asked.

"Fine, Roger." Abby smiled at him. "Are *you* okay?"

He nodded. "Yeah. I shouldn't admit it, but yesterday freaked me out. I watched the news today and it's great — you fished Helen Long out of the river last night!"

"We've seen her, Roger, and she's doing well," Malachi told him.

"Did she solve everything?" he asked.

"She's in the hospital, so we're trying to give her time to feel better before getting her to remember details," Abby said.

Roger nodded. "Hopefully she'll have what you need."

"What are you doing here?" Abby asked him. "Did you just happen by?"

"I came to meet Bianca for lunch. But she's late."

"I'm sure she'll be along in a few minutes," Abby said.

"I really like her," Roger murmured.

Abby suddenly heard a mental echo of her own voice. *I'm sure she'll be along in a few minutes.*

But she might not be.

She glanced at Malachi, who was studying Roger. "Why don't you give her a call, see what's holding her up?" Malachi suggested.

"I have. She's not answering her cell. I

tried her bed-and-breakfast, too. Couldn't reach her."

The possible explanation seemed to hit Roger as he spoke. His knees gave out; he would've fallen if Malachi hadn't leaped to his feet to bring a chair around for him.

Roger stared at the two of them. "He's got her!" he cried. "Call the police! I've got to call the police. You *are* the police. No, you're the feds . . . Oh, God. What do I do, what do I do?"

Malachi already had his phone out. "First, don't panic. People do run late. Cell phone batteries die. But under the circumstances, we'll get all the information we have on Bianca to David Caswell."

Roger looked as if he'd been hit by a brick. While Malachi spoke to David on the phone, Abby asked Roger, "Her name is Bianca Salzburg, right? She said she was transferring here from Chicago. Is she from Chicago? This is important, Roger."

"Salzburg, yes," Roger answered. "She was born in Chicago and went to Northwestern. She works for a small shipping company that handles delicate items — Pack-A-Gram, it's called. They're opening an office in Savannah. She was staying at the old Hayden house. You know the place, Abby. It was owned by Jimmy Hayden until last year when he died. His niece Shelly came back to take over the property and turned it into a B and B. She fixed it up nicely."

There was little emotion in his voice, he was so distracted.

Abby thought, but didn't say, that — like the known victims — Bianca had eaten at the Dragonslayer.

Malachi ended his call and made another before returning the phone to his pocket. "David's on it and he'll be here soon. We've reported the situation to our colleagues, as well. Bianca could show up in a few minutes, but we'll get started on the information we need, just because we're all concerned these days. So, how late is she, Roger?"

Roger glanced at his watch. "Now? Almost forty minutes."

"My colleague Angela Hawkins is on her way here to wait with you. Meanwhile, Jackson Crow is hitting the national databases to get all the information we can on Bianca. Let's hope she shows in a few minutes, apologizing for being late and explaining that she didn't charge her phone."

Roger jumped to his feet. "Helen! You have to get Helen to tell you what's going on. I'll go to the hospital. She'll talk to me — she'll tell us what happened. You saved her, right? She owes you, Abby. You have to make her tell you!"

Malachi rose and set his hands on Roger's shoulders. "Look at me, buddy. You panicking will not help Bianca. We've spoken with Helen, and we'll speak with her again, see if we can't get some details that might help. But listen to me and try to understand. We can't force Helen to tell us what she doesn't know."

"But," Roger protested, "she's alive! She *has* to know —"

"She says she saw a pirate," Abby said.

"What?" Roger demanded.

"She thinks Blue Anderson attacked her."

"Blue Anderson?" Roger repeated, looking at her blankly.

"Roger," Malachi said in a firm voice, "relax. Sit down. You'll wait here for a while longer. We'll stay until Angela arrives. Then we'll head out and start searching for her, okay? Every cop in the city will be on the lookout, too."

Roger shook his head. "She's underground somewhere. Or she's being held on a ship. It's not like they'll be able to see her."

"We'll do everything we can," Malachi said.

Abby put a hand on Roger's arm. "I'm going to get you one of Gus's old fixes, okay? A cup of tea and whiskey. Calm those nerves a bit."

"Yeah," Roger said huskily. "Yeah, okay."

By the time Abby snagged their waitress and got the tea for Roger, Angela had arrived. Tall, beautiful, controlled, she quickly had Roger talking to her, telling her about Bianca, how they'd met, and how great she was.

"Let's go," Malachi told Abby.

"Yes, get going," Angela said. "Roger and I are fine here."

"The check," Abby began.

Angela waved a hand. "Roger and I may have something else while we're here. And Jackson may come by soon. He's already got fliers into the hands of the police, and they'll get them out right away. Of course, we could really be jumping the gun, but . . ."

Abby gave Roger a kiss on the head. "It's going to be okay," she whispered.

He nodded. He still looked as if he'd been hit by a brick.

Malachi took her arm and they walked down the length of the riverfront to the parking area.

"Do you actually think she's been taken?" Abby asked.

Malachi pursed his lips. "I don't know. Maybe she's just blowing him off, but we

284

can't risk it. We'll stop by the bed-and-breakfast first and then go back to the hospital to talk to Helen. We'll see if we can get some kind of clue from her. Do you know the woman who's taken over the Hayden house? Shelly, he said her name was."

"Yeah, Gus knew everyone in town. Shelly actually lived up in Charleston. I hadn't heard that she'd turned the house into a bed-and-breakfast but I'm not surprised. It's a big old colonial and they put in a pool about ten years back."

"Tell me where to go."

Malachi was driving. He had a good grasp of the city's grid layout, with the squares bordered by streets.

When he'd parked, Abby ran up the walk. The front door was open; she went in. The Hayden house had a broad foyer with a staircase that went straight up to a second-floor balcony. Shelly had set up a reception desk in the foyer.

"Hey, Abby!" Shelly smiled as she greeted her. She came around the desk to give her a big hug. They didn't know each other that well, since Shelly was about five years older than Abby. But whenever she'd been in town, they'd seen each other often enough. Slim and attractive, she must have made a complete aboutface in her life because she'd worked in Charleston as a graphic designer.

"Shelly, it's good to see you," Abby said, returning the hug.

"Congratulations, Agent Anderson. I understand you're full-fledged now."

"More or less," Abby said. Malachi was behind her by then. She saw Shelly's eyes widen as she looked at him and then at her. She wondered how she hadn't realized from the beginning what she clearly saw now — he was an extremely attractive and arresting man. Other women seemed to respond to him instinctively.

Of course, she was doing that herself.

She gave herself a mental shake. Whatever private relationships they had, she couldn't forget her position, her chosen vocation and what they were here to do.

"Hi," Shelly said to Malachi. "You two are together?" She evidently approved.

"Shelly Hayden, Malachi Gordon. He's a private investigator and a consultant with the FBI," Abby explained. "We're here because one of your guests didn't show up for a lunch appointment, and we want to be sure she's all right."

"Oh. Oh!" Shelly said. "Which guest? Oh, it has to be Bianca Salzburg. She's registered, and then I have two retired couples and a family of four. She was fine this morning. I made quiches for breakfast and she was so sweet, really loved them. She was cheerful when she left here."

"When was that?" Malachi asked.

"About eleven," Shelly told him.

"Did she say where she was going?"

"No, and I'm afraid I don't grill people when they leave," Shelly said. "Sometimes they ask me about a tour or a carriage ride — but if they're going out for the day, well, I don't feel it's my place to ask questions."

"Were your other guests down here when she had breakfast?" Malachi asked next.

"Yes, the Mortons were sitting with her at one of the tables on the patio. I serve breakfast outside by the pool when I can."

"Are they still here?" Abby asked.

"Out by the pool."

"May I?" Abby gestured, indicating that she wanted to walk through.

"Of course," Shelly followed Malachi as he kept pace with Abby. "I heard they found the girl who was working for Dirk on his *Black Swan*. Do you think Bianca might have been . . . kidnapped and assaulted by the same man? Or . . . I mean, it's just been a few hours. Can she really be missing?" She sounded both puzzled and concerned.

"We're not taking chances," Malachi said.

"This is *so* distressing!" Shelly murmured.

The Mortons were a handsome couple in their late sixties or early seventies, who both looked fit and tan. Abby envied them for a minute. They appeared to be the kind of people who'd worked hard, raised their children — and survived to enjoy their golden years together.

She quickly introduced herself and said that Bianca Salzburg was probably fine, but with the sad state of events lately, they were trying to make sure.

Mrs. Morton gasped softly. "Oh, that lovely, lovely girl!" She turned to her husband, "Henry, she was so pleasant, wasn't she? She joined us for breakfast." As he nodded, she looked at Abby. "This is Bianca's first trip to Savannah. She's from Chicago, you know. Loves Chicago — her family's there — but she was offered a chance to manage the new office for her company if she moved to Savannah. She says that since she got here, she's been absolutely thrilled, the city's so beautiful. We told her we'd been coming for years. Can't move from Philly, since our grandkids live there, but we love to spend a month in Savannah every year."

"It's one of the most beautiful cities in the world," Abby agreed. "Did Bianca say anything about her plans for the day?"

"Why, yes. She said she'd met a nice local

fellow and that she was having lunch with him. Down by the river somewhere. I forget — what did she say, Henry? The Irish pub?"

Henry Morton murmured. "Yes, Connie. The Irish pub."

"Henry, if you know something, you have to speak up," Connie Morton said.

"You seem to be doing fine for both of us," Henry said.

Connie rolled her eyes. Her husband smiled at her.

"Shelly is pretty sure she left around eleven," Malachi told them. "Does that sound about right?"

"Yes, precisely right," Connie said. "She waved to us as she was walking out."

Abby thanked them; when Henry expressed serious concern about Bianca, she promised they'd call the bed-and-breakfast with any news.

They bade Shelly and the Mortons goodbye and headed out.

"They were a lovely couple," Abby said as they walked to the car.

"Yes." He nodded thoughtfully. "I have a feeling they've been together for years — and that they're still in love."

"I envy them in a way."

He flashed her a smile. "You're too young to envy anyone yet. The world's out there for you."

"Yes, I know. They just made me think of my parents. The world was once theirs, too. But they died before they made it to where the Mortons are now."

"And yet," Malachi said softly, "what they had was probably better than what many people get even if they live to be over a hundred."

That was true, but Abby missed her parents and her grandparents as much as ever and found it painful to talk about. She changed the subject back to work.

"So, we're going to see Helen?"

"Yes." When they drove alongside Colonial Park Cemetery, she was surprised when he suddenly saw a parking space and slid into it.

Abby frowned. "Helen's at the hospital. Why are we here?"

"I know. I thought we'd stop for a minute."

"Oh. Okay."

He was already out of the car. She followed as he walked through the main entrance, beneath the arch and the great eagle. He kept moving toward the back, making straight for the bench where he'd seen the ghostly old couple and pointed them out.

They weren't at the bench. They were

standing by a grave.

Abby hung back and watched. She saw Malachi approach them, not speaking at first. He stood by the grave and bowed his head.

After a few minutes, Abby inched closer. Malachi spoke quietly. "Good afternoon," he greeted the pair. "I'm sorry for your loss. Your son?"

The man appeared startled and looked at his wife. Then he looked at Malachi again and Abby heard his voice, like paper shifting on the wind.

"You are speaking to me, young man?"

"I am," Malachi said. "If you'll forgive my intrusion."

"Of course." The woman nodded. "Yes, it is our son."

"He is gone, you know. And you could be with him," Malachi told them.

The elderly man shook his head. "Soldiers came here," he said. "They defaced Josiah's grave. Scraped off his name with their knives. We must stand guard, lest they come again."

"If you tell me what should be on the gravestone, I can see that it's fixed," Malachi promised. "The soldiers won't come again. They were bitter because so many of their own died in the war and they behaved badly.

But that war is long over — it ended a century and a half ago. I swear, I will see that the gravestone is repaired. If you tell me his name and what you wish written on it, I give you my solemn vow that it will be set to rights."

"You can do that?" the woman asked.

"With her help," Malachi said, gesturing at Abby.

She walked over to join them. "Savannah is my home. I know the people who can get this done," she told them.

The man turned to her. "You would really help us?"

"Of course."

"You two are always here," Malachi said.

"Always." The man took his wife's hand.

"You must notice what goes on around here," Malachi remarked.

"We watch. We watch over this grave," the wife said.

Malachi nodded. "A mother's love, a father's dedication. But perhaps you could help *us*, too. People are disappearing. I know the city is crowded, that tourists come daily. But . . . late at night, or even during the day, do you see things?"

The man studied Malachi for a long time and then slowly lifted his arm, pointing. "There is something — there, on the corner

— something that is odd."

"Not truly odd. It was dug years and years ago," the woman said. "It is part of the old drainage system."

"And it was abandoned years ago!" the man added.

The woman sniffed. "Abandoned. Sealed after the horror of the yellow fever! But there were things that went on then that . . . I believe they thought if they could get the bodies out of the city through the sewer system, they would not infect others. They dug deep tunnels by the old hospital. But there was more that went on than was ever recorded."

"Have you seen anything there?" Malachi asked.

"Shadows at night. By day, who knows?"

"People move around," the old woman said. "There is an alley behind the first mausoleum. Sometimes a tall figure goes there . . . and does not come back. But there are many of us here. Many, many walk the city. Our kind. We are like shadows. And shadow-walkers may be restless by night. So what we've seen . . . I am not sure. But we will watch for you," she said anxiously. "If you wish, we will watch for you."

"That's very kind."

"My son . . . he fought bravely in the War

of 1812. Please. His marker should read 'Lieutenant Josiah Beckwith, born April 9, 1790. Died for his country, September 12, 1814, at the Battle of North Point during the War of 1812. Beloved son, husband and father. A patriot.' "

"We'll see to it," Abby said, jotting the details on a small notepad. She prayed she could keep her promise.

The man's arm was around his wife's shoulder. He started to offer his hand, but let it fall. "I am Edgar Beckwith. This is my wife, Elizabeth."

"Malachi Gordon," Malachi said. "And Abigail Anderson."

"Anderson?" the woman said, looking at her. "Are you related to the family that owns the tavern?"

She nodded.

"Your family are good people, Ms. Anderson."

She thanked them, and Malachi took her arm. They left the old couple gazing sadly at their son's tombstone. Abby saw two young women standing by a red brick aboveground grave — watching her and Malachi. She felt her cheeks growing red.

As she glanced at Malachi, embarrassed, he smiled. "Don't worry!" he said.

"They think we're crazy, that we talk to

imaginary friends," Abby muttered.

Malachi laughed. "These days? Everyone looks crazy because half the time they have headsets on or they're on the phone and they seem to be talking to themselves. So . . ."

"Do you think the Beckwiths really saw something in the alley?"

"I think they did and that they'll lead us where we'd eventually have gotten — except we'll get there more quickly now."

"Get where?"

"Back beneath the ground," he said.

10

Malachi called David, asking him to send a few officers to the alley. Then he called Jackson, suggesting he get someone to do historical and architectural research on the area.

In the meantime, he told Jackson, he and Abby would drive back to the hospital to talk to Helen.

"Any word on Bianca Salzburg?" she asked.

He repeated her question to Jackson; no, Bianca hadn't appeared.

He and Abby got into the car and headed back to the hospital.

"What made you want to stop at the cemetery and talk to that couple?" she asked him.

He sent her a warm smile. "You."

"Me?"

"When you talked to the Mortons and then told me how you envied them, I started to think about these two in the cemetery. They're there for the long haul. Some people don't care — dead is dead. You move on. Others . . . well, honor was a big thing to them. They need that tombstone fixed."

"How am I going to convince city council and the staff in charge of the cemetery that I know how that gravestone should be corrected?" Abby asked.

"We'll pull something out of a history book somewhere," Malachi assured her. "Or some old record."

Abby stared ahead, looking tired and grim. He reached over and took her hand.

"I'm worried about Bianca."

"He holds his victims. We have time to find her."

"He assaults his victims," she said.

He couldn't argue with that.

"We'll see what Helen can tell us now that she's a little more removed from the situation," he told her.

At the hospital they learned that Helen was resting comfortably. Kat had been sitting with her; when Abby and Malachi came, she rose and stretched. "I'm off for a bit — walk around, maybe grab some coffee."

"We'll stay until you get back," Malachi said. As she moved toward the door he

297

asked quietly, "Has she given you any information?"

"She's been asleep for the past hour. I suggested she try to remember details, but I'm sure she's telling us everything she remembers — or what she thinks she saw. Maybe you can get more."

Kat left, and Abby sat beside the hospital bed. Helen's eyes flickered open and, for a moment, they registered fear — until she saw Abby. "Hey," she said weakly.

"Hey, yourself. How are you doing?"

"Okay. Dirk came to see me." She smiled. "With Aldous and Bootsie. Aldous is a sweetheart. He told me he's been so worried, he almost grew back some hair."

Abby laughed, then glanced at Malachi.

He nodded, letting her know she should do the talking for now.

Abby drew a deep breath. "Helen, we think he's taken another woman."

Helen's eyes closed; she went gray, trembling visibly. "I'm so sorry!" she whispered.

"You're the only one who can help us."

Helen shook her head. "I don't know how," she said, her voice raspy. "I just . . . don't." Her eyes opened and she stared at Abby. "I never believed in ghosts before. And I know he was supposed to be a gentleman pirate, and that Errol Flynn and Johnny

Depp made pirates seem cool, but . . . it was Blue, Abby. I *know* it was Blue Anderson. He's dead, but somehow . . ."

"Helen, it wasn't Blue. And even if he came back as a ghost, he'd *never* do anything like this. It's someone dressing up as Blue."

"But . . ."

"Think about it, Helen. You know that has to be true."

Malachi stepped forward, dragging a chair closer to Helen, across from Abby. "Helen, you were hurt. You were hit on the head. You were abused and kept in a dark place. You're being wonderful, but what we need you to do is try to remember every little detail. What happened right before Abby pulled you out of the water?"

Helen's forehead wrinkled with her effort. "I remember hearing water. I remember it being dark, and I remember the man . . . Blue."

"It wasn't Blue. It was someone dressed as Blue," Malachi said again. Abby frowned at him, but Helen let out a breath.

"Someone dressed as Blue," she agreed listlessly. "I — I only saw him briefly. He put something on my eyes."

"He blindfolded you?" Abby asked.

"Yes."

"You remember him being in the room," Malachi said. "What kind of room?"

"It was . . . I think it was a cabin." Tears welled in Helen's eyes. "Touching me," she said with a whisper.

"That's okay. You don't have to remember that part right now," Malachi said. "But did he wear cologne or aftershave? Do you remember anything about his voice?"

"It was gruff — like a pirate's voice."

"Do you remember any other sounds? Did you ever hear people?" Malachi asked.

Abby glanced at him and set a gentle hand on Helen's. She carefully avoided the IV dripping fluids into a vein in Helen's arm, but tried to comfort the young woman.

"I didn't hear people . . ." Helen said. Then she bit her lip. "Yes, once . . . but it was early on. I thought I heard people. Maybe music. And tapping. A rhythmic tap . . . tap . . . tap. Only sometimes. Maybe it was a band . . ."

"Thank you, Helen," Abby said.

Malachi took over again. "What do you remember about being held captive?"

Helen shuddered; Abby reached over and smoothed down a lock of her hair.

"I was in the bed . . . the bunk . . . whatever. It wasn't comfortable. He said I was a captive who'd fallen in love with him.

But he repulsed me. He . . . he made me want to vomit. I gagged or choked and then . . . then he was angry. He told me I was a bad captive."

"Helen, was he with you all the time?" Malachi asked.

"I don't . . . I don't know. I remember lying there . . . my hands were bound and my feet were tied to something and I couldn't move. He'd go away . . . and then he'd be back. And then he'd touch me again. So . . . so disgusting. I couldn't — I couldn't pretend. I couldn't be what he wanted, couldn't even pretend to be in love with him. He was very angry. My hands were still bound, but then . . . then he untied my feet . . . my ankles, I guess. He jerked me up and wrenched my hand around and . . . I felt one of his hands holding mine down on a table or something and then —"

She broke off with a sob.

"He cut you," Abby said quietly.

"He cut off my finger!" Helen sobbed. "I can still hear the sound. There was a whoosh . . . and then I felt the slam of it . . . and I felt the pain. I was still blindfolded but I knew . . . I knew it was my finger." She continued to sob.

"Oh, Helen!" Abby said, stroking her cheek gently. "I'm so sorry. I'm so, so sorry."

Malachi apologized to Abby with his eyes but she obviously understood that he had to press forward. "Helen, he took your finger while your blindfold was on. What then?"

"He dragged me along the floor," Helen began. "Maybe . . . maybe there was music again. I heard a beat . . . tap, tap, tap. And I thought I heard laughter across the water. I — I felt the night air on my skin. I knew he had a knife and I thought he was going to stab me. But he cut the ropes — and then I was in the water. I was suddenly in the water, and I was trying so hard to swim, but I was in pain, and my arms . . . they were so stiff. I got the blindfold off. I . . . I don't know what happened to it. I don't even know what it looked like. I couldn't swim. I felt so heavy, I was all tangled up in something. . . ."

"You were found wearing a wench costume," Malachi told her. "Do you recall changing into it, or when you were changed into it?"

Helen shook her head, tears welling up in her eyes again. "I'm so sorry. I should just be grateful to be alive!"

"Helen, it's okay," Abby said. "You were assaulted, you were nearly killed. That's a terrible trauma, and you'll probably need counseling to get over it. But don't worry now. You're safe here, protected by people who'd die before they let anything else happen to you!"

"I owe you both my life," Helen said.

"You owe your life to your own will and strength, Helen," Malachi said firmly. "You are a survivor. You're going to be fine. And don't apologize for the pain you feel, and don't ever apologize for crying. You have real inner strength, and you're going to get through this."

Helen managed a shaky smile.

There was a knock at the door. A tall, brawny male nurse was there; Malachi wondered if he'd been specially chosen to watch over Helen, just in case there was trouble. He didn't doubt that Jackson Crow might have seen to such a thing.

"There are a few people out here asking to see Ms. Long," the nurse announced.

"Oh?"

"I told them only two at a time. There's a fellow out here named Roger English and a couple of others — Jack Winston and Blake Stewart." He shrugged. "Earlier, they said it was fine for Mr. Johansen to see her with his friends. But I was told to check with whoever's here from enforcement."

Malachi could see that Abby was about to

get up and prevent anyone from coming near Helen.

"Abby, could you talk to Roger for a minute? Tell him Helen's had it very rough and that he shouldn't push her. I think it's okay for the other two gentlemen to come in right away. But, of course, that's up to Helen." He turned to her.

Helen nodded. "Yes, of course. I want to see my friends, but I — Abby? Would you run that brush through my hair?"

"Of course!" Abby hastened to do as she was asked.

When she was finished, Helen said, "How silly — I'm lucky to have my life and I'm worried about how I look."

"That's not silly," Malachi assured her. "That's life-affirming."

"And you look beautiful," Abby said.

"Wenches are supposed to be tough, aren't they?" Helen asked.

Abby smiled, glanced at Malachi and hurried out. A minute later, the two young actors who worked for Dirk came into the room. Malachi studied them. They looked very different from the way they had when he'd seen them on the *Black Swan*.

Jack Winston, the older and more confident of the two, was dressed in a T-shirt that advertised Guinness and a pair of stylishly threadbare jeans. He was well-built and had a naturally cocky way about him, but his eyes were filled with tenderness as he walked in. Blake was younger and his heart appeared to be prominently displayed on his sleeve as he followed Jack. Tall and lanky, he wore jeans as well, but had on a polo shirt.

"Helen!" Jack said.

"Hi," Blake greeted her. Jack kissed Helen on the cheek; Blake stood awkwardly beside the bed.

"Hey, you two!" she said.

Jack didn't seem to recognize Malachi. He walked over to him and thrust out his hand. "I'm Jack Winston and this is Blake Stewart. We work with Helen. We've been worried sick. We, uh, called the hospital and they said it was okay to visit."

"Sure. Helen needs to see her friends," Malachi said, shaking hands with Jack. Blake seemed confused, as if he should know him but didn't. Malachi smiled. "Malachi Gordon. I'm a private investigator working as a consultant with the federal unit down here."

"Oh, uh, great," Blake said. Still confused, he turned back to Helen.

Jack did the talking; he was a good bedside guest. He regaled her with tales of kids who'd been on the ship and told her how much she'd been missed. Blake listened, just staring at Helen, his infatuation evident.

He sat down, taking the place Abby had been in before. "Helen . . . oh, God. Oh, Helen, we missed you so much! We're so glad . . . Anything, anything you need or want, you let us know. We'll get it for you!"

"I'm going to be okay, Blake. Abby and this gentleman here, Mr. Gordon — they saved me."

"I wish it had been me, Helen!" Blake said passionately. "I wish I could have saved you. If I ever find out who did this, I swear, I'll kill him!"

His words hung in the air for a minute. "You can't say that," Helen told him. "You . . . you have to let the law take care of him."

"Don't worry," Malachi said. "I understand how you feel, Blake. But she's right. You have to leave this in the hands of the law."

Blake didn't answer.

Jack placed a hand on his shoulder. "They'll get him, Blake. They'll get him. Don't upset Helen."

"I'm fine," Helen said softly. Malachi thought she was; seeing how Blake felt meant something to her. His affection made her stronger.

Just then, Abby came back into the room with Roger English, Roger looking duly chastised. He went over to Helen and bent down — then straightened abruptly and asked, "Is it all right if I kiss your cheek? It won't hurt you or anything?"

"I would love a kiss on the cheek," she said.

"I'm so glad you're okay, Helen." Roger kissed her cheek with great care.

"Thank you, Roger."

He nodded, stepped back and looked at Malachi. He didn't say anything else.

Malachi rose. "Come on, Roger, let's go get some coffee."

"So, Helen, we're hoping you'll be back with us soon. I mean, we want you to get rich and famous in a zombie movie, but we'd like you back with us, too," Jack said.

Roger came forward again. "Helen, he's taken another girl. Her name is Bianca Salzburg. You might have met her. . . . She took some of the local tours and she might have been on the *Black Swan*. Helen, you have to remember —"

"Stop it! Leave her alone!" Blake said.

Malachi got up, stepping between the two of them and glancing at Abby.

He clapped Roger on the back. "Kat

should be back soon," he told Abby.

He was done at the hospital; he'd gotten from Helen everything he thought he could, and it was time to start going over what she had said, and trying to put the pieces together. Now, Helen deserved a little peace.

As soon as he was outside the room with Roger, he said, "You were very good in there — at first. But we already told Helen that another woman is missing. She wants to help. I'm glad you came to see her, but badgering her won't help. Abby explained that to you."

Roger was red-faced but he nodded dully. "They haven't found Bianca yet. She hasn't been back to her B and B, and she isn't answering her cell."

Malachi didn't tell him he was sure the police had put a trace on the phone. "We're going to do everything we can" was all he said.

"Can I tell Helen I'm sorry?" Roger asked.

"I think it's best if you don't. She's had enough for today."

"All right," Roger said. "Is there anything I *can* do?"

"Take a walk. See if you can think of anything. If you do, call me." Malachi presented a card. It had nothing on it but his cell phone number.

"You don't even have a name on this," Roger told him.

"Doesn't need it. You have my name. Call if you need me."

Roger nodded and glanced wistfully toward Helen's hospital room. The uniformed officer on duty by the door stood there with his arms crossed looking at Roger.

"I'm going," Roger muttered, heading toward the elevator. "I guess I'll check out the Dragonslayer."

Malachi watched him leave. As he did, an elevator door down the hall opened and Kat stepped off. She tried to keep the doors from closing but she didn't move quickly enough. She apologized to Roger, who mumbled something, pushed the call button and stood there, waiting.

Kat came down the hall. "Everything all right?" she asked Malachi.

Malachi nodded, still watching Roger. "I think Helen's had all the visitors she can handle for the day," he said.

"She has visitors in there now?"

"Jack and Blake — the pirate actors she works with on the *Black Swan.*"

"Ah. You let them in on purpose, I take it."

"I did."

"Suspects?"

309

"I don't think so. I think they're just friends. No ulterior motives. But we can't be sure yet."

"I'll get the nurse to shoo them out. He's a great guy and a major help. His name is Byron. He'll do twelve-hour days — switching with Bruno, another nurse Jackson found here — and one who fits his name well," Kat said.

Malachi nodded, keeping an eye on Roger, who continued to wait by the elevator. "Leave it to Jackson Crow," he said, and smiled. "Did Will see or hear anything on board the *Black Swan*?" he asked.

"No, but he got along famously with Dirk," Kat said. "And with his buddies, Bootsie and Aldous."

"Is he back at the house on Chippewa now?"

"Spelling Angela on the cameras, yes."

"I'd like him to follow Roger English," Malachi said.

"You think *Roger* is responsible for all this?" Kat asked. "Isn't he the one who's going crazy looking for Bianca?"

"Yes and no. I don't believe he's a killer. But he'd be interesting to watch. He's in love. And he knows the city. He may lead us someplace he suspects might be a haven for the killer. He may even have an idea he isn't willing to share. He doesn't feel any of us wants to find Bianca Salzburg with the same desperation he does."

Kat pulled out her phone. Malachi waited while she put through the call to Will, who promised to get to the tavern quickly and start following Roger. Kat spoke for another minute or so and hung up.

"Jackson was about to call you. He's at a place near the river called the Wulf and Whistle. It's by that alley you told him about. He wants you to go there as soon as you can," she said.

"We're on it." Malachi paused. "Kat, what do you think the killer is using to hack off fingers?"

"A very sharp object, one with some heft. He's taking them cleanly."

"So, maybe something like an old pirate's boarding ax?"

"Could be," Kat said.

"Thanks."

Kat reached for the door to Helen Long's room. "I'll send Abby out — and sic Byron on our visitors."

Soon after, Abby joined him in the hall.

"Helen is doing fine," she said. "I told Roger we'd talked to her and that she'd given us everything that she could. I warned him not to push her."

"I know. Come on. Jackson asked us to meet him at the Wulf and Whistle."

"It's in front of the alley our ghosts pointed out to us this morning." Abby hesitated. "Malachi, what do you think she heard — aside from the music. If she was on the river, she might've heard the entertainment from any of the tourist boats. But the sound she heard, like a beat. She didn't say it was drums, exactly, but something like that."

Tap, tap, tap.

He didn't know, but he felt he should. It was there, hidden somewhere in the back of his mind.

The Wulf and Whistle was in one of Savannah's historic buildings; it had gone up about ten years before the yellow fever epidemic. Abby had been inside many times. Business owners in the city could be a tight group; what was good for the city was good for everyone, and Gus had been close with the people he saw as his colleagues rather than competitors. Right now, the restaurant and bar was owned by Samuel Mason, who lived in Florida. His manager, however, was Steve Rugby, a man in his mid-forties who ran the place with friendly ease. Abby had always liked Steve and the Wulf and Whistle.

When the building had first gone up, it had been a tavern with apartments above it.

It was still a tavern with apartments above it. Peanuts were served in shells, the walls were decorated with old advertisements and the feel of the establishment was warm and congenial.

As soon as they entered, the hostess directed Abby and Malachi down to the rum cellar. Once, it had probably housed little more than rum. Now, it still held the old casks, but there were also endless rows of wine, and cases and stacks of fine bourbons, whiskeys, rums, gins and other alcohol, too.

Steve, a barrel-chested balding man, was there with Jackson Crow, David Caswell and a number of other officers. The shelves had been removed from one wall and Steve had been showing the police and Jackson a section of that wall.

Jackson and David hailed Abby and Malachi when they arrived.

"We sent some officers out on a door-to-door," Jackson explained. "And Steve called to tell us about the tunnel."

"So there *is* a tunnel here?" Abby asked. "I never knew about this one, either!"

Steve joined the conversation. "None of

us knew about it. We did some renovations down here about three months ago," he said. "When we did, we had engineers in — you know, you have to make sure these old places are safe. Anyway, they were looking at the pilings and found that we had a false wall here. They knocked it down. My assistant did some research for me, and we're putting the info on our new menus," he added proudly. "The owner during the War Between the States was a heartfelt abolitionist, and this place was a stop on the Underground Railroad. Anyway, they must have kept the entrance hidden behind rum casks back then. And by the time we got to it, the false walls had been painted over again and again. But, like I was showing the police, we had our entrance here sealed as part of the renovation."

It might have been sealed before, Abby thought, but not anymore. The police had taken sledgehammers to it.

Now, a dark hole gaped before them, running beneath the earth. The artificial light from the cellar faded into the far reaches. David Caswell held a large searchlight and started moving slowly into the dank tunnel.

"Shall we?" Jackson asked, pulling out a flashlight, as well.

Abby felt Malachi's hand on the small of

her back as he guided her forward.

Light played over the walls of the tunnel. There were places where the earth had fallen in and other places where plaster or wooden walls remained to shore it up.

They walked for about fifty feet and came to a dead end.

Jackson, David and Malachi tapped on the solid wall of earth they'd reached, listening for a hollow sound that would indicate the tunnel had been blocked but continued. Malachi used the end of his light to dig at the earth. He hit more earth.

They tried, moving along, casting the light in different directions, tapping and searching, but an hour later, they remained frustrated.

"Nothing," Jackson said. "I could've sworn there'd be something,"

"Me, too," David Caswell agreed.

"We can get some engineers down here tomorrow," Jackson said, "and see if we're missing anything. For now . . ."

"For now we have to give it up?" Abby asked.

"An engineer will uncover what we can't," Malachi told her.

"Right." Abby felt deflated; she'd been so certain they'd find *something*.

They trudged back out of the tunnel.

Steve and the other officers remained in the cellar.

"We'll call it a night and get someone in here tomorrow," David announced.

Jackson stepped forward to thank Steve for all his help. "Hey, it's my city," Steve said. "And it tears at my heart to hear about the bad things that are happening. Whatever I can do . . ."

"Sorry about wrecking the wall," Jackson reminded him.

"Easy to fix," Steve assured them. "Don't worry about it."

They left, going up to the tavern and out to the street, where David, Jackson, Malachi and Abby stood together, looking at one another.

They resembled kids who'd been playing in the mud, Abby thought. "Well," David said with a wry grin. "Time to hit the showers."

"Bianca Salzburg hasn't surfaced, has she?" Abby said. It wasn't really a question.

Bianca, her disappearance, had to be the reason for tonight's exertions.

"No," David admitted. "She's still missing."

"He has her," Abby said.

David turned to Jackson. "We traced her cell phone. The signal disappeared somewhere around here. That's why we needed to tear everything up at the restaurant. But I have men on the riverfront. We might go broke on overtime, but we're leaving nothing unturned. We have police vessels out on the river and the coast guard, too. We're doing everything we possibly can."

Abby nodded. "But —"

"We have to quit for tonight," Jackson said decisively. "Everyone needs to sleep."

They wished one another a good night. Then Abby and Malachi returned to the Dragonslayer.

Grant Green was at the desk when they walked in. "My God!" he said, staring at the two of them, mouth agape. Guests were still having dinner in the dining rooms; a few people — along with the trio of Bootsie, Aldous and Dirk — were at the bar. Grant hurried around the host stand to meet them. "What have you been *doing*?"

"Playing in the dirt," Abby said facetiously.

"Okay, never mind." Grant sighed. "How's Helen?"

"Doing well."

"What about the other girl? The one Roger was seeing?" Grant asked.

"No one knows yet," Malachi told him.

"That — that bastard!" Grant sputtered.

"He takes a new one the minute he . . . loses one. Can't you stop him?"

"We *will* stop him," Malachi said.

"Are you getting any closer?"

No! Abby wanted to scream. *How is he doing this? How is he eluding this kind of manhunt?*

"I believe we are," Malachi responded. "Thanks to Abby, one girl is alive. And with the police prowling the river now and all the searches taking place out there . . . he'll be caught."

"Soon, I hope!" Grant said.

"Every criminal makes a mistake at some point," Malachi insisted. "That's when we'll get him."

"Uh, you might want to clean up first," Grant said, looking pointedly at Abby.

"I'm going upstairs now. Oh, Grant, can you ask the chef to make us something to eat?" she asked. "You can send it up —"

"Or," Malachi interrupted, "we can eat at the bar. Join Dirk, Bootsie and Aldous."

"Okay," Abby said. "But first, a shower."

Malachi came with her, but didn't seem to notice that she was shrugging out of her muddy clothing as they entered the apartment. He repeated his inspection, making sure no one was inside, under the beds, in the closets. He headed back to the bank of computer screens to watch what was going on in the restaurant.

Abby cleared her throat. "I'm hopping in the shower," she told him.

He nodded; he didn't even glance up. So much for her appeal.

Hot water had seldom felt so good. Well, other than the night before, after she'd plunged into the river . . .

It felt sensuously good. Despite everything they were frantically doing in their desperate new search to find another young woman, she wished Malachi would join her.

She almost *needed* him.

She pictured him walking into the bathroom, stripping off his clothing, imagined the sleek feel of his naked flesh and his hands on her breasts.

But he didn't come in.

She emerged, feeling a little embarrassed. When she returned to the living room area, having donned jeans and a T-shirt to head back down for dinner, Malachi was still studying the screens, fixated on them. But he immediately sensed her standing behind him.

"The soap . . . You smell wonderful," he told her. There was a husky note in his voice and a darkening in the hazel of his eyes as he watched her; it made her knees tremble.

"You would've been welcome to join me," she said.

He smiled, an ironic twist to his lips. "I had to know that this apartment was safe."

She smiled. He stood and started to touch her but drew back. "Go down and join our friends at the bar. Try to casually find out what they've been doing all day."

She wanted to argue with him. Bootsie, Dirk and Aldous — these men were bulwarks in her life. They couldn't be guilty of anything. Will Chan had been watching Dirk and the *Black Swan.* Bootsie was old. Aldous . . .

Aldous was healthy and fit — and not all that old. He'd always looked like a pirate with his gleaming bald head and single gold earring.

He had money. Enough money to do whatever he wanted. His business was a shipping company; he had ships and boats at his disposal.

She didn't say anything, but Malachi gave her another rueful smile. "I see your mind working," he said.

"Aldous?" she asked.

He nodded.

"I'm sure your FBI friends have checked out everything they possibly can on him. As far as I know, he's never even had a parking ticket."

His grin deepened at that. "Hey, *you're* the one who's actually a fed at the moment," he reminded her.

Abby rolled her eyes. "I'll be downstairs," she said, and left him in the apartment. She was grateful to see that Grant had ordered dinner for her and Malachi. Two covered plates were set on the bar, next to Bootsie. Aldous was sitting between him and Dirk.

Abby kissed the three of them on the cheek, hitched herself onto the bar stool beside Bootsie's and took the cover off her food. Chicken potpie. It smelled wonderful.

"You doing okay?" Bootsie asked her, his eyes grave.

"I'm just feeling sick that this killer may have taken another young woman," she said.

"But," he said, lifting a glass of ale to her, "you saved Helen. She seems to be doing just fine — minus a finger, unfortunately. But you can live perfectly well with one less finger. I should know. I've lived most of my life without a leg."

Dirk bent over the bar to speak to her across the other men. "Did you see Helen again tonight? She's really doing well?"

"She's really doing well," Abby assured them. "So, what about you gentlemen? What have you been up to today?"

"We went with Dirk to see Helen," Aldous said, looking at her as if she should have realized that.

"That was this morning," Abby said. "How about later? Have you been sitting on these chairs all day?"

Frowning, Dirk surveyed the restaurant and said, "Abby, you know I've been back on the *Black Swan.* That handsome young Asian fellow, or whatever he is, has been working with me. You know that," he repeated.

"Will Chan."

"Yeah, Will. He's a good guy. A great performer."

"I don't really know him but I have heard he's a pretty talented magician, as well," Abby said.

"Yeah, he's something else. He pulls doubloons out of kids' ears, has 'em laughing. Wish I could keep him," Dirk said. "He was with me for the afternoon tour. I assume he's keeping an eye on me, right?"

"An eye on the guests, the river . . . everything, Dirk."

"Yeah. Like I'm a suspect!" Dirk said, sounding a little bitter.

Sullivan walked up to Abby. "Water? Beer, soda — anything to drink?"

"Just water, thanks, Sullivan," Abby told him.

"And not to worry — these old barflies haven't been here all day!" Sullivan said, grinning. "They've only been back for about three hours now."

Three hours. So, ever since Dirk had berthed the *Black Swan.* There'd been at least three hours when they could've been doing anything. Separately or together.

And of course, there were two hours between sailings on the *Black Swan.* Right around lunchtime . . .

Right around the time Bianca Salzburg had disappeared.

"Is your food okay?" Sullivan asked.

"Yes, it's fine. I just started talking and got distracted."

"Ah, there's your colleague," Sullivan said. He waited as Malachi, fresh from the shower, came to join her.

"Hello," Dirk said in greeting. The others echoed him.

"Gentlemen." Malachi took his seat next to Abby.

"Cops, FBI people wasting their time watching me and God knows who else," Dirk muttered. "And they've come up with . . . nothing."

"Sometimes a killer's never caught," Aldous reminded him.

"They'd better catch this one, or Savannah will run out of women," Bootsie commented.

Malachi turned on his bar stool to face them. "You don't feel the police are doing everything they can?" he asked.

"Killer hasn't been caught," Bootsie said. "And they're hounding good people, like our friend Dirk here."

"Oh, they'll catch this killer," Malachi spoke with all the confidence he could muster. Grant had moved over toward the bar. Sullivan remained where he'd been, right behind it. All five men stared at him. "This killer . . . well, he's pretending to be Blue Anderson."

"Yeah, I heard. The media got hold of Helen Long's story about being attacked by a 'pirate,' " Sullivan said. "So he's pretending to be Blue?"

"Here's the thing," Malachi went on. "And I'm not talking out of line. The police want some of Helen's information out there to prevent other women from being taken. The man who lured her to the abandoned church had given her a business card with the name Christopher Condent on it. I'm sure you gentlemen know who the real Christopher Condent was?"

"A pirate. A brutal pirate who got away with it," Sullivan said.

"He died in France, right?" Dirk asked.

"Rich as Midas, from what I've read," Aldous added.

"Yes, I think our killer believes he can do whatever he wants, get away with it and then sail off into the sunset. Christopher Condent. Students of piracy or local history might know the name, but it's not like Blackbeard or any of the really well-known names. So, he amuses himself by using the name and the business cards, but then dresses up as Blue. Everyone in this area knows what Blue looks like. There are dozens of paintings of him, including the replica of him right here in the dining room. But there's a problem with that."

"What?" Bootsie asked. "Other than the guy getting his pirates confused."

"Well, Blue, of course."

Everyone stared at Malachi. "What do you mean?" Aldous asked.

"I mean the real Blue won't stand for it."

Bootsie began to laugh. Dirk let out a choked cough that became a chuckle.

"Blue Anderson's been dead for two and a half centuries!" Sullivan said.

"Blue is here in spirit," Malachi told them all.

"Yep — in all the spirits behind this bar," Sullivan said, grinning.

"Oh, no, my friends. Don't kid yourselves. Blue is very much here, in every brick and beam of this tavern. And his anger will grow — and when it does, the killer had best beware."

11

"I bet they've decided the FBI has brought in a certifiably crazy person as a consultant," Abby said as the door to the apartment closed behind them.

Malachi smiled, shrugged and immediately pulled her to him and into his arms.

She felt . . . The only word was *melting.*

They needed to talk, of course. His words downstairs had been met with laughter, then blank stares and awkwardness. Sullivan had started cleaning the bar. Grant had cleared his throat and walked away. Dirk said he'd had enough to drink for the night, and Aldous and Bootsie had quickly agreed. They were out the door before Abby and Malachi had made it to the stairs.

But now . . .

Nothing seemed to matter. Her body's memory kicked in, a physical memory that resided in her skin, her muscles, her very cells. Sliding against him, she felt guilty for a millisecond, but she was doing everything she possibly could to assist the police and Krewe unit in finding the killer. Jackson had said they needed sleep. But she needed *this* more than she needed sleep.

And Malachi obviously wasn't giving a second's thought to Jackson's advice.

They began to shed their clothing, their lips meeting as shoes and fabric went flying. They touched, then broke away, helped each other and moved slowly down the hall, still kissing. Soon they were back in the bedroom, tangled in the sheets, and she wasn't thinking about anything but this man — the taste of his flesh, the feel of his lips and hands upon her. His kisses warmed her where they fell; her body sparked to life with the brush of his fingers. The pressure of his body was vital and arousing, and she returned his passion with an urgent hunger of her own. The thundering of her heart seemed shockingly loud.

They moved, then kissed again. They looked at each other, and they whispered words that meant everything, although they were unintelligible. They broke apart to deliver hot wet kisses, then arched together, teasing and arousing, until he thrust into her and their pace became frantic. Moments later, it slowed, building to a sweet crescendo, exploding fiercely, and taking them into an even sweeter spiral of release. Their bodies gradually relaxed, and the glow of completion merged with the indefinable sensation of being with someone who meant so very much. . . .

This pleasure, being in such a state, feeling like this with another person, was nothing she'd ever encountered before. Abby smiled; she pushed away the thought that they hadn't even known each other until this had begun, that their homes were in different places and that she had no idea what the future would hold. But life seldom had such perfect moments and she was going to cling to these.

She wasn't sure what she expected him to say. Maybe something about its being damned good sex, if not something more intimate and personal, like, *My God, that was the most extraordinary experience I've ever had.*

Maybe that was her line. The words whispered silently in her head.

Malachi raised himself up on one elbow and looked down at her, a smile playing on his lips as he quizzically said, "Certifiably crazy?"

Shift gears! she told herself.

"*I* know you're not certifiably crazy. I just

don't know what *they're* going to think," she said. "You never cease to amaze me. I've been warned my whole life not to mention the fact that I see a ghost, and it sounds like you've never said anything, either — and then you announce to a bunch of murder suspects that the ghost of Blue Anderson is wandering around."

"You don't think it was a good idea?" he asked.

"They all looked at you as if you'd lost your mind," Abby said.

"Hmm."

"Hmm?"

"If they're innocent, of course, they'll figure I'm crazy. But if the guilty party was among them, then that guilty party will start thinking. Because I planted it in his mind, he'll start to worry that ghost of Blue just *might* be around," Malachi told her. "He'll start looking over his shoulder."

"So there's a method to your madness?"

"There's always a method to my madness." Dark hair fell in a swath across his forehead. She thought he was more endearing, lying there, than any male could be. "Sadly, however, there's little method to my social skills," he said. He bent over and kissed her lips with a lingering wistfulness. "You're . . . incredible. That's lame. But you are."

She smiled. "Incredible isn't so lame."

He lay back down, pulling her against his chest. She felt cherished, and yet . . .

She felt respected, as well. He would want to shield her from danger, she knew. But she sensed that he would also have faith in her.

But as happy as she was with her personal situation, she couldn't stop thinking about what was going on. She wanted to jump out of bed and find the young woman who'd probably been taken. She felt she should rush to the river again, run up and down the street, do *anything* rather than nothing. And yet she knew that such feelings were worthless; she'd learned about patience, being precise, following clues — controlling the impulse to become so emotionally involved that you couldn't act. Or acted recklessly.

Trust was important. She had to trust that David Caswell was a good cop and that Jackson Crow knew what he was doing.

And still her mind raced.

"Tap . . . tap, tap, tap," she murmured.

"That's exactly what I was thinking," Malachi said.

"Really?" She rose up to meet his eyes. He stroked her hair thoughtfully.

"It means something," he said. "I keep thinking that, soon enough, I'll figure out what."

"And you still include Dirk and Roger in your suspect list?" Abby asked.

"I do. If they make any movements tonight, we'll know."

"Oh?"

"Will's been keeping an eye on Roger since he left the tavern this afternoon. He didn't stay here long, had a quick drink, then took off." He shook his head. "I believe his emotion is real. If it turns out he's our killer, I'm losing my touch. But, for now, don't worry. Lie down. We have officers out there watching and searching. On the riverfront. Cruising around city hall . . . down the east and the west sides of the city. There are people out there, Abby. Let them do their jobs."

Nodding, she lay back down beside him.

Music. Helen had heard music. She'd been thrown into the water not long before Abby saw her.

That meant the killer had been out on the water. He'd been within their grasp.

Tap, tap, tap.

She felt Malachi stir and moved deeper into his arms.

She dreamed of making love again.

They fell asleep.

Malachi lay awake, smiling when he heard Abby's easy breathing. She was exhausted. There was an emotional toll in all of this, especially since it came right after her grandfather's death. She hadn't really had time to mourn his passing before a connection between his death and that of the recent victims had become plausible and apparent to her — and now the body count was adding up. He rolled onto his side and turned to watch her sleep, studying the contours of her face. He found himself wondering why certain people fell into such a profound attraction, why the physical act could mean something so different, depending on how you felt about that person. He reached out, just to touch her hair, but started when he heard his phone ringing.

He scrambled from the bed and searched for the jeans he'd discarded somewhere. He hurried down the hall until he found them and dug into his pocket.

The caller was Will Chan.

"Roger English is on the move," Will said. "I'm following him now. He left his house and he's headed toward Bay Street if you want to join me."

"Has he seen you?" Malachi asked.

"Hasn't made me yet. He was walking fast but then he stopped, pulled out his phone, looked at it — muttered to himself — and then began walking again."

"I'll be there in a few minutes!" Malachi said.

He started to slide back into his clothing. Hopping into his jeans, he turned and nearly crashed into Abby. Her hair was a tangle; her eyes were wide. "Where are we going?" she asked.

"After Roger."

She frowned but said no more. He had to hand it to her; she could dress fast. She was dressed — slipping her Glock into her waistband — while he was still tying his shoes.

The Dragonslayer was silent as they crept down the stairs. It was after the night crew had left, before the morning crew came in. They hurried out and he waited to make sure Abby locked the front door.

He took her hand as they ran across the parking lot and toward Bay Street. He saw no one there, and Malachi quickly drew his phone from his pocket and called Will back.

"Where are you?"

"In front of city hall, on the river," Will replied. "He's pacing by the water. Keeps looking out at it. Pulls his phone in and out of his pocket."

"Come on," he told Abby, catching her hand again.

They ran up onto the embankment to reach the river walk and crossed by closed stores, restaurants and taverns, staying close to the shop fronts to meld with the shadows. As they moved silently closer, someone stepped out from the buildings.

Will. He beckoned to them and they joined him behind a pillar.

The three stood there silently as they observed Roger English.

Roger paced and then stood still and stared out at the river. Malachi looked down the length of shops. There were other people in the shadows, he realized.

True to his word, David Caswell had officers on surveillance. Watching the river.

And now, watching Roger.

Was he about to call someone — someone out on the river who had a captive?

They waited what seemed to be a very long time while Roger walked up and down, continuing to stare out at the water.

He clutched the cell phone and pulled something from his pocket, then stuffed it back. He began to dial.

Who was he calling?

Malachi jumped as he felt his phone buzz

in his pocket. Stepping back, he looked at it.

Roger was calling *him.*

He glanced at the others and hurried a distance away, then answered his phone.

"Roger?" he whispered.

"Yeah, it's me," Roger said. As Malachi watched, Roger glanced at his phone, as if trying to figure out how Malachi had known it was him.

"I haven't given this number to many people," Malachi explained.

"Oh, yeah? Well, thanks. Look, I'm sorry to wake you. I know what time it is but . . . you said to call. I'm down on the riverfront, right near city hall. Dumb, I know. But I couldn't stand it. I couldn't stand doing nothing. And I realize there are cops out here, too — I believe someone is on this 24/7 — but I think I can see something out on the water. I think it's a rowboat. There's nothing else out there, but can you get here?"

"Yeah. Give me two minutes. I'm up and I'm close. I'll be right there." *A rowboat.* He thought of what Blue had said.

Roger turned; Malachi didn't know how, but he seemed to home right in on his location.

He walked toward him. "Malachi?" he asked.

Malachi walked toward Roger at the same time. "You said it. People are watching the river."

"Have you seen anything?" Roger asked.

Will and Abby came out of the shadows, coming over to join them. "*Everybody's* watching the river?" Roger asked. Malachi wasn't sure if he felt reassured, stalked or just mystified.

"What is it you saw?" Malachi asked.

"Come here. Come straight to the edge and you'll see. It's moving with the current," Roger said.

"I'll get Jackson." Will stepped aside to make the call.

"Do you see it?" Roger demanded.

Malachi did; it was dark out on the water and the current was moving, but every few seconds, the moonlight touched down on something. He understood why Roger had stared out at the water for so long. It was there, and then it seemed to disappear in the darkness.

"We need to go out there and get it," Roger said.

Abby put a hand on his arm. "Will's calling for a boat to tow it in, to find out what's going on. Maybe you should —"

"Should what?" Roger shouted. "Go home? I can't, Abby. Come on — you know I can't do that!"

"I'm sorry, Roger. You're right. We'll just stay here and wait." She came to him as a friend and slipped an arm around him, standing by his side.

Only seconds later, they saw a marine patrol boat with lights flashing streak along the river. They saw it slow down and circle the object. The moon went behind a cloud and as it reappeared, they saw an officer tossing out a towrope.

Malachi's phone rang. He answered immediately.

Roger stared at him.

"It's a rowboat and there's nothing in it," he told Roger. "Possibly, it just broke away from a dock. They'll tow it in. It might have no connection to the case."

"Empty," Roger repeated dully. Then he grew animated again. "That could mean that . . . she's in the river. Tell them . . . tell them they have to search the water. They have to search the water until they find her! Like when Abby saw Helen. What if he threw her out of that rowboat? If he did, she's in the water somewhere!"

"Roger," Malachi said, placing his hands on the man's shoulders and focusing on his eyes. "There had to be someone in the rowboat to throw someone else in the water. There was no one in the boat."

Roger seemed to deflate. His shoulders slumped. "Yeah, you're right. I guess you're right. But . . . but she could be out there."

"So is the patrol," Malachi said.

"Yeah, I know," Roger said. "I've got other people running my tours for me. I'm available if there's anything I can do. I mean, hell, I'm here whether you want anything from me or not. I'll be walking around. I'll be looking. I can't give up."

"Rog, how well did you know Bianca?" Abby asked. "I mean, everyone's on the lookout because of what's been happening, but she could have lost her phone or decided not to . . . pursue the relationship."

"I might've just met her," Roger said, "but there was something there, Abby. I don't believe Bianca blew me off and disappeared."

"Okay, I'm sorry," Abby murmured.

Mollified, Roger looked back at the river. "I guess . . . I guess I'll go home for a while. Sleep."

"Come on. Let's all walk back," Malachi said.

"You guys don't need to babysit me," Roger protested. "You sure don't need to go out of your way."

"I'm staying at Abby's house on Chippewa," Will told him. "I'll walk back with you, Roger."

"My place is just past Abby's."

"Yeah?" Will said. "Then we're going the same way."

The two of them started walking ahead, but Roger stopped and turned back. "I thought you all were watching the river?"

"Shift is over. New crew coming on," Malachi said to him.

Roger nodded and then saw Abby. He came back and threw his arms around her in a warm hug. "Thank you," he said.

"Love ya, Rog."

"You, too." He nodded, then turned, hurrying to catch up with Will. Malachi's phone vibrated; he grabbed it quickly and heard Jackson's voice. "When you get back in the Dragonslayer, take a look at the footage on the computer screens."

"Anything wrong? Anything I should worry about?" Malachi asked.

"No, nothing wrong. But a little bizarre. Interesting. Have a look, then get some sleep."

"What?" Abby asked as Malachi slipped his phone into his pocket.

"Nothing. Jackson's just checking in," he said.

He and Abby walked slowly behind Will and Roger, coming along the riverfront and then hiking over to Bay and down toward the Dragonslayer.

When the other two split off, heading to the center of the old town, Abby waved. "I feel like such a jerk," she said. "Roger and I went to school together from the time we were kids."

"And you're being a good friend. Remember, part of shadowing people is to clear them," Malachi reminded her.

As they returned to the Dragonslayer, he noticed that the sun was just coming up.

"Let's get a few hours' sleep," he said huskily.

Abby nodded. "Good idea."

The morning crew had yet to arrive. Abby unlocked the door and they trudged up to the second-floor apartment. She started for the bedroom; he wanted to follow.

"I'm just going to check the screens. I'll be right there," he told her.

He sat down and looked at the various views of the Dragonslayer. Nothing. He ran the footage back, quickly at first. Then he reran it, closely studying the screen that showed the front of the Dragonslayer.

He saw himself and Abby leaving. They went out of view.

He glanced to see the time; they were gone about ten minutes when someone else approached the Dragonslayer.

Head down.

Most of the time when a person or persons couldn't be identified on video, it was because of a sweatshirt with a hoodie.

But this person wasn't in a hoodie. He wore a sweeping hat and a cloak. A long black cloak.

But the figure reached the Dragonslayer and seemed about to try the door, then abruptly stepped back. The hat still blocked any view of the face. "Look up, you bastard!" Malachi muttered.

But the person didn't look up. Apparently, something at the Dragonslayer had spooked him.

Malachi went through the footage of the bar area and saw a shadow appear just inside the front door.

"Blue," Malachi whispered. "Blue, you *are* watching over this place."

He typed a message to Jackson. Maybe Will could enhance the footage in the morning; maybe there was some information they could get.

Jackson was still at the computer in Abby's house.

Police closest to the area were dispatched. They were there in minutes but the person was gone, and out of camera range almost immediately.

While we were by the river.

Yes.

Do you think the cameras scared him off?

Don't know. Camera would be pretty obvious if it was someone who knew the Dragonslayer.

Any hope of enhancing the footage?

I'll get Will on it later in the morning. Rowboat taken to the forensic lab. I'll report as soon as we learn anything.

OK. Grabbing a few hours sleep.

I'm on for the next few hours here. Angela spells me at eight. Police know to call at any time. I'll keep you posted.

Malachi signed off and walked down the

hallway to Abby's room. He went in and tiptoed over to the bed.

Abby was sound asleep. She'd set her gun on the dresser — hadn't even taken off her clothes. He pulled a blanket over her, stripped and lay down himself. He stayed awake for a few minutes, once again wondering about the mysterious noise Helen had reported.

Tap, tap, tap. He knew it meant something. But *what*?

Abby woke up with a jolt. It felt very late, and although the drapes were drawn, she could feel the warmth of the sun pouring in.

She dashed out of the room and found Malachi sitting at the computers.

"Good morning," he said.

"What time is it?" she asked.

"Ten."

"Ten! We should be up and doing something."

"You'll notice that I am," he said with a laugh. "But when you're ready, we'll go back to the area around the cemetery and the Wulf and Whistle."

"All right. I just have to send a few emails before we go."

"Okay, take your time."

"Take my time?" Abby echoed. "No, no, I slept a lot. We have to get started! If this guy is following his usual timelines, Bianca doesn't have much longer. But if we're going back to the cemetery today, I have to live up to my promise about having that tombstone repaired."

"Do you know who to contact?" Malachi asked.

"I know a few people on the city council. I'll write the emails to get things started." She walked over to the desk near the balcony, where she'd left her laptop, and then paused, looking at him. "So, how am I going to explain why I know all this? We don't really have an opportunity to research it."

"Just say it came up when the bureau was investigating. They won't ask anything else if you do that. I'll tell Jackson. He really can get someone on the research," Malachi said.

Abby nodded and she retrieved her notepad before she quickly sat down.

" 'Lieutenant Josiah Beckwith,' " she read. " 'Born April 9, 1790. Died for his country, September 12, 1814, at the Battle of North Point during the War of 1812. Beloved son, husband and father. A patriot.' I have it all — yes?"

"Yes."

Abby looked through her list of email

contacts, selected a few of the influential people she knew on city council and wrote something vague about finding the information while investigating the cemetery on an FBI case. She asked that the situation be rectified, that the gravestone defaced during the Civil War be repaired.

As she typed, Malachi walked over to her.

"How many people around here dress up as pirates?" he asked. She realized that he was holding a cup of coffee for her, which she accepted gratefully.

"*Lots* of people dress up as pirates," Abby said. "Why?"

"Come on back to the computers when you're done there," he told her. "Finish your emails first."

She did, and when she approached the computer screens, she saw that Malachi had frozen a frame of the video. It showed someone standing in front of the Dragon-slayer.

Someone who looked very strange.

She could see nothing of the actual person. A massive, plumed pirate hat hid the face, and a sweeping black cloak encompassed him to a degree that hid his size. If it *was* a him. Abby thought that it was — the person appeared to be tall.

"When was that?" she asked Malachi.

"At 3:32 a.m.," Malachi told her.

"When we were down by the river," Abby said.

"He was trying to get in here?"

"So I assume. But he stopped."

"Did he try the door? Or did he not even reach it?"

"Never tried it," Malachi said, leaning back. "They saw it on the screens at your house on Chippewa, too, of course. They called the police right away, but by the time a couple of officers arrived . . ."

"He was already gone," Abby concluded with a sigh.

"Yup. And I don't think he was afraid of the cameras. I think he knew about them and that's why he was smart enough to keep his head down. I think he was afraid of Blue."

Abby stepped back. "You saw Blue? Was he on one of these screens?"

"No," Malachi told her. "But . . . here's an image the camera did pick up."

Abby looked over his shoulder as he replayed the footage of the host stand and bar area, along with the front of the restaurant.

A dark shadow appeared just behind the entry door.

"Is that a trick of the video, of the light?

Or is it . . . something?" Abby asked.

"Well," Malachi mused. "It's definitely something."

"Do ghosts record this way?"

He smiled at her. "Maybe. I don't really know. But . . . I do believe that Blue is watching over this place."

"And you believe this . . . killer is someone who spends a lot of time in the Dragon-slayer. And it's the guy in the plumed hat."

He nodded. "Let's head over to the cemetery. We'll see what our old folks have to say."

Macy was at the host stand, and Abby went over to her. "Is everything all right?"

"Yes, of course, Abby. What about you? How are you doing with all this?"

"I'm okay."

Macy glanced past Abby at Malachi and smiled. "I'm so glad you're here — all of you. For Abby."

"Thank you, Macy," Malachi said. "By the way, do you remember much about the day before Gus's funeral?"

"Um, it was pretty much a day like any other. We had the signs up, that the restaurant would be closed the next day. There was an announcement made at the service that the mourners were welcome to join us here after, and we wanted to limit it to the people who'd known Gus well, not have casual tourists wandering in."

She seemed perplexed, uncertain about his reasons for asking.

"I'm talking about the time just after Helen Long left the restaurant," he said. "Do you remember anyone who might've left soon after she did? How about our barflies?"

Macy looked at him blankly for a moment. Her lower lip trembled slightly. "Helen's been found. Abby saved her."

"Yes, but another young woman is missing and Helen hasn't been able to give us much information. I'm hoping you can help us." He leaned on the host stand, meeting her eyes. He really had a curiously charming way about him, Abby thought. More so, perhaps, because he had no idea.

"I'd love to help you!" Macy said. "I wasn't down here the whole time. I was going back and forth, between the restaurant and supply room. And we were so distracted that day, too. But . . . oh, I think both Aldous and Bootsie left in the early afternoon. And wait! Yes, I know Dirk left even before they did because he took his ship out. He worked the *Black Swan*'s morning and afternoon shifts because he knew he wouldn't do either one the next day. But . . .

I could be off on my times."

"Terrific, Macy. Anything else?"

Macy shook her head. "No, I was here. Later Sullivan went up to do an inventory to get our orders in, since we knew everyone would be preoccupied the next day. More than that, I can't say."

"You've been very helpful, Macy," Malachi told her. "Thank you."

"If there's ever anything I can do . . ." Macy's voice trailed off.

Malachi thanked her again and turned to leave; Abby followed. They walked the few blocks to Colonial Park Cemetery.

That day, Abby let herself really look around the cemetery and *see*. She saw the old couple, vigilant as ever on their bench. A young woman in a long white gown seemed to float behind a live oak that dripped with moss. A grinning soldier stood behind a group of tourists; he blew on a girl's neck and his grin broadened when she spun around, looking for the prankster. Across the way, hovering by one of the monuments, two young women in early-nineteenth century clothing seemed to be taking a casual walk through the stones.

Malachi, she thought, noticed them all. He was, however, fixated on the older couple.

"Good morning," he said, pausing by the bench.

"Good morning, young sir," the man said, standing politely.

"We wanted to let you know that Abby has written the necessary people about your son's gravestone. We are in the process of getting the situation rectified," Malachi told him.

"We thank you sincerely." The man bowed. "My love," he said to his wife, "a great dishonor will be set right."

The woman rose, as well. She looked at them, and Abby could almost believe there were real tears in her eyes.

But she wasn't there. Except as . . .

Heart, soul, spirit?

"I wish I could set every situation right." Abby decided not to add that, through the years, gravestones hadn't just been defaced, some had disappeared altogether. She wanted to tell them that cemeteries were really for the living. The dead remained alive in their loved one's memories.

"We found a tunnel in an old building," Malachi said. "Right down the street, in the area you kindly pointed out to me. But it brought us to a dead end. Have you noticed anything else?"

"You looked inside, not in the alley?" the

351

man asked.

"We'll go back," Malachi said. "We'll keep looking. Inside and out."

"There was a time, not long after the war — the war that took our son — when the dead were often taken beneath the ground. The dead and dying. The yellow fever . . . they did everything they could to fight it. And when it was over, I believe they tried to hide the epidemic and how many it claimed." He spoke thoughtfully. "We were the South. Our economy was cotton — and the river. The cotton plantations, of course, depended on slaves. But there were those who hated slavery. Early on before the other war, I heard they began to use some of those tunnels to hide people who were escaping. We, my wife and I, we closed our eyes. I was a merchant here, and I knew how the plantations worked, but . . . in my heart, I also knew it was wrong. If I remember . . ." He looked at his wife. "If I remember, we saw people in the night back then. Hurrying down the streets. Disappearing into the alley, into the darkness."

"Thank you," Malachi went to shake the man's hand; Abby watched a ghostly hand touch Malachi's in return.

She lowered her head, smiling. He thought he was awkward with people. He wasn't.

352

He was very good.

With the living *and* the dead.

"Thank you," Abby echoed. She and Malachi hurried across the cemetery to leave by the main entrance. They passed tour groups and couples, parents and children.

They walked back toward the Wulf and Whistle. The buildings on the street were flush with one another; space here was at a premium. But a narrow alley stretched between streets, an alley that was no longer passable by any kind of conveyance. A tree that had taken root blocked it at the sidewalk. Malachi and Abby crawled over the roots that sprouted through the concrete, and they stood in the narrow alley behind the Wulf and Whistle.

"Who knows exactly what was going on when," Malachi murmured, studying the building. "But there *was* a tunnel in the Wulf and Whistle. Presumably, during the yellow fever epidemic, they were bringing the sick and the dead down to various tunnels and underground rooms. Then, when the Underground Railroad became active, they reopened the tunnels. After the war — the Civil War, this time — the local owners, aware of what went on at the cemetery, which was now under military rule, might have hurried and covered up their secrets."

"But we went down into the Wulf and Whistle. You tapped all the walls in the tunnel there yourself."

"Yes, but an entry from the tavern might have been sealed off. That doesn't mean there aren't more tunnels beneath us."

"And how are we going to find one? And if it's all blocked off, how's a killer using it?"

"The killer, obviously, knows where it is," Malachi said. "And, somehow or other, he's opened it."

Abby turned around in the little space. Behind the Wulf and Whistle was a wooden portico and a gate that sectioned off an area. She realized that was where the tavern kept their garbage.

"Hey!" she said.

She went to the gate and opened it. She saw a bin there and threw it open. Inside it was another bin that could be removed to dump the garbage.

"Malachi!" she called.

He hurried over to her. "They'd never need to move this," she said. "They obviously always lift out the inner bin when they have to empty it. Steve must have some of his employees take it to the end of the alley for garbage pickup."

Malachi walked around behind the giant bin. Planked grating supported the bin and stretched about two feet behind it. He bent down and raised the wooden planks.

"There's a hole," he said. "A big black hole. Shall we?"

12

The hole went straight down. At some point, Malachi thought, the tunnel must have been dug as part of a sewage system. Maybe those dealing with the yellow fever outbreak used it, and for the Underground Railroad any route was better than no route. It was good to think that there'd been those willing to risk everything to help others, just as it was chilling to think about the fear escaping slaves must have felt when they slipped into the tunnels. He could imagine them praying that they'd reach a ship, and that the ship would take them north without being stopped and searched.

The tunnel smelled dank. Malachi thought about death and disease and human misery as he crawled down the treacherous earth ladder that led to the floor below. Hitting the ground, he dug in his pocket for his flashlight, then shone the light over the length of the tunnel. Like the others, this one appeared to head straight for the river.

"Careful," he told Abby. "The grips are old and weak." He set his flashlight on the ground and reached up to help her make her way down.

"Plus wet and nasty," Abby murmured.

"Yeah. But let's see where this goes."

"Should we have called it in?" Abby asked.

"No. The killer could well have seen all the commotion going on at the Wulf and Whistle. He might be amused now, assuming we had it completely wrong. I don't want him to know we've found this place. If he doesn't know, he might try to make use of it again."

Abby nodded. She had a small flashlight herself and she waved it before them, letting the light fall over the earth walls.

As they moved along the length of the tunnel, it began to narrow. Halfway down, they came across a break in one of the walls.

The fork and the main tunnel stretched ahead, both stygian in their darkness. They looked at each other in the eerie glow of the flashlights. "No splitting up," Malachi said.

"I wasn't about to suggest it. Good agents trust in their partners and their backup."

"Then I say we go right."

Abby considered where she was for a moment. "I'm trying to figure out where we are — where we'd be if we were on street level. We'd be heading back to the Dragonslayer."

"Yes," he said.

"Let's go."

The tunnel was narrow; in places, dirt was falling in. They walked for what Abby estimated was at least a block.

After that, they walked for the equivalent of another block. As they did, she heard their feet scraping on the rough ground. Malachi stopped and touched the walls.

"Are these tunnels solid?" she asked.

"They seem to be. They were dug properly, support beams were set in . . . we're safe. They seem to be in better shape than half the new housing you'll see," Malachi remarked.

They kept walking, their flashlights illuminating the way. And then they came to a solid wall of earth.

"Well, this is great," Abby complained.

"Actually, it is," Malachi said, stepping back.

"Why do you say that?"

"You know about where we are?" he asked.

"Yes," she said slowly. "We're almost at the Dragonslayer."

"Start at the very end, then back up. Feel the walls. Feel them, tap them . . . tell me when you feel something different. Let's put the lights down and shine them on the walls."

They did so, one light facing left, the other pointed toward the right.

Abby moved along the walls, testing them. They seemed to be earth, but the long-gone architects of the tunnels had given them support beams and arches. Dampness had damaged some of the wood that shored up the walls, but she assumed they would have used a hardwood that didn't easily decompose. After all, they'd lasted this long.

She was so intent on her work that she was startled when she heard Malachi shout, "Aha!"

She turned around. At first, all she saw was darkness and the glare of the light — but then she realized that the light was creating *shades* of darkness. Malachi had found another fork in the tunnel.

"How . . . There was wall there before!" Abby said.

"That mud patch with the vine attached is like something I have at my house in Virginia. In the house, it's called a pocket door. The wall slides into a pocket in the rest of the wall."

Abby picked up her flashlight and stood by his side. She gasped. "Malachi — that's the end of the tunnel that leads from the Dragonslayer!"

"That's what I figured," he said. "So, our killer's been able to access the Dragonslayer from the Wulf and Whistle, the Wulf and Whistle from the Dragonslayer and the river from either of them."

"We can shut off the bastard, cement him in," Abby said bitterly.

Malachi shook his head. "Not if we want to find him while Bianca is still living."

"So what do we do?"

"Right now, we go back. We pretend we've never been here — and we get Will to bring in some cameras. We need to follow this killer wherever he's going. That's how we'll rescue Bianca."

Malachi stepped through the hole he'd created in the tunnel wall. He inspected the pocket into which he'd slid the wooden door that had originally seemed to be just more earth-and-hardwood tunnel wall. "At my house," he told Abby, "this kind of door was used to turn the place into a tavern by night — a way stop for travelers — and then back into separate rooms for working and sleeping. Thomas Jefferson's family had apparently been involved with the building of my house. I really have one of those places where you get to say 'Washington slept here.' But I believe this technique must've been common during colonial days."

"I guess these tunnels were used at various times, for various reasons," she mused.

Malachi nodded. "City planners might have started them, pirates might have continued to use them — to shanghai others or to effect their own escapes. And then they became important to the Underground Railroad during the Civil War. At other times, the city or property owners sealed up entrances, as well as these secret doorways from one tunnel to another. Remember, governments — federal, state and municipal — usually do whatever is cheapest. You don't need a tunnel, then seal up the entrance. If you know the city and you've heard about its history all your life — and studied it — you might realize where to look for these entrances."

"I know the city!" Abby said.

"Yep, and you knew about the tunnel under the Dragonslayer because it was *your* tunnel. You knew about the hospital tunnels because their existence and the history of what went on during the yellow fever epidemic was recorded — sketchily, yes, but there were records," Malachi said. He offered her a dry smile. "Since you were never looking for a way to kidnap people and take them out on the river, you probably never tried to explore underground Savannah as thoroughly as our killer did. Come on, let's go back to where we came in. I don't want to use the Dragonslayer tunnel and the tavern stairs. The dining room will be full right now, and I don't want to be seen."

"Let's hope nobody sees us crawling through the garbage," Abby said.

"Yeah," Malachi agreed. "I'm going to give Jackson a call so he can arrange for someone to watch the entrance here. Someone in plain clothes who won't be noticed. Jackson will have to talk to David Caswell, get someone he trusts implicitly." He had his phone out, tried to call, then made a face at her.

"Well, that was dumb. No signals down here. Come on. Let's go back up as smoothly as we can and get someone down here." He grinned at her. "After that, we need to shower again. Another reason I'd rather not go to the Dragonslayer — I don't want to be seen like this. We'll go to your house on Chippewa, okay?"

Abby nodded. Malachi closed the pocket door, and they made their way back through the tunnel.

Abby's flashlight reflected off something on the floor. She instinctively started to pick it up and then didn't. She hunkered down and took a closer look; Malachi hunkered down next to her. "Gum wrapper," he said. "Or part of a gum wrapper."

"Fingerprints?"

"Possible, yes," Malachi said. He glanced at her. Even in the eerie light, there was a beauty, a strength, in his face. Not only that, she couldn't remember being able to communicate with anyone as she could with him.

It was the ghost thing.

It was the sex.

It was whatever made him unique.

"Certainly not an eighteenth- or nineteenth-century object," he said. He was prepared; he reached into his pocket and she saw that he had a little envelope. He turned it inside out to pick up the ripped gum wrapper, secured it without touching it and slid it into his pocket. He took her arm, drawing her up. "Okay, let's get out of here now."

He hoisted Abby up and out of the hole. She turned around to help him, but he'd gotten a grip on the tenuous ladder to get himself up.

"Wow," he said, looking at her. "Let's hope we don't run into anyone we know."

"That's not easy here. I know a lot of

363

people."

"We'll just hang back for a minute. Let me call Jackson and get him talking to David. I'll tell him what we've found and why we don't want to make it public yet." He put the call through to Jackson, who said he'd be there soon, and then leaned against the wall as they waited. The alley smelled of rotting garbage.

"Great place to hang around," Abby said.

Malachi grinned. "I've been in worse."

He stared at her and she asked, *"What?"*

"You even look good festooned in dirt."

"So do you!"

He smiled, but his smile faded. His mind, she realized, was always moving, often along a number of different tracks at once.

"Timing is everything in a crime like this," he said. "It's not that it's difficult to get around. We've been within blocks of the same area, so someone who needs to get from place to place with very little time can do it easily. But still, if we could just pinpoint who was where when . . . At least we could eliminate people."

"Do you believe that Roger is really in the clear?" Abby asked.

He shrugged. "I do. There isn't any proof."

A moment later, Jackson Crow walked into the alley. He was with a man who was close to six feet with beautiful café-au-lait skin, thirty-five or so, and wearing an *I Love Savannah* T-shirt, the kind sold in dozens of tourist shops.

"Officer Dale Kendrick," Jackson said, introducing him. "He'll be keeping an eye on the alley. And he transferred in from Atlanta recently, so it's not likely he'd be recognized by anyone here."

They shook hands with Kendrick. Malachi handed the gum wrapper over to Jackson, who would bring it to Forensics. Will was back on the *Black Swan,* and Angela and Kat were spelling each other on the screens. Will had enhanced the footage showing the strange figure approaching the Dragonslayer the night before. But no matter how enhanced, the face was hidden. However, they could eliminate anyone under six feet. Jackson left them to head down to the station; he was due to meet with David at Forensics to see if anything had been discovered regarding the rowboat they'd found in the river. He left them.

"On to Chippewa Square," Malachi announced.

He shook hands with Kendrick again, thanking him. "It's my job," Kendrick told him, waving as they walked off.

They hurried to the house, hoping no one

would notice them in their dirty, disheveled state. Luckily, tourists were distracted by their own destinations or the beauty of the homes, the street and the moss-draped live oaks.

Angela came to the door and looked them up and down, a trace of amusement on her face. "Cute. You're like children out of a very dirty sandpile."

"That's something to think about," Malachi said.

"What's that?" Abby asked.

"The dirt. This person has to come out of these tunnels dirty — unless he's going all the way through, and not coming back until he's been out on whatever vessel he has on the river."

"Good point," Angela said. "And, by the way, Will worked with the city and got a camera up on the exit to the riverbank from the Dragonslayer. They were careful setting it up so they weren't seen doing it. We won't want to scare anyone off. No one will be able to use that venue again without being instantly visible. Come into the dining room and I'll show you."

They followed her. There'd been another camera set up; it looked out over the embankment where Abby had plunged into the river to save Helen Long.

"That's good. See anything?" Malachi asked.

"A lot of tourists," Angela said with a sigh. She smiled at Abby. "So, you're thinking about joining us?"

"What?" Abby asked, startled by the question.

"You've already been through the academy. I'm assuming you're expecting an assignment when this is over. I believe Jackson intends to suggest you join us."

"Be — be part of the Krewe?" Abby stammered.

"The rest of the bureau may talk about us behind our backs," Angela said, "but we're actually considered a pretty elite group."

Abby glanced at Malachi. He'd known, she thought. He was watching her, waiting for her reaction.

"I guess we should get through this first," Abby said. She turned quickly. "I'll go up and shower," she said. "Oh." She looked at Malachi. "I have a few clothes here. But —"

"Malachi and Jackson are about the same size. It's not a problem," Angela said. "If it was, one of us would just run over to the tavern. So, go and shower. There's nothing like a shower to wash away dirt and to clear the mind."

"Here's hoping," Abby said, and sped up

the stairs to her own room.

She'd given the Krewe carte blanche with her house; she noted that they'd apparently recognized this room as hers and chosen other ones.

She looked around. She'd rented it furnished and during her most recent visit, with the place empty, she'd brought her old treasures back to this room, out of nostalgia more than practicality. Maybe because her life was on the verge of change . . . The bookshelves were filled with her beloved fiction — and the books she'd devoured on law enforcement, the FBI, profiling, unsolved cases and the minds of killers.

I must have been a pretty scary kid, she thought.

The guitar she'd never quite learned to play sat, once again, in its stand near her closet. A stack of board games lay on a table in a corner. The room was still decorated in royal blue with black trim, nothing girly or frilly about it.

She had never owned a doll.

She examined her old CDs and DVDs, which she'd arranged on one of the shelves. She'd collected some weird and obscure music and some classics. She'd been in love with the Traveling Wilburys and the various band members and their solo careers and work. She'd watched everything ever done by M. Night Shyamalan.

She'd also owned *Blythe Spirit,* which her father had taken her to see on Broadway, and *Ghost, The Ghost and Mrs. Muir . . .*

Because she had her own ghost?

She smiled a little bitterly. "Blue, I do have my own ghost — so where are you? It's you and me now, you know?"

Her half smile cracked some of the dried mud on her face.

The shower. She went in and turned the spray on hot and hard. A shower felt great on the body and great for the mind, as Angela had suggested.

However, it didn't really do much for *her* mind. Although it did make her forget — for the moment — that they were in a battle against time if they were going to find Bianca Salzburg.

It made her wish she wasn't in the shower alone.

She winced.

She was becoming obsessed with Malachi. A good thing? Or not? What if they'd just discovered each other simply because of the circumstances? What if what she felt wasn't real and what if their personal relationship fell apart and they both became part of the Krewe?

She needed to think carefully.

She still wished he was there in the shower with her.

A shower could clear the mind.

Malachi didn't really want his mind cleared; he wanted to put everything within it in order.

First. Theories he was convinced could be proven, or were, in effect, proven by what they knew.

Like his belief that the killer was someone who knew Savannah, knew it extremely well, and knew the history of the city.

Second. The killer thought he was a pirate or wished he was a pirate in days gone by. He'd given Helen Long a card with a name on it, Christopher Condent, and Condent had been a brutal pirate who'd never faced justice, eventually becoming a rich man.

Third. The killer was dressing up as Blue Anderson.

Because there were so many good images of Blue? Or because of the sweeping hat Blue had worn, his long dark hair and the facial hair that could hide a real identity? And did the motivation involve his theory that the killer wanted to discredit the real Blue Anderson? If so, was there any connection to the fact that the victims had all been to the Dragonslayer before they were abducted?

Fourth. A mental note, really. He thought he had the killer narrowed down; he'd be shocked if he was wrong. It was someone close to Abby. Someone who was close to the Dragonslayer and had known Gus well. Someone familiar with the legends of Blue and other pirates, and, perhaps, someone in a solid business position. He'd need a certain amount of money to move about easily, to join others at a bar, to appear to be part of the everyday community. Perhaps he wasn't young or attractive, but he would know how to make others think he was kind and nice. He was dressing up and proud of the fact that he was fooling people, including his own peers. No one knew him when he went into pirate mode to attack his victims.

Malachi got out of the shower. Angela had left him several pieces of Jackson's clothing. He didn't want to look like an agent but he wanted clothing that didn't advertise the fact that he was carrying a weapon. He chose jeans, a polo shirt and a navy windbreaker. He was going to drink with the barflies today, get them talking, learn more about them. And he'd do it with Abby, who would know what was true and what wasn't and if any of the trio — or even Sullivan, Macy or Grant Green — behaved strangely.

Downstairs, he was glad to find Kat Sokolov at the dining room table, watching the screens that patrolled the Dragonslayer and now the river embankment, too.

"Kat, what about the victim from the tunnels? Have they identified her yet?"

Kat shook her head. "They have her DNA and took dental X-rays, but there's nothing to compare them to. I received some possible candidates from the database, but nothing definitive."

Malachi sighed. "A woman's murdered and we don't even know who she is."

"Do you think it would help us find the young woman who may still be alive if we did know who the other victim is?"

"Maybe not. But the thing is we have three dead women, one who escaped and a dead man. We also believe Gus was a victim. We assume that both men were killed because they stumbled onto something. The women were new to Savannah, although Helen Long had been here for a while. They were all attractive — all beautiful female captives. But I suspect the killer saw them, watched them, before he took them. I suspect he's looking for a woman to be the perfect mate in his life of pirate crime."

Abby had come down and stood in the doorway.

"He has a whole fantasy built up," Abby said, continuing Malachi's narrative. "He's the pirate who seizes a captive and the captive falls in love with him, eschews her old life and joins him on the high seas. Perhaps the killer thought he had the right woman with Helen — but she kept saying she was repulsed by him. She didn't want him to touch her, and she couldn't pretend. That's what happens when he gets to the point where he feels rejected, he kills. And then he searches for another woman."

The others nodded.

Abby lifted her hands. "How does this help us, though?"

"It *does* help us. We watch for someone who . . . watches," Malachi told her. "Let's head back to the Dragonslayer."

"Because we're going to find the killer there?"

He studied her for a moment. She was obviously trying to keep the bitterness out of her voice.

"Yes," he said. "Because we'll find him there."

It was late for lunch, but the Dragonslayer was still doing a booming business. Macy

373

was at the host stand, and Bootsie and Aldous were at the bar. Abby got up onto the stool next to Aldous. He'd just finished a plate of fish and chips, and while she affectionately called him a barfly, he wasn't drinking; he sipped from a cup of coffee.

"How are you holding up?" he asked, nodding at Malachi, who sat beside Abby.

"I'm fine, Aldous. Just confused — like everyone else. And scared. There's another girl out there somewhere, and I'm hoping we can find her, as we did Helen. Alive, I mean."

"Yeah, alive. It's a sorry thing, huh? And your friend Roger English — is he broken up over it!"

"I know. They'd just started dating, but he felt he'd found the 'one,' " Abby said.

Bootsie did have a beer in front of him. He let out a snort. "Roger, ah, that boy! Well, she was — sorry, is a pretty girl. But I don't think she's the one for him. Roger is falling apart now, but that boy is a passionate soul. He loves the city, he loves dress up and history. She's a little namby-pamby for him. He'll figure that out."

"Let's hope he gets to figure that out," Malachi said.

"Let's hope," Aldous repeated. "He's here now — over there, at a table. With your

374

other high school bud, Abby. What's that other kid's name? The one he works with?"

"Paul Westermark?"

"Yeah. Apparently the girl playing Missy Tweed isn't available tomorrow — she's up in Charleston for her mother's birthday. You said the show was to go on, so . . . I guess they're trying to come up with someone to fill in or rewrite or whatever."

"That doesn't sound like a problem," Malachi said. "They have Abby. She's a wench at heart, the best wench ever, I'd think. She's related to Blue Anderson. His descendent, I should say."

"He was my great-great-great-whatever uncle."

"Still, the whole swashbuckling thing is in the genes," Malachi said. "It sounds like great fun. I'd love to get in on it, too."

"Lad, I'm betting they'd welcome you!" Bootsie assured him. "There's nothing like playing pirate."

"Aye-aye!" Aldous said.

"Not when you have to do it every day and make drinks in costume and wash these bleached cotton shirts all the time!" Sullivan chimed in. He'd finished preparing a tray of drinks for one of the waitresses but was listening to them and now walked down on his side of the bar to join them.

"You don't really mind, do you?" Abby asked him. "The pirate and wench outfits here have become tradition. Maybe I could spruce them up, though. We haven't changed in while. Maybe get you a nice new frock coat?"

Sullivan laughed, running his fingers through his red hair. "It's not so bad, Abby. I'm just bitching. Well, we could spruce up some of them. I'm not sure I want a frock coat. It can be hot as hell in Savannah." He looked at Abby anxiously. "Were you planning to make a lot of changes?"

She smiled. "No, Sullivan. I love the Dragonslayer, and Gus handled it brilliantly by leaving things alone. I won't be here all the time, anyway. And Macy and Grant do a great job. But I'll okay new uniforms if we can improve on tradition."

Sullivan seemed pleased. "Cool. I love my job here. And I agree that the costumes add to the ambience. One day, I'll save enough to buy my own place. Oh, I'm not going to compete with you — it won't be pirate-themed! Maybe I'll go with a high-Victorian type of place. And it won't be for years."

Abby couldn't help laughing at his conciliatory tone. "Savannah abounds with fine places and the Dragonslayer is only one of them. When you open your own place, Sullivan, we'll all celebrate."

"Thanks," he said. "I'll make my bartenders dress to the nines! I know — I'll have them look like the butler in *Downton Abbey*. Grant will love it — whoops, don't worry. I won't steal him away."

"I'm not worried," Abby shook her head.

"You might want to worry about Rog over there, Abby," Bootsie murmured. "He's down in the dumps."

"Yep, he's broken up about that girl," Sullivan said. "I don't blame him. She seemed to be nice. He was so pleased and proud to introduce her around."

"I'll go talk to him." Abby slid off her bar stool. She walked over to the tables in the dining room with the Blue Anderson statue by the grate. Roger and Paul Westermark were there. She wasn't sure what they were talking about because they glanced up at her approach and grew silent. Paul quickly stood and gave her a hug. Roger did so more slowly. He looked at her anxiously.

"Anything?" he asked.

"Not yet, Roger. But the police are following new leads."

"New leads?" he asked. "Like what?"

"They're inspecting the rowboat we found last night. They're still combing the river and the ships and boats. They *will* find her,

Roger. You have to have faith and . . . and keep living your life," Abby said.

"Abby just lost her grandfather," Paul reminded him. "One of the greatest old guys on earth. And she's *doing* things. She's not sitting around moping."

"That's hardly the same thing!" Roger waved a hand in the air. "Besides, Abby wanted to be a cop. Or an agent. She's good at this. I'm not."

"Nobody's good at worrying about someone they care about, Roger. It's a terrifying situation," Abby told him. "But you do have to keep on with your life while we're searching."

"So, yeah, are we doing the street show tomorrow?" Paul asked. "We did it every Saturday until . . . well, until Gus died."

"Gus would want it go on, of course. Yes — and I'll be your Missy Tweed."

Paul sat back, grinning at her. "Wow. I was afraid you'd come back here thinking you were above such things."

"Hey, this is my heritage we're talking about."

"You remember the lines and everything, right?"

"More or less. It's half ad-lib, anyway," Abby said, rolling her eyes. "It was never my favorite role. Missy Tweed just screams a lot and gets tossed from man to man."

"The crowds love Missy Tweed. Look at me — I get to play Scurvy Pete. I've had people throw stuff at me," Paul said. "And I had such high Shakespearean hopes!"

Abby smiled at that. "Paul, you act beautifully and you always seem to have work, here or in commercials or with your singing. I heard you're going to start recording."

"Yeah, I'm planning on getting into a studio. A producer showed up at one of my performances in the Irish bar. He's going to finance it for me. I'm pretty happy with that," he said.

"I used to be happy," Roger moaned.

"He's had a few beers," Paul told Abby in a low voice.

"Did you eat anything?" Abby asked.

"Yes, Mom, I did."

"Okay, I'll get into the wench costume and we'll do our pirate act," Abby said. "We'll make Gus proud, huh?"

"You bet, Abby. You bet." Paul nodded vigorously.

"Yeah, Abby, of course. I'm sorry," Roger said.

"Don't be sorry, just be strong," she told him. She gave them both a slightly grim smile and returned to the bar.

Things here had changed.

Aldous and Malachi were gone; Will Chan had come in with Dirk Johansen and they were now seated next to Bootsie.

"Where did Aldous and Malachi go?" Abby asked.

"Oh, Aldous has some business to check on. Malachi . . . I don't know. I think he was going upstairs. Or maybe he went outside. I'm not sure," Bootsie said.

"How did everything go today?" Abby looked past Dirk to Will Chan.

Chan's features gave away nothing of his thoughts; his smile and mannerisms were consistently pleasant. "I'm having a great time as a pirate," he said. "And the ship sails on as always, right, Dirk?"

"Yeah, Chan, you're an excellent addition. The Chinese did make good pirates," Dirk said.

"Actually, I'm Trinidadian, with a real mix of ethnicities," Will told him.

"Oh, yeah? Well, Trinidadians made great pirates," Dirk said.

Dirk had a glass of beer, and Bootsie, who was being a bit garrulous, had ordered a fresh one. Will Chan seemed to have the situation in hand. She told him, "I'm going to run upstairs and check on some paperwork. Unless anyone needs me for any-thing?"

"Ah, Abby, you are a delight!" Bootsie said. "In fact, there's never been a better descendent of old Blue. Other than Gus, of course. I'm always proud to have you at my side. But we're pretty used to you being gone now. We'll carry on — Sullivan over there, Dirk and me. We'll carry on!"

Abby glanced at Will, who nodded. She had a feeling that someone in the bar was a cop, following Roger. Will was sticking close to Dirk, and he couldn't possibly follow two men, no matter how good he was.

She rose, curious to find out where Mala-chi had gone, but when she ran upstairs, he wasn't in the apartment. She looked into the offices, the employee areas and the storeroom with its long rows of restaurant supplies, but he wasn't anywhere to be found.

He'd gone out — without leaving word.

She quickly dialed his number from her cell.

When he answered, she asked, "Where are you?" She tried not to sound anxious.

"Tailing Aldous."

"Oh. I would've come with you. Me show-ing you the city might have kept you from looking obvious."

"Don't worry. I won't look obvious," he promised her.

"Okay." She realized she was a little lost without him, although she was the one who was actually an agent. But Malachi had real-world experience, as a cop and a private investigator, and as one —

As one who could see beyond the surface.

"I'm willing to bet he eventually ends up back at the Dragonslayer," Malachi said. "But right now, we're going toward the river. Seems like he's heading for a yacht. Nice piece of work. Beautiful boat. Looks like it's about thirty-three feet."

"That's his pleasure craft. She's called the *Lady Luck,*" Abby told him.

"Okay. I'm trying to keep up. I'll talk to you soon."

Abby bit her lip as he ended the call. The police, she knew, had already searched the *Lady Luck* when Malachi and Jackson insisted the Dragonslayer "barflies" be investigated.

She walked back to her apartment and opened the door. As she did, she discovered that she hadn't locked it when she'd gone to the storeroom.

As she shut it behind her, she saw someone standing by the windows that opened out onto the balcony.

Instinctively, she set a hand on her Glock.

But the person turned. "Abby," he said softly. And then, as if testing her name, "Abigail Anderson."

13

Aldous walked with a determined pace, apparently oblivious, careless of whether anyone watched him or not. He seemed to have purpose and went straight from the Dragonslayer to River Street.

Malachi kept a careful distance as Aldous walked along the river and stopped at the private dock where the *Lady Luck* was docked.

He used his owner's key in the slot, as well as his code, to gain entry and only then did he turn around to see who else was nearby. Malachi had ducked behind a handy SUV.

It was still early; people were out in droves. That seemed to please Aldous. He walked onto his yacht, whistling.

Malachi waited to see if he intended to take the vessel out.

He couldn't tell; Aldous went down into the cabin.

Malachi put a call through to Jackson.

Before he could explain what was happening, Jackson sprang some information on him. "They've identified the rowboat we brought in last night."

"Yeah?"

"She's from the *Lafayette* — a merchant ship."

"How did she wind up in the water?"

"No one knows. But we didn't need a warrant. The captain assured us we could search the ship and of course we did. He also told us she'd already been searched. The cops have been on almost every ship, boat and floating anything on the water."

"And nothing? So it was just an unconnected accident?"

"Not really. The *Lafayette* is owned by a giant parent company, and the CEO happens to be one of the Dragonslayer's main barflies."

"Aldous Brentwood?"

"Yeah. That's why it was searched the first time."

"I'm on the riverfront watching him now. He just went out to his private yacht, the *Lady Luck.* He locked the gate behind him. I'm going in."

"Malachi, hold on. There are officers near you. I can be there —"

"I'm taking a dive, Jackson. If he does

have her on that yacht, he's torturing her right now. Get here as fast as you can."

He hung up before Jackson could argue, then he moved to a public area, shed his jacket and shoes and dove in. He swam around hard and fast to the *Lady Luck* and caught hold of the mooring rope to swing himself up on deck.

Aldous was nowhere in sight. Malachi tiptoed around the deck to look down into the cabin, but it was a large one and his view was blocked. He had to take the steps.

The yacht was luxurious. The steps led to a galley and dining area, with a captain's chair and all kinds of electronic gadgets to the left.

Still no sign of Aldous. There was a hallway that stretched toward the aft. He followed it, then quietly opened the first door. The room was a head, complete with shower. The second door opened to an elegantly appointed cabin. Empty. He tried the door across from it. Also empty.

One cabin remained. The master storeroom. He strode the last two feet down the hallway and listened. Logic told him that no woman could be captive there — unless she was dead. If she'd cried out at any time, she'd have been heard by someone on a nearby boat or even someone walking on

River Street.

Tap, tap, tap.

Helen's words still haunted him.

There was no tapping, just the rhythmic lap of water against the hull. He could hear a band playing at a riverfront club, but that wasn't the noise he was listening for.

He heard the cabin door opening; he skirted back, sliding into the head, cracking the door slightly.

Aldous Brentwood walked down the hallway and went topside. Malachi couldn't see him, but it sounded as if he'd hopped back onto the dock. He waited a moment longer and hurried down the hall to the aft.

He threw open the cabin door.

Abby stood still, wondering if she was really seeing what she thought she was. Maybe she *wanted* to see Blue so badly she'd envisioned him there.

But Malachi saw Blue. In fact, Blue had spoken to him.

And now, he'd actually spoken to her.

"Blue." She said his name, wondering if he'd disappear. But the image remained. The spirit of the man she'd seen for the first time, years and years ago, when she and her grandparents and the Dragonslayer had been in danger.

He had led her to Gus; he had led her to save Helen.

She walked closer, but not too close.

"You helped me," she told him.

He inclined his head. "Of course, but there is little I can do when no one sees. *You* see. Quite remarkable, Miss Abigail," he said. His voice was like a dry wind. He didn't speak often, she thought. She suspected it wasn't easy for him.

"Did you see Gus . . . die?" she asked him. "And Helen — how did you know? What have you seen? We need your help again, Blue — we so desperately need your help."

He shook his head and in that motion he seemed to impart great sadness.

"I came upon Gus. I tried to keep watch after I realized someone had opened the grate and knew about the exit by the riverbank. I was too late to realize that the Dragonslayer was being used. I was too late with Gus — but I began watching, walking a vigil around the Dragonslayer, up and down the tunnel, out to the river. I saw — from a distance — something. There was nothing I could do, no boat I could take. But you followed me, and the woman lived."

She nodded. Hoping he'd be able to give her a name had probably been too optimistic.

"You're still keeping watch," she said. "And you saw someone approach the Dragonslayer last night in the middle of the night, when we were out. You scared that person, Blue. You made him leave."

"I tried to see who it was. He left too quickly." Blue moved with a flourish of his frock coat; he was evidently indignant. "He wore a cape as I sometimes wore. He pretends to be me!" He looked as if he'd say more, as if he'd unleash a spate of curses but determined not to — not with a great-great-whatever niece standing there. He waved a hand in the air. "The young gentlemen pretend to be me in your theatricals, but I find that quite charming. I appear heroic and honorable, do I not?"

"Very honorable," Abby assured him.

"To be depicted so is palatable. For a killer such as this coward to take on my persona — that is beyond despicable. To torment and slay young women as he does . . . This is a monster. A monster, Abigail, and I will help you in every way that I can."

"Thank you," she said. "We need you."

He nodded. "I continue to keep watch here. I watch over you as you sleep. I am here, in this hall, or below." It sounded as if he attempted to clear his throat. "Times have changed, of course. And yet heinous murder remains heinous murder. And few people are so cruel and brutal as this . . . this piece of human refuse."

He seemed to be fading.

"Blue," she called out. "Why have you never spoken to me before?"

"Because there was no need," he said. "You knew I was here. And you followed me each time, as I prayed you would. I . . . I need to rest now. This is . . . difficult for me. Perhaps one learns . . . Still, throughout the years, there are not so many who can see me, and fewer still who hear me. But, Abby, I am with you."

Except, as he spoke the last words, he wasn't. He disappeared as if he'd never been there.

Abby realized she was shaking.

She sat down on the chair in front of the computer screens. She gazed at them for a moment, her mind strangely blank and her hands still trembling. She clenched them into loose fists.

The screens showed her that Sullivan remained behind the bar, Macy chatted with customers, Bootsie raised a beer to his lips.

Will Chan sat and watched.

In the dining room, Paul and Roger were still at the table. Paul was speaking earnestly to Roger; Roger nodded and kept drinking.

He was going to play an interesting Blue the following day if he didn't stop.

She left the computer screens, knowing that someone at the house on Chippewa was always watching them. By the time she came downstairs, Bootsie and Will were gone. Sullivan worked behind the bar, putting away glasses.

Macy was off-duty, and Grant Green had taken her position at the host stand.

"Hey, girl," Grant said to her. "I'm glad you're here. You getting any rest?"

"Yeah, I'm fine," Abby said.

"No luck on the missing girl, huh?"

"Not yet."

He leaned toward her. "I'm having the waitress bring a check to Paul and Roger. I'm pretty sure Paul wants to get Roger out of here. At least the two of them won't be driving."

"Thank God for small mercies," Abby said.

"It's all right to . . . hurry them out?"

"Grant, yes of course. You're the manager. You can and should refuse to sell to anyone who appears inebriated. That includes my high school friends."

He smiled. "Thanks. It's just kind of . . . Well, we're entering a new era at the Dragonslayer. We all need to adjust."

She refrained from telling him that, at the moment, the running of the tavern was the last of her concerns.

"But you know what? I'm here. I'll take care of this," she told him.

She walked over to the table where Paul and Roger were still sitting. She slid in next to Roger and took his hands. "Look at me, Roger."

When he did, she said, "You're going home now. Go to bed and get some sleep. We're doing the pirate show for the crowd tomorrow. I need you to be in good shape. You and Paul. I'm not an actor. I can only do it because I grew up here — and because I have the two of you. Okay?"

He smiled at her a little blearily. "Yeah, you know about Missy Tweed, don't you?"

"She was ransomed," Abby said.

"But she fell in love with Blue. She wanted to stay with him. He did save her — he came back to his ship to find that bastard, Scurvy Pete, trying to attack her. Scurvy Pete told him she was a captive and they were pirates and he was being a fool. So Missy thought Blue was her savior. Of course, Blue *had* seized her off her father's ship, but that didn't stop Missy from loving him. He was a businessman, Abby. Blue was a businessman. He only attacked ships that belonged to England's enemies. He took her off her father's ship when he saved the crew because the ship had been caught in a storm and wrecked and began sinking. So . . . Blue actually saved Missy twice," he concluded.

"It's a great story, Roger. And we'll do it well tomorrow. *If* you go home now."

Paul looked at her with gratitude. "Come on, Roger. I'll get you home."

Paul helped him up and they left together, arm in arm. As Abby watched, a man in a colorful tourist shirt rose from his table and followed.

Abby smiled. The police were at work; she knew the man had to be a plainclothes officer, doing his job.

Following Roger English.

"I busted into an empty cabin," Malachi told Jackson. "And I'm afraid I dripped water all over that beautiful yacht. But I did find this."

He hadn't heard anything in the cabin and hadn't really expected to find Bianca Salzburg. If she'd been there, she would've made some sound — unless she'd been gagged and Helen hadn't said anything about being gagged, just blindfolded.

So, no Bianca. But what he *had* found was more than a little suspicious.

Maybe not under normal circumstances. But under these circumstances . . .

He handed Jackson the scarf. It was a large pirate-themed scarf, the kind that was sold all over the city. It had been crumpled and kicked half under the bed. He wondered if it was used as a blindfold by someone.

Aldous?

The man was big and burly. He looked like a pirate. He was rich. He owned ships and a private yacht. He was in the prime of his health.

"Where did he go when he left here?" Malachi asked, sitting on a bench to get his shoes back on as they spoke.

"He was followed to his house. There's an officer outside now," Jackson said.

"Did they get anything off that partial gum wrapper?"

"Testing isn't in yet."

Malachi nodded. Fingerprints, if there were any, weren't necessarily easy to match, since they might not be in any law enforcement database.

Malachi stared out at the river. One of the big paddle wheelers was going by; the music and laughter traveled all the way to shore.

People looked at him curiously as they

394

passed. On the riverfront, it was growing late. But tourists, in smaller numbers, were still passing by. The news of a missing woman — and the murders — was surely disconcerting to them. But if they traveled as couples or in groups, the horror was removed. They could sympathize, but this wasn't their home, and it wasn't their friend, lover or child who'd been killed or was missing.

No person could embrace every tragedy. It would make life unbearable.

There was nothing Malachi could see on the river. Not then.

"I guess I'll call it a night." He turned to Jackson. "They'll watch him through the night?"

"There'll be a man on his house at all times," Jackson said.

Malachi nodded. "Good." Then he frowned, shaking his head. "Jackson, something is bothering me. Helen talked about a sound. Tap, tap, tap. Does that mean anything to you?"

Jackson looked tired. "They weren't taken by the ghosts of Fred Astaire or Gene Kelly," he said. "Tap, tap, tap. I don't know. I'll try to think of things that could make that kind of sound. And I'll see that the whole team is aware."

"It's hard," Malachi said. "Situations like this always are. But," he admitted, "it's better when you work with others — the right others."

Jackson managed a smile. "So, you're in? As more than a consultant?"

Only if we find Bianca alive, Malachi thought.

"Assuming we solve this," he said.

"We'll solve it," Jackson vowed. "We have to. And we will. We have a perfect record so far."

They left the riverfront together, parting ways on Bay Street. Jackson had brought his car and Malachi didn't want a ride for the few blocks to the Dragonslayer. He could dry off enough walking back, then he'd slink up the stairs before anyone noticed him.

The Dragonslayer was still open when he returned, but he didn't pause to speak to anyone; he just started up the stairs. Grant, at the host stand, saw him and waved, and he waved back. None of the barflies was present, nor did he recognize anyone at the tables.

When he entered the apartment, Abby came rushing over to him and threw herself into his arms.

"I can't wait to tell you what happened!"

she said excitedly before drawing back. "Ugh. You're all wet!"

"I went swimming," Malachi said. He was sorry the moment he said the words. Hope sprang into her eyes.

"You found Bianca?" she asked excitedly.

"No. I dove into the river to get to Aldous's yacht." He inhaled. "Abby, the rowboat Roger saw on the river — it belonged to a ship owned by one of Aldous's companies. The police searched the ship, welcomed by the captain."

"Does that prove anything?" she asked. "Other than that a rowboat from a big ship broke away?"

"Maybe that's all it is. But I also found a scarf on his yacht that might . . . that might've been used as a blindfold."

"*Might* have been used as a blindfold. And that would hold up in court?" she asked.

"Abby, we're searching for a killer. We're not in court. We're trying to find a young woman while she's still alive."

Abby let out a breath. "I know," she said, meeting his eyes.

"Nothing's been proven — we're watching Aldous, Dirk, Roger, among others — and keeping an eye on Bootsie, of course."

"He's seventy!"

Malachi nodded. "But we have to watch

everyone, Abby. Everyone who was familiar with Gus — and the Dragonslayer," he went on. "Gus knew something because of what he'd seen here. There's no way out of that. Don't forget he found one victim's finger."

She nodded again. She looked deflated but seemed to have accepted the truth. "So much time is going by. Bianca doesn't stand much of a chance, does she?"

"She's strong and resilient. She may be playing it just right," Malachi said. "He wants a captive who will fall in love with him. He's trying to live out a fantasy."

"If he doesn't give himself away somehow, we'll never find him," Abby muttered.

"We will," Malachi said with assurance. "He was afraid when he came to the Dragonslayer the other night. Why he came when he did, I don't know. Maybe just to prove that he could."

"The only people with keys are —"

Malachi interrupted her. "How closely did Gus watch his keys around his friends?" he asked.

She pursed her lips and then sighed. "He kept his keys on a hook behind the bar," she said. "I guess anyone could have *borrowed* them and had copies made."

"Anyone who knew how casual he was with them."

"But the grate to the tunnel —"

"Was opened by someone who knew the combination."

"At least we have a new lock — with a new combination." She frowned. "But if we're sure it was one of those three, why don't the police just bring them all in?"

"I believe they'll bring Aldous in for questioning tomorrow. We're trying to be very careful. We don't want to catch him but lose Bianca."

"Of course."

She stood there, dejected again, raven's wing hair like a mourning cape around her slumped shoulders.

He walked over to her. "You were going to tell me something," he reminded her. He started to embrace her, remembered he was still soaked and stepped back. "What? What was it you were going to tell me?"

"Blue," she said. "Blue was in here, right after I talked to you on the phone. He spoke to me. He had a real conversation with me. But even though he's been haunting the tavern for years, he's not good at drawing whatever energy he needs to speak. I'd hoped so badly that he knew something. But, like you've said, ghosts or spirits seem to be the same as we are. They aren't omniscient. They only know what they've seen. He didn't see what happened. He just knew that the tunnel was being used. But he promised me he's watching now."

Malachi touched her hair, brushing his fingers down the silky length of it. "Blue is your ancestor," he said. "It's you he cares about."

"He must have cared deeply about Gus. And the others who came before Gus and me."

"I'm sure he did, but you're his focus now. He'll do anything to protect you — and the Dragonslayer." He stepped back. "I'll get in the shower."

He left her in the living room and walked down the apartment hallway to the bedroom, shedding his wet clothes. He went into her bathroom; the Dragonslayer might be old, but Gus had had the bathrooms modernized. The faucet released a hard spray of steaming hot water.

He let it pound down on him, just standing there for several minutes.

And then he felt her. She'd stepped in behind him. She held the soap in her hand and worked it slowly over his body.

A shower can clear the mind. . . .

In a radiant spray of heat he became lost in the sheer sensual pleasure of being with this extraordinary woman while the water pulsed, hot and vibrant, searing into his muscles.

They more or less made love. They teased and aroused, and teased and aroused again as they left the shower and halfway dried themselves, then fell into bed together.

Being together like this was sweeter every time. There was nothing arbitrary about it, nothing that didn't seem to offer promise, nothing that brought back the pain of memory and the past.

He'd never really thought it possible. He was falling in love again.

Abby had never really liked playing Missy Tweed. To her mind, Missy had been an idiot. History said she'd fallen in love with Blue Anderson and that she'd cried when she was returned to her father. She disappeared into history after that, but Abby always felt she'd probably been a spoiled teenager and that, once home, she'd simply fallen in love again.

But here she was . . . playing Missy Tweed.

Paul, as Scurvy Pete, stood beside her on the platform. Roger, sober and seriously in "Blue" mode, was wearing his pirate best. They'd drawn a huge crowd; the little reenactments and the way the players talked and related tidbits of history were well documented and well-known, a high point in most tour books for their area.

Will Chan had taken on the role of narrator that day, dressed as a swashbuckling pirate himself. He talked first about the history of the city of Savannah and the early days of piracy. He told the crowd that pirates had found their way into coastal cities, often snubbing their noses at a royal governor and whatever military or local law might be in effect.

He told the story of Blue as if he'd been a true gentleman with the people of Savannah.

And then he told the story of the floundering of Missy Tweed's ship and how the crew had been saved — and the damsel taken for a fair ransom. Blue believed that asking a ransom for Missy was well within the law; after all, he'd saved the lives of an entire crew. And if asking for the ransom wasn't quite within the law, then so be it. He would still be paid. However, on his ship, every man knew that captives were not to be molested or harmed.

But Scurvy Pete had brought his own pirate ship flush with Blue's; he'd wanted in on the action. And when he'd seen the delectable Missy, he'd wanted much more. Thus began the drama that the crowd was about to witness.

With a flourish, Will left the makeshift stage. Abby dutifully let out the scream of distress, which brought the pirates to action, Scurvy Pete accusing Blue of being less than a man and a blot on the rugged truth of piracy. Blue, in turn, ridiculed Scurvy Pete, telling him he was due to swing from a yardarm, that he wasn't just a blot on piracy but a blot on the entire human race.

Abby could see that the rest of the Krewe who were in Savannah were scattered through the crowd. They were there because their suspects were there, except for Dirk, who was out on the *Black Swan.* Dirk was not alone, although he undoubtedly thought he was. A plainclothes policeman was on board; Abby knew that Jackson and Malachi both believed they were drawing close to a resolution and that everyone needed to be watched.

"You fool! I will have your captive, and I will return the lass as I see fit!" Paul told Roger. "You will fall beneath my steel!"

"One day I'll fall, but I will fall to the law on the high seas and not to the likes of you, Scurvy Pete!" Roger said. "I will go with my ship — and not with the dregs of the sea!"

"To the death, Blue Anderson! To the death!" Paul bellowed, and the two began to thrust and parry with their swords, to the delight of the crowd.

Abby screamed appropriately — like a girl — and fell back. Will Chan came to slip his arms around her and help her from the stage so the sword battle could continue.

The two men were very good at what they did. The crowd grew, with everyone entranced. Finally, Blue caught Scurvy Pete with a fatal blow.

Paul died, emoting dramatically. Will took to the stage again to do a follow-up, and then the crowd broke into applause.

Abby was immediately besieged by a number of children in the audience. She posed for pictures with them and answered what questions she could about Savannah and piracy.

She looked up at one point, aware that she was being watched. Malachi had been waiting for her to notice him.

She made her way through the crowd to approach him.

"I'm heading to the station. They've just brought Aldous in," he said quietly.

She felt her heart sink. "All right. I'll join you there soon."

"Don't worry. Jackson and I will question

him. David will go in and out. We'll find out where he's hiding Bianca."

"You're *sure* it's him?" she asked.

"No, but the evidence points to him."

"Do they have anything definitive?"

Malachi nodded. "DNA on the scarf I found on his yacht," he told her.

"DNA?"

"From tears," Malachi said. "The scarf was around the eyes of Felicia Shepherd at some point before she was killed. They were able to extract DNA and it matched Felicia's."

Malachi had to hand it to Aldous. When he'd first been brought in, accused of the murder, he'd been belligerent and angry. Then he'd look incredulous.

Now, he looked scared.

"You want to take it for a few minutes?" Jackson asked Malachi, who'd been observing the interrogation. "David thinks we can handle this better than he can."

"Sure."

Malachi walked into the room. Aldous Brentwood raised his head; he was pale. His bald head gleamed in the bright light overhead, his gold earring glittering.

"You," Aldous muttered. He shook his head as if in disgust.

"Aldous, you shouldn't be aggravated with *me*. I didn't want to think you could be guilty of something like this."

"I'm not!"

"One of your rowboats was found out on the river. Forensic teams are going over it now. I believe we're going to find some organic matter that will prove the boat was used to dump the bodies of those who were killed."

Aldous leaned toward him. "I'm not stupid, Agent Gordon. You can't prove I ever had that rowboat. I own the ship, yeah, but I don't work on it."

"I'm not an agent," Malachi told him. "Just a consultant."

"Consult yourself out of here. My attorney is going to make mincemeat out of all of you." Aldous sat back, crossing his arms over his chest. "You've got nothing on me. Does Abby know you've brought me here?"

"She knows. And, Aldous, I'm afraid we have more on you than that."

"What? That I go to the Dragonslayer? That I was friends with Gus?" He shook his head. "You'd have to arrest half the city."

"Didn't they tell you what this is?" Malachi asked. A pirate scarf — the one he'd found half under the bunk in the yacht's master cabin — was on the table between them, carefully folded in a plastic bag.

"It's a scarf in a plastic bag."

"*Your* scarf," Malachi said. He watched the man intently for his reaction. Aldous Brentwood didn't appear to be anything other than perplexed.

"I don't buy those stupid tourist scarves!" he said.

"But you did. This one was found on your yacht."

"What? It was not! I let the police search my yacht. I've cooperated since this whole thing began. I am *not* guilty of anything! Hell, what's the matter with you? I'd never have hurt Helen. I was crazy about Helen. *Am* crazy about her."

"Maybe you liked her too much."

"You're sick!" Aldous spat.

"Am I? You've bought into the legend of pirates and their swashbuckling adventures since you were a kid. Look at your normal mode of appearance. You're not married and never were. You own all kinds of ships. You're rich, and you're rich because of the sea. You know the Dragonslayer, you know Savannah and the river. And you know your pirate history. Come on, Aldous. You want to live a fantasy. You probably imagined from the first that you could kidnap a girl and convince her you were a charming rogue, an Errol Flynn or a Johnny Depp. But you could never get the right girl."

Aldous Brentwood's eyes widened with incredulity as he stared at Malachi. "I don't know what the hell you're talking about!" he shouted. "And I sure as hell don't know what this scarf — that isn't mine — means!"

"It was used as a blindfold, Aldous," Malachi said. "Poor Felicia cried — cried in fear and terror and despair — when she was bound in a cabin on one of your ships. She cried, and she left traces of her DNA to prove that you were her killer."

"I'm not — and that wasn't on my yacht!" Aldous protested. "The police were on my yacht." His eyes narrowed. "They didn't find anything there — unless it was planted!"

"Planted by the police?" Malachi asked, raising an eyebrow.

"By the police," Aldous agreed energetically. "Or . . . or someone!" He pointed at Malachi. "Or you. You! We don't know you — you don't belong here. You're not one of us. Maybe you planted it on the yacht!"

"Aldous, get over it. I was the one who found the scarf, but I wasn't in Savannah when this spree of kidnapping and murders began," Malachi told him.

"But *you* found it, right? You went on my boat illegally. I don't know the law all that well, but I know you can't use evidence in court when you got it illegally. And don't you get it? You're harassing the wrong person. I didn't do any of this. I'm innocent — I swear it!"

Malachi decided wearily that he believed him. Aldous was passionate in his denial. But he pushed a little further.

"Actually, I'm not a cop. I'm a civilian and I thought I heard you screaming on your yacht. I went out to see if you needed help. I saw that scarf, and took it in case you'd been kidnapped or injured — one victim was a man, you know — and it meant something. I gave it to the police."

"That's the biggest crock I've ever heard," Aldous sneered.

Malachi shrugged. "Maybe. We know you have all the right credentials — and a rowboat and a scarf with a victim's DNA."

Aldous shook his head. "But . . . it's not me. I didn't do it."

"So, how did your rowboat wind up loose and how did the scarf wind up on your yacht?"

"I don't know! I'm telling you, someone put them there," Aldous said. "I swear to you, I know nothing about that scarf."

"Who else is on your yacht on a regular basis?" Malachi asked.

"I have a cleaning crew that comes in once or twice a month." He paused. "There are ten berths there, so one of the other owners could have gotten on my yacht. And, then, of course —"

Aldous broke off. He looked ill.

"And then, of course — what?"

"Gus, Bootsie and Dirk. The three of them had keys to the dock," he said. "They're my best friends. They were always welcome on my yacht."

Something cold hardened inside Malachi. *Aldous could be lying, trying to shift the blame.*

But he didn't know; he didn't have a definite sense that yes, he was guilty, or no, he was innocent. He believed Roger, and even though he wasn't completely certain, he leaned toward believing Aldous.

That left Dirk or Bootsie.

Or . . .

Someone else who was always at the Dragonslayer, someone who knew everything about the way it ran, day in and day out.

Grant Green, Macy Sterling, Jerry Sullivan.

Macy? Doubtful — unless she was someone's accomplice. Grant? Not around during the day. And yet, that could mean he

410

was able to be anywhere else, without even having to slip away.

Jerry Sullivan, the bartender, friendly, ever listening, knowing everything and everyone. Always there from lunch until closing.

"Aren't there any cameras around that river that might've been aimed at my *Lady Luck*?" Aldous asked him. "I'm telling you — someone was on my boat and planted that scarf."

"Say it was planted, and the police didn't do it. Who would it have been?"

Aldous shook his head, lost and dejected. "I . . . I don't know. All I can tell you is that I've never attacked anyone, I just happen to be bald, and I don't have any fantasies about being a pirate," he said.

"I'm going to see what I can do for you, Aldous." Malachi got to his feet.

"You're going to let me go?"

"I'm going to ask that you stay here for the moment. They'll get you some coffee."

"Yeah, sure, if it's going to clear me. I'll drink coffee and play Tiddlywinks all night if it'll make you people believe me."

"Great. I've got to go."

Malachi was anxious to be on the move.

They only had one real connection to the killer. Helen Long. He had to talk to her again.

There had to be some clue in her story. There was something he should be seeing clearly, but couldn't, not yet. The answer to the riddle was in the back of his mind somewhere; he just hadn't figured it out.

Tap.

Tap, tap.

Tap, tap, tap.

14

"Pirates were really bad, right?" a little boy asked Abby, his smiling mother beside him. She might have been portraying a girl who was an utter nitwit, but the audience seemed to have sympathy for the damsel in distress.

"Hmm. Well, yes, piracy is bad. There are still pirates out there today, and they're very bad," Abby said, crouching down to his height. "But Blue Anderson walked a middle ground. He started out as a privateer. That means, more or less, that he was asked to be a pirate."

"People can *ask* you to be a pirate?" The towheaded boy stared at her, eyes wide.

"Back then, we weren't a country yet. We were a group of colonies governed by the English. England and Spain always seemed to be at war. So the king or queen of each country would allow men to seize ships — as long as they were ships that sailed under the enemy's flag. So, Blue was a privateer to begin with. He never did seize an English ship. You remember the story in today's show? He actually saved the crew of a foundering ship, but kept Missy because he thought he was owed something for his work."

"What happened to Blue?" the boy asked.

"Tyler, you're driving the lady crazy," his mother said apologetically.

"Not at all," Abby assured her. "Blue never begged for a pardon, but he wasn't a bad guy. Legend had it that the Royal Navy could have sunk his ship several times, but they let him sail by. Whether that's true or not, I don't know. One day he sailed out — and he never came back. No one heard from him or any of his crew again, so history records that he was caught in a storm at sea and went down with his men and his ship."

"Wow, cool!" Tyler said. Gripping his mother's hand, he asked, "Can we go in there — to Blue's tavern — and have lunch? The menus for kids are supposed to be *pirate hats!*"

"Paper pirate hats, but yes," Abby told him.

"Yes, lunch!" his mother said. "Come on now. Thank you . . . Missy."

Abby grinned. "My pleasure."

Standing, she looked around. Will Chan

was heading into the restaurant; Jackson Crow was keeping an eye on her and talking on the phone.

Roger and Paul were still talking to tourists.

Aldous, she knew, was at the police station.

She went into the restaurant herself — and saw Dirk just ahead of her and glanced at her watch. The *Black Swan* would have finished the first tour of the day.

He was probably on his way to the bar for lunch before the second tour.

Abby quickened her pace. The show was over; she wanted out of Missy Tweed's voluminous gown and into her own clothing — and she especially wanted her Glock.

She walked into the tavern. It took a moment for her eyes to adjust to the dimmer light.

Grant and Macy were at the host stand, talking. She assumed Grant had come in to make sure that their return to the Saturday-morning theatrical events went smoothly.

But, as she watched, Grant gave Macy a kiss on the cheek. Macy walked over to the bar where Bootsie and Dirk were now seated together. She sat down next to Dirk and let out a sigh.

"How was the show?" she asked.

"It went very well," Bootsie said. "Very well. You and Grant are keeping everything moving along. Gus would be pleased."

"I'm relieved." Macy shrugged. "Why I thought anything would be different . . . I don't know." She sighed again. "I miss Gus."

Abby hurried over to where Macy was sitting. "We all miss him," she said.

"Oh, Abby! I didn't see you there." Macy turned, touching Abby's arm. "I'm sorry — I mean we all miss Gus, but he was your grandfather. We don't have the same right to miss him that you do."

Abby smiled at that. "Macy, you were just as much family. Miss him all you like — and I'm grateful that you do!"

"I wish you were staying around, Abby," Sullivan said.

"You don't need me," Abby assured him.

Grant came striding over, watching the host stand as he did, but grinning. "We have to let her move on, you know!" He lowered his voice to a whisper. "I think love is in the air."

"Love!" Bootsie scoffed. "Love? Who are you in love with, young lady?"

"Tall, dark, handsome and somewhat mysterious — seems to almost read minds," Grant said, teasing Abby.

"Love! Bah. Abby and that fed, they're

both cops," Bootsie muttered.

"Cops fall in love," Macy said.

Dirk winked. "And everyone falls in lust from time to time."

"Come on, Abby," Grant said. "What's the deal with the tall, dark and handsome G-man?"

"You mean Malachi?" she asked innocently.

"Let's hope — or else our girl's become a home wrecker," Dirk said. "I get the impression that the cute little blonde G-woman is with tall, dark, exotic actor G-man. And the pretty blondish one is with tall, dark, handsome and Native American G-man. That leaves intriguing G-man who's staying up in the apartment."

"Now, why would you be worried about my love life, anyway, huh?" Abby asked Dirk, avoiding the question.

"We'll always worry about you, Abs," Bootsie said.

"We're like the great-uncles you're really glad you never had," Dirk told her, which made Abby laugh.

"Hey, I'm just the bartender," Sullivan said lightly.

"You guys know I dreamed about working for the federal government, that all my life I wanted to be an agent," Abby said. "You know I'll go back to work with a unit, wherever I'm assigned."

"Yeah, but I looked this unit up," Grant said sagely. "They're the Krewe of Hunters."

"What does that mean?" Bootsie asked.

"They ask the dead questions — and the dead help them find the killers," Grant explained.

Macy giggled at that. "Seriously? Come on, Grant. The one woman is a medical examiner. If they could talk to the dead, she'd just ask the corpses who . . . who turned them into corpses. Oh, I sound terrible — I'm concerned, really. I'm grateful you found Helen, Abby, and praying that Roger's girlfriend will be found, as well. But it's not looking good for her, is it?"

"We don't have any real answers," Abby said.

Bootsie made a sound of derision. "All those feds and cops — and nothing. You people, all that schooling — and a pirate's walking all over you." He raised his beer. "Ask the dead questions, my ass!"

"Bootsie," Dirk remonstrated quietly.

"It's just us here," he said. He looked around. "Hey, where's our third? I haven't seen Aldous all day."

"I'm sure he'll be around," Sullivan said, pushing away from the bar to get a drink order from one of the waitresses.

"Yes, I'm sure he will," Macy agreed.

"Hey, you make a great wench, Abby," Grant told her.

"Gee, thanks. Which reminds me, I want to go and get out of this now." Abby turned but then paused, looking back. "Do me a favor, will you, Macy? Why don't you and Dirk go out on a date instead of staring at each other all the time? It's not like you just met or anything."

Macy's face went bright red. "Abby!"

Dirk was silent.

"Now there's a sensible question," Bootsie said. He gave Dirk a nudge. "Here's your chance, boy. Ask her out."

"Um . . ." Dirk said.

Macy found her voice. "Dirk, I don't know what these people are doing, but don't you dare feel obliged to ask me anything."

"I don't feel obliged, Macy."

"Good."

"But . . . we *should* go out sometime. To a restaurant. We're in a restaurant. I mean, a different restaurant. One where you're not working. Or we could go dancing. Or . . ."

"Dirk Johansen, are you asking me out?" Macy demanded.

"I guess I am. Except you don't have to feel obligated or anything. I'm not trying to put you in a bad position —"

"I would *love* to go out with you, Dirk!" Macy said.

"Thank God! That's settled," Bootsie said. "Now, can we get back to sitting around the bar and bitching about everyone we see? Macy, shoo! Go back to work."

Macy smiled and walked back to the host stand. Grant took a seat at the bar.

"That," he announced, "was really cool. Good work, Abby!"

"Thank you, thank you. Now, I'm finally going to get out of this ridiculous outfit!"

Leaving them at last, she ran up the stairs as quickly as she could, encumbered by the skirts that had defined her as Missy Tweed for a few hours.

Helen was doing much better.

When Malachi arrived, her police guard was seated in the hallway, reading the newspaper.

Angela Hawkins was in the room with Helen, as were her coworkers, Jack and Blake. They were still in their pirate attire from the morning sail of the *Black Swan;* Malachi assumed that, like Dirk, they usually took the two hours between sailings of the "pirate" vessel to either have lunch or get their errands done.

Helen seemed to be beaming; she was, he thought, maybe a year or two older than Blake — the one who was so obviously — and awkwardly — in love with her.

But that afternoon, she was thrilled by his attention.

"Malachi!" she said, greeting him with a warm smile.

He bent down to kiss her cheek. "Helen, you look wonderful."

"I'm feeling good," she said. "And the doctor said I'm doing well, right, Angela?"

"He said you're almost ready to go home."

Helen frowned. "You need to talk to me again, don't you, Malachi?"

"If you don't mind," Malachi said. "When you're ready."

"I think that's a hint to the two of us, Jack, but that's okay," Blake said. He'd been sitting by her on the other side of the bed. "Jack and I have to get back for the afternoon sail of the old *Black Swan*. We'll be back, Helen."

"I may not be. Hot date tonight." Jack grinned. "With a pretty, pretty — and I do mean pretty! — redhead who sailed this morning. She agreed to do me the honor of joining me for dinner this evening. So, my beloved colleagues, it might be tomorrow before I stop by. But I'll bring you delicious details!"

"Get out of here! If she's smart, there won't be that many details!" Helen joked.

"I'll be here tonight," Blake promised.

"Thanks. You really help the time pass," Helen said softly.

Blake beamed. He and Jack left, waving as they walked out the door.

Malachi sat next to Helen. Angela sat on her other side, taking her hand. "You're very strong, Helen." Angela smiled, encouraging her. She looked over at Malachi. "A therapist was in to see her. She's doing brilliantly, he says."

"He also said I'll never forget," Helen told him. "And he said . . . he said I'll be able to go forward again, have a good time, even have a relationship again."

"Of course you will. We'll get him, and you'll know we did it because of you. You'll know you saved others. He had you, but you beat him, Helen," Malachi said.

She gave him a weak smile. "It's strange. I always thought I was so liberal. But if I had a gun and he was in front of me, I'd want to shoot him. I want him strung up, I want his skin flayed from his body . . ." Her voice broke.

"That's human nature, Helen." Malachi spoke as reassuringly as he could.

"Is it? I hope so."

"Helen, I'm not a hypnotist or any kind of therapist. But I want you to try to relax when we talk," Malachi said. "Angela is here. We're both here. You're protected. I know it hurts, that it's painful, but I really need you to try to remember every detail."

"I wish I could remember more," she said. "I went into the church . . . and I remember the searing pain in my head — and then nothing."

"And then, the lapping of water against a cabin. You were in a ship's cabin."

"I think so," Helen said.

"What made you think it was a ship's cabin?" Malachi asked.

"There was a lot of wood. Paneling. I was in a bunk."

"Big cabin or little cabin?"

"Tight . . . it was a tight cabin. When he was in it, I could feel him as soon as he came in." She kept her eyes closed.

"And you remember a sound?"

"Yes."

"Tap, tap, tap?"

She frowned. "Yes, it was an odd sound."

"Was he with you all the time when you heard it?"

"No . . . sometimes, he wasn't." She thought for a moment. "But . . . when I heard it, I was so afraid."

"Why?"

"It meant he was coming for me."

Up in the apartment, Abby turned on the television in the living area for company while she ran down the little hall to her room and changed out of her pirate clothing. She chose jeans, a T-shirt and finally a denim jacket — a perfect way to hide the Glock she didn't intend to leave behind.

She was anxious to call Malachi and see what was going on. Had they found something that proved Aldous could be the killer?

Had Aldous confessed?

She felt shaky and weak considering the possibility. Aldous seemed like a good man, as well as a powerful one. He was rich, but he'd always spent a lot of time working for various causes. How could a good man, who was willing to donate his money and his labor when needed, prove to be such a heinous criminal?

But it made her shake, too — thinking that it could be someone she'd known most of her life. That she might have gone to school with someone who'd grown up to be a killer.

As she came down the hallway and went back into the living room area, she heard the television. She suddenly stopped; a newscaster, a sleek, attractive blonde, was speaking from an anchor desk while an insert on the screen showed a scene at the police station.

"While the Savannah police are not making any statements at this time, inside sources, choosing to remain anonymous, have stated that a suspect in the infamous River Rat murders is in custody and being questioned. The River Rat Killer — so dubbed because of his ability to disappear on the water or under the ground — is suspected to have taken the lives of one man and three young women, to have kidnapped and tortured a fourth young woman and may possibly be holding another captive, even as he's being questioned by the police. While our information has not been verified, it seems that the city of Savannah may soon breathe a huge sigh of relief. Our source has told us that the evidence in this case is based on hard science from the forensic lab. We'll be back with more information the minute it's available. Stay tuned."

Abby had to sit down. *Aldous.* It seemed impossible.

Her hands were trembling when she pulled out her cell phone to call Malachi. He answered immediately.

"Hey, wench," he said. "Is the show over?"

"It is. Where are you? What's going on? The media are announcing that the man suspected to be the killer is in custody."

"The media have it already?"

"They do," she said. "And I assume they're referring to Aldous."

"I imagine. He's the only suspect. He's not really being held. So far, he's actually there voluntarily. I suggested to him that he didn't want to leave yet."

"You don't really think it's Aldous, do you?"

"I think it's important that people — especially the real killer — believe the police are convinced the killer's in custody."

"But if the killer *isn't* in custody . . . or if he is, for that matter, Bianca is still out there somewhere."

"I'm at the hospital. I'm on my way back, though. I may walk around for a while. I'm trying to clear my head. Are you all right?"

"Of course. I'm fine. I'm in the apartment. I just got out of pirate-wench mode."

"Who's there, at the Dragonslayer?"

"When I came up? Roger and Paul. They were still pirates, talking to diners. Bootsie and Dirk were at the bar, although Dirk will have to leave soon. Macy and Grant Green are both here."

426

"Just go down and be friendly, okay? They should start questioning the fact that Aldous isn't there. Isn't there a TV behind the bar?"

"Yes, for games and events. It wasn't on."

"Make sure it's on. See what happens when your patrons watch the news about the suspect who's being held. I'll be there soon."

Abby ended the call. She stepped out of the apartment and carefully locked the door. Straightening her shoulders, she hurried down to the bar.

Macy was at the host station, Sullivan behind the bar.

Roger was seated at a table with a family, entertaining their three children. Paul was in the dining room as well, speaking with a young couple.

Neither Bootsie nor Dirk was at the bar.

"Where are our favorite barflies?" she asked Sullivan.

"Who knows?" Sullivan shrugged. "I guess Dirk went back for the afternoon sailing of the *Black Swan*. Bootsie went with him. Maybe he's sailing with Dirk today. Aldous hasn't shown up, so he might have wanted to hang with a friend."

"Possibly." Abby nodded. "Can you turn on the TV, Sullivan?"

"Sure. Anything special?" he asked.

"Whatever. How about news?"

Sullivan picked up the remote and switched on the flat-screen television that hung over the low etched mirror behind the call-brand whiskeys.

Abby had no idea how much good it was going to do, the two barflies who were supposed to see the news weren't there.

But the same newscaster came on, reporting that a suspect was being held in what was now called the River Rat case. She didn't have anything new to add, but she rephrased things so that it almost sounded as if she were telling her audience more.

Looking up at the screen, she could sense people walking up and crowding behind her. Roger and Paul were suddenly beside her; so was Macy. Abby hadn't even known Grant was still there, but he was with the group staring up at the screen.

"They caught him?" Macy breathed.

"But they're not revealing a name," Sullivan said.

"What about Bianca?" Roger asked. "They're not saying anything about Bianca!"

"They don't seem to really know anything," Grant commented. "They know the cops are holding someone and that's it."

"No news about Bianca is good news, Roger," Macy said gently.

But Roger shook his head as he stared glumly up at the screen.

"No news . . . But they have to find her!"

"If they have a suspect, they can make him tell where he's keeping her," Sullivan said. He looked at Abby. "Right? Hey, wait — Abby, you must know who it is."

She wasn't comfortable lying but she had no intention of telling the truth.

"I've been here playing wench. All I can do is connect with the feds and see what they know."

"Well, call Malachi!" Macy insisted.

"I just talked to him. He wasn't at the station," Abby said. "He isn't involved with what's going on there."

"But he's an FBI agent."

"Consultant," Abby corrected.

"Okay, then *you're* an FBI agent!" Grant said.

"I just passed the academy. I don't have an official assignment," Abby said.

Grant shook his head. "Then you're running around helping those guys for free?" Grant asked. "Gus should've taught you to be a better businesswoman."

Abby frowned at him. "Grant, business has nothing to do with it. I tried to get them down here because they're part of an elite unit who seem to solve situations no matter what."

"They need to hurry," Roger said, walking over to Abby. "Bianca's out there! She's not going to last much longer," he said dully. "If she's still alive, if she isn't floating somewhere we haven't found her yet. Or like that poor Jane Doe they've got at the morgue. Shoved into an old crypt some-where."

Abby very much wanted to say something reassuring to him. But the killer almost certainly had her. He'd taken Helen, and attempted to kill her within a few days. She'd failed to fall in love with him, failed to welcome him as her heroic lover.

How long could Bianca play the game before he got tired of trying to make her love him? Or before he realized that even if she *was* playing the game, she was lying and despised him?

The clock was ticking.

Malachi parked the car at the back of the Dragonslayer parking lot but he didn't go in. Abby was watching the Dragonslayer. He'd just heard from Jackson, who was still at the police station. Will Chan was aboard the *Black Swan*.

A plainclothes detective had followed Dirk and Bootsie. Bootsie had returned to his own home, riverside of Colonial Park Cemetery; he'd gone in and was still there.

Malachi began to walk along the river, back along Bay Street and then into the old section, where Oglethorpe had planned his original streets and squares.

What was he missing? Tap, tap, tap.

He started, quickly moving aside, as his distraction almost caused him to walk into a man. "I'm sorry, excuse me," he muttered. Then he paused as the man stopped — and he realized he was looking at a soldier, a man in a Union uniform. It wasn't tattered and torn, so he must've been wearing his parade best, dark blue adorned with gold braid.

Cavalry, Malachi thought, the analytical part of his mind making the first judgment.

Dead, was his second thought.

He was near the cemetery, but the last burial in Colonial Park Cemetery had been in 1853.

Then again, ghosts didn't usually haunt cemeteries. They haunted the places where they'd lived and found happiness, where they feared for those who lived after them, or where they had met trauma.

He continued to stare at the ghost, incredulous and curious.

The young ghost stared back at him — incredulous, too, and very curious.

A couple passed him on the street, clearly disturbed by the way he seemed to stare at some invisible entity. Maybe they felt a strange cold in the air, as well.

The woman shivered, looked at Malachi as if she feared there was something seriously wrong with him and the couple moved on. Malachi was alone with the young man under the shade of a live oak.

"I'm sorry," Malachi said. "I didn't see you at first. Can I . . . can I do anything for you?"

"You are talking to me?" the ghost said.

"Yes, sir, I am."

"You . . . you see me. You hear me."

"Yes. My name is Malachi Gordon."

The ghost smiled. "Lieutenant Oliver Mackey. No, sir. There is nothing you can do for me. I was just going home."

"Near here?" Malachi asked. "Not Colonial Park Cemetery?"

"That cemetery has been closed to burials for years, sir. I'm sorry to say I died of a fever before ever proving my mettle in battle. While I was despised in life, sir, for my abolitionist views, I was, in death, returned to the arms of my family and laid to rest in my family plot." He pointed toward a house around the corner from the Wulf and Whistle. He shrugged, looking at Malachi. "The coffin was never opened here. The war had begun, so I might well have been stripped, tarred and feathered, even burned to ash, had they done so."

"The war is long over."

"But I know that the fight for real equality, which this country must stand for, continues." He shook his head. "Broke my heart not to be loyal to my state, but I couldn't help my beliefs. Slavery was morally wrong, against my God."

"Many people agree with you, Lieutenant. But the world is changing, although it changes slowly."

"Laws are one thing — it's harder to change the human mind."

"I have faith in the future, but yes, you're right." He gestured at the cemetery. "Lieutenant, I didn't know there were still family vaults or burials in the city area."

"There are not. They built over the few graves in my folks' yard years ago. I am afraid my bones and those of my wife are broken and scattered. Where the earthly remains of my parents and grandparents might be found . . . I have not yet discovered."

"I'm sorry," Malachi said.

"They rest, sir, in a far better place. That I know."

"So why do you stay?"

"I stay . . ." The young soldier started to speak and then broke off, as if perplexed himself. "I stay because I wait to see a better world. Then I will rest."

You might well haunt these streets for eternity if you're waiting for all men to embrace one another, Malachi thought.

But he said, "Noble indeed, Lieutenant. I wish you well. I believe we are on the way. I honestly believe most men seek the right to life, liberty and happiness for all. But to end all prejudice — the whole world has a way to go. Where one hatred dies, another often springs to life."

"Perhaps," the lieutenant agreed. "Sir, it was a pleasure — you cannot imagine what a pleasure — to make your acquaintance." He tipped his cavalry hat and started to walk on.

"Excuse me, sir. Perhaps you could help me."

The lieutenant paused, looking at him. "I would be happy, of course, to be of assistance to a visitor to my fine city."

"Do you know anything about the tunnels around here? Tunnels that lead to the river?"

434

The lieutenant smiled broadly. "I knew quite a bit. My wife, although scorned by society for doing it, still managed to help many a man and woman to escape via the river. Captain Emanuel Vance used to bring a ship in, laden with supplies. He pretended to run the blockade, but what he did was carry many to freedom."

The question had brought out enthusiasm in the young lieutenant. "The Dragonslayer, of course, was known for its tunnels since the days of the pirates. As was the Pirates' House. But a network was dug during the yellow fever. I saw the morgue myself as a young lad. No longer in use at the time, of course, but the remnants were there. Still are, I believe. But what we used for the Underground Railroad, sir, were the tunnels through the vaults. The vaults do not exist anymore, but the tunnels do."

"What vaults?"

"Very old burial vaults," the lieutenant said. "The one behind my house is gone, but it connected to a vault beneath a tavern."

"The Wulf and Whistle?"

"Indeed. You know the place?"

"Yes. I went down to the tunnel, which led to the Dragonslayer — and from there, to the river."

The lieutenant smiled. "Oh, sir, there are other branches in that tunnel. Savannah's secret society of abolitionists knew that tunnels could easily be discovered. There are little pockets, twists and turns down there. Before the shelling of Fort Sumter, those who believed in freedom for all were secretly working down here. Some of the finest engineers in the country were below the ground, along with some of the finest engineers from Europe. Those tunnels are extensive. Explore, but take care. If you are buried in any kind of collapse, sir, I fear you will not come out."

Malachi thanked him, furious at his own stupidity.

They'd found the damned tunnel underneath the Wulf and Whistle. Why hadn't they broken down all the walls?

Malachi saw the young lieutenant off, then hurried back to the alley. A man in jeans and a polo shirt leaned against the wall, reading a tourist guide. Malachi walked up to him. "Officer?"

The man looked at him quizzically; Malachi produced the ID Jackson had given him to use while working the case.

"Yeah, Shubart. Officer Mike Shubart."

"I'm going down," Malachi said. "If I'm not back up in an hour, alert the troops."

"Yes, sir. You got it."

Malachi walked to the tunnel and phoned Jackson, telling him what he was about to do. He reached the wooden cover, moved it and crawled into the tunnel. Hitting the ground, he pulled out his flashlight.

He patted his side, making sure the Colt .45 that was his favorite weapon was exactly where it should be. Then he played his light over the darkness that swallowed even that glow. He proceeded slowly.

Abby couldn't get hold of Malachi. His cell went straight to voice mail and his recorded voice said, "Leave your message, please."

"It's Abby. A very annoyed Abby. Where are you? What's going on?" she demanded, and then ended the call.

Police work, any kind of law enforcement work, could be tedious. Much of it involved watching. And waiting. Endless waiting.

She was watching at the Dragonslayer. *Could be worse,* she tried to tell herself. If she got hungry, at least there was food. And the seats were comfortable. The climate was nice.

And there was enough coffee to keep her wired for a week.

But try as she might to stay calm, she grew increasingly anxious. She sat at the bar, watching. Waiting.

Roger and Paul seemed to have nothing to do that day. Maybe Roger was watching her as she watched him. He probably assumed that if anyone was going to know anything, it would be her.

Every so often, news about the suspect in the River Rat case came on. Everyone went still and stared at the screen.

And then they turned to Abby.

She shrugged. "I haven't been able to reach my colleagues yet," she told them. That was true in a way. Malachi wasn't answering.

To escape them all, she returned to the apartment to make her next phone call. Still no answer when she tried Malachi.

So she called Jackson next. "Don't worry. I talked to him. He's searching the tunnel by the Wulf and Whistle again. Seems he met up with a Union soldier while walking, a man who had worked with the Underground Railroad. The tunnels go all over, according to the soldier. I'm standing at the entrance to the river as we speak, watching from this end, waiting."

Watching and waiting. Of course. She hesitated. "Someone's here, in the Dragonslayer? A cop in plainclothes?"

"You have the cop of all cops on the way

over to spell him. David Caswell is coming. For dinner, naturally."

"Naturally," Abby said. "Thank you, Jackson. If you hear from Malachi —"

"I'll get in touch right away, Abby. We keep close tabs on one another. It's what keeps us all alive."

"I know," she said softly.

She left the apartment and came downstairs, to discover that David Caswell had arrived — and Bootsie and Dirk Johansen were back. The *Black Swan* had finished her afternoon sail.

David was by the bar, being grilled. Dirk looked as if he were in despair. He turned to Abby, his eyes filled with sorrow. "They think it's Aldous!" he said.

"I'm so sorry, Dirk," she murmured.

Dirk shook his head. "I *know* Aldous. He's one of the best men out there. I refuse to believe the worst of him. He never had to join the military because his family was always rich. He did his stint, anyway. He could've sat back on his ass his whole life, but he gave money to charitable projects and worked on them, too. I *won't* believe he's a killer."

"We would have known," Bootsie insisted. "You're wrong, young man," he told David Caswell.

439

"I'm afraid we have physical evidence against him," David said. "But this is America. Every man is innocent until proven guilty." He looked at Abby and inclined his head. She thought he'd been called by Jackson Crow, therefore knew where Malachi had gone — and what she was about to do.

"Well, we'll see." Abby shrugged. "I guess I'll take a stroll through and talk to a few of the guests."

She did. Most of the diners were tourists, and they were intrigued by the case going on in Savannah.

They were relieved the police had a suspect.

She made her way into the second dining room and over to the image of Blue. He stared at her with unseeing eyes.

But he was there somewhere, she knew. *Watching.*

That thought made her smile.

She pretended to adjust the image of Blue and then stepped inside the little fence that surrounded the grate.

She slipped down into the tunnel without a backward glance.

Malachi came to the fork in the tunnel; he knew that one path led to the Dragonslayer and then to the river.

He hadn't thought much about the other, because it didn't lead to the river.

Or, he realized, it didn't *appear* to lead to the river. He moved in the other direction, his light bouncing over the walls.

He came to a heap on the floor and paused, ducking down to look.

Bones.

Bones caught in fragments of cloth, with the remnants of feet in ancient boots.

This was no new murder victim. He couldn't really tell what he was seeing, the remains had been there for so long. They'd almost returned to ashes and dust, as the saying went. But the fact that they were here was interesting; this was clearly a pathway someone had used at some time. There was little he could tell from the stained bits of fabric and crumbling bone, but he had a feeling this dead man had been here at least two hundred years. Had he been abandoned where he lay as a warning to others?

He tried to imagine the days of the Civil War lieutenant and the slaves who would have been led through the tunnels to escape. Perhaps, at that time, these bones had been left so that if the tunnel was discovered, it wouldn't be considered an escape route, and those who tried to use it would face the law — or worse.

He straightened and kept walking.

His light revealed something else ahead of him, something white, like a woman's gown, an elegant nightgown. He hurried toward it.

Then, a grunt of astonishment burst through his lips. He took a step — but there was no ground. He crashed down into a deep hole. His body slammed hard on the earth and rock below.

Abby slowly walked the tunnel to the river; she saw nothing. It didn't seem anyone had been down recently. But of course they'd kept the grate locked with a new combination lock since last week. She, Malachi and Jackson Crow were the only people who knew the combination to the new lock.

But she'd learned that the tunnel from the Wulf and Whistle connected to this one. There'd been a guard on at the Wulf and Whistle, though. No one could have used these tunnels since the situation was discovered — not without being seen. And if she looked at it the way the police and Malachi and Jackson's Krewe were looking at it, all the suspects were currently accounted for. Aldous was at the station; the others were in the Dragonslayer.

It took her a few minutes to work the

catch on the false or pocket door that led from tunnel to tunnel. She wished she'd paid more attention when Malachi had opened it. But, eventually, she heard the catch give and then the pocket door gave, as well.

She moved farther, running her light carefully over the walls. First, she retraced the steps they'd taken when she came down with Malachi.

When she reached the junction, where the second tunnel branched off, she hesitated, casting her light to either side. She saw nothing. Then she heard a cry. Ragged, throaty.

"Help . . . help."

The sound was weak, but it seemed to ricochet off the tunnel walls.

"Malachi?" she called.

No response.

She instantly took out her phone to call for help. Of course, there was no signal. She was so angry she nearly threw the phone against the wall but refrained, sliding it back into her pocket. "I'm here!" she shouted. "Where are you?"

Still no response. She was sure the sound hadn't come from behind her, so she started forward, into the second tunnel, calling out, "Malachi!"

"Abby, stop!" she heard him call back, but it wasn't with the same voice she'd heard before.

"Where are you?" she cried.

"Don't move any farther. I'm in some floor trap in the tunnel."

"I'll get you out," she said, moving carefully, step by step.

"It's a trap in the floor. I walked right into it," he said with disgust. "There aren't any holds here, anywhere. Get help. Go get Jackson. I'm okay."

His voice had become clearer, louder. She must be almost on top of him. She fell to her knees and crawled ahead, carefully covering the distance, feeling the ground as she did so. She'd just about reached him when she heard something behind her.

It wasn't a tap, tap, tap . . .

It was a thump, thump, thump.

"Abby!" she heard Malachi yell.

She started to turn, started to reach for her Glock.

That was when the object slammed into her head, and only then did it register exactly what the sound was.

"Abby!"

Malachi heard the thud. Abby made a sound — not a scream but a gasp of surprise and pain. He pulled out his gun but he was afraid to fire; he couldn't see from the depths of the hole and he was afraid he'd hurt her.

He shouted out instead. "Let her be. We all know who you are now. It's over!"

"Ah, me hearty young lad! No, no, I think not. They'll hang old Aldous for my sins, and it's a shame, but that's the fate of seamen such as ourselves!" came the answer.

Malachi began to scrabble at the earth. The killer had her. He heard the soft thunk, thunk, thunk, as the killer moved away with Abby.

And Abby . . .

Abby hadn't let out another sound.

Swearing, Malachi scratched and clawed at the earth, desperate to find a handhold.

At some point while she was being jostled, Abby started to come to.

Bootsie had used the hard end of an old blunderbuss to strike her. She was astonished that she had come to, although her awareness was dulled by the sharp pain in her head.

Thump, thump, thump turned to *tap, tap, tap,* and then she felt herself thrown down. She was in a boat. Yes. *Thump, thump, thump.* The sound of Bootsie's peg leg. The sound she'd been told about.

And now . . . a rowboat.

Blue had said something about a rowboat. When the rowboats were out . . .

She could hear laughter and conversation but it seemed to come from far away. She heard another sound — the splash of oars. She was on the water.

She tried to open her eyes without betraying that she was awake. Raising her eyelids slightly, she could see the riverfront easing away from her. Bootsie was facing her as he rowed. She realized that he'd tied her wrists together. He'd used sailor's knots. Struggling would only tighten her bonds.

Police were all over the riverfront! Why hadn't they seen her?

She tried to calculate where she was. South on the river — south, and that was why the sounds of life were so distant. They'd come up well below the customary tourist area and she thought he must have kept the tiny boat beneath one of the docks. It wouldn't have been obvious, and therefore probably hadn't been searched. It was a rowboat, and there was nowhere to hide a woman in a rowboat.

He'd easily eluded the police time and time again.

Not now, she told herself. *Not now.* He was

caught. He hadn't stopped to kill Malachi. Maybe he thought Malachi would die in the hold. That no one knew he'd gone below the earth. But Jackson and the Krewe did, and they'd find him.

Before he killed her?

Bootsie. Her grandfather's old and dear friend. Bootsie.

A man she'd known most of her life.

The killer . . . the River Rat . . . was Bootsie. Robert Lanigan.

Impossible. Bootsie was nearly seventy. He didn't fit any profile. What had suddenly turned him into a murderer? And when?

The questions that seemed to arise in a flurry didn't matter. Her life was at stake. Bootsie wasn't stupid; she was sure he'd taken her Glock and her cell phone. What he'd done with them, she had no idea.

That particular question was quickly answered. She heard two splashes in the water and knew her phone and Glock were about to meet the river bottom.

She feigned unconsciousness.

Which didn't bother Bootsie. He began to talk. "Ah, pretty girl, pretty girl! You always were the best wench, Abigail. I have been searching and searching, but I didn't see, didn't realize. *You* were the real beauty, the prize of the river — of the whole vast sea.

You're the one I've searched for, Abigail. Aye, we've only now to chuck the other. She wasn't worthy, so we'll toss her into the water. It will be a fitting end for such a one! Women, you see, can be evil. Protect the women and the children! Bah, vicious little bastards — that be the children! And wicked, horrid creatures — that be women. Most of them, anywise. But now, perhaps, we'll sail the seas together, eh, Abby? As it should be."

Chuck the other . . .

She hoped that meant Bianca was still alive.

And that he was taking her to wherever he had Bianca.

A moment later, the rowboat hit something. Hard. Opening her eyes a little, Abby saw that it wasn't a ship; they'd come to a rickety old boathouse on the river.

Clip, clip, clip . . .

That was the sound Bootsie's peg leg made against the wood of the rowboat as he beached it and then grabbed her.

The sun was dying as he threw her over his shoulder and began to walk, his gait jagged as he sank a bit on the left side of his body each time he took a step.

She heard the bang of a door and they entered the shack. It was old — Civil War era, she thought. He threw her down and she continued to feign unconsciousness. When he'd hobbled off, she looked around. She was on a flat surface. Old boats in various stages of disrepair littered the ramshackle structure. There was a door that led to a room, an old office or such.

The cabin Helen Long had told them about?

That had to be it.

And somehow, she had to stop him before he drowned the other young woman.

Malachi didn't waste his breath screaming or shouting. He forced himself to be calm, trying to find anything that could serve as a grip.

He was startled when things started to fall on him.

Dirt . . . an old box . . . even the old bones . . .

He looked up. In the spill of light from his flashlight, lying on the ground by his feet, he saw a face appear before him.

He'd hoped for a cop.

Or anyone living, for that matter.

It was Blue.

"Get me help, Blue. I'm begging you, get me some help. Find my friends from the agency — they'll see you, Blue, they'll get me out."

"There's no time. He has Abigail," Blue said.

"What are you doing?"

"Building up the ground. He would not mind. The bones belong to Blackheart Mc-Cready. He went to the devil long ago, my friend. Use them, step on them, use everything you have."

Blue fell flat on the ground, pushing in more dirt, dirt and rocks.

Malachi understood what he was doing. Piling up all the refuse Blue sent down to him, picking up his flashlight to use as a tool as well as for whatever illumination it could provide, he set to work. He built the refuse up and clawed at the walls above, creating a handhold for himself. He created a foothold next, and gripped the earth wall with his toes. The bones of the long-dead pirate helped him dig into the earth walls. He hollowed out another hold and then another. Blue reached down to him; they both knew that the ghost had no real ability to grab him and yet . . . he felt as if he was helped, pulled upward.

He rolled onto the ground. "Which way, Blue? Where the hell is he taking them?"

"This way . . . and then . . . follow me!"

He ran after Blue, who was speeding

through the darkness as if he were a bolt of fire. They seemed to run forever, until they came to a series of steps dug into the ground many years ago. They were far down the river. Dusk had fallen, and he could see nothing on the water.

"Blue, where?" he said desperately.

"He comes out here . . . There are boats under that old dock."

Malachi stared at the river. And then he saw it — an old boathouse on a jut of land that curved about fifty feet into the water.

He began to run again.

Abby felt she must have been doing a decent job of feigning unconsciousness. Bootsie walked around — *tap, tap, tap, tap, tap* — muttering. She had to find a way to take him by surprise — difficult when her hands were tied.

He was old, for God's sake, close to seventy. But he was in good shape, good health — except for his mind, obviously — and he was decked out with a blunderbuss and sword.

How the hell had he gotten those weapons? Where and when had he changed into the frock coat and hat he was wearing?

He couldn't have come from the Dragon-slayer. David Caswell would have seen him

— would have followed him, would have stopped him.

She heard Bootsie still moving around, still muttering to himself. "Ach, I'll worry about this one later . . . We'll need time. Best wench, yes, I have Abby now, and she is the one. I should have known before, yes. This will work. But I must get the other one out of the cabin . . . get rid of her now, out in the river. Poor lass — not good enough. She'll have to die. . . ."

He was going for Bianca. He walked toward the closed room in the boathouse. At this moment, she was alive. But he was going to take her out and kill her. Bootsie didn't keep more than one woman at a time. He had taken *her* that night, Abby thought, because he'd had the opportunity.

Because he was losing control.

Tap, tap, tap, tap . . .

He was going for Bianca.

She heard Bianca's muffled scream as the door was thrown open. Abby twisted around and got to her feet, looking for a weapon. At least he'd tied her hands in front of her. If he'd tied them behind her . . .

She could see nothing in the shadowy expanse of the old boathouse except a discarded fishing pole. It was better than nothing. With her head still pounding, she took a step and staggered. She froze, afraid he'd heard her, willing herself to find her balance. Bianca screamed again. Bootsie must have reached her.

She hunkered down for the fishing pole and got it in her hands, then rushed for the door. Bootsie was inside, hauling Bianca over his shoulder.

He had powerful shoulders, a powerful physique he'd maintained all the years she'd known him.

The room in the boathouse was just as Helen had described it — small, paneled, like a cabin on an old sailing vessel of days long gone. A pirate's vessel, perhaps.

Bootsie started to turn; she slammed the fishing pole over his head with all her strength. He lurched backward, dropping Bianca. She struck him again with the fishing pole, and he fell against the wood, almost on top of Bianca.

But as Abby drew back, ready to strike again, Bootsie recovered his balance. Blood poured from a wound on his forehead and he was infuriated. He bellowed out a curse and came after her. Abby lifted the fishing rod again, but he caught it and wrenched it from her hands. She backed away, faltering only a little, watching him with the same fury.

"Ah, lass! I will break you, you will see!"
He walked toward her, bringing them to the
main room of the boathouse. "There is no
defying me! I am the king of the seas.
Governments fall down before me, none
may rule me. And you will obey me or you
will die! I am Blue Anderson! I am Blue
Anderson, and I will rule the seas from here
to eternity."

"You're not Blue! Blue didn't hurt anyone!"

"You're not hurt! You're a captive, and
you want to stay with me!" he roared.

Abby stared at him in shock. But he
seemed to believe what he was saying —
that he was Blue Anderson.

"You will. You will be the wench, and you
will want me!"

He walked over to her; she raised her
hands in self-defense. He was incredibly
strong — slapping her arms down and
throwing her back to the floor. Again, the
world seemed to spin. He wrenched her up,
gripping her arms with viselike strength.

"Don't want to scar you, lass, but I won't
mind beating you within an inch of your
life," Bootsie told her. "Now, I'll have to be
hog-tying you until I get rid of the other
one."

"Touch her again and you're dead!"

The threat rang out with cold assurance.
Relief filled Abby.

Malachi.

He was soaked and muddy; he'd apparently crawled up to the boathouse from the river. He had his gun trained on Bootsie and his eyes were centered on the man.

But Bootsie didn't release her. He spun her around in front of him, whipping something from his pocket. She suddenly felt steel against her neck.

"Can your bullet move fast enough to stop the blade of my knife, boy?"

Malachi strode closer to Bootsie. "Let her go."

"Fight for her. Fight for her like a man, Scurvy Pete! You won't take my woman!"

Malachi frowned.

"He can't fight you, Blue," Abby said. "He has no weapon with which to fight. Blue wouldn't fight him without a weapon. It's a pirate's honor!"

"He's got himself a mighty pistol there," Bootsie said. She felt the knife scratch against her throat.

"Give him a sword. He'll put the pistol down."

Malachi must have seen the madness in Bootsie's eyes. "A sword! No pirate captain would claim his captive without a fair fight!"

He shoved his gun back into the shoulder holster. "Leave your hostage. Play out the scene, Blue Anderson. Give me a sword!"

Bootsie wasn't crazy enough just to let her go. He dragged her with him, backing toward one of the chests. "Here — take your sword. Throw the gun to the corner of the room and take up your sword, Scurvy Pete!"

"I've put the gun away," Malachi began.

"No! Throw it across the floor!" Bootsie commanded.

Malachi took his weapon from the holster, bent down and let it slide across the floor to a corner of the room.

"My sword now, sir! Blue Anderson, it will be a fair fight."

Bootsie, still holding his knife against Abby's throat, thrust her away from the chest. "Get your weapon, Scurvy Pete, get your weapon."

His eyes never leaving Bootsie's, Malachi reached into the chest, piled high with swords and knives. He chose a sword.

He stepped back, lifting the sword. Abby saw him judge her position and that of Bianca, who'd sidled back against the cabin door and sat there now, eyes wide with shock, not making a sound.

"Shall we, Blue?"

Bootsie pushed Abby from him, sending

her to her knees. He turned. Malachi was
ready, and still Bootsie went after him with
a vengeance that was startling.

Malachi fought hard. She didn't know
where he might have learned about this kind
of sword fighting — and perhaps he knew
nothing. At first, he struggled just to defend
himself from the fury of Bootsie's attack.
And then, finally, he began to move forward,
managing to attack rather than merely
defend. The two men dodged and maneu-
vered about the room.

Abby rolled away from the action, coming
at last to where Malachi's gun had ended
up. He carried a Colt .45.

She got her hands around it. It was a
larger gun than hers with a higher caliber
bullet, but she wasn't afraid to fire it.

She tried to take aim; the men kept moving about.

Tap, tap, tap, tap, tap . . .

Bootsie could move fast with his peg leg;
he could all but dance.

Malachi lunged forward, slamming
Bootsie's weapon, and the sword went flying across the room. Malachi staggered
back, wearied by the fight.

"Stand down, Blue, stand down!" he cried.

Bootsie seemed to falter. Abby realized he
was reaching down to his thigh — to grab a

knife from its sheath.

She had a clear shot.

She fired as he drew the knife, about to throw it into Malachi's heart.

The sound was deafening; the recoil sent Abby flying back, her arm in agony.

Bootsie froze. Then he crashed to the floor, his peg leg moving at an awkward angle as his twisted body fell.

Malachi rushed to Abby, drawing her into his arms, loosening the ties that bound her wrists. As he did, they heard sirens.

A floodlight suddenly lit up the interior of the boathouse.

"You are surrounded. Put down your weapons. Come out with your hands up!" someone ordered over a megaphone.

Bianca gave a strangled sob and Malachi started toward her.

Thankfully he didn't have to leave Abby.

Police were pouring in, Jackson Crow and David Caswell at the head of the group.

Since Bootsie was dead, it was difficult to put together the complete history of what had happened — where his madness had begun and exactly how he'd managed all his feats of kidnapping, disappearances and murder.

David Caswell told them they might never

know; it was sad to say, but there were people who might remain missing forever — and there were bodies that might never be found.

A search of his house led them to a stairway, which went to the cellar. There they discovered a pocket door that opened into the labyrinth of tunnels — and his hidden store of frock coats, breeches, hats and pirate weapons.

As the Krewe and David Caswell sat around the table at Abby's house on Chippewa, they learned that the police had been examining other unsolved cases they'd had over the years. They couldn't be sure. But Bootsie might have started his murder spree as much as a decade before. Back then, he might have lived out his fantasies at a slower rate. His wife had been alive then; she'd probably kept him from totally indulging in his longing to be a pirate captain who kidnapped women and tried to get them to fall in love with him. But they'd always wonder about a number of other situations. They'd uncovered a drowning victim in their records from ten years earlier. Foul play had been suspected, but the case had grown cold. Two years later, the body of a young woman, decomposed beyond recognition, had been found south of them, off

North Hutchison Island in Florida. There were missing-person cases that had never been solved in the following years. So, yes, it was possible that Bootsie had begun killing slowly — and had then escalated into his mad world of piracy, seizing young women and killing them at a more frantic rate.

"Here's what I don't understand," Abby said. She was glad to be at the table; she'd stayed at the hospital the night before because of the concussion she'd received. "Why didn't Helen recognize Bootsie? He approached her with a business card identifying him as a man named Christopher Condent. But Helen *knew* Bootsie. And he didn't use Blue's name. He used the name of a different pirate."

"I was in the behavioral unit for years before the Krewe," Jackson said. "I've taken so many courses on the human mind that I should have answers. But I don't believe any of us have ever gotten to the core of what can make a man — or woman — so twisted. How they can be insane and yet behave sanely. He dressed up and hid his identity so well she didn't know him."

"She said there was something familiar about him — that she felt she *should* have known him," Malachi said. "That's why I suspected one of the men who hung around the Dragonslayer. That, and the fact that every victim had eaten at the tavern."

"But Dirk would have been on the ship at the same time the so-called businessman, Christopher Condent — aka Bootsie Lanigan — was on board. And Dirk didn't recognize him, either."

"That just goes to show how skilled he'd become at disguise," David remarked.

"But Bootsie had a peg leg!" Abby said. She looked at David and then murmured, "Oh. Right."

"Exactly," David said. "He had his peg leg, which he preferred to use. But we know he also had several newer prosthetics."

"I knew that, too." Abby nodded. "He claimed to like his peg leg best, said he hated the newer so-called 'real' prosthetics."

"A peg leg is best for a pirate," Kat said quietly.

"Playacting." Will shook his head. "It can become far too real."

"In Bootsie's case, definitely," Kat said. "And he was taking the fingers from his victims because it was part of — of being a pirate?"

"Obviously we'll never be able to ask him," Jackson replied, "but whether much of what we hear is legend or not, it *is* known that Blackbeard — among others — didn't hesitate to cut off a man's finger when he wouldn't hand over a diamond ring. This might be a detail Bootsie added later on. The earlier potential victims weren't missing any fingers."

They all talked about their theories, what they could and couldn't have done.

David was remorseful over the fact that they searched ship after ship — boat after boat — and never thought to look in the old ramshackle boathouse. A records check, of course, showed that it belonged to a corporation owned by a holding company Bootsie was involved with.

"After Abby pulled Helen Long from the water, and after Helen's testimony, we were all convinced he held the women on a boat or ship." Angela smiled at Abby. "Thanks to you, though, two women lived. Helen and Bianca."

"Yeah — but I got myself hit on the head," Abby said.

"Only after I fell down a hole," Malachi reminded her dryly.

"Bianca will live. She's traumatized, and it'll take time. But Helen's already out of the hospital, and Bianca . . . well, at least she kept her finger," Kat murmured. "And, hopefully, the police will soon discover the identity of the one girl who remains a Jane Doe."

"It's good to know that, for Bianca, the future has real promise. For one thing, she has Roger, who hasn't left her side since he was allowed in," Jackson said. "We'll take all the good we can get."

Abby felt her phone vibrate; she knew it signaled an email and meant to ignore it. She liked sitting here with the Krewe. They'd be leaving soon, and although she'd be happily accepting the position offered to her, she wouldn't reconnect with them for a while. They were in Savannah now, and she didn't want to be distracted.

She glanced at the new email, anyway — and gave a little cry of delight. The others went silent.

She smiled. "Sorry. I just got a note from a friend of mine on the city council. She had her assistant go into the records after I wrote to her, and they're going to see that the gravestone in Colonial Park Cemetery is repaired. The proper information will be carved on it. The name had been damaged when the stone was vandalized by soldiers when Savannah surrendered to General Sherman."

"That's great," Jackson said, a knowing smile on his lips. He looked at Malachi.

"Perhaps the two of you would like to go make that statement at the cemetery?"

"Sounds good. Let's take a walk," Malachi told Abby.

"One minute. I want to print out this email to bring to Josiah's folks," she said, hurrying off to do that.

She and Malachi left the group with the Krewe planning their last evening in Savannah; they'd have a barbecue at the house on Chippewa Square. Will said he thought it was fine for Kat to shop for the barbecue, but someone else might want to do the cooking. Kat was indignant, and Angela did her best to mollify them both; while Jackson watched with amusement.

Abby and Malachi walked the few blocks to the cemetery. It was late afternoon, just as it had been when they'd gone into the tunnels the day before.

It was a beautiful time of day. The live oaks dripped moss that stirred and moved in the breeze.

Abby was grateful to be alive.

On the one hand, she could still shudder, remembering the fear she'd felt when she realized she'd been taken. But fear wasn't entirely a bad thing. Jackson wanted them to feel fear — not debilitating fear, but the kind that made them careful and smart.

They had managed well, especially since they'd never clearly identified a suspect. They'd had to use what they knew about both the living and the dead to see the situation through to its conclusion. They'd successfully played into the fantasy of a man who'd become a homicidal psychopath. Abby was glad the rest of the Krewe seemed proud of her and Malachi. The Krewe had come to Savannah because Jackson Crow had recognized something in her plea to him. He'd found Malachi and, together, they'd found her. She knew the right future stretched before her now.

"There they are," Malachi whispered as they entered the cemetery. Josiah's parents were sitting on their customary bench, as if they mourned someone only recently gone. Perhaps, to them, the sorrow was as deep as if it had occurred yesterday.

Abby walked over to them, her printed email in hand. "Good afternoon, Mr. and Mrs. Beckwith," she greeted them.

Edgar Beckwith immediately stood, bowing to her. Elizabeth rose by her husband's side, clutching his arm and looking expectantly at Abby.

"Anything?" Edgar asked.

"Abby will read it to you. This message is from someone with the power to help,"

Malachi said.

Abby smiled and read the email out loud. She saw that Edgar and Elizabeth Beckwith smiled, too, as they heard the news. Elizabeth stepped forward to touch Abby's face with a gentle hand. "Thank you," she whispered. "Thank you."

"There will be a little ceremony when the work is completed," Abby told them. "We'll be here for it."

They bade Edgar and Elizabeth Beckwith goodbye, leaving the couple to stand by the grave, expressions of happiness and relief on their faces.

"That felt wonderful," Abby told Malachi.

"Yes," he agreed. And it had. But one thing still troubled her, and Malachi seemed to sense that.

"What?" he asked her softly.

She drew in a deep breath. "We've pulled a few good endings out of this, but . . . how did Bootsie kill Gus? The autopsy showed that Gus died of a heart attack."

"I wish I could give you a definitive answer. I can't. But here's what my instinct tells me. Gus was a fine man, the kind of man who cared about others. I believe he was searching the tunnel, that he suspected something," Malachi said. "When he stumbled on Bootsie, his heart probably gave out when Bootsie attacked him. Gus died trying to save others, Abby."

Abby nodded. She knew it would be years before everything Bootsie had done was uncovered. And it was shattering to think that he'd been killing people and coming to the Dragonslayer, becoming more and more convinced that he was the living embodiment of various pirates — including Blue Anderson. Maybe he'd tried out different roles at different times. Blackbeard, Christopher Condent. Henry Morgan. But above all, he'd wanted to be Blue.

And she'd kissed his cheek, cared about him, thought of him as Gus's dear old curmudgeonly friend . . .

He had come to Gus's funeral. Made himself at home in the bar afterward, just waiting to seize another woman.

She shuddered. It was still too hard to believe.

"One more question," she said. "Everyone was certain we should be searching for Bianca on a boat or a ship. How did you figure out that he was hiding her in the boathouse?"

Malachi turned to her. He smiled and told her, "Blue. The *real* Blue Anderson."

EPILOGUE

They'd needed a change of scenery. And Jackson had given them two weeks. Actually, he'd given *Abby* two weeks; she was already official. When the two weeks were up, Malachi would have to go through classes at the academy. That was just the way it was. Unless he preferred to stay a consultant, which had its up and downs. But Abby wanted him to be a full part of the Krewe, and he knew Jackson thought that was best, too. So what the hell? He'd go through the academy.

But before that, they had two weeks.

So Malachi and Abby had packed up and come to his home southwest of Richmond and, as he'd hoped, she loved the house and its surroundings. The area was remote, but she didn't mind. She appreciated the country around them, the richness of the trees and the beauty of the crystal rivers and streams. They spent their time hiking, playing in the lake down the hill from his property and exploring Virginia. They went to a Civil War reenactment and to Richmond to visit some of the sights, and they traveled down to Colonial Williamsburg and took a day to do something that was sheer fun — Busch Gardens.

Abby was a glutton for roller coasters.

Mostly, they slept in mornings. They watched DVDs and listened to music. They indulged in each other and wondered if they'd always feel the need to be so close and so intimate. He talked about his marriage, and she told him about her few relationships, and they'd sympathized over their past experiences.

Their time was drawing to a close late one night — or early one morning — when he woke to find that she wasn't at his side. Rising, he slipped into a robe and walked out to the hall. "Abby?"

She didn't answer, so he went down the stairs. And then he saw her. She was seated by the fire and she was deep in conversation. That was why she hadn't heard him.

Zachary was there, looking extremely pleased. Malachi hadn't seen him since he'd come to the house with Abby. Knowing Zachary, he'd been making his own judgments before presenting himself.

Abby glanced up and saw him. She smiled. "Zachary and I have met. We've been talking."

Zachary stood. "She's delightful!" he said, gesturing at Abby.

Malachi walked over to Abby, who rose. He slid an arm around her. "Delightful? Well, she's a crack shot, no-nonsense, a brilliant agent — and she can play a great wench. I think I'll keep her."

"You will, of course, be a perfect gentleman," Zachary said in a stern voice.

"I can try, of course. And will," Malachi added hastily. "But she's stubborn, and she has her own mind."

"I like that in a woman. My dear Genevieve was always ready to share her opinion. We lived in difficult times and she was ready to rise to any occasion. In fact . . ."

"In fact?"

"If you can make this work, I could perhaps move on," Zachary said. "And join my dear Genevieve."

"Abby, he wants me to ask if you'll marry me." Smiling, Malachi looked at her.

Abby laughed. "We have, indeed, discussed that possibility, Zachary. We think marriage might be right for us in the near future. I'm not a big fan of diamonds, but we *have* a lovely ring with an emerald —

one that belonged to Malachi's mother. It happens to be my birthstone. So, for the moment, we'll move forward, learning about our future, using what talents we have to help others. And when the time is right, there will be a lovely wedding. We'll have it in Savannah. I think Blue needs to give me away. It'll be interesting to see that with a crowd observing, but I'll know he's by my side and that's the important thing. So, Zachary, you'll have to come to Savannah."

"Savannah! A beautiful city. I — Yes, I will manage to do that, and then, perhaps . . ." His voice trailed off. "I believe I've waited these many years, trusting that someone like Malachi would come along, and now . . . knowing that what we've had as a family will go on."

Malachi wasn't sure how Abby did it; she stood on tiptoe at just the right height and moved just the right amount of distance. It appeared she placed a perfect kiss on Zachary's cheek.

"The children are going to be beautiful!" Zachary said happily.

"But no rushing us now!" Abby insisted.

"I promise," Zachary assured her. He turned to Malachi. "I must go tell Genevieve!" he said, and headed toward the family cemetery in back.

Abby looked at Malachi with amusement. "I think he approved of me. It took him long enough to decide."

"Zachary? Ah, yes, he can be difficult to impress, but he does seem bewitched," Malachi said. "With you."

"Well, I'm grateful he does approve."

He lifted her chin and kissed her lips. "What matters more is that you approve of me," he told her.

She clasped his hand. "I'm wide-awake. If you want to follow me upstairs, I can tell you all about my approval. Or, rather, I can show you." She grew serious. "These moments, this time . . . all precious, I think."

"Very precious. We have to value such precious moments," he said. "They define our lives." He kissed her again and they started up the stairs.

"Think they're going to like each other?" Abby asked.

"Zachary and Blue?"

"Yes."

"I'm sure they will. They'll be like two wonderful old grandpas, shedding a few tears as we say our vows," Malachi said. They'd reached the door to his room. "For now, however, back to showing me that approval . . ."

She released his hand and walked into the

room. He paused and watched her for a moment.

"What?" she asked, turning back.

"Nothing. I'm just grateful that you're here, that you walked into my room."

She laughed softly, a sound that seemed to make the world right. "And I'm just grateful that you walked into my life."

ABOUT THE AUTHOR

New York Times bestselling author **Heather Graham** has written more than one hundred fifty novels and novellas, has been published in nearly twenty-five languages, and has over seventy-five million copies in print. An avid scuba diver, ballroom dancer, and mother of five, she still enjoys her south Florida home, but loves to travel as well. Reading, however, is the pastime she still loves best, and is a member of many writing groups. For more information, check out her Web site, theoriginalheathergraham .com.